# VALLEY
## *of the*
# MOON

Melanie Gideon is the bestselling author of *Wife 22* and *The Slippery Year: A Meditation on Happily Ever After*, as well as three young adult novels. *Wife 22* has been translated into thirty-one languages. She has written for the *New York Times*, *San Francisco Chronicle*, *Shape*, *Marie Claire*, *The Times*, and other publications. She lives in the San Francisco Bay Area with her husband and son.

You can connect with Melanie Gideon at melaniegideon.com, facebook.com/MelanieGideonAuthor, or on Twitter @MelanieGideon.

Also by Melanie Gideon

*Wife 22*

*The Slippery Year: A Meditation on Happily Ever After*

# VALLEY
## *of the*
# MOON

## Melanie Gideon

HarperCollins*Publishers*

HarperCollins*Publishers*
The News Building
1 London Bridge Street
London SE1 9GF

www.harpercollins.co.uk

This paperback edition 2017
1

First published in the USA by Ballantine Books, New York 2016

Published by HarperCollins*Publishers* 2017

Copyright © Melanie Gideon 2016

Melanie Gideon asserts the moral right to
be identified as the author of this work

A catalogue record for this book is available from the British Library

ISBN: 9780007425532

Set in Adobe Caslon Pro

Printed and bound in Great Britain by
Clays Ltd, St Ives plc

For Sarah and Vasant Gideon

Life can only be understood backwards, but it must be lived forwards.

—Søren Kierkegaard

# Valley
# of the
# Moon

# JOSEPH

❧

*Valley of the Moon, California*
*1906*

The smell of buttered toast was a time machine. I stepped inside
it and traveled back to 1871. Back to London. Back to my childhood kitchen, to the lap-bounced, sweets-chunky, much-loved seven-
year-old boy I once was, sitting on a stool while Polly and Charlotte
flew around me.

Whipping cream. Beating eggs. Chopping parsley and thyme. Oh,
their merry gossiping! Their pink cheeks. Nothing scared them, not
mice, spiders, nothing. Shoo. All the scary things gone.

"More biscuits, please," I said, holding out my empty plate.

"No," said my mother, working the bread dough. She wiped her
damp forehead with the heel of her hand. "You've had enough."

If you'd walked into the kitchen at that moment, you'd have had
no idea she was the lady of the house, working right alongside the
servants. My mother, Imogene Widger Bell, was the only daughter of
a knocker-upper. Her father had made his living by rising at three in
the morning to knock on the windows of his customers, waking them
like a human timepiece. My mother herself had entered service on
her twelfth birthday. She was cheerful, hardworking, and smart and
ascended quickly through the ranks. From laundry maid to scullery
maid. From kitchen maid to under cook. When she was sixteen, she
met my father, Edward Bell (the son of the gardener), by a stone wall.
She, enjoying a break, the sun beating down upon her face, the smell

of apple blossoms in the air, an afternoon of polishing silver in front of her. He, an assistant groundskeeper, coiled tight, knee-deep in brambles, and desperate to rise above his class.

Besotted with my mother, he presented a lighthearted façade to woo her, carefully hiding the anger and bitterness that fueled his ambition. His only mistake as he saw it? To have been born into the wrong family. My mother did not see things that way. Her belly was full every night. She worked alongside honest people. Her employers gave her a bonus at Christmas. What more could one ask?

They were terribly ill matched. They never should have married, but they did. And though it took many years, my father eventually did what he'd set out to do: he made a fortune in textiles. He bought a mansion in Belgravia. He hired staff. A lady's maid and a cook for my mother. A valet for him. They attended concerts and the opera. They became patrons of the arts. They threw parties, they hosted salons, they acquired Persian rugs for every room.

And in the end, none of it mattered: they remained outsiders in the class that my father had hoped to infiltrate. His new "friends" were polite to his face, but behind his back referred to him as "that vulgar little man." He'd earned his fortune, it was not passed down to him—they would never forgive him for it. All the bespoke shirts in the world couldn't hide the fact he was new money.

"Joseph, five minutes and then back upstairs to your schoolwork," said my mother. "Did you finish your sums?"

"Yes," I lied.

"No," said Madeline, the governess, who had appeared in the doorway and was holding out her hand to me. How long had she been standing there?

I groaned and slid off the stool.

"Don't you want to go to university one day?" asked Madeline.

I should have been in school already. That my mother had convinced my father to allow my sister's governess to give me lessons at home was a miracle. My father consistently reminded me this would come to an end and I would soon be sent away to a proper school.

If only he knew what really happened at 22 Willoughby Square once he left the house every morning. My mother sailed us out of the sea of oligarchy and into the safe harbor of egalitarianism. We became a community of equals. Titles evaporated. Young Master, Little Miss, Cook, Girl, Mistress, Governess. Poof, gone. Polly, Madeline, even Charlotte, the lowliest kitchen maid, called my mother Imogene.

As a result my education was broad. I was taught not only how to multiply and divide, to read and recite, but how to blacken a stove, how to get candle wax out of a tablecloth, and how to build a fence. Some of the lessons I disliked more than others. Egg gathering, for instance: the chickens terrified me. They'd run after me, pecking at my feet.

"I hate the chickens," I said to my mother. "Why do you make me go out there?"

"How else will you learn what you love to do?" she said. "You don't have to like everything, but you must try."

What my mother loved was greengage plums.

The most sublime-tasting plum in the world, she always said, but the tree had a fickle temperament and was notoriously difficult to grow. She had a small orchard in the back of our garden. I had never tasted one of her greengage plums, or if I had I couldn't remember. The last time her trees had fruited, I was a baby. Every July I'd ask if this was the year the plums would come.

"You must be patient," she told me. "Everything good takes time."

I was a greedy boy. I stamped my foot. I wanted a plum now.

"How to wait," she said, looking down at me with pity. "It's the hardest thing to learn."

I was always waiting for my mother to come home. Most afternoons she left the house to attend one meeting or another. She was devoted to many causes. Education. Women's rights. Land reform and the struggles of the working class. She made signs. She marched in the streets. Once she even went to jail with a group of her fellow suffragettes. Much aggrieved, my father went to retrieve her, paying the exorbitant two-pound bail to set her free. When they walked in the door, my mother looked shy and triumphant. My father was enraged.

"You've made me a laughingstock in front of my friends," he spat at her.

"They are not your friends," she said, taking off her gloves.

"You have forgotten your place."

"And you have forgotten where you came from."

"That is exactly the point!" he bellowed.


They slept in different bedrooms that night and every night thereafter. My father had done everything he could to erase his history and pull the ladder he'd climbed up behind him. He forbade my mother to join any more organizations. She agreed, and instead began holding meetings at the house while he was at work. In her mind, everybody deserved a better life and it was her responsibility as a woman of means to help them achieve it. Unmarried women with children, spinsters, laundresses, jakesmen, beggars, and drunks all traipsed through our doorway and were led into the parlor to discuss their futures.

When I was eight, my mother left. She told me she was going on a painting trip to Provence. She'd been unable to bring herself to tell me the truth: my father was admitting her to an institution. He did it without her consent. He needed only two signatures to have her committed, his and his lawyer's. Her diagnosis: unstable due to overwork and the inability to handle domestic responsibilities. She was gone for four months.

She returned fifteen pounds lighter and the color of curdled cream. She used the same light, cheery voice she always had with me, but I wasn't fooled. There was no joy in it anymore. She spoke as if she were standing on the roof of a building in which somebody had forgotten to build the stairs. She'd fight to sustain eye contact when we spoke, but as soon as we stopped our conversation, her gaze would fall to the floor.

It was Charlotte, the kitchen maid, who finally took pity on me and told me the truth. "Painting, my arse. She got locked up by your father. Sent away to the loony bin."

I didn't believe her, but the governess corroborated the story. Polly, the cook, too.

"Don't tell her you know," said Polly.

"But what do I do?"

"Treat her exactly the way you've always treated her," she said.

"But—she's different," I whined. I wanted my real mother back. The playful, optimistic, bread-making, injustice-fighting, eye-glinting woman who called everybody by their first names no matter what their stations.

"She'll come back," said Polly. "You just have to be patient. Sit with her. That's all you have to do."

It was easy to sit with my mother. She rarely left the house anymore. Most days, after breakfast and a bath, she retired to the parlor.

"I've taken up some lovely new pursuits," she said. No longer did she work in the kitchen alongside Polly and Charlotte. Instead she sat on the chaise and embroidered, the curtains drawn, the lamp lit, her head bent studiously over her work.

"Shall I read to you?" I asked.

"No, thank you. I prefer the silence."

"Shall I open the curtains? It's a beautiful day."

"I don't think so. The light is too bright for me."

"Then I'll just sit here with you."

"Wonderful," she murmured.

I lived on that "wonderful." A crumb, but I swallowed it down, pretending it was a four-course meal.

She would come back. Polly said she would. I just had to be patient.


Over the next year she stopped leaving the house altogether. Twilights were especially difficult. Once my mother was a sunflower, her petals spread open to the sky. Now, one by one, her seeds fell out of their pod.

It was a cold day in November that she told me she would be wintering in Spain. She'd developed arthritis, she said. A warmer climate would suit her.

I'd overheard my father talking to his lawyer, making the arrangements, so I knew she was lying—he was sending her back to the asylum. He'd institutionalized her because he wanted an obedient wife who was satisfied living a quiet, domestic life. Instead she'd been returned to him a ghost. He didn't know what else to do.

I didn't know what to do either, but even though I was only nine, I knew locking her away again was not the solution. I threw my arms around her and begged her not to go.

"I'm sorry, I don't have a choice." She looked down at me as if I were an inanimate object—a book or a shawl.

"You're lying. You're not going to Spain."

"Don't be silly, of course I am." She pushed me away. "And you're far too old to be acting this way."

"Mama," I whimpered.

For a split second her expression softened and I saw my old mother gazing back at me with empathy and love. But a moment later the light drained out of her eyes.

"Take care of your sister," she said.

"You must run away," I cried, desperate. "Someplace he won't be able to find you. Leave tonight."

She pursed her lips. "And where would I go?"

"Anywhere."

"There is nowhere else," she said.

I wept silently.


A week later, the night before she was due to leave, her bags already packed, my mother lay down on her bed in a long dress like the Lady of Shalott, drank an entire bottle of nervine, and took her last breath. In an instant everything changed. Polly became Cook. Charlotte became Cook's Girl. Madeline became Governess. I reverted back to Young Master; my sister, Little Miss. And my father packed me off to boarding school.

I would never see the greengage trees fruit again.

❧

My toast had grown hard. The butter congealed. The consequences of time travel.

"A girl," reported Martha, walking into the kitchen. "Ridiculously long lashes. Dark hair. Looks just like her mother."

My American wife was an herbalist and midwife, as were her mother and grandmother before her. She carried soiled linens into the scullery.

"Are they still planning on leaving?"

"I assume so."

"Did you ask them?"

"No, I didn't ask them, Joseph. I was in the middle of delivering a baby. And it was a breech, at that." She lowered the sheets carefully into the copper. "Thank you for filling it."

Getting the water was my job. The scrubbing of the stains out of the linens was hers. I was progressive in all matters, including women's suffrage, but I had my limits.

She stirred the sheets with a wooden spoon and sighed. "I'm sure they haven't changed their minds."

Greengage had lost more than a few families in the past year. I suspected it came down to the siren call of modernity. Electric lights. Steamships. The cinema. They were afraid of missing out.

When Kathleen O'Leary was a few months along, her husband, Paddy, had let me know they were moving back to Ireland.

"You understand," he said to me in his thick brogue. "We're not from here. We must stop our fooling around and go home. If we stay any longer, we'll never leave."

As if Greengage had been nothing but a holiday.

Martha was a tiny thing. When I was sitting, we were practically the same height. She put her cheek next to mine. She smelled of lavender soap. Soon she'd also smell of the chicken fat she used to moisturize her red, chapped hands.

"There isn't anything you can do about it," she said. "Greengage is your dream, Joseph. It's not everybody's dream. You have to remember that. Besides, maybe they'll come back."

"This optimism is quite out of character for you."

"Yes," she mused. "There's something about a birth. One can't help but be hopeful."

❧

After boarding school, I had attended Pembroke College at Cambridge, where I'd graduated with a dual degree in classics and economics. Then my father insisted I embark upon a Grand Tour. I thought it an antiquated rite of passage, but he thought it a necessary rounding out of my education. How he prized worldliness! He wouldn't be able to pass as gentry, but damn it, his son would.

I traveled to France, Italy, and Germany. The Netherlands, Belgium, and Switzerland. I was supposed to go back to London then, to officially join Bell Textiles as my father's second-in-command; instead I dropped down into Turkey and then made my way to Egypt. From there I went to the Far East, and after that, to Russia. I finished in Greece, spending a few weeks in Athens before finally returning to England.

I was gone for over a year. It took me that long to realize how depressed I was at the idea of my future—sitting in a glass room looking down at the unlucky souls on the factory floor. The women spinning and operating the looms. The men weaving and carding. The boys sweeping the floor, dust and lint choking the air. My father's employees labored twelve hours a day, six days a week, amidst deafening noise for paltry wages. And why was I sitting in that glass room rather than on the floor? Not because of hard work, but because I'd been born into the right family.

This was not the life I wanted.

I couldn't stop thinking of those shimmering days before my father sent my mother away. The world she created. Between the hours of eight and seven, the household hummed and buzzed joyfully. No job was valued more than another. There were no delineations between rich or poor. To be useful, to do good work with people that you respected, that's what was important. But that world did not exist anymore.

I'd have to go out and create it.

———

It was in June of 1889 that I stepped off the train in Glen Ellen, California, steam curling around my ankles, the smell of fate in the air. I took a deep breath. A perfume of mountain laurel, ripening grapes, and chaparral danced on the breeze, deepened with a base note of sun-baked rocks and ferns.

My requirements for our new home? Close to a train—there were two train lines that ran through Glen Ellen. Near a large city—Santa Rosa and San Francisco were not more than a few hours away. Arable land—the hills were veined with springs.

I was enchanted as soon as I stepped off the train. As were the hundreds of others who got off the train with me who were now in the process of climbing into buggies and wagons, en route to the dozens of resorts, enclaves, and tent campgrounds in the area, where they would soak up the sun, get drunk on Cabernet, swim and picnic in the druidy redwood groves while reciting Shakespeare.

I climbed into a wagon and was driven off by a Mr. Lars Magnusson to view the old Olson farm. We traveled a mile or so into the hills, past oak glens, brooks, and pools of water, past manzanitas, madrones, and trees dripping with Spanish moss. Sonoma Mountain was to the west; its shadow cast everything in a soft purple light. When we finally reached the farm and I saw the luscious valley spread out in front of me, I knew this was it. *Greengage.* It would be a home for me and Martha at first, but I hoped it would soon be something more. A tribute to my mother and her ideals; a community in which she would have flourished, where she would have lived a good long life.

*Greengage.* The burbling creek that ran smack down the middle of the property. The prune, apple, and almond orchards: the fields of wheat, potatoes, and melons. The pastures for cows and sheep. The chicken house and pigsty. The gentle, sloping hills, mounds that looked like God's knuckles, where I would one day plant a vineyard. I was done with fancy trappings, done with servants, with balls and hunts, with titles, with soot, with my Cambridge pals, the stench of the city streets, with war. I was about to cast off my old life like a tatty winter coat.

"Did you know the Olsons?" I asked Magnusson.

"We emigrated from Uppsala in Sweden together."

"Why are they selling?"

"Dead."

"Dead? Of what, may I ask?"

"Husband, diphtheria; wife, scarlet fever."

"I'm very sorry to hear that."

"One right after the other."

"Really?" My mouth twitched in sympathy. "How difficult that must have been for you."

Magnusson scowled. Compassion from a Brit was both an unexpected and unwelcome intrusion. "You plan to use this farm for a commune?"

"A commune? Who told you that?"

"Jake Poppe. The proprietor of the general store."

"No. He is mistaken. It will be just me and my wife. At first," I added, not wanting to mislead him. There were already twelve people waiting to join us. Three farmers and their wives, four children, a carpenter, and a stonemason.

"You will need help. It's a large property," he said.

"I'll get help."

"You will pay well?"

"Yes." And I would pay for everything to get the farm up and running, but hopefully it would eventually pay for itself. That was my plan.

"Look, what is your price?" I asked, unwilling to reveal anything more to him.

Magnusson stared stonily down into the valley as if I hadn't spoken. I couldn't have guessed that this gruff, withholding Swede would not only join my endeavor but eventually become my indispensable right-hand man.

"Five thousand dollars," I blurted out. "That's more than fair. Fifty dollars an acre."

In a matter of weeks, on my twenty-fifth birthday, I would come into my full inheritance, and that would fund not only the purchase but all the other initial costs. My father would not be pleased. I would rarely speak to him again once he heard of my *cockamamie* plan.

Five thousand dollars was a fair price. The farm had gone to seed;

it would take a lot of work to bring it back. Magnusson snapped the reins, growled *ja,* and just like that I was the proud owner of one hundred acres of the promised land.

Within a few years Greengage was well under way. Word quickly spread of the farm in the Valley of the Moon where residents would not only be given a fair wage (men and women paid equally no matter what the job) but share in the eventual profits.

Was I a dreamer? Yes. Was it a foolishly naïve scheme? Possibly. But I was certain others would join me on this grand adventure, and it turned out I was right.

Our numbers rapidly increased. We built cottages for families and dormitories for single men and women. We erected a schoolhouse and a workshop. We repaired the chicken coop and the grain silo. The jewel in the crown, however, was the dining hall. The hub of the community, I spared no expense there. In the kitchen there were three iceboxes, two enormous Dutch stoves, and a slate sink the size of a bathtub. The dining room was a bright and cheery place: southern exposure, redwood floors, and five long trestle tables. Greengage was still small back then, only a few tables full at mealtimes, but I hoped one day every seat at every table would be taken.

&

"Please don't tell anybody about the O'Learys leaving," I said to Martha.

"No goodbye party? You just want them to sneak out in the middle of the night like thieves?"

That's exactly what I wanted. Leaving was contagious. In 1900, we'd had nearly four hundred people living at Greengage Farm. Now, in 1906, we were just under three hundred.

"They deserve a proper goodbye."

"A small party," I conceded. "Let's have it here, rather than the dining hall."

"No," said Martha, putting an end to the conversation. "It will be in the dining hall just like all the rest of the parties."

After she went back upstairs, I pulled a small tablet out of my breast pocket. In it, I kept a roster. I found the O'Learys' names and put lines through them with a pencil. I would just have to look for a new family to replace them.

The O'Learys left on a beautiful day in April. I'd gone to their cottage before the party I couldn't bring myself to attend, said my goodbyes, then made my excuses. An upset stomach. I said I was going off to the infirmary in search of an antacid. Instead I climbed up into the hills.

A hawk circled above my head. I soothed myself by looking down upon Greengage, which looked particularly Edenic that morning, bathed as it was in the late morning sun. All was as it should be. The hens were fat and laying eggs. Sheep grazed in the pastures and bees collected nectar.

I could see Matteo Sala working in the vineyard. He leaned back on his shovel and wiped his brow with a hankie. He came from a family of Umbrian vintners and was doing what he was born to do—what made him happy and fulfilled. That was the entire point of Greengage. Why would anybody want to live anywhere else?

The bell gonged, announcing the start of the party. People walked toward the dining hall. Fathers carried their children on their shoulders. Women strolled arm in arm. What was on the menu? Butter and cheese and apples. Mutton stew. Lemonade and beer. The smell of freshly baked sponge cake was in the air.

I'd worked hard over the years, carefully cultivating relationships outside of Greengage, gaining a solid reputation as a fair and honest businessman. We sold much of what we grew to restaurants in San Francisco and Glen Ellen. It wasn't difficult. Our produce was magnificent. When asked how we did it, I talked about nitrogen-rich cover crops, compost, some of the traditional Chinese farming methods that we employed. I didn't tell them our secret: contentment. We were a happy lot.

"Joseph!" called a woman's voice from down in the valley.

My sister, Fancy, had caught sight of me. Now I was doomed. I would have to attend the party.

"Get down here, you cranky old man!" she shouted.

She stood in the meadow surrounded by a group of children who all craned their heads up and began shrieking for me as well. My heart filled at the sound of their voices.

If only I'd brought my camera. I was not a sentimentalist, but I would have liked to have captured that moment. To freeze time in my lens. To be able to gaze back at the image of the party just beginning. To remember precisely how it felt when the pitchers of lemonade were full. When the cake had not yet been cut, and the afternoon stretched out in front of us.

Early the next morning, before dawn, I went outside to relieve myself. As I was walking back into the house, the floor began to shake. A temblor. I froze in the foyer, waiting for it to stop. It did not.

Martha shouted from upstairs. "Joseph!"

"Come down!" I yelled. "It's an earthquake!"

Martha appeared at the top of the stairs in her nightgown, her eyes wide. The staircase rattled, the banister undulated.

"Hurry!" I held out my hand as she ran down the stairs. I threw open the front door and we stumbled into the yard. The full moon was a bone-white orb in the sky.

The sounds that followed next could only be described thus: a subterranean clap of thunder, an ancient sequoia splitting in two, a volley of bullets, the roaring of a train coming into the station. A preternatural *whoosh, whoosh, whoosh,* a lasso spinning through the air.

We'd been through many earthquakes and I knew one thing for certain. Never had there been one like this.

It was April 18, 5:12 A.M. We clung to each other on the front lawn and waited for the shaking to stop.

When we walked back into the house, Martha gasped. Nothing had been disturbed. No painting had fallen off the wall, no porcelain jug had bounced off a counter. No books had slid out of a bookshelf. No brick had cracked in the chimney. Everything looked just as it had before. It was incomprehensible. In every earthquake, no matter how minor, we'd sustained some damage. This temblor was clearly a monster and yet . . .

"Quickly," said Martha. "We must see how the others have fared."

We all knew the emergency drill. Fire or quake—congregate at the dining hall.

The sky slowly brightened, from indigo to a robin's-egg blue. We walked through Greengage in a state of disbelief. No trees were downed. No chasm rent a field in two. The schoolhouse, the cottages, the dormitories, the winery, the barn, the cooper's shed, the workshop, every structure was intact.

Martha, who rarely showed her affection for me in public, picked up my hand and threaded her fingers through mine. It was not a romantic gesture. It did not make me feel like we were husband and wife. Instead it stripped me of my years and made me feel as if we were two orphan children wandering through a vast forest.

You might think our behavior odd. Why weren't we rejoicing? Clearly we'd been spared. But I was a realist, as was Martha.

Something was very wrong.

Everybody was present and accounted for, and there wasn't so much as a single scratch or a scraped knee. If there were wounds, they were not the visible sort.

The only thing that was different was the towering bank of fog that hung at the edge of the woods.

"Glen Ellen," Magnusson reminded us.

"Yes," said Martha. "Of course, our friends in Glen Ellen." She clapped her hands together and shouted out to the crowd. "We can't assume they've been as fortunate as us. We must go to them."

I stopped a moment to admire my spitfire of a wife. Barely five feet tall, maybe ninety pounds. Butter-yellow hair, which was loose around her shoulders, as the earthquake had interrupted her in mid-sleep. Martha was not a woman who traded on her beauty. It shone through, even though she eschewed lipstick and rouge and wore the plainest of serge skirts. I felt a sharp prick of pride.

It took us nearly an hour to organize a group of men and a wagon full of supplies.

"Be careful," said Martha nervously as I climbed up on my horse. "There could be more aftershocks."

"The worst is over," I said. "I'm sure of it."

"I don't like the look of that fog," she said. "It's so thick."

It was a tule fog, the densest of the many Northern California fogs. When a tule fog descended upon Greengage, spirits plummeted, for it heralded day after day of unremitting mist and drizzle. But these fogs were vital to the vineyard as well as the fruit and nut trees. Without them the trees didn't go into the period of dormancy that was needed to ensure a good crop.

"I know the way to Glen Ellen. I could get there blindfolded." I smiled brightly in order to allay her fears. "We'll be back before you know it."

Within seconds of entering the fogbank, I fell off my horse, gasping for air. Disoriented, confused, my chest pounding. A profound, fatal breathlessness.

The two men who had gone before me were already dead.

I was lucky. Magnusson pulled me out before I succumbed to the same fate. Friar, our doctor, came running. He later told me that when he felt my pulse, my heart was beating almost four hundred times a minute. Another few seconds in the fog, and I would have died, too.

In my experience, when the unthinkable happens, people respond in one of two ways: they either become hysterical or are paralyzed. Greengage's reaction was split down the middle. Some panicked and screams of anguish filled the air; others were mute with shock. Only a minute ago we'd ridden into the fog, as we'd done hundreds of times before. And now, a minute later, two of our men, husbands and fathers both, were dead. How could this be?

I preferred the wails; the silence was smothering. People covered their mouths with their hands, looking to me for answers. I had none. I was as shocked and horrified as anybody else. The only thing I could tell them was that this was no ordinary tule fog.

———

We put our questions on hold as we tended to our dead. The two men had been stalwart members of our community, with me since the beginning. A dairyman and a builder of stone walls.

Magnusson tossed a spadeful of dirt over his shoulder.

"Let me help," I said to him, feeling a frantic need to do something.

"No. You are not well."

"Give the shovel to me, I'm fine," I insisted.

Nardo, Matteo's sixteen-year-old son, took the shovel from Magnusson. "You're not fine," he told me. "You're the color of a hard-boiled egg."

He was right. Whatever had happened in the fog had left me utterly exhausted, and my rib cage ached. It hurt to breathe.

"Thank you," I said.

The boy bent to his grim task. Digging the graves.

That afternoon, time sped by. It careened and galloped. The men were buried one after the other. People stood and spoke in their honor. People sank to their knees and wept. Grief rolled in, sudden and high, like a tide.

Then it was evening.

I lay in bed unable to sleep. I felt hollow, my insides scraped out. I sought refuge in my mind. I turned the question of this mysterious fog over and over again. Maybe we were mistaken—perhaps the fog was not a fog, it was something else. Had the massive temblor released some sort of a toxic natural gas that came deep from the belly of the earth? If it *was* a gas, it would dissipate. The wind would eventually carry it away. By tomorrow morning, hopefully.

During breakfast in the dining hall, I relayed my theory. The gas was still there, as dense as it had been yesterday, though it didn't appear to be spreading. There was a little niggling thought in the back of my mind. If it was a gas, wouldn't it also emit some sort of a chemical, sulfurous odor?

I divided us into groups. One group set off to investigate the wall of gas further. Where did it start? Where did it end? Probably it didn't encircle all of Greengage, but if it did, were there places where it wasn't as dense? Places where somebody fleet of foot might be able to dart through without suffering its ill effects?

Another group conducted experiments. The gas had to be tested. Was there any living thing that could pass through it? The children helped with this task. They put ants in matchboxes. Frogs in cigar boxes. They secured the boxes to pull-toys, wagons, and hoops. They attached ropes to the toys and sent them wheeling into the gas.

The ants died. The frogs died. We sent in a chicken, a pig, and a sheep. They all died, too. The wall encircled the entirety of Greengage, all one hundred acres of it, every square foot of it as dense as the next. Whatever it was made of, it did not lift. Not the next morning. Or the morning after that.

The first week was the week of unremitting questioning. Wild swings of emotion. Seesawing. The giving of hope, the taking of hope.

Was it a gas? Was it a fog? Why had this happened? What was happening on the other side of it? Were people looking for us? Surely there'd be a search party. Surely somebody was trying to figure out how to get through the fog and come to our aid.

The second week was the week of anger. Bitter arguments and grief.

Why had this happened to *us*? What had we done to deserve this? Were we being punished? Why hadn't any rescuers arrived yet? Why was it taking so long?

People grew desperate.

Late one night, when everybody was asleep, Dominic Salvatore tiptoed into the fog, hoping if he moved slowly enough, he would somehow make it through. He got just five feet before collapsing.

We lost an entire family not two days later. Just before dawn, they hitched their fastest horse to their buckboard, hid under blankets, and tried to race their way through the fogbank. The baker was the only one awake at that hour. The only one who heard the sound of their wagon crashing into a tree. The horse's terrified whinny. The cries of the children. And then, silence.

After that, nobody tried to escape again.

The third week, the truth of our situation slowly set in. Meals at the dining hall were silent. Appetites low. Food was pushed away after one or two bites. Everybody did their jobs. What else could we do? Work was our religion, but it also produced our sustenance. It gave us purpose. It was the only thing that could save us. The cows were milked. Fields plowed. Everybody thought the same thing but nobody would voice it. Not yet, anyway.

Help wasn't coming. We were on our own.

# LUX

❧

San Francisco, California
1975

I sat in the passenger seat holding a squirmy Benno on my lap. He had a ring of orange Hi-C around his mouth. I'd have to scrub it off before he got on the plane; it made him look like a street urchin. He sucked on the ear of his stuffed Snoopy while his sticky hand worked the radio dial.

He spun past "Bennie and the Jets" and "Kung Fu Fighting."

"But you love 'Kung Fu Fighting,'" I said.

He vehemently shook his head and Rhonda laughed, her Afro bobbing. An X-ray technician at Kaiser, she'd left work early to drive us to the airport and help me see Benno off. We'd been roommates for the past three years, and she was the closest thing I had to family in California. Right now she seemed to be the only person in my life who wasn't keeping a constant tally of my failures (perennially late everywhere I went, maxed-out credit cards, beans and toast for dinner three times a week, musty towels, and an ant infestation in my closet due to the fact that Benno had left half an uneaten hot dog in there that I didn't discover for days).

Benno stopped turning the dial when he heard whistling and drumming, the opening instrumentals for "Billy, Don't Be a Hero." He nestled back into my chest. Within a minute, his eyes were welling up as the soldiers were trapped on a hillside. He moaned.

"Change the station," said Rhonda.

"No!" shouted Benno. "The best part's coming. The sergeant needs a volunteer to ride out." Tears streamed down his face as he sang along.

"God help us," I mouthed to Rhonda.

"Babe, is this a good cry or a bad cry?" I whispered to Benno.

"G-good," he stuttered.

"Okay." I wrapped my arms around him and let him do his thing.

Benno loved to feel sad, as long as it wasn't a get-a-shot-at-the-doctor kind of sad. He loved, in fact, to feel. Anything. Everything. But this kind of emotion, happy-sad, as he called it, was his favorite flavor. Tonight I would indulge him. We wouldn't see each other for two weeks.

Rhonda took one last drag of her cigarette and flicked the butt out the window. She was no stranger to this kind of melodrama. The song ended and Benno turned around, fastened himself to my chest like a monkey, and buried his head in my armpit.

I stroked his back until he stopped trembling. He looked up at me with a tear-streaked face.

"Better?" I asked.

He nodded and ran his finger across the faint blond down on my upper lip. He made a chirping sound. My mustache reminded him of a baby chick, he'd once told me. I told him you should never refer to a lady's down as a mustache.

I'd given Benno my mother's maiden name—Bennett. I loved the clean, bellish sound of it. She'd flown out for his birth; my father had not. At that point he and I had been estranged for more than two years, and my choice to have a son "out of wedlock" was not going to remedy that situation.

My mother, Miriam, had been campaigning for Benno to come east for a visit for months. I'd said no originally. The thought of shipping Benno across the country to my hometown of Newport, Rhode Island, land of whale belts, Vanderbilt mansions, and men in pink Bermuda shorts, was unthinkable.

"Please," she said. "He needs to know where he comes from."

"He comes from San Francisco."

"He barely knows me."

"You visit three times a year."

"That's not nearly enough."

She upped the ante. She promised to pay for everything. The airfare, the escort who would accompany him on the plane. Finally I relented.


I'd met Nelson King, Benno's father, in a bar a week before he shipped out to Vietnam.

"You're not from here" was the first thing he said to me.

I'd been in San Francisco a little over a year at that point and thought I was doing a pretty good job of passing as a native. I'd worked hard to shed my New England accent. I'd traded in my preppy clothes for Haight-Ashbury garb. The night we met, I was wearing a midriff-baring crocheted halter top with white bell-bottom pants.

"What makes you say that?" I asked.

"You hold yourself differently than everybody else."

"What do you mean? Hold myself how?"

He shrugged. "Stiffer. More erect."

I puffed out my cheeks in irritation. He was an undeniably good-looking man. Pillowy raspberry lips. Luminous topaz skin. He could be anything. Persian. Egyptian. Spanish. Later I'd learn his mother was black, his father Puerto Rican.

"That wasn't an insult," he said. "That was a compliment. You hold yourself like somebody who knows their worth."

I was nineteen, in between waitressing jobs, and desperately searching for an identity. That he saw this glimmer of pride in me was a tiny miracle. We spent every day together until he shipped out. It wasn't love, but it might have blossomed into that if we'd had more time together.

After he'd left, I'd written him a few letters. He'd written back to me as well, echoing my light tone, but then we'd trailed off. Three months later, when I'd found out I was pregnant, I'd written to him again, but didn't get a reply. Soon after, I discovered his name on a fatal casualty list in the *San Francisco Examiner*.

Although his death was tragic and shocking, the cavalier nature of our relationship and that it had resulted in an unexpected pregnancy was just as jarring. We'd essentially had a fling, a last hurrah that had allowed for a sort of supercharged intimacy between us. A quick stripping down of emotions that I imagined was not unlike the relationship he might have had with his fellow soldiers. The details of our lives didn't matter and so we'd exchanged very little of them. We'd just let the moment carry us—to bars, to restaurants, and to bed.

In an instant, the dozens of possible futures I'd entertained for myself receded and the one future I'd never considered rolled in.

I was pregnant, unmarried, and alone.

"What do I call the man?" asked Benno as Rhonda pulled into the airport parking garage.

"What man?"

"The man who lives with Grandma."

"The man who lives with Grandma will be away when you visit," I said.

The man who lived with Grandma, a.k.a. my father, George Lysander, would be spending the last two weeks of August at his cabin in New Hampshire, as he'd done for the last forty-something years. My mother had timed Benno's visit accordingly.

"I met him before," said Benno.

"You were only two, Benno. Do you really remember meeting him?"

"I remember," he insisted.

My father had been in San Francisco for the Association of Independent Schools' annual conference (he was dean of admissions at St. Paul's School in Newport). He'd arranged to stop by our apartment for dinner: it would be the first time he'd met his grandson.

"For you," he'd said to Benno, handing him a loaf of sourdough bread.

Benno peeked out from behind me, his thumb in his mouth.

"Say thank you to your grandfather," I prompted him.

"He doesn't have to thank me," said my father.

"Yuck crunchy bread," said Benno.

I watched my father taking Benno in. His tea-colored skin. His glittering, light brown eyes.

"I don't like it either," my father said. "How about we have your mother cut off the crusts?"

Benno nodded.

"We can make bread balls."

It was an offering to me. Bread balls were something my father and I did together when I was a little girl. Plucked the white part of the bread out of the loaf and rolled tiny little balls that we dipped in butter and salt and then popped into our mouths. It drove my mother crazy.

That was all it took. Benno adored my father. He climbed into his lap after dinner and made him read *The Snowy Day* three times. I washed the dishes and fought back tears of relief and resentment. Why had it taken him so long to come around?

But he hadn't—not really. When Benno was standing in front of him in the same room, he came around. But when he was three thousand miles away from us, back home in Newport, the distance grew again. His contact with Benno dwindled to a once-a-year birthday card. The incongruity between our realities, the life I'd chosen and the life he'd wanted for me, was too great to reconcile.

"What if he's there?" asked Benno.

"He won't be."

"But what if he is? What do I call him?"

"Then you call him Grandpa," I said. "Or Grandfather. Or Mr. Lysander. Or George. Christ, Benno, I don't know. You'll have to ask him what he wants to be called, but I don't think it'll be an issue. You won't see him."

My father had never missed his precious two weeks at the lake. He would not be missing them now.

———

I hated airports. They were liminal space. You floated around in them untethered between arrivals and departures. A certain slackness always descended upon me as soon as I walked through the airport doors.

"Are you scared?" I asked Benno.

"There's nothing to be scared of, kid," said Rhonda. "You're going on an adventure."

"I'm not scared," he said.

"Look, babe. The days will be easy. It's the nighttime that might be hard. That's when you'll probably feel homesick. But just make sure you—"

"Can we go up the escalator?" he interrupted me.

I stopped and crouched down. "Benno, do you need a hug?"

He blew a tiny spit bubble. "No, thank you."

"Don't do that, that's gross."

He sucked it in.

"Well, may I please have a hug?" I asked.

"I'm busy."

"You're busy? Busy doing what?"

"Leaving, Mama," he sighed.

Abortion wouldn't be legal in California for another three years, but even if it were, I never would have terminated the pregnancy. Perhaps given different circumstances I'd have chosen differently, but for this baby my choice was life. Of course I didn't know he'd turn into Benno. *My* Benno. I just knew he needed to come into the world.

Everybody thought I was crazy. Not only was there no father in the picture, but the father was black. How much harder could I make it for myself—a single white mother with a mixed-race child?

He brought me such joy. I never knew I was capable of loving somebody the way I loved him. Purely, ragged-heartedly. I couldn't imagine my life without him in it.

But my life with him in it was also ridiculously hard. I was a parent twenty-four hours a day. Every tantrum, every cry of hunger, every question was mine to soothe, to feed, and to answer. I had no spouse to hand him off to. No partner to help pay the bills. I could never just walk away. I was the sole person in charge of resolving every issue in my child's life, from how to deal with bullies, to *Is that rash serious?* to *He's three years old and still not using a spoon properly—what's wrong with him?*

I wasn't stupid. I'd known that raising a child on my own would be challenging. It was the isolation that blindsided me. The intractable, relentless truth was that I was alone. I could meet other mothers on the playground. We could talk bottle-feeding and solid foods, how to get rid of cradle cap, the best remedy for diaper rash. We could laugh, commiserate, watch each other's babies while somebody ran to the bathroom. But at the end of the day, they went home to their husbands and I went home to an apartment that was dark until I turned on the lights.

When we got to the gate, I was panicked but doing my best to hide it. I'd never been separated from Benno for more than a night.

"You must be Benno," said the stewardess when we checked in. "We've been waiting for you!" She picked up the phone, punched three numbers, and spoke softly into it. "Jill, Benno Lysander is here." She hung up. "You are going to adore Jill. She's a retired stewardess. She's got all sorts of activities planned for you, young man. Crossword puzzles. Hangman. Coloring books. A trip to the cockpit to meet the captain, and if you're very good, maybe you'll get a pair of captain's wings."

Benno's eyes gleamed. I was on the verge of tears.

"Stop it," Rhonda whispered. "He's happy. Don't screw this up." She pulled her camera out of her pocketbook. "Let's get a Polaroid of the two of you before you go."

Five minutes later Benno was gone.

We walked out of the airport silently. Rhonda waved the Polaroid back and forth, drying it. When we got to the car, she handed me the photo.

I'd forgotten to wash Benno's face. His mouth was still rimmed with orange.

Later, back at our apartment, Rhonda poured me a shot of Jack. Then she looked at my face and poured me a double. "It's only two weeks," she said.

I pounded the whiskey in one swallow. "What was I thinking? He's a baby."

"He's an old soul. He's a forty-year-old in a five-year-old body. He'll be fine. Give me that glass."

I slid it across the table and she poured herself a splash.

"I forbid you to go in his room and sniff his clothes," she said.

"I would never do that," I said.

"Hmm." She took a dainty sip of the whiskey.

*Elegant* was the word that best described Rhonda Washington. Long-necked, long-legged. An Oakland native, Rhonda had five siblings. All of them had *R* names: Rhonda, Rita, Raelee, Richie, Russell, and Rodney. Rhonda's mother said it was easier that way. All she had to do was stick her head out the window and yell "Ruh" and all the kids would come running.

"Now, what's your plan? You aren't just going to sit around the house moping," she said.

"I've got this week off, then I'm working double shifts all next week." I waitressed at Seven Hills, an Irish pub in North Beach.

"So what are you going to do this week?"

"I'm going camping."

"Camping?" said Rhonda. "Like, car camping? With a bathroom and showers?"

"No, middle-of-nowhere camping, with a flashlight and beef jerky."

I'd given a lot of thought as to how I was going to spend my first week of freedom in five years. I let myself fantasize. What if I could do whatever I wanted, no matter the cost? Where would I go? How about Paris? No, too snooty. Australia, then; Aussies were supposed to be friendly. Oh, but I'd always dreamed of seeing the Great Wall. And what about the Greek islands? Stonehenge? The

Taj Mahal? Pompeii? I pored through old *National Geographics*—
I rarely let myself dream anymore. My list quickly grew to over fifty
places.

In the end I decided on camping right near home. Yes, it was all I
could afford, but I wasn't settling; before I'd had Benno it had been
my escape of choice. I'd been to Yosemite, Big Sur, and Carmel. Closer
to home, I'd camped on Mount Tam, at Point Reyes, and in the Marin
Headlands. If I was depressed, angry, or worried, I headed for the
hills. If I didn't get a regular dose of nature (a walk in Golden Gate
Park didn't count), I wasn't right. I needed to get away from the city.
Sit by myself under a tree for hours. Fall asleep to the sounds of an
owl hooting rather than the heavy footfalls of my upstairs neighbors.
I was competent in the wilderness. Nothing frightened me. I wanted
to feel that part of myself again.

Rhonda tossed her head. "Okay, nature girl."

"What? I *am* a nature girl."

"Using Herbal Essence does not make you a nature girl, Lux.
When's the last time you went camping?"

"A few months before Benno was born."

"Do you still remember how?"

"You don't forget how to sleep in a tent, Rhonda."

"This just seems impulsive. Is it safe to go alone?"

"Yes, Rhonda, it is. I can take care of myself. I know how to do
this." My father was an Eagle Scout. He taught me everything he
knew.

"Fine. Why don't we make a list of what you'll need."

"I already have a list."

I knew what Rhonda was thinking. *Here goes Lux again, just throwing things together and hoping for the best.* That was how I lived my
daily life, from hour to hour, paycheck to paycheck. This was the only
Lux she knew. I wanted to show her another side of me.

"I've been planning this for months, you know," I said.

"Really?"

"Really."

"Well—good," she said. "Good for you."

I walked around the table and threw my arms around her. "Admit it. You love me."

"No."

"Yes. You love me. Silly, flighty me."

Rhonda tried to squirm out of my grasp, but she grinned. "Don't ask me to come rescue you if you get lost."

"I won't."

"And don't take my peanut butter. Buy your own."

"Okay."

I'd already packed her peanut butter.

I did go into Benno's room at midnight. I did lie down on his bed and bury my face in his pillow and inhale his sweet boy scent. I fell asleep in five minutes.

Rose Bennedeti and Doro Balakian were my landlords, the owners of 428 Elizabeth Street, a shabby ("in need of some attention but a grand old lady," said the ad I'd answered in the classifieds) four-unit Victorian in Noe Valley. A lesbian couple in their seventies, they occupied the top-floor flat. We lived on the second floor, the Patel family (Raj, Sunite, and their daughter, Anjuli) lived on the first, and Tommy Catsos, a middle-aged bookstore clerk, lived in the basement.

I loved Rose and Doro. Every Saturday morning, I'd go to the Golden Gate Bakery to get a treat for them. When I rang their bell, the telltale white box in my hands, Rose would open the door and feign surprise.

"Oh, Lux," she'd say, hand over her heart. "A mooncake?"

"And a Chinese egg tart," I'd answer.

"Just what I was in the mood for! How did you know?"

This Saturday was no different, except for the fact that the two women wore glaringly white Adidas sneakers and were dressed in primary colors, like kindergartners. They were in their protesting clothes.

"We're going to City Hall. Harvey's"—Doro meant the activist Harvey Milk; they were on a first-name basis with him—"holding a rally, and then there's to be some sort of a parade down Van Ness. Come with us, Lux."

"We shall be out all day, I would think," said Rose.

Rose and Doro were highly political, tolerant, extremely smart (Doro had been a chemist, Rose an engineer), and believers in everything: abortion rights, interracial marriage, and the ERA. *Why not?* was their creed.

"You'll join us, of course," said Doro.

I frequently gave up my weekends to march, picket, or protest, dragging Benno along with me. I believed in everything, too.

I put the bakery box on the counter. "I can't. I'm going on a camping trip."

"Oh, how wonderful!" said Doro. "Good for you, Lux. A Waldenesque sojourn into nature."

"Would you like to bring a little . . . ?" asked Rose. She put her thumb and index finger to her mouth and mimed inhaling.

"You smoke?"

"No, dear, we don't partake, but we like to have it for our guests. Shall I get some for you?"

I wasn't a big pot smoker.

"Just one joint," said Doro. "You never know."

Only in San Francisco would an old woman be pushing pot instead of a cookie and a nice cup of tea on you.

"All right," I agreed.

"Marvelous!" they both chimed, as if I'd told them they'd just won the lottery.


I'd purchased five Snoopy cards from the Hallmark store to send to Benno in Newport. I didn't want to overwhelm him or make him homesick. I just wanted him to know I was there. Filling them out was a surprisingly difficult task. I was going for breezy, with an undertone of *Mommy loves you so much but she did not sleep in your bed last night*. Here's what I came up with:

Benno, I hope you had a great day!
Benno, Hope you're having a great day!
Benno, I'm sure you're having a great day!
Benno, Great day here, I hope it was a great day there, too.
Benno, Great day? Mine was!

I asked Rhonda to mail a card each great day I was gone.

I wanted to camp somewhere I hadn't been before. I chose Sonoma, about forty miles from San Francisco. Wine country. Also referred to as the Valley of the Moon. When I read about it in my guidebook, I knew this was where I would go. Who could resist a place called *Valley of the Moon*? It was an incantation. A clarion call. Just saying it gave me goosebumps.

It was the Miwok and Pomo tribes who came up with the name *Sonoma*. There was some dispute as to whether it meant "valley of the moon" or "many moons" (some people claimed the moon seemed to rise there several times in one night), but that wasn't important. What was important was that the Valley of the Moon was supposed to be enchanting: rushing creeks and madrones, old orchards and wildflowers. The perfect place to lose myself. Or find myself. If I was lucky, a little of both.

By the time I'd finished packing, it was just after noon and 428 Elizabeth Street was empty. Rose and Doro were still at the rally, Tommy was working, Rhonda had taken the bus across the bay to visit with her family, and the Patels had gone off for a picnic in the park. I threw my pack in the trunk of my car and hit the road.

An hour and a half later, I pulled into the parking lot of Jack London State Park.

I relied on instinct out in the woods; I depended on my gut. I could have made camp in a few places, but none of them was just right. Finally I found the perfect spot.

The scent of laurel and bay leaves led me to a creek. I trekked up the bank to a small redwood grove. Sweat dripped between my shoulder blades. I was in my element; I could have gone another ten miles if needed. I dropped my pack. Yes, this was it. The air smelled of pine needles and cedar. The clearing felt holy, like a cathedral. I punched my arms in the air and hooted.

I experienced the absence of Benno (not having to hold him as a fact in my mind every minute) as a continual dissonance. I had to remind myself: *He's not here. He's okay. He's with Mom.* I hoped the shock would lessen as the days went on and that I'd not only acclimate to the solitude, but relish it. Nobody needed me. Nobody was judging me. I could do or act or feel however I wanted.

I peeled off my sweaty tank top. I stood there for a moment, barechested. It was warm now, but once it got dark the temperature would drop. I draped the tank top over a bush to dry and put on a clean T-shirt.

I pitched my tent. Beside my sleeping bag went *The Hobbit,* a pocket-size transistor radio, Doro's joint, a book of matches, and a flashlight.

For dinner I ate two Slim Jims and some peanut butter. By this time the woods were purpling with dusk. I crawled into my sleeping bag. In the pages of *The Hobbit* I'd tucked the Polaroid of Benno and me. I kissed my fingers and pressed them on his image. *Good night, sweet boy.*

I thought about reading. I thought about taking a puff of the joint. I did neither. I put my head down on the folded-up sweater that served as my pillow and instantly fell asleep.


I awoke in the middle of the night. It was freezing; I could see my breath. I slid on my jeans. I had to pee badly.

I unzipped the tent and stepped outside. Fog had enveloped the campsite, a fog so thick I couldn't see three feet in front of me. I gingerly walked a few yards from the tent, pulled down my jeans, squatted, and peed. The fog cleared for a moment and a glorious full moon bobbed above me in a star-studded sky. Seconds later the fog descended and my stomach clenched. I felt trapped.

I saw a light off in the near distance. It blinked once and disappeared. I stared steadily at it. It blinked again. Somebody must have a cabin out here.

Suddenly I was desperate not to be alone.

It seemed like only minutes, but it must have taken me hours to find that light, because when I broke through the fog, it was day and the sun shone brightly.

I stood at the edge of a meadow. This was no cabin; it was a large, barnlike structure, wood-shingled with red trim. Through the open doors, I could see dozens of people sitting at long tables. Silverware clinked. The smell of bacon wafted through the air.

A pang of loneliness struck me, seeing them all there, dining together. I frequently felt this way when I came upon groups, at the beach, at Seven Hills—the worst was the Christmas Eve service at Grace Cathedral. As if everybody but me had people. I guess I had people: Benno and, sometimes, Rhonda (on the rare nights she was home—she had quite a social life), but what I really wanted was a tribe.

I don't know how long I stood there, spying on them, wishing somebody would see me and invite me over. Finally I screwed up my courage and began walking across the meadow. I had nothing to lose. They'd either welcome me or send me on my way.

# JOSEPH

❧

*Valley of the Moon*
*1906*

A young woman stood at the threshold of the dining hall. A stranger. One moment we were eating breakfast, the next moment she was standing there. There was an air of impermanence about her. Was she an apparition?

"Um, hello," she said, blinking.

"Finally!" cried Fancy, jumping up from the bench. "You're here! I never doubted you'd come. I never gave up hope!"

Before I could stop my sister, she ran to the woman and embraced her. "Are there others? Is it just you? Why did it take you so long?"

Four months had passed since the fog had encircled us. In public I was always careful to use the word *encircled* rather than *trapped*. It left the door cracked open a bit. And through this open door had come—

"I think you've mistaken me for somebody else," the woman said, her cheeks flushed. "I mean, I'd like to be the one you expected. But I don't think I am."

No, she was not the one I expected; I never could have dreamed her up. Why was she dressed so strangely? Was she going to some sort of a costume party? Unlike the Greengage women, who wore their hair neatly pinned back, hers was loose, with a fringe so long it nearly covered her eyes. Instead of a skirt, she had on dungarees that clung to her pelvis and thighs. She wore a shirt that said KING'S ALE—SMILE IF YOU HAD IT LAST NIGHT.

"Look, Joseph," said Fancy, beaming, as if she herself were responsible for the woman's appearance. "Look!"

I walked over to them, fighting a vertiginous sensation. I felt exactly as I had just after the earthquake, when Martha and I discovered everything and everybody in Greengage was intact. Utter disorientation. As if my cells were being forcibly rearranged.

"I'm Joseph Bell," I said, introducing myself.

"Lux Lysander," she said, shaking my hand firmly.

Her eyes darted around the room, taking us all in. She had the same bewildered look on her face that I'm sure I had on mine.

"Are you shooting a film?"

*Shooting* a film? "How did you find us?" I asked.

"I saw your light through the fog."

"You came through the fog?"

She rubbed her upper arms and shivered. "It was so thick."

"So you weren't looking for us?" asked Fancy. "You just stumbled through the fog? And stumbled upon us here?"

Lux raised her shoulders somewhat apologetically.

"Did the fog make you feel ill?" I asked.

"Ill how?"

"Shortness of breath? Heart palpitations?"

"I felt a little claustrophobic, so my heart was probably racing, but no, I didn't feel ill." She looked around the room as 278 pairs of puzzled eyes stared back at her.

"I think I should leave," she said. "Obviously I'm interrupting something."

She backed out of the room, turned quickly, and started walking across the meadow.

"No, wait!" I shouted. I caught up with her, grabbed her elbow, and spun her around. "Please indulge me. Allow me to ask you a few more questions about the fog."

She looked alarmed. "Why? What's the big deal about the fog?"

"As you said, it's an unusually thick fog. And it's been here for a long time."

A group had gathered around us, desperate for information. I'd hoped to be able to question the stranger privately, but I could see that would not be an option.

"Please. May I ask you a few more questions?"

"Okay. I guess so," said Lux slowly.

"Thank you. Can you estimate how large an area is fogged in?"

"I'm bad at estimating distances."

"All right. How long did it take you to come through the fog?"

"Well, that was strange. It felt like just minutes, but it must have taken me much longer, because it was midnight when I left my campsite, but then when I got here it was morning."

Again that stomach-dropping feeling.

"You walked through the fog for a few miles?"

"Um—probably."

"You were camping? Where?"

"In the Valley of the Moon. Jack London State Park."

Jack London had his own state park? I knew he was doing well (he'd just spent thousands procuring a neighboring parcel of land), but I didn't know he was doing *that* well. A park named after himself? He'd always been a bit of a narcissist.

"Was the fog there when you arrived?"

"No, it was a beautiful clear night. I didn't get fogged in until after midnight, as I already told you." She was getting irritated at my line of questioning.

I was about to ask her about the earthquake—How had Glen Ellen and Santa Rosa fared? And what about San Francisco?—when Magnusson came up behind me and whispered in my ear, "Test the fog."

Yes. Whatever the woman said would be moot if we could now travel through the fog freely as she just had.

"Nardo!" I yelled.

A young man with a head of thick black hair made his way up to me. Our resident pig-keeper.

"We need a piglet," I said.

"Berkshire or Gloucestershire?"

"Gloucestershire. Get a runt."

I smiled at Lux, trying to put her at ease, and she shifted her weight from her left to her right foot nervously. "Are we done here?"

"Almost," I said.

Nardo disappeared and a few minutes later returned with a piglet, pink with black spots, tucked under his arm.

Lux lit up at the sight of the pig. "Oh, he's adorable."

"Give the pig to her," I said.

Nardo handed him over. "He's scared. Hold him close. Let him feel your heart beating."

"Will you do me one last favor?" I asked Lux. "Before you go."

But she was preoccupied with the piglet. "You need a name. I'm going to name you Wilbur," she said, stroking its silky ear. "You know, from *Charlotte's Web*."

I nodded impatiently. "Will you step into the fog for a moment? With the pig?"

"Why do you want me to do that?"

"I need to test a hypothesis."

"What hypothesis?"

I'd have to tell her the truth—a partial truth anyway. "The fog makes us sick. But it didn't make you sick."

"Why does the fog make you sick?"

I couldn't think of a lie quickly enough. "I have no idea," I said.

Her face softened. "Oh. Okay. So you're wondering if something's changed. That's why you're all looking at me this way. Because I came through and I'm fine and now you're wondering if you'll be fine, too?"

"Exactly."

"You want me to test it out for you. With the pig?"

"If you wouldn't mind."

Everybody had left the dining hall now and was standing just a few feet behind us, listening carefully to our conversation.

"Please," said Fancy.

"All right. But then I really have to go," she said.

I pulled out my pocket watch. "Sixty seconds. I'll let you know when it's time to come out."

"You're not worried I'll run away with your prized pig?" she joked.

That was the least of my worries.

She entered the fog. A minute later I called to her and she stepped back into the sun. The pig lay still in her arms.

"You—it's dead," she stammered. She glared at me. "It's your fault. You did this. You made me kill it. Why did you do that?" she cried.

"I'm sorry. Listen, it's only a pig," I said, thinking at least it wasn't one of us.

She shook her head, angry. "I have to leave right now. I've got to go home." Clearly rattled by the pig's death, she blathered on. "It's almost time for my son to start school. I haven't even bought his school supplies."

"But it's only August," I said.

As I said it, I was struck by a foreboding which I realized I'd been trying to fend off from the moment she arrived. But now it overtook me, filling me with trepidation.

"Mid-August," she said, "practically late August. The sixteenth. Nineteen seventy-five—in case you've forgotten," she added, looking me up and down. My trousers and suspenders. My boots and linen shirt.

I could sense everybody behind me stunned into silence, holding their breath. I finally said, "Well."

*Well* was a workhorse of a word that could mean so many things. *Well, nice to have met you. Well, this certainly has been an illuminating conversation. Well, a madwoman had found her way through the fog to Greengage.*

"I don't feel so good," said Lux.

"What's wrong?" asked Martha. She was using her clinical voice, firm and calming. It made you want to tell her everything.

"I'm dizzy," said Lux. "I think I'm going to puke."

She swayed and slid to the ground, the pig falling out of her arms. Then she went very still. Martha sank to her knees and pressed her fingers to the side of her neck, seeking out her pulse.

Dear God! Had I done this by forcing her back into the fog? Had I killed her?

"She just fainted," said Martha, sitting back on her heels. "She'll be fine. No thanks to you, Joseph. Asking her all those questions. Scaring her half to death. What were you thinking?"

Fancy, dumbstruck, said, "Nineteen seventy-five?"

Fancy's comment triggered the crowd and everybody started speaking at once.

Martha ignored the hysterics.

"Let's get her home," she said to me.

I bent and lifted her into my arms. Lux. This stranger.

Her name meant *light*.

We were halfway to the house when Martha said, "It was a full moon yesterday, wasn't it?"

During the four months we'd been trapped, it seemed that full moon days passed differently than all the rest of the days of the month. Just after midnight on the day of the full moon, time began to race by. Like a record on a gramophone played at ten times the normal speed, we sped up, too. Hours seemed to go by in minutes. The sensation lasted for twenty-four hours. It was only on the morning after the full moon that time resumed its natural pace.

"The earthquake happened on the day of the full moon," she reminded me.

"What are you implying?"

She made the irritated face she always made when she hadn't quite figured something out.

"Obviously she's mentally unstable," I said.

"That's just it. She doesn't seem unstable to me. Joseph—" She stopped. "What if she's perfectly sane?"

"Put her in the wing. The back bedroom," said Martha.

I laid Lux on the bed and she did not wake. Since she was unconscious, the two of us took the opportunity to survey her openly.

"What is the meaning of her shirt?" asked Martha.

"Something . . . sexual?" I guessed.

"Maybe. But why does she wear it?"

"Perhaps she likes drawing attention to herself."

"How can she breathe in those trousers? That can't be good for her reproductive organs. I wonder if she has any identification on her? I'm going to check her pockets," Martha announced.

She approached the bed and slid her hand into Lux's left dungaree pocket. Nothing. From her right pocket she pulled out a wrinkled-up sweets wrapper. *Jolly Rancher*. She smelled it.

"Cherry," she said. "Admit it, Joseph."

"What?"

"You've never seen any woman dressed like this."

"Yes, because I do not make a habit of cavorting with the insane."

"Oh, stop it. Something about her isn't right, but it isn't that she's crazy. There is no mercantile on earth that sells clothes like this in 1906."

"You're saying she's telling the truth?"

"I'm saying you have to open your mind. The unexplainable has already happened. We've been trapped by a fifty-foot wall of fog for four months. If we try to walk through it, we die. We must consider other"—she whispered, as if it hurt her to say it—"possibilities."

I sat down in a chair.

"What are you going to do?" she demanded.

"I'm going to wait until she wakes up."

"And then?" she pressed me.

"And then I'll ask her some more questions," I said, trying to sound as if I had a plan.

# LUX

❧

The sheets smelled of sun. The man who'd made me kill poor innocent Wilbur stood looking out the window, his back to me. I coughed and he turned around.

"You're awake," he said.

Joseph, that was his name. He was about six feet tall, with dark hair and eerie light blue eyes. His face was tanned and a bit weathered; he was middle-aged, probably in his forties, but he was in good shape. He bristled with vitality.

"What happened?" I asked.

"You fainted."

"I did?"

"You don't remember?"

"I remember feeling dizzy."

"And how do you feel now?"

I took stock. No headache, no dizziness—I was hungry, however. "Starving."

"When did you eat last?"

"Around seven last night. A couple of spoonfuls of Jif."

He made a funny face and I was embarrassed, as well as intimidated. He had a posh English accent.

The room was furnished impeccably in nineteenth-century farmhouse décor; not a detail had been overlooked. There was a washstand with a basin and pitcher. A rag rug. A lantern hung on the wall. The floor was hardwood, studded with black nails. The mattress rustled beneath me. Horsehair.

Why was the house outfitted like this? And why was this man dressed like Pa from *Little House on the Prairie*? Was this a movie set? Was he an actor? My mind kept scrabbling for purchase. The only thing that made sense was that they were in the middle of filming a scene when I arrived. But why didn't they stop acting when I'd barged onto the set? And why did the pig die when I entered the fog? That wasn't a special effect. The pig had really died; I'd felt its limbs go slack.

My heart started to pound. I put my hand on my chest to try and slow it down.

"Rest," he said. "I'll go get you something to eat."

The thought of being left alone panicked me. I grabbed ahold of his arm. "No, please don't leave."

He stared down at my hand, seemingly taken aback that I'd touched him, and I forced myself to loosen my grasp.

"I'm only going downstairs. I'll be back in a few moments," he said.

I looked at him wild-eyed.

"I promise, Lux."

He had a deep, resonant voice that immediately comforted me. It told me this was a man who did what he said he was going to do. Still, I didn't want to be left alone.

"I'm coming with you."

"You should stay."

"Nope, I'm coming." I slid my legs over the side of the bed.

When he saw that it was useless to try to stop me, he helped me to my feet and led me out of the room and toward the stairs. He pointed out the landing window. "That's Martha, my wife."

A woman knelt in the garden, her back to us. She tossed a pile of weeds in a basket.

"You live here? You and your wife?"

"Yes."

"For real? All the time?"

"It appears so," he said wearily.

"Dressed this way? Sleeping on horsehair mattresses on purpose?" He stuck his head through the open window. "Martha!" he shouted.

She swiveled around. It was the woman who'd asked me what was wrong just before I'd fainted.

"For God's sake, she's awake, come inside!"

Martha got to her feet, wiping her hands on her apron. She, too, was attired head-to-toe in period garb. An ankle-length skirt, a long-sleeved blouse, and button-up boots.

"You're not an actor? This is not a movie set?"

"No," he confirmed.

"I don't understand. Why would you choose to live like you're in the nineteenth century? Are you a religious sect? Is this some sort of a commune?"

I didn't really think they were a religious sect, but I hadn't yet landed on any other plausible explanation. Oddly, he seemed as confused as I felt. His pupils enlarged as he took in my jeans and hiking boots; my appearance was just as shocking to him as his was to me.

"Come down!" Martha called up from the bottom of the stairs. "I'll make you a sandwich."

Martha brought a bowl of plums to the table. She was a petite woman, so small that from a distance she looked like a child. Her blond hair was parted in the middle and pulled back severely, but she had a kind face.

"Are you still hungry?" she asked. "Have some fruit."

I'd already devoured my sandwich. "No, thanks, I'm good."

We were making small talk but the atmosphere was dense. Questions were gathering like storm clouds. I had questions, too, but they could wait. Their need to know seemed more urgent.

"We are not actors. We are not a religious sect. This is not a commune," said Joseph.

"I didn't mean to insult you. I was just trying to understand what was going on. Where I was," I said.

"You're at Greengage Farm," said Martha. "In the Valley of the Moon. You've heard of Greengage?" she asked.

"No."

Martha turned to Joseph, her eyebrows knit together in worry, no longer able to hide her emotions. "But we've been here for seventeen years. Everybody knows who we are."

I shrugged. "I'm sorry. I live in San Francisco. That's probably why I've never heard of you."

Joseph picked up Martha's hand and squeezed it.

"It's 1975?" he asked me.

"Yes," I said, baffled.

He gave me a grave look.

"What is the problem?" I asked.

He hesitated. "It's 1906 here."

Joseph told me their story. It was simple enough. The earthquake. The fog. Stuck here for four months. Then I arrived.

What wasn't simple—believing it.

"You can't expect me to buy this," I said.

"It's the truth," said Joseph.

"Well, if it's the truth, I need proof."

"Where's your proof you're from 1975?" he asked.

"Look at me," I said, pointing to my shirt.

"Look at us. That's your proof as well," said Joseph.

"Show her your passport," said Martha. "In the parlor desk. Right-hand drawer."

He sighed, but left to retrieve it.

"I'm sure this must be quite shocking," said Martha. "But I assure you we are just as shocked."

I stared at her and shook my head. They were dressed this way because they were from the past? Because they'd somehow got stuck in time? It was laughable. But Martha didn't look crazy. She looked completely sane.

"I'm sorry. I don't mean to be rude. But what you're asking me to believe is impossible," I said.

"I know," said Martha.

"It's preposterous."

"Yes," she agreed.

Joseph returned with his passport. It wasn't a booklet, like our current-day passports; it was a piece of paper pasted into a leather folio.

*By order of Queen Victoria, Joseph Beauford Bell is allowed to pass freely and without hindrance into the United States of America* ... blah, blah, blah, antiquated language. His date of birth. July 20, 1864. And at the bottom of the page—a photograph.

Unmistakably him.

When I was a child, my father forbade me to read science fiction or fantasy. Trash of the highest order, he said. He didn't want me muddying up my young, impressionable mind with crap. If it wasn't worthy of being reviewed in the *Times*, it did not make it onto our bookshelves.

So while my classmates gleefully dove into *The Lion, the Witch and the Wardrobe*, *A Wrinkle in Time*, and *The Borrowers*, I was stuck reading *Old Yeller*.

My saving grace—I was the most popular girl in my class. That's not saying much; it was easy to be popular at that age. All you had to do was wear your hair in French braids, tell your friends your parents let you drink grape soda every night at dinner, and take any dare. I stood in a bucket of hot water for five minutes without having to pee. I ate four New York System wieners (with onions) in one sitting. I cut my own bangs and—bam!—I was queen of the class.

As a result I was invited on sleepovers practically every weekend, and it was there that I cheated. I skipped the séances and the Ouija board. I crept into my sleeping bag with a flashlight, zipped it up tight, and pored through those contraband books. I fell into Narnia. I tessered with Meg and Charles Wallace; I lived under the floorboards with Arrietty and Pod.

I think it was precisely because those books were forbidden that they lived on in me long past the time that they should have. For whatever reason, I didn't outgrow them. I was constantly on the lookout for the secret portal, the unmarked door that would lead me to another world.

I never thought I would actually find it.

While I examined Joseph's passport, Martha did some quick calculations on a piece of paper.

"Joseph, if she's telling the truth, sixty-nine years have passed out there, but only four months in Greengage. That means almost three and a half of her hours pass per minute here. She's been here half an hour at least. That's about four and a half days she's been gone. Her people will be panicked. We've got to take her back to the fog immediately."

*If she's telling the truth.* They didn't believe *me*? Martha looked stricken with worry. Real worry, not fake. Three and a half hours passing per minute? Come on! Part of me wanted to laugh. I half expected a camera crew to come busting out of the pantry. But what if they were telling the truth and three and a half hours were passing per minute here? Oh God. If I stayed in Greengage just another hour, almost two weeks would have gone by at home.

"I've got to go!" I cried.

"Yes, you do," said Martha.

"No, you don't," said Joseph firmly. "There's no need to panic. You're on regular time now. I'd stake my life on it."

"We can't take that chance, Joseph," said Martha.

"What the hell are you two talking about?" I asked, getting more and more confused.

"Come," said Martha. "We'll take you to the fog. We'll try and explain as we're walking."

I looked back and forth between the two of them. If they were acting, they were putting on an amazing show.

We walked at a brisk pace, just short of a jog.

"That feeling we've had on full moon days, Martha . . . that sensation," Joseph said. He trailed off—whatever it was he was trying to describe was not easily articulated.

"Let me ask you something, Lux. Does it feel like time is racing by right now?" he asked.

"I don't know. I don't think so."

In fact it felt like the opposite. My anxiety was making time feel as opaque as stone.

"It feels like it's passing normally, correct?" he prompted.

"Well, it's not exactly zipping along," I said.

"For you, too, Martha?"

"Yes."

"But yesterday, before she came?" he asked Martha.

They exchanged solemn glances.

"What? Tell me," I said.

"Yesterday the day was over in what felt like an hour," she said. "It's been like that every full moon day since the earthquake."

"We knew it, we just didn't want to acknowledge it. The existence of this young woman confirms it," Joseph said to Martha. "Time *has* been speeding up on full moon days and to the tune of approximately fourteen years. But *only* on full moon days." He turned to me. "The rest of the days of the month—like today—time passes here exactly as it passes out there on the other side of the fog."

He nodded at me. "I don't think you're in any danger, Lux. You made it through the fog perfectly fine. And unlike us, it appears you can leave anytime. You can leave right now if you want to."

We had reached the meadow. The wall of fog still hung there.

"I think she should go," said Martha. "We don't want to take any chances."

I thought of Benno with my parents. Day two of his vacation.

"Please, go," pleaded Martha.

"If I go, will I be able to come back?"

"I don't know," she said.

I'd always had a sixth sense about Benno being in danger. I knew moments before he fell off the jungle gym that he was about to fall off. I would often wake in the middle of the night just before he woke with a nightmare. We were that close, that connected. I tried to reach out to him, to feel him three thousand miles away in Newport. I sensed nothing but good, clear energy. He was probably sitting on the couch with my mother, eating apple slices.

"I want to test out the fog once more," I said. "Make sure I'm okay in it. That I really can leave whenever I want."

Martha gave me a concerned look.

"I'll stay in there just a minute," I said.

"You have somebody—at home?" Joseph asked.

"Yes."

"If you decide not to come back, we'll understand," he said.

Heart thudding, I walked into the fog. It was thick, but I had no trouble breathing. In fact, it seemed completely indifferent to me. I turned my back on Greengage and tried to peer through the fog to my campsite. I saw the faintest of glows, which comforted me: it was daylight in my time just as it was daylight here. I listened carefully and heard the hum of Route 12. And then a song. A car radio as it drove by. The unmistakable chorus of Captain and Tennille's "Love Will Keep Us Together." That song reassured me like nothing else—it was on a constant loop on every station in 1975.

"A minute's up," said Joseph.

I hesitated, then stepped into the past.


"You're sure?" I asked Joseph, back at the house. "That unless it's the day of the full moon, time passes regularly here?"

"As sure as I can be."

Martha frowned. "I still think she should go back."

Now that I'd convinced myself time was passing normally on the other side of the fog, I didn't want to go, and I didn't want them to force me to. I had something to offer them. Information. I would parcel it out to them while trying to figure out what was really going on.

"We studied the earthquake in school," I said. "It leveled San Francisco. The city went up in flames. It was an eight-point-something on the Richter scale."

"The Richter scale?" asked Joseph.

"It's a way to measure the magnitude of a quake."

"Eight points is high?"

"It's a monster."

"We kept waiting for somebody to rescue us," said Martha. "We were well known in Sonoma. We sold our produce to every restaurant and grocery store within fifty miles of the farm. Why didn't people come looking for us?"

Joseph rubbed his temples and sank lower in his seat. I could see the depression enveloping him. Crazy or not, I had to do something.

"When I go home, I'll get help."

"What kind of help could you possibly get?" he asked.

"I don't know. Who could figure out a way to get you out of the fog? A physicist?"

He gave me a skeptical look.

"Maybe a meteorologist?" I said, attempting a joke. "Look, I'm not kidding. There's got to be a solution." Even though part of me was still not accepting the reality of all this, I forged ahead. "What about if I got some sort of a vehicle here? We could drive you through the fog."

"We tried that," said Joseph. "We have a Model T. Magnusson built a compartment for it. It was airtight. It didn't work."

The front door opened and footsteps pattered down the hallway.

"My sister, Fancy," said Joseph.

The woman who'd hugged me when I first arrived walked into the room. Her dark hair was cut in a pixie. She wore crimson silk pants and a green kimono top. Compared to Joseph and Martha, she looked like a circus performer.

"Is it true?" she asked Joseph. "Is it true?" she asked me, not waiting for her brother's reply. "Are you really from 1975?"

"I am."

Tears sprang to her eyes. "I've missed everything," she cried.

I understood what it was like to feel like life was passing you by.

"Did women finally get the right to vote?" she asked.

"Yes."

"What year?"

"Nineteen twenty, I think. Here in the States, anyway."

"Oh goodness, it took that long, did it? I have so many questions.

Is she going back? Are you going back?" She looked at me with a desolate face, handing me something folded up in a cloth napkin. "I brought you a treat. A bribe, really, to induce you to stay. Some of Elisabetta's almond sponge cake."

I opened the napkin. A square of golden cake was nestled into the cloth. "No inducing necessary," I said. "I'm staying."

I was still far from convinced it was 1906, but I wasn't leaving without looking around a bit more.

"For the day," clarified Martha.

"Goody!" said Fancy, clapping her hands. "There's so much we have to talk about."

Suddenly I was aware of how bad I must look. My shirt was smeared with mud. I smelled of Wilbur, of barnyard. I tried to smooth my hair down, untangle it with my fingers, but it was hopeless.

"You'll want to clean up," said Martha.

"I'd love a quick shower," I confessed.

Martha filled two large pots with water and put them on the woodstove. "Fancy, help me with the tub. It's in the scullery."

The two women carried a tin tub into the kitchen. There was no such thing as a quick shower here.

"I didn't mean for you to go to all that trouble. I'll just wash up at the sink. Or in the bedroom," I said, remembering the basin and pitcher.

"Nonsense," said Martha.

She emanated calm. She was a woman who dealt with the facts. I was here. I was dirty. I needed a proper bath.

"Your clothes will have to be washed. Get her something to wear in the meantime, Fancy," said Martha.

"You mean like a corset?" Was Martha wearing one right now? Her waist was tiny.

"I don't wear corsets and neither should you, Lux," said Fancy. "Constricts the lungs and the liver. Death traps. I believe in a more natural look."

The conversation had taken a disturbingly intimate turn.

"You may find me in the parlor when you're done," said Joseph, disappearing.

"There is nothing natural about your look, Fancy," said Martha.

Fancy's brightly colored silks were definitely not the norm, but I appreciated them.

"It's the latest style, I'll have you know. From Shanghai," she sniffed.

Once the water was hot, Martha poured the contents of the two pots into the tub, retrieved a towel and a cake of soap, and handed them to me.

"Martha makes the most brilliant soaps," said Fancy.

I smelled the soap. Lavender.

Martha abruptly left the room without speaking. Had I done something wrong?

"Don't take it personally. She's not good with hellos and good-byes," said Fancy. "We are going to be friends, I just know it." She smiled. "Would you like to know a little about me? I'm sure you're very curious."

She gazed at me expectantly.

"Of course," I said.

"Well, I've never been married. I've come close. I was engaged to Albert Alderson, but I called it off at the last minute, and do you want to know why? He had horrible breath, like blue cheese. Edward, my father, was so angry. He said, 'You're calling off a marriage because of halitosis? Give the poor man a mint! Or breathe through your mouth.' Yes, Father dear, I'll breathe through my mouth for the next fifty years. Ah, poor Edward. I'm afraid both his children gravely disappointed him. Are you married, Lux?"

I hesitated. "Yes," I lied. If she really was from an earlier era, I didn't want to put her off.

"Really, you lucky girl! There's nobody interesting here. What's your husband's name? Tell me all about him." She leaned forward, her eyes bright.

"Oh. Well, I sort of misspoke. I was married, but I'm not anymore."

Her face fell. I could tell what she was thinking. Was I a divorcée? To her, that was probably even worse than having a child out of wedlock.

"I'm a widow. I have been for a while. He, my husband, died years ago."

Who knows? Maybe Nelson and I would have gotten married if he'd lived. It was another lie, but it wasn't that much of a stretch.

"Oh, Lux, how awful."

"It's okay, we don't have to talk about it."

"I'm so sorry. How rude of me to interrogate you like this when we've only just met." She stood. "I'll go upstairs and gather up some clothes. You have a lovely, long soak."

I didn't have time for baths at home. Something about the experience made me feel like a child. I trailed my hands through the warm, soapy water and took inventory of the room. Pots of herbs lined the windowsill: chives, tarragon, and mint. On the shelves, stacks of simple white crockery. On the wooden table, bowls piled high with fruit and vegetables: peaches, plums, a basket of corn. It was so perfect—I still couldn't shake the feeling I was on a movie set.

My mother once told me impossibility was a circle. You started at the top and immediately fell, plunging down the curve, all the while saying to yourself, *This can't be.* Then you reached the hollow at the bottom. The dip. A dangerous place. You could lose yourself. Stay there forever, devoid of hope, of wonder. Or you could sit in that dip, kick your legs out and pump. Swing yourself clear up the other side of the curve to the tippy-top of the circle, where impossibility and possibility met, where for one shining moment they became the same thing. I pointed my toes underwater in the tub and gave a kick, so small it barely disturbed the surface of the water.

When had I grown so cautious?

The clothes were surprisingly comfortable. A pale blue blouse, velvety soft from being laundered so many times, and an oatmeal-colored cotton skirt, loose enough that it didn't bind at the waist. I felt strangely liberated wearing the outfit, grateful to leave my jeans behind. Fancy had given me a tortoiseshell clip, but I had no idea how to use it to pin my hair back. Instead I braided it loosely and bound the end with a bit of twine I found on the counter.

Finally I made my way to the parlor, where I found Joseph sitting in a leather chair, his eyes closed, listening to opera on a gramophone. An Italian soprano keening in a minor key.

The room felt intimate and cozy. Floor-to-ceiling bookshelves. A piano and a large mahogany desk that was covered with letters, papers, a microscope, sheet music, and—was that an ostrich egg? The air smelled pleasantly of candle wax and tobacco.

"All freshened up?" he said.

How long had he been watching me?

"It's a beautiful room. Inspiring."

"Inspiring? How?"

"I don't know. It just makes you want to do things. Discover things. Get out into the world."

"Ah," he said.

I was tongue-tied, seemingly incapable of saying anything intelligent while still occupied with casting about for an explanation. I needed to find some sort of strategy to calm my mind. I decided I would act as if this was really 1906, without truly accepting it. In that duality I was able to move forward.

"Are you feeling all right?" he asked.

"I'm fine."

"You look—" He trailed off, as if he thought better of what he was about to say.

"Shell-shocked?" I offered.

He nodded. "You find this impossible to believe."

"Well—yes," I admitted.

He sat erect in his chair. "How can I help?"

*How can I help?* Had anybody ever asked me that? He had such a calm, steady presence about him. His gaze didn't flit away from mine. He looked directly into my eyes without blinking. I was hanging on a rock face, searching desperately for my next handhold. He was offering to throw a rope up to me, to be my belayer.

"You're not lying, are you?"

"I don't lie," he said.

"You really believe it's 1906."

"It's 1906, Lux."

"Do you believe I'm from 1975?"

"I must confess I'm struggling a bit with that."

"You think I'm lying?"

"No. I think you believe it's 1975."

"Then you think I'm crazy."

He hesitated and then said, "It has crossed my mind."

"So we're both thinking the same thing. That the other is a lunatic."

I don't know who began laughing first, but the laughter was contagious. I stood ten feet away from him, but that distance closed rapidly, our communal astonishment at the madness of our situation serving as a bridge, connecting us to one another.

Finally he stood. "I think a tour of Greengage is in order."

"You want to give me proof that this place is really what you say it is."

"Proof and a chance to show the farm off."

"You're the one in charge? The owner?" I suspected he was—everybody looked to him.

"I bought the original parcel of land, but as far as I'm concerned we all own Greengage Farm equally."

"Greengage? Oh, because of the plums? You must grow them. I love greengage jam."

"We don't grow greengage plums. They are notoriously hard to grow."

"Then why did you name the farm Greengage?"

He frowned ever so slightly. "Would you like a tour?"

"Sorry. Yes, please," I said. *Stop asking so many questions, Lux.*

As we walked, Joseph explained to me what he'd set out to do, what kind of a community he'd envisioned: a residential farm where all jobs were equally valued and all jobs, whether done by men or women, paid out the same wage.

"Women still don't get paid as much as men," I said.

I watched his reaction carefully. Would he be surprised to hear that fact? He didn't seem to be.

"You were quite forward-thinking for your time, then," I said. "A real feminist."

"A feminist?" He raised his eyebrows.

"Somebody who supports women's rights."

"Yes. Yes. Of course."

Unless he was a brilliant actor, he'd never heard the word *feminist*. You couldn't open a newspaper or magazine in 1975 without reading an article about feminists protesting some inequity or another.

Despite my skepticism, my heart lifted. What he was describing was a truly egalitarian society. I was in the presence of an honest-to-God idealist. I wanted to share with him that I was an idealist, too, but the idealist in me had been driven underground. Buried by the past five years of a shitty, low-paying job, and my inability to figure out how to better my and Benno's lives.

*Please let him be real. Please let this place be true,* a little voice inside me said.

It was August and the fields were high with corn. In the orchard the last of the peaches clung to their branches and the apples were showing their first pinkish blush. The vegetable garden overflowed with produce: peppers, green beans, zucchini, tomatoes, cucumbers, and squash. It was the farm's busiest season, he explained.

There were people hard at work everywhere. Some ignored me when he brought me by; others stared boldly. I didn't sense unfriendliness, more of a stunned curiosity. Would I help them? Would I hurt them? I tried to appear as unthreatening as possible. I said hello whenever I caught somebody's eye; still, I knew they were relieved when I moved on. I felt like a voyeur. Perhaps they felt like an exhibition.

"How do you decide where to put people to work?" I asked.

An elderly man picked corn. For every ear of corn he put in the basket, the woman beside him picked a dozen. It obviously wasn't an easy task for him.

"I don't decide, they decide," Joseph said. "If they want to be on the garden crew, they're on the garden crew. If they want to be on the animal crew, they're on the animal crew."

"But what if everybody wants to be on the animal crew and nobody wants to be on the garden crew?"

"That's never been the case. The numbers always work out."

"But what if somebody isn't suited for the particular kind of work they want to do?"

"There's always some way they can contribute. If you tell a man he's useless, he becomes useless."

*Yes. And if you tell a woman she's only good enough to clean up people's dirty plates, she'll always be cleaning up people's dirty plates,* I thought.

"How many crews are there?" I asked.

"Garden, fields, orchard, brambles, animals, building, medical, domestic, kitchen, winery, and school," he rattled off. "There's also the herb garden, but that is Martha's domain—she works alone."

"Brambles?"

"Blackberries, raspberries, strawberries, too, even though they're not technically a bramble. The bramble crew is mostly children, who end up eating practically everything they harvest. But it's a fine first job for them. They have to learn how to pick around the thorns."

"How many people live here?"

"Two hundred and seventy-eight: 55 children, 223 adults."

"And you can produce enough food to feed you all?"

"More than enough. In fact, since the fog, we've let some fields and gardens go fallow."

He led me into a large two-story building. "This is the workshop, the building crew's home base, although most of them are out on the grounds this time of day."

The workshop was cavernous. Tucked into the corner was a blacksmith station. Every kind of tool imaginable was neatly hung or stacked against the back wall. There was even a horse mill.

Maybe Greengage was a living-history museum, like Old Sturbridge Village or Colonial Williamsburg, where the employees were paid to dress up and stay in character no matter what.

A man sanded a plank at one of the tables. It looked like he was putting together a tiny house.

"Magnusson!" Joseph called out.

The man stalked across the workshop floor. He was an intimidating figure; he towered over Joseph. His hair was white-blond, his eyes cornflower blue.

He stared at me, clicking his massive jaw.

"For God's sake, don't be a cretin. Be polite and say hello," said Joseph.

"Hello," he grunted.

"What are you building? A house for elves?" I said nervously.

Magnusson rolled his eyes.

"A privy," said Joseph.

A privy. Right. No flush toilets here.

"Sorry," I said, then cringed. *Act normal, Lux; they're just people.* I was surprised how badly I wanted them all to like me.

"What do you mill?" I asked.

Magnusson walked away without a word, done with me and my ridiculous questions.

"Grain," answered Joseph. "Oats. Wheat and corn."

"Oh," I said in a small voice. "I'm sorry. I live in San Francisco. I don't know how you do things on a farm."

"That's fine. I love talking about what we do." He led me out of the workshop.

"I'm afraid I made a bad impression on your friend."

"Magnusson is a Swede," he said, as if that explained everything.

We walked past pretty little cottages and two dormitories. On our way to the schoolhouse, Joseph told me they didn't keep to a regular school year. When the children were needed to help with a harvest, school let out. When the community work was done, school was back in session again.

The schoolhouse was empty today. Written on the chalkboard was a Walt Whitman quote.

*Now I see the secret of making the best persons: it is to grow in the open air and to eat and sleep with the earth.*

Sun streamed through the windows and birdsong filled the air. How I would love for Benno to go to school in a room like this. How I would have loved to have gone to a school like this. Against my better judgment, my spirits soared.

"Whitman is Martha's patron saint," Joseph said.

"Did you and Martha meet here on the farm?"

"We met at a lecture on cross-pollination methods for corn."

Was he serious? He didn't crack a smile. Yes, apparently he was serious.

"Is she from California?"

"She's from Topeka, Kansas. A farmer's daughter."

He told me how Martha had been raised by her Scottish grandmother, a feisty old woman who ate bacon sandwiches, befriended the Kiowa, rode bareback, and practiced herbal medicine, as had her mother, and her mother before her. It was this grandmother who made sure Martha knew her digitalis from her purple coneflower, this grandmother who transformed her into a gifted herbalist.

"Martha's a midwife as well," he said.

"Wow. So she takes care of everybody?" Two-hundred-something people? That was a lot of responsibility.

"We have a physician here, too. Dr. Kilgallon, better known as Friar. They have an agreement. If it bleeds or is broken, it goes to Friar. Everything else goes to Martha."

"So she treats people with what—tinctures?" I'd seen the row of tinctures at the co-op. I'd always been intrigued, but I was doubtful they'd work as well as Tums or Tylenol.

"Not just tinctures. She makes eye sponges and wine cordials, fever pastes, catarrh snuffs, blister treatments. But more often than not, her prescription is simple. Chop wood. Eat a beefsteak. Kiss your children," he said.

"That works?"

"You'd be surprised. Never underestimate the power of having somebody pay attention to you."

I wanted a Martha in my life.

He took me to the wine cave. Past the hay shed and the chicken coop, the sheep barn and the horse barn. We climbed into the hills and he proudly showed me one of the four springhouses on the property. Then he proceeded to give me a long lecture on gravity-propelled irrigation systems while we gazed down upon the farm, which was set in the bowl of the valley, a verdant paradise.

I was enchanted. My chest ached with longing. There was something here that was familiar, that I'd been missing but I hadn't had any idea I'd been missing until this man had shown it to me.

"Well, if you have to be trapped, this is the place you'd want to be," I said.

His face transformed into a mask of incredulity. "Good God." He quickly walked away, leaving me to follow.

# JOSEPH

❧

I t was exhausting, trying to act normal around her when what I really wanted to do was ply her with questions. Instead she plied me with questions—clearly she'd never spent time on a working farm. Still, she was not a prissy woman. She didn't hold her breath in the pigsty, or shudder when she learned she would have to relieve herself in a privy. I could see she was fit. Her hands were red and rough like Martha's; she used them to make a living.

"Where in San Francisco do you reside?" I asked.

"Noe Valley."

"Where do you work?"

"At a pub."

"You're a barkeep?"

"I'm a waitress, but don't look so shocked. Women bartend, too. Where are we going?"

She was afraid I was taking her back to the fog. I have to admit, if I'd been told I'd traveled back in time nearly seventy years, I'd have run back to my own time as fast as I could. That would be most people's natural reaction. Instead she'd worked hard to keep an open mind. She listened intently and soaked up every little detail, and gradually, over the course of the afternoon, I'd seen Greengage cast its spell on her. She hadn't said anything to that effect, but it was written on her face—awe.

Despite my misgivings about her, I was heartened to see Greengage had lost none of its charms. Indeed, it had a beauty and goodness that seemed to transcend questions like the ones we were grappling with today. If she really was from 1975 (and I still wasn't convinced), I couldn't begin to imagine the things she'd seen. The kind of life she lived. That our simple community had dazzled her gave me hope.

All at once I realized how badly I wanted for her to be real. To be who she said she was.

"I'm taking you to the house for a rest. I'm sure you must be fatigued."

She smiled. "I am. I am fatigued."

"We eat early. The dinner bell rings at six."

Her face clouded over. "I don't have any money to pay for dinner. I didn't bring any with me. I'm sorry."

That was four times in the last hour that she'd apologized. I couldn't hold my tongue.

"You must stop saying you're sorry every other minute. It's—there's simply no need for it." I stopped myself from saying how unattractive it was to hear a woman apologizing all the time. "There is no fee for dinner. You are our guest."

I hadn't laid my hand on any currency in four months. That had been one of the unforeseen boons of our strange circumstances, not having to worry about money, dispensing it or making it.

She stared at me, her color high.

"I didn't mean to offend you," I said.

"You're right. I apologize too much. I hate that about myself." She looked off into the middle distance. "I'll help clean up, then."

"That's not necessary."

"But everybody here pulls their weight. You just showed me that. I can't take something from you without giving something back."

"You are our guest," I repeated. "We don't expect anything in return."

Her eyes welled up with sudden tears.

———

"Joseph, you old boot," said Fancy. She sat on the front porch, waiting for us. "You've monopolized Lux for far too long. Give somebody else a chance."

"We were on a tour," I said.

"What did he show you? The boring workshop? The chicken coop? I would have taken you to meet Dear One."

Dear One, known to everybody else as Eleanor, was the daughter of Polly Bisbee (our childhood cook) and was Fancy's closest friend. *Dear One* as in "Dear One, would you get me a cup of tea?" "Dear One, would you mind ever so much closing that window?" She'd been Fancy's companion until my mother died, and then she became her lady's maid. Fancy would never refer to her as a maid now. My sister had been slower to evolve than me, but eventually she had come around.

Fancy and Eleanor were not permanent residents of Greengage. In fact, they'd arrived for their annual visit just days before the earthquake. It had taken them four weeks to travel by steamship from London to New York and then another week on the train from New York to San Francisco.

"I would love to meet Dear One," said Lux.

Fancy jumped up from her chair. "We're off, then!"

"No, she is in need of a rest," I said.

Lux nodded at me gratefully. She'd been too polite to turn down Fancy's invitation, but she really did need to sit down. She looked quite pale.

"I suppose you've had quite a shock," said Fancy.

"Well, you've had quite a shock, too," said Lux.

Fancy was usually steadfastly upbeat, it was one of her great strengths. But this was not one of those times; she now slumped in despair. I drew my sister to me. She laid her head against my shoulder and sighed.

"Yes, I guess we have," she said.

Dinner was a strange affair. Some people came and paid their respects to Lux; they bobbed and curtseyed and welcomed her, making me feel I was sitting next to royalty. Others avoided her like a leper, going out of their way to bypass her, walking down another row so they wouldn't risk having to say hello.

It was terribly awkward. Twice I got up to leave and twice Martha stopped me.

"They are looking to you to set an example," she said. "They're nervous. They don't know how to make sense of what's happening. Give them some time."

Lux was polite. She greeted everybody with the same warmth. She looked them in the eyes and shook their hands like somebody who wanted desperately to be accepted. She started on another round of *I'm sorries*—"Sorry for what's befallen you," "Sorry it hasn't befallen me," "Sorry I'm free and you're not"—but I kneed her under the table and she immediately stopped.

"Sorry," she said to me under her breath. "This is just so weird. I don't know what to say."

"Do something," said Martha to me.

I stood and clinked on my glass with a knife. The room quieted.

"Listen up," I said. "These are the facts. This is what we know. This woman, Lux, accidentally found her way here through the fog. It seems she can come and go through the fog, though we cannot."

I couldn't bring myself to voice the unfathomable, that according to Lux, on the other side of the fogbank it was 1975. I paused, expecting somebody to start interrogating me about it, but the room was complicit with silence. We all needed some time to grapple with this news.

"I know you want answers. You want to know what's happening. What does this mean? Her arrival." I took a deep breath. "I don't think it means anything."

This was a lie. Her arrival changed everything and we all knew it, but because we didn't know what it *really* meant for us, everybody agreed to let this lie stand for now.

"Not for us, anyway. For us life goes on as it has for the past four months. Nothing has changed. We will get up in the morning and meet with our crews and put in a good day's work, and then we will sleep, knowing we've earned our rest. And the next day we will wake up and do it all over again."

"Is she staying?" Matteo asked.

I looked down at Lux.

"I'd like to stay a few days, if you'll let me," she said quietly, so only I could hear.

I fought to keep a neutral expression on my face, as if it didn't matter to me whether she stayed or left.

"For a while," I confirmed. "Treat her like one of us."

"Yes, please," said Lux. She got to her feet. "I don't want any special treatment."

Oh, but she was special; this was clear the moment she stood. Even if she wasn't from the future, she could travel freely through the fog and we could not. She blinked once, twice, and took her seat.


I sat on the porch in the dark. I couldn't sleep; I'd been sitting there for hours. I heard Lux before I saw her. The sound of her bare feet creeping down the stairs. The squeak of the door opening. She padded to the railing in a muslin nightgown (Fancy must have lent it to her), put her hands on the railing, arched her back, and sighed.

I cleared my throat, announcing myself, and she jumped.

"You could have told me you were there," she said.

"My apologies," I said.

My eyes had acclimated to the night long ago, so I took the opportunity to survey her unseen. I estimated her age as somewhere in her twenties. Her face was without wrinkles, her complexion fair but tanned by the sun. Her brown, shoulder-length hair had fallen out of its braid. She impatiently pushed her fringe to the side, exposing dark straight brows. She had a small but sturdy frame and was of medium height. I could smell Martha's soap on her skin; it was unnerving.

"Can I have one of those?" she asked.

I gave her one of my precious cigarettes. She leaned forward and I lit it with a match. She inhaled deeply, held the smoke in her lungs and blew it out.

"Do you still think I'm mad?" she asked.

"I'm on the fence."

"Well, how do we get you off the fence?"

"Do you have any identification?"

"Not on me." She thought for a moment. "Everything's at the campsite."

"You could answer a few questions," I said.

"Okay. Shoot."

"Who's the president of the United States?"

"Gerald Ford," she said without hesitation.

"What number president is he?"

"Thirty-eight."

"Who's the prime minister of England?"

"I have no idea. But I can tell you that in 1914, England, along with France, Russia, and Japan, will declare war on Germany. America will try and stay neutral, but finally in 1917 we'll join the fight and help win the war, but at a terrible cost. Something like seventeen million people will die. Trench warfare. Gas. U-boats." She shuddered. "World War I."

"World War *I*?"

She looked at me calmly.

"That implies there's a World War II."

"From 1939 to 1945," she said. "Something like seventy-five million casualties."

"Dear God. World War III?"

"Not yet. But America just wrapped up a war with Vietnam." She took another puff of her cigarette. "Oh, yeah, and a man walked on the moon."

I grunted with skepticism.

She grinned. "I'm not pulling your leg. Neil Armstrong in 1969. Do you want to hear more? I could tell you about the Depression, about Prohibition, about the civil rights movement, about Martin Luther King, about *Roe v. Wade*. Abortion is legal now, by the way."

I held up my hand. "That's quite enough, thank you. A few minutes of quiet, if you don't mind."

"Of course. You'll want to take that all in," she said a little smugly, pleased to have put on such a convincing show.

The crickets chirped. A moth batted its wings futilely against a closed window. My mind reeled.

"Don't you want to ask me any questions?"

"My questions were answered today when you took me on the tour," she said.

"Are you saying you believe me?"

"No. Yes. I mean kind of. What else can I do? At some point you just have to sort of commit, right?"

"Commit to what?"

"This. Us. What's happening. That I'm here. That you're here. That this can't be, and yet it is. It's beyond the laws of nature, but until some other evidence surfaces to disprove you, I'm going to go along with all this, and maybe you'll go along with it, too. What other choice do we have?" She shrugged.

She'd just expressed the same conclusion I'd been coming to. Continuing to mistrust each other seemed like a waste of energy, at least for now.

"Do you think we did something? To bring this on?" I asked.

"Like what? What could you have possibly done?"

She was right. We had done nothing but work hard to be self-sufficient and treat each other fairly and equitably.

"You were happy?" she asked.

"We were happy."

Clarification: *most* of us had been happy. The O'Learys hadn't been happy. Paddy's last words? "If we stay any longer, we'll never leave." How right he had turned out to be.

"So. That's not a crime. That's what everybody wants." She took another deep pull on the cigarette. "I have a joint back in my tent. I wish I'd brought it."

"A joint?"

"Pot. Marijuana. Um, cannabis—I guess that's the proper name. What do you call it?"

"Hashish."

"Is it illegal? It's illegal now."

"You could mail-order maple sugar hashish candy in the Sears, Roebuck catalog."

Lux laughed. "You're kidding."

"No, I'm afraid I'm not."

She flicked the ash of her cigarette over the railing.

"Are you married? Do you have children?" I asked her, changing the subject.

She sat down in the rocking chair next to me. "I'm a widow. I live with my son, Benno. He's five."

She said this dryly, with very little emotion.

"My condolences."

"Yes, well, it was a while ago."

"Still, that must have been very difficult."

"He was in the army. He died in the war."

"The war with Vietnam?"

"Yes."

"Where is your son right now?"

"He's with my mother."

"You live with your parents, then? Siblings as well?"

She gave me a strange look. "I live alone. Well, I have a roommate, Rhonda, but she's barely ever home."

"Where do your parents reside?"

"In Newport, Rhode Island."

"Across the country? Why aren't they with you? However do you manage on your own without help?"

She stood, walked down the stairs, and threw her cigarette in the dirt. "I manage just fine. Nobody lives with their parents anymore. Everybody leaves home. Everybody. It's just what you do."

This was the moment when I fully believed she was from a different time. She could relay an encyclopedia's worth of historical facts to me; she could tell me of every scientific, mathematical, and medical advancement; she could describe the plots of award-winning novels that hadn't yet been written, hum the tunes of unheard operas and symphonies, tell me of new planets, new cocktails, new styles of clothing—but none of it would convince me more than this simple fact. She was alone, she and her son. This would have been a very rare scenario in my time.

Lux walked back up the stairs. "I've got to get some sleep. What time do you wake up in the mornings?"

"Five."

"Everybody gets up then?"

"It depends on the crew."

"What crew will I be on?" She tipped her chin up, looking defiant, as if I were about to deny her the opportunity to be put to work.

"What crew would you like to be on?"

"Garden," she said.

"Fine. Garden starts at seven, but the breakfast bell rings at six."

"I'll be up at five-thirty," she said.

"Do you have a watch?"

"No, do you?"

"I don't need one. I wake up the same time every day."

"Same," she said proudly. "See you at dawn."

# LUX

I woke to the sound of something being poured, Martha filling the washbasin with hot water. Through the window I could see the first streaks of red in the sky. The sun hadn't risen yet.

I sat up in bed. "You don't have to do that. I can do it myself." I didn't want her to wait on me—it made me uncomfortable.

"It's chilly in the mornings. You won't be used to the cold house."

I pulled back the covers and put my bare feet on the floor. The wood was freezing. I gave a little gasp.

Martha dragged the rag rug to the side of the bed. "That's where it belongs, not in the middle of the room." She scowled and I felt guilty, as if I had been the one who moved the rug, though I wasn't.

"Joseph says you want to join the garden crew today."

"Yes, if that's okay. Unless I'm needed elsewhere."

She looked impeccable, her hair swept back neatly into a bun. She wore a gray skirt and a spotlessly clean apron.

"Where you work is entirely up to you, as I'm sure Joseph explained." She eyed my skinny ankles suspiciously. "Although it's a busy time of year in the garden. You'll be harvesting. It's backbreaking, repetitive work. Kneeling. Stooping over, picking, hauling baskets to the wagon."

"That won't be a problem. I'm a waitress. I carry platters of food all day long. I can even carry a keg of beer up from the basement." A pony keg, but still.

She cocked her head as if trying to imagine me with a keg of beer on my shoulder. "The water's getting cold," she said.

"Thank you. And next time—"

She waved dismissively at me. "Yes, yes, you'll get your own water. Don't worry, I have no intention of being your servant."

I dressed in the same outfit I'd had on yesterday. Skirt, blouse, and hiking boots. When I got downstairs, I found Fancy waiting for me.

"Good morning!" she piped. "Did you sleep well?"

I hadn't slept much at all. I'd been too revved up after my conversation with Joseph, which for some reason had left me feeling exposed. Also, I couldn't stop thinking about Benno. Day three without him. I missed him desperately.

"I slept okay."

"Wonderful," said Fancy. "Let's go to the dining hall. I'm starving."

"Should we wait for Joseph and Martha?"

"They left ages ago," she said, linking her arm through mine.

A few minutes after we set out, the bell rang. Families streamed out of their cottages and the dormitories emptied. Children ran ahead of their parents, dogs at their feet. Roosters crowed. Horses pushed their velvety noses into fresh hay.

I could smell the pancakes from a hundred feet away. My stomach grumbled.

"Everybody's looking at us," said Fancy. "At you."

They were looking at me but something had changed since last night. Their faces seemed more open, less guarded.

"It's odd, isn't it?" said Fancy. "How quickly something unbelievable becomes believable."

I was thinking the very same thing. Yesterday I'd spent the day riding waves of surreality and shock. Thinking *This can't be happening*. Today, just twenty-four hours later, those waves were still coming in but the time between sets was much longer. This *was* happening. I *was* here. I saw the same acknowledgment on people's faces.

"What crew are you on?" I asked Fancy.

"Much to my brother's dismay, I'm a flutterbudget. I just can't seem to settle on one thing. Where are you working today?"

"The garden."

"Oh," she groaned. "Poor girl."

"I chose it."

"Mmm, let's see how you feel about it tonight, shall we? When that lovely complexion is the color of a beet and your clothes—my clothes—are soaked through with sweat."

"You should come with me," I said.

"How I wish I could. I have just the perfect hat, with a lovely blue satin ribbon." She looked at me sadly. "Alas, I've already committed myself to the entertainment crew."

"The entertainment crew. Joseph didn't mention that."

"That's because I'm starting it today. You're welcome to join—I have all sorts of things planned. I thought our inaugural event would be an old-fashioned country dance. The Scottish reel, lots of lively skipping up and down in rows just like in *Pride and Prejudice*. Then a strings concert; as it happens, the beekeeper is a violinist and there are two cellists on the building crew. And perhaps a bimonthly lecture series. There is a great deal of untapped knowledge here at Greengage. And why, you, Lux! Oh my goodness, why haven't I thought of you? You must be our first lecturer. You can fill us in on what we've missed. Tell us all about the twentieth century. Will you do it? Please say you'll do it. Please?"

"Fancy," said Joseph. "She hasn't even had her tea yet." He'd suddenly materialized beside us.

"Good heavens," said Fancy. "Must you always be popping up like that? It's so uncivilized, not to give a person some warning. And stop interfering. We're the most bosom of friends already. Isn't that right, Lux?"

Nobody had ever referred to me as a bosom friend before. I felt tears come to my eyes, which was completely ridiculous, especially under the circumstances.

"You are overwhelming her," said Joseph, peering at me with concern.

Twice now he'd seen me tear up. What was wrong with me? Why was I so emotional here?

"I am not overwhelming her."

"She's not. She's not overwhelming me," I said, although the idea of giving a talk to 278 people made me feel faint.

Fancy squeezed my arm.

"Come on, you two," said Joseph, leading us into the dining hall. "Fancy, make sure you eat a proper breakfast. You have a long day ahead of you, installing the new privies."

Fancy snorted, "I will be doing no such thing."


Martha was right. Being on the garden crew was backbreaking, repetitive work—but I loved it all the same. They started me in strawberries, me and all the kids; I guess they thought I couldn't be trusted with proper vegetables yet. The children sat in the dirt, and for every strawberry they picked, another went into their mouths. None of them spoke to me for a while, although they did their share of staring, and then one little boy asked, "Don't you like strawberries?" and that broke the dam of silence.

"I love strawberries," I said.

"Then why aren't you eating them?" asked a girl.

"Because I'm not hungry."

"Why aren't you hungry?"

"Because I just ate breakfast."

"What did you have for breakfast?"

"Pancakes, just like you."

"Do you have pancakes at your house?"

"All the time."

"Do you have children?"

"Yes, I have a son, just about your age, maybe a little younger. His name is Benno."

"What kind of a name is Benno?"

"It's short for Bennett."

"Why isn't he with you?"

"He's on vacation."

"Vacation?"

"A holiday. With his grandmother."

They looked horrified, their faces smudged with dirt, their fingers sticky with strawberry juice.

"Then why are you here? Why didn't you go with him?"

Why, indeed? Suddenly I was hungry. I stuffed three strawberries in my mouth.

After lunch I graduated to tomato picking. Nobody spoke to me for an hour. Finally a woman who looked to be in her fifties said, "You don't have to be so gentle."

She was referring to the way I was handling the tomatoes. Tenderly placing them in the basket, being careful not to bruise them, which slowed my picking down quite a bit.

"They're just going in the pot," she explained. "Those"—she pointed a few rows away—"we baby."

She walked over to the other row, picked a tomato, came back, and handed it to me. "Taste."

"I don't have a knife."

"Just bite into it," she instructed me.

I bit into it like an apple; juice splattered on my chin. The skin was warm. It tasted of sun and earth and rain.

"Now eat this," she said, handing me one of the tomatoes I'd picked.

Even though it was a deep red, it had none of the depth of flavor. It didn't explode on my tongue, it just sort of sat there.

"You see the difference? These are for canning. Those are for eating."

"Yes."

"Good." She knelt down again. "My name is Ilsa."

"Hi, Ilsa, I'm Lux."

"I know. You don't have to introduce yourself. Everybody knows who you are."

My basket was nearly full. I picked more tomatoes, quickly this time, and stood. The wagon was a good quarter mile away. I arched my back and stretched, preparing for the walk. The basket weighed at least twenty pounds.

"Do you have moving pavements in San Francisco?" asked Ilsa.

"Moving pavements?"

"Sidewalks that carry you everywhere so you don't have to walk," she explained. "You just step on them and—whoosh!—off you go."

This was what people in the early twentieth century thought the future would bring? I guess it was similar to me wishing that one day there'd be a tiny record player I could carry around in my pocket so I could have music wherever I went.

"Oh. God. No. That would be nice, though, wouldn't it? There are so many hills in the city. But there is something close. Moving stairs. Escalators."

"What about personal flying machines?" asked a man who'd been eavesdropping on our conversation.

"You mean like a car—an automobile that flies?"

He nodded.

"No, but we have commercial airlines. TWA. Pan Am. They fly hundreds of people in one airplane. You can travel from San Francisco to Boston in around five hours."

He cried out in surprise. From then on, the rest of the afternoon flew by. I was deluged with questions. People gasped at what they heard. They also laughed and made fun. How strange. Why would anybody need to blow-dry their hair? Or use an electrified toothbrush? Or sit in front of a small screen in their living room watching something called *The Rockford Files*?


At the end of the day, the garden crew climbed into the empty wagon. I didn't know what time it was, but it had to be well after six; the sun was low in the sky and the air had a hint of coolness in it. Slowly we made our way back to the dining hall. My fingernails were edged with dirt, my back was tight and my calves sore from all the bending and lifting, but I felt a kind of grounded satisfaction that I hadn't felt in years. A pleasant ache in my solar plexus. The steady thrum that only comes from working outside.

We were packed into the wagon, sitting thigh to thigh. I now knew everybody's name. Claudette, a six-year-old girl with a red birthmark on her neck in the shape of China, crawled into my lap, and in the ten minutes it took us to get to the dining hall, she fell asleep.

"Do you mind?" asked Ilsa.

"Not at all." I enjoyed the weight of her head on my shoulder. It reminded me of my sweet Benno. I wondered what he was doing this very minute. How many days was it until I'd see him again? Eleven? Twelve?

"Is she yours?" I asked.

"She's my granddaughter."

"Oh, your daughter is here, too?"

Ilsa looked off into the distance. "She was."

Later I'd learn that Ilsa's daughter had left Greengage the night before the earthquake to spend a few days with her cousins in Alameda. Would Claudette ever see her mother again? No matter how enchanting a place Greengage was, what had happened to them was ghastly.

After dinner that night, when nobody was looking, I stepped into the fog. I was anxious to confirm that nothing had changed—that time was still passing regularly in my world. Once again, I heard the hum of the highway. And once again, I caught the briefest snippet of a song from a car radio. "The Hustle." An image of Benno and me in the kitchen popped into my mind, the two of us doing the bump. The happiest of memories. He was fine. I was fine.

I would ask Joseph if I could stay a few more days.

I woke at midnight. Unable to fall back asleep, I went out on the porch. Joseph was there. We'd barely spoken at dinner, although I'd caught him looking at me a few times.

The red tip of his cigarette glowed in the dark.

"We have to stop meeting like this," I said.

He didn't answer.

"Can I have a puff?" I asked.

He handed the cigarette to me. I took a drag and tried to give it back to him. "Keep it," he said. "How did it go today?"

I didn't realize until he asked me the question how I'd been long-ing for him to inquire about my day.

"Good. I like the garden crew."

"Do you?"

"You sound surprised."

"You didn't mind laboring in the heat for eight hours?"

"I loved it."

"You *loved* it?"

"You don't believe me?"

"I doubt you're used to this kind of life."

What kind of life was he referring to? The kind of life where you spent the day outside, playing and working alongside people who knew you, really knew you?

"When I was a kid, my father would take me to Lapis Lake in New Hampshire," I said. "Greengage reminds me of there."

Joseph held his hand out for the cigarette.

I gave it back to him, surprised that he didn't mind sharing with me.

"Were you happy at Lapis Lake?" he asked.

"I was. For a long time."

"Until you weren't."

Right.

"When were you there last?"

I had to think. "Nineteen sixty-four," I said finally.

⚜

"Absolutely not," said my mother. "It would break your father's heart. You're going." She handed me a jar of Pond's. "By the way, just be-cause you'll be swimming every day doesn't mean you shouldn't cleanse your face properly every night."

I tucked the Pond's into my suitcase. "I'm only talking about going up a couple of days late. This weekend is Meg's birthday party. Her parents are renting out the entire rec center. We'll have the pool all to ourselves. After that I can go join Dad at the lake."

I didn't tell her the party was co-ed and that Meg had invited a bunch of sophomore boys.

"I can take the bus to Portsmouth on Monday and Dad can meet me there."

"He needs your help opening up the cabin."

"He can open it himself."

My mother sighed.

"Please. It's only two days. Nobody will miss me."

"Everybody will miss you. The McKinleys. The Babbitts. They'll be terribly disappointed if you don't show up with your dad for Saturday night dinner. And what about that new family that bought the cabin next to the Hineses last year?"

"The Harrises," I said.

"Yes, don't they have a girl your age?"

Beth Harris. We'd bonded last summer. We were as opposite from each other as could be, but our differences fell away at Lapis Lake.

My mother folded a blouse. "You'll have great fun once you get there, you always do." She eyed my blue jean shorts. "You're not wearing those today, are you?"

My father and I were leaving for the lake tomorrow, but today the three of us were attending the New Parents' Reception at St. Paul's School.

"It's just a bunch of parents."

"A bunch of very excited parents who are thrilled and grateful their children will be attending St. Paul's in September, thanks to your father." She rifled through my closet and pulled out a blue dress with a white Peter Pan collar. "This will do nicely."

"No," I groaned.

"I'm sorry, darling, but you're going to have to get used to dressing conservatively. If you think you're under a spotlight now being the dean's daughter, wait until you're the headmaster's daughter."

The headmaster of St. Paul's was retiring and my father was the obvious choice to replace him; the board had been considering the appointment for months. He had the seniority and he was deeply committed to his job. He was popular as well. Kids adored him; they always hung out in his office. Grateful mothers sent him plates of cookies; grateful fathers, bottles of scotch at Christmas. He left the house at seven-thirty each morning and often didn't return until seven o'clock at night. He loved his work.

"Can I bring a book?" I asked.

"That would be rude."

"If I sit in the very back?"

"What book?"

*"House of Mirth,"* I lied. I was in the middle of Updike's *Rabbit, Run* and couldn't wait to get back to it.

"Fine," she capitulated.


There were benefits to being my father's daughter, and the moment we stepped onto campus they accrued to me. We were like celebrities. Parents called out their hellos. Many times, on our way to the chapel, people stopped us.

"Is this your daughter?"

"Yes, this is Lux," said my father.

"Oh, she's just lovely," they said. "A junior, senior?"

My father looked appalled.

My mother said, "Oh, no, Lux is just entering her freshman year." I was breathless, thrilled they thought I was older than fourteen.


I didn't end up reading *Rabbit, Run* at the New Parents' Reception. My father, preaching the gospel of St. Paul's School from the pulpit of the chapel, was too riveting. Like everybody else in the audience, I was swept away by the force of his charisma. I prayed for his eyes to fall on me, to choose me, to mark me as special. But foolishly I'd chosen to sit in the back row. It was impossible for him to pick me out in the sea of blue dresses.

At least that's what I told myself; I wasn't ready to admit the truth—I was afraid my shine had worn off for him. Things had become awkward and forced between us over the past year. Most of my friends already had that distance with their fathers, it was built into their relationships; they'd always been much closer with their mothers. But in my house, it was the opposite. It was my father and I that were inseparable. His darling girl; that's what he called me. He understood me—his bright, easily bored, passionate, underdog-defending, in-need-of-large-doses-of-physical-activity-and-changes-of-scenery daughter. And more important than understanding me, he liked me. He was most proud when I took the road less traveled by.

It wouldn't be exaggerating to say I lived for the look of delight and surprise in his eyes when I accomplished something out of the ordinary. Beating him at chess. Reading the unabridged version of *Anna Karenina* when I was ten. Starting a campfire with nothing but a flint and a knife.

But now it seemed our father and daughter skins were growing too small. I still craved his attention and approval, but he gave it more sparingly. Our long, rambling conversations about everything and anything—the speed of light, the Cuban missile crisis, how many minutes on each side to grill a perfect medium-rare steak—had petered out, replaced with the most quotidian of inquiries: *Is* Gunsmoke *on tonight? Is it supposed to snow tomorrow? When's the last time the grass was cut?*

It was mostly my fault. I'd created the distance. Or puberty had done it for me. Along with my new body (Breasts! Hair! Hips! Pimples!) came disorientation. What was charming behavior when I was a girl wasn't always so charming at fourteen. Also, my adventurous nature didn't set me apart anymore. The rest of my friends had finally caught up with me. Not only were they doing the daredevil things I'd always done, but they were doing those things on a grander, if more subversive, scale. They lied, they sneaked around, they hid their real lives away from their parents. They said they were going to the beach; instead they took the bus to Providence. They said they were sleeping over at a friend's house; instead they spent the night on the beach with a boy. I was a good girl, I still asked permission to do practically everything, but for the first time in my life my father had started to question my judgment. He'd loved my precociousness when I was young. He'd let me roam free my entire life, in fact he'd encouraged it. Now, just when I was on the cusp of truly being able to handle the independence, he wanted to shut me in.

More and more we stood on opposite shores, or, worse than that, he wasn't on the shore at all. Instead it was my mother who'd taken his place, waving at me from across the sea that separated parent from child, imploring me to wash my face and moisturize every night.

"I'm going to miss you two," my mother said the next morning, watching me zip up my suitcase.

Jeans. Shorts. Shirts. Bathing suit. Underwear. Sneakers. What was I forgetting?

The phone rang downstairs.

"I've got it!" shouted my father.

"Why don't you come with us?" I asked.

She plumped up the pillows on my bed. "Me, sleeping on that mildewed mattress? All those bugs? Rats running around in the eaves at night and God knows what else?"

Lapis Lake was no Lake Winnipesaukee. It was a dozen or so uninsulated fishing cabins clustered around a small lake. It was at the base of Mount Fort, a tiny mountain, more of a hill, really. My grandfather Harry, who worked as a pulper at the paper mill in Rumford, Maine (until he died of lung cancer at forty-eight), had made the exodus to the lake every summer, as had a group of other mill families. When my grandfather's generation passed, the cabins had been handed down to my father's generation, who in turn brought their sons and daughters every August. Or *daughter*, in my case.

My mother had gone with my father to Lapis Lake a few times, but after I was born she'd stopped. She wasn't a snob (she sent Christmas cards to all the other lake families every year), she just wasn't outdoorsy. She much preferred to stay home in Newport. When Dad and I were gone, she met her friends for drinks and dinner. She waded through thick books, ate at odd hours, and went to the movies. She had no problem keeping herself busy.

"I've never seen a rat," I said. There were, however, plenty of mice.

There was a loud thud from the kitchen and my father yelled, "Jesus!"

We ran down the stairs and found him in his jeans and undershirt, barefoot, coffee and broken pieces of mug all over the floor.

My father's left leg was almost two inches shorter than his right; he usually wore his lift from the moment he got out of bed to the moment he climbed back in at night. This structural defect (he referred to it that way, as if he were a building) had prevented him from participating in any kind of athletics when he was a boy, and when he was a man it had kept him out of the war. It hadn't barred him from academia, though. He'd gotten his undergraduate degree in English at the University of Maine and his graduate degree in public policy at URI. Education was everything to him. It was the only path up and out.

Now thirty-nine (with lifts for every kind of footwear imaginable, including his slippers), my father was confident and handsome, his dark hair Brylcreemed, his face smelling of Pinaud-Clubman aftershave. He didn't have a belly like lots of the other fathers. He boxed at McGillicutty's gym in Middletown three times a week to stay in shape.

"What a mess," my father said.

"I'll get it." I grabbed a dish towel and wiped up the spill.

"Who was that on the phone?" asked my mother.

"Manny. He'll be here to cut the grass on Thursday."

"You already told me that," said my mother.

"Did I?"

My father smoothed the hair back from my mother's face, tipped up her chin with his finger, and looked into her eyes. When my father turned the spotlight of his gaze on you, it was like you were the only person alive.

It was a quiet ride north. My father and I often didn't speak when driving to the camp; it was a transitional time and we honored it. But this silence felt oppressively heavy. Had my mother told him I wanted to come late?

"Are you okay?" I asked when we rolled through the New Hampshire tolls.

He shook a cigarette out of its pack. "I'm fine. Just tired."

"Looking forward to getting to the lake?"

"Mmm-hmm." He punched the cigarette lighter in.

An hour later we turned onto Rural Road 125. The woods were lush and green.

"Smell that?" said my father, inhaling deeply. "That is the smell of freedom."

*And dead mice,* I thought as we walked into the cabin.

"Christ," said my father. He put down his suitcase and immediately began opening windows and shutters. "Get me a bag."

I got a paper bag from under the sink and he went around the house retrieving mousetraps. I got one look at a desiccated ball of gray fur and covered my eyes.

"Next year this is your job," he said.

I took the dust covers off the furniture and swept the floor free of mouse droppings. I grabbed sheets and, on my way to make the bed, reread the framed newspaper clippings that hung on the wall. My parents' wedding announcement. An interview with my father on the seventy-fifth anniversary of St. Paul's School.

It wasn't a fancy cabin, but it was ours. One tiny bedroom and an open kitchen with a pullout couch. We had electricity and running water, but no heat besides the woodstove. No toilet, either, just an outhouse in the backyard.

I'd been going with my father to Lapis Lake since I was four. Over the past ten years, he'd taught me how to fish, how to track deer, and how to read the night sky. We spent our days working around the camp, swimming, canoeing, hiking Mount Fort, and playing board games. Dinners we ate at the clubhouse with all the rest of the lake residents; families took turns cooking and cleaning. But the late evenings after everybody retired to their cabins were the best part. Each summer Dad would pick one novel from "the canon" and we'd sit out on the porch and he'd read aloud to me. He started with *Treasure Island.* We'd read *Moby-Dick* and *Lord of the Flies.* This year he'd chosen *The Great Gatsby.*

"George, is that you?" somebody shouted from out on the porch. It was Gary Thibodeux, with his seven-year-old daughter, Lily. We went out to greet them.

"Lux, you've grown. I'da barely recognized you," he said, squinting at me.

That was a compliment, right? He meant I looked mature? Pretty?

"Lily's been waiting for you to get here, haven't you, Lily?" he said.

Lily chewed nervously on a strand of hair. Last summer I'd spent practically every morning with her in the lake, teaching her how to dive off the raft. I'd known her since she was a baby.

"Remind me what grade you're going into," I said.

"Second."

"I can't believe it. I thought third or fourth for sure."

She glowed. There was nothing little kids liked more than to be mistaken for somebody older. Clearly, I still hadn't outgrown that particular pleasure either.

"Hello, Gary," said my father, coming down from the porch to shake his hand.

"Well, you're the last to arrive," said Gary. "We're full up now."

My father grinned. "Let summer begin."

"Began a few hours ago by my watch," said Gary, a can of Pabst in his hand.

Fish sticks, french fries, baked beans, and salad. Pound cake with strawberries and Cool Whip. Saturday night dinner. Normally I sat with the kids my age, a group of teenagers, including Beth Harris, who, like me, had changed in the last year, though not in a good way (she looked like she'd gained twenty pounds). But the first night back was always sort of awkward. I took a seat next to my father at the adult table for the first time ever.

"Don't you want to eat with the pack?" he asked.

"Not really." I was feeling shy.

"You should go eat with them."

"I want to eat with you."

He gave me a pinched smile.

I'd known all the adults sitting at the table since I was little. Since I was the only kid, they spent the meal indulgently asking me questions. I hadn't planned on being the center of attention, but I can't say

I didn't like it. I could sense all the kids watching us, eavesdropping. I was popular at school, but I was even more popular at Lapis Lake. In their eyes I led an exotic life in ritzy Newport. My father was the dean of a private school. Their fathers all worked at the mill.

How was ballet? Great. I'd just gotten my first pair of toe shoes.

What was the school play this year? A musical, *Guys and Dolls*. I played Sarah Brown, the lead.

Who was my favorite band? Was it still the Beach Boys? No, it was Ray Charles.

Instead of beaming, being proud of my exploits, my father grew uncomfortable. He tried to change the subject, get them to talk about their children, but somehow the conversation always meandered back to me. Now I understood my father's reticence at having me sit at the adult table. I'd disrupted the unspoken order; I'd forced myself into the spotlight. I, along with all the other kids, belonged in the corner at the card table with the rusted metal legs, the table that had grown increasingly more silent as the evening went on.

"I didn't mean for that to happen," I said when we got back to the cabin.

The last thing I wanted was to start our vacation off on a sour note. I'd hoped our two weeks together would be an opportunity to reconnect, to recover the old ease we'd had with each other. And just how was I going to accomplish this? My plan was to show off a little. Dazzle him. Remind him of the old Lux. And now, only a few hours into our vacation, it seemed I'd done the opposite: I'd embarrassed him. I'd already blown it.

He was banging around in the kitchen, getting the coffeepot ready for the morning. "If you want to be treated like an adult, you have to act like an adult," he said.

How wasn't I acting like an adult? I'd made every attempt to be polite, to answer every question, to have impeccable manners.

"You may think you look grown-up, but you're not," he added.

"I—I know that," I stammered. "You think I don't know that?"

He dipped his head, flustered, and I realized he was as thrown as

I was to find us here, in this new place where neither of us spoke the language.

"I'm sorry, Dad. I didn't mean to offend you."

"You didn't offend me," he said, sitting heavily in a chair.

"Did I offend anybody else? Please tell me. I'd feel terrible if I did."

"No. No," he said. "That's not it. You're missing the point."

I sat down at the table with him. "Then tell me the point, please."

He breathed loudly through his mouth. "People couldn't talk freely. Not with you there."

"But that's not my fault. I didn't stop them from talking."

"Why did you insist on sitting with us?"

I longed for his touch. A hand on my shoulder. A squeeze of my arm. I needed him to be my gravity, to pull me back down to earth.

"It was the first night. I hadn't even had a chance to say hi to anybody. I wanted to sit with you," I said softly. "I'm sorry. I didn't think. I should have noticed I was the only kid."

My father sighed.

"I'm sorry," I said again, my voice breaking.

"I know," he finally said.

He clasped his hands and squeezed his eyes shut.

"Are you all right, Dad?"

"It's just—I've been looking forward to this all year."

"Me too," I said.

My father was a different person at Lapis Lake. The minute we got here, he changed; his power sluiced off him like water. At the lake he was content to be part of the group. I'd always thought this humbleness was a bit of an act, but tonight I saw that it wasn't. It was actually a relief. Who he allowed himself to be at Lapis Lake was who he really was. He'd grown up with these people; he was at heart one of them. Maybe the dean was the act. This was an astounding realization for me.

He got up from the table and poured himself a glass of water. He always poured himself a glass of water right before bed. Was he going to bed?

"What about *Gatsby*?" I said, alarmed. "Aren't we going to start tonight?"

He looked at me wearily. "I'm exhausted, sweetheart. I'll see you tomorrow."

Adrenaline surged through me—why were all our rituals changing?—but I grabbed onto his "sweetheart" like a life preserver. He hadn't called me that in a long time.


The next morning the phone rang.

"It's your mother," my father said from out on the porch. "Will you get it?"

I grabbed the phone. It wasn't my mother, it was Meg, calling to tell me what a fun party I'd missed.

"Everybody was asking where you were."

"What did you tell them?"

"I told them your father was holding you captive in a fishing shack in the middle of the Maine woods."

"New Hampshire."

"What's the difference? Cooper Henderson was there."

I'd had a crush on Cooper for two years.

"Was he with Candy?"

"No, he was alone. They broke up a few weeks ago."

They had? I couldn't believe I'd missed the party. And for what? A moldy, mice-ridden, yes, *fishing shack,* in the middle of mosquito-infested woods.

My father walked into the room and held his hand out for the phone. I cupped my palm over the mouthpiece. "It's not Mom, it's for me."

He looked at his watch. "Hurry up. We're clearing brush from the trail this morning."

We usually spent the mornings on some sort of a work detail with other families. The afternoons were reserved for fun.

"I gotta go," I said.

"Any cute boys there?" Meg asked.

"If you think pimple-faced mouth breathers in Wranglers are cute, then yes."

We called it lake time. It always took a few days to settle into it. The hours slipped and slid, and when they finally broke free of their constraints, we stopped looking at the clock and began living by the weather and whim.

It happened for my father on the second day. I saw it surface on his face while he was twirling spaghetti on his fork. A sort of peaceful look. Quiet. Inward. He lifted his eyes and smiled at me. I felt jealous—I wasn't there yet.

I didn't get there the next day or the day after that either. A week went by.

I started to pay attention and focus on my senses. There were things that reliably brought lake time on. The smell of Coppertone lotion. The billowing smoke of a charcoal grill. The slap of a tetherball against a sweaty hand. A wet bathing suit hanging from a clothesline. Still I couldn't get there. Something was keeping me out.

"What's wrong?" asked my father. "Why are you so antsy?"

I'd rummaged through the fridge three times in the past twenty minutes.

"Go outside," he said, waving his hand at me, annoyed.

I put shorts and a T-shirt on over my bathing suit and clopped noisily down the porch stairs in my flip-flops. As soon as I left, he turned on the record player. Sam Cooke. "You Send Me."

I walked the waterfront, past the Meriweathers' and the Hineses' place. Beth Harris sat on her porch reading.

"Hiya," I called out. "What are you reading?"

She showed me the cover.

"Proust," I said, making sure to pronounce it the correct way.

"You look surprised."

"Why would I be surprised?" I asked, trying to cover up my surprise. "Are you reading it for school?"

"No, for pleasure," she said.

I couldn't tell if she was serious. We'd barely spoken since I'd arrived. I'd caught her staring at me more than a few times. Sometimes I thought it was an admiring look; sometimes she seemed angry and judgmental. Maybe she was mad. After last summer we'd promised to be pen pals, but although we'd written to each other regularly throughout the fall, we soon tapered off. Then she sent me a Valentine's Day card; I hadn't sent her one. I was sort of repulsed. Weren't we too old to be sending each other Valentine's Day cards?

"Want to go swimming?" I asked.

I could see a group of kids down on the beach.

She shrugged. "Give me a sec. I'll get my suit on."

Five minutes later the screen door swung open and she appeared in a Hawaiian print bikini, a towel in her hand. Her thighs were dimpled with cellulite. The top barely contained her breasts. She had rolls of fat on her belly.

"Um, do you want to get your cover-up?" I asked.

"I don't have a cover-up."

At first I'd felt bad for her, but now I felt angry. I'd have to walk with her, looking like that. She was still new to Lapis Lake; they'd only started coming last year. She hadn't grown up with the other kids. Didn't she know she was an outsider?

If there was such a thing as karma, I suppose it was then that my karma sat up and took notice. Flush with my lake insider-ness, it never occurred to me that in the future I'd be the one on the outskirts, having made choices that would keep me on the fringes.

"Do you want to borrow my T-shirt?" I asked.

Her eyes narrowed to slits. "You know it won't fit me."

"Sorry, just thought I'd offer."

"I'm sweating to death. Let's go," she said.


I was right. When we got to the beach, the other kids parted like she was Moses and they were the Red Sea. They snickered. Beth's face grew pink, but she threw her shoulders back.

"Fuck you," she said under her breath.

At first I thought it was directed at all of us, then I realized it was directed just at me. She'd sent me a Valentine's Day card and signed it *XOXOXOXO Hope You Have a Super Day,* and I was about to leave her beached on the shore.

She marched into the water. Nobody joined her; it was as if they thought they'd catch fat cooties if they went in with her. She stayed in a long time. Finally she got out. We couldn't take our eyes off her. I was part of the group, but it was no longer a group I wanted to be a part of—still, I couldn't pull myself away.

I heard my father's voice behind me: "Beth."

He walked to the water's edge with her towel. He draped it over her shoulders.

"Thank you, Mr. Lysander," she said.

"My pleasure," said my father. He strolled with her up the beach and turned on the charm. Within a few minutes I heard her laughing.

My father didn't mention the Beth incident when I walked in the door. Instead I found him filling his canteen with water, preparing to go on a hike.

"Can I come?" I asked.

I wanted to tell him why I didn't stand up for Beth, why I'd let the others treat her that way, but I didn't know what to say. I had no defense other than that I couldn't afford to align myself with her. I was constantly negotiating the border between in and out, and the gentlest of breezes could push me into either camp. I had to stay alert. I had to stay vigilant. Being fourteen was exhausting.

"I'd prefer some time to myself," he said.

My throat tightened. "Okay," I said in a small voice, the realization that he didn't want to be with me fully sinking in. But I didn't want to be with him either, not really.

Two days ago we'd spent the night camping on Mount Fort. We cooked our dinner over the campfire, made a shelter out of pine boughs, and slept in a tent. I found it incredibly tedious. He was so regimented about it all. Everything had to be done in a certain way. I'd made the mistake of forgetting to do one last cleanup around the campsite to make sure we hadn't left anything behind. He held up a Jolly Rancher candy wrapper. My mother had sneaked a few into my Dopp kit.

"Is this yours?"

"No."

He shook his head gravely at me and tucked the wrapper into his pocket. "Travel lightly and leave no trace."

That was his mantra. He'd been telling me that since the day I was born.

"I didn't leave any trace. I told you, it isn't mine."

He didn't believe me.


My father was gone the entire afternoon. Without him there, the cabin felt weightless, like it was floating in the trees. I pretended to be sick that night so I didn't have to go to supper. I opened a sleeve of saltines and sat on the porch listening to the rattle of silverware, the rising and falling of voices coming from the clubhouse.

The sounds of the Beatles' "I Want to Hold Your Hand" carried over the water. It must be dessert time; the kids always cranked up the music after dinner. I felt like Beth must have felt when she walked into the water, every eye watching her, judging her. Why was it that everything I did these days seemed to go wrong?

I could fix this. All I had to do was go to the dining hall and say I was feeling better. Sit down at the kids' table next to Beth, strike up a conversation, and invite her over to the cabin after dinner for s'mores. And that night, when my father picked up his copy of *Gatsby*, I would tell him I was sorry. I didn't know why I couldn't find myself here, or why I felt so lost.

But I couldn't get my legs to stand up. Time slowed down. The minutes were hours long. Darkness began to fall; the first stars appeared. Finally I saw my father winding his way home through the trees.

"I thought you'd be in bed," he said, and my words dried up in my mouth.


The following morning I asked, "Could we go out for supper tonight? I'm stir-crazy."

I couldn't hide my restlessness anymore. I'd come to the conclusion that I'd outgrown the lake. It was like I'd rounded a point on some invisible coast, and now that I'd come around the headland, I knew the truth. These people, this world, was too small for me.

"When we drove in, I saw a new hamburger place in town. The Rathskeller."

"That wasn't a restaurant, it was a bar," said my father.

"A bar that serves hamburgers."

I poured myself some water and mixed in a spoonful of Tang.

"Aren't you tired of hot dogs? Please," I begged.

"All right," he said after a while.

I spent all afternoon getting ready. When I walked into the living room wearing a sundress with kitten heels, he visibly startled.

I'd transformed myself. My hair, bleached light brown from the sun, spilled down my back. My shoulders were tanned, the color of walnuts. I'd cinched the waist of my dress with a thick black belt and put on Jean Naté body splash.

I wanted him to be shocked at my metamorphosis. I wanted him to compliment me.

Instead he grabbed his keys off the counter and said, "Let's go."

People stared at me when we walked in. I wasn't imagining it.

"Your daughter," said the waitress. "What beautiful eyes. They're the exact color of the lake. She must drive the boys crazy."

"Mmm," said my father. "Can you bring me a whiskey?"

"Sure. What about you, hon? A Coke?"

"Yes, please."

"No Coke—she'll have a glass of milk with her burger."

I glared at my father. "Yes, I'll have a glass of milk with my burger. Because I'm five."

"All righty," said the waitress, taken aback by the tone of my voice.

"For Chrissakes," said my father when she was out of earshot. "What the hell is wrong with you?" He got up and headed toward the bathroom.

I waited till he was out of sight, then bolted up. "I'll get his whiskey," I said to the waitress, who passed me looking stressed, her tray piled high with plates of food.

"Thanks a bunch, hon." She called out to the bartender, "She needs a whiskey neat for her dad."

I sat down at the bar. The bartender wore a UNH sweatshirt. He poured the drink. Impulsively and without thinking, I grabbed the glass and drank it down, the liquid burning my throat. I tried not to grimace.

He poured me another, a smile playing on his lips.

"I go to UNH, too," I said. "What year are you?"

"Junior, you?"

"I'm a freshman—well, about to be a sophomore."

"Do you live in Alexander Hall? Mills?"

"Mills."

"Better finish that off before your father comes back."

I looked at the drink: I was having second thoughts. "I can't. It's disgusting."

He laughed, filled a mug with Coke and poured a shot of rum into it. "I think you'll like this a little better."

I took the Coke and the glass of whiskey back to the table. My father joined me a minute later and noticed my soda.

"I thought I told you to get milk."

I could already feel the effects of the whiskey. My limbs felt loose. My face hot.

"The waitress brought it. I think she must have gotten my order confused."

He flashed me a skeptical look, picked up the glass of Coke and sniffed it. His eyes darkened and he took a sip. Carefully he set the glass back down on the table and wiped his mouth with his napkin.

"I didn't order it, Dad. I swear. The waitress just brought it."

"Did you have a sip?"

"No!" I cried.

He glared at me.

"Okay, yes, but then I realized there was liquor in it and—"

"What kind of an idiot do you take me for?" he hissed.

He got out his wallet, threw a ten-dollar bill on the table, slid out of the booth, and walked away, leaving me sitting there.

The bartender, who'd been listening to the entire conversation, raised his eyebrows at me. "Better get going," he said. "You're gonna miss your ride."

I woke the next morning to the sound of my father whistling. The woodstove crackled, the coffee brewed. I could tell by the sound of his footsteps he was in a good mood.

"Get up, lazybones. I'm making your favorite, blueberry pancakes. The blueberries freshly picked by yours truly."

I didn't answer him. I pulled the covers over my head. He came into the room a few minutes later.

He'd given me the silent treatment all last night. Now he wanted to be nice?

"Lux. Time to get up."

"I don't feel good."

He felt my forehead. His skin smelled like the lake. His brow creased. "Lux, I'm sorry, I over—"

I cut him off. "Cramps," I said.

"Oh. Okay. Do you have what you need?"

"Just leave me alone for a bit. They'll pass."

He checked on me every hour, a look of increasing concern on his face. He brought me tea. Lemonade. A boiled egg. A deviled ham sandwich. He brought in Monopoly, a deck of cards, *The Great Gatsby*, but I refused to play or listen. Each time he opened and shut the door, he shrank a little, and I was glad of it. He'd gone too far. I'd misbehaved plenty of times. Done stupid things. He'd been disappointed with me, but never ashamed. This was different. I'd felt scorn from him. Contempt. It had a completely different smell than disappointment. Like something scorched, an iron left a second too long on a blouse.

That night, after my father had gone to sleep, I sneaked out and went back to the Rathskeller.

"You again," said the bartender.

I'd dressed more conservatively this time, not wanting to draw attention to myself. Jeans, flats (it was a mile walk from the cabin to the bar), and a gingham shirt, tied tight at my waist.

"Me again."

"Where's Daddy?"

I shrugged.

"Ever had a margarita?" he asked, already pouring the drink. He watched as I took a careful sip.

"It tastes like limeade."

"Like it?"

"Oh, yes," I breathed.

His eyes drifted to the TV mounted above the bar. "Damn Sox. Can't get anything going this year."

I felt his attention waning. I gulped the rest of the drink.

"Make me something else," I said.

"Like what?"

"A martini, dry, two olives." That was my mother's drink.

"You shouldn't mix liquors. A girl like you, weighs nothing, you'll be drunk in no time."

"And that would be a bad thing?"

He grinned. "That would be a very bad thing."


Two hours later he drove me home. I was looped—I'd never had that much to drink before. My mind felt skittery, like marbles on a wooden floor.

"Stop here." I didn't want him to pull in the driveway; I couldn't chance waking my father up.

I launched myself across the seat and tried to kiss him on the lips. He turned his head at the last minute and I ended up kissing him on his jaw.

"Whoa," he said, pushing me away. "I was just being nice. I'm not—interested in you. You're a kid."

"Oh God," I said, mortified.

"How old are you, anyway?"

"I told you, I'm a freshman."

"Not at UNH you're not. Mills is not a freshman dorm." He got out of the car, came around my side, and opened my door. "Go home," he said, not unkindly.

In front of our cabin was a beautiful old maple tree. It provided shade on a sunny day and filled the house with its sweet leafy smell. A big bough extended out over the lake. You could walk across it like a dock.

I did so now. Drunk, I navigated it carefully like a trapeze artist. Then I sat down and dangled my feet in the water.

*Go home.*

I pulled my Swiss Army knife out of my pocket. My father had given it to me for my tenth birthday. I flicked it open and carved LUX WAS HERE into the soft wood of the bough. It felt so good and right. Like I was restoring order to the night.

The next morning, when I came out of the bedroom, my head pounding with my first ever hangover, my father handed me some sandpaper and pointed to the tree.

"Erase your fucking name," he said.

When we got home, my father told my mother the truth. The phone call he'd received the morning we'd left for the lake had not been Manny the gardener, but rather Herbert Jeffers, the president of the St. Paul's board. Jeffers had broken the news to my father that he'd been passed over for the headmaster job. In the end they'd decided to go with somebody else, a legacy. A Princeton grad. A man whose family had attended St. Paul's for the last fifty years.

I wanted to go to him, hug him, say the right thing. *It doesn't matter, Dad. Who cares. Screw them. You're a great dean.* I could have done that. *Before.* But this was after. We'd cast each other off at Lapis Lake.

We were worlds apart.

# JOSEPH

❧

"I've never been to New Hampshire," I said to Lux.

"You're not missing much. Where are you from, anyway? I mean, where in England? Obviously you're British."

"London."

"Where in London?"

"Have you ever been there?"

"No."

I wasn't in the mood to tell her my life story. "It's not a time I care to remember."

"Do you mind?" She gestured to the chair beside me.

Where were my manners? "Please."

"I understand about the past," she said, sliding into the chair. "I have plenty of things I don't want to remember either."

I changed the subject. "What did you think of the garden crew?"

"Oh, I liked them very much. Especially Ilsa."

Poor Ilsa, whose daughter, Brigette, had been in Alameda on the night of the earthquake.

"It must be agony for her, wondering if Brigette kept trying to get back to Greengage," said Lux.

I'd wondered about this, too. How could Brigette not have returned? Lux showed us how easy it was to get here. All she had to do was walk through the fog. Why hadn't Brigette done the same?

"I have a theory," said Lux. "I think she didn't come back because there was no way for her to come back. Because the fog wasn't there."

"It was there when you came."

"Yes, but it wasn't there when I first arrived. Remember I told you it rolled in after midnight?"

Actually I'd tried to forget that fact. It taxed my brain too much to contemplate it.

"Okay, so add that information to what we already know. Time speeds up only on full moon days. And sixty-nine years have passed out there, even though only five full moons have happened here, so we can extrapolate that every full moon night, fourteen years pass, correct?"

"It's 13.8 years if you want to be precise," I said.

She frowned. "Fine—13.8 years. So maybe the reason Brigette never made it back to Greengage is because the way back—the fog—is only there on my side once every *13.8* years. Brigette would have had to have been in the exact right place at the exact right time to stumble upon the fog. And what are the odds of that? Minute. Practically nil. That would explain why nobody came to rescue you, too. They couldn't find you. You weren't there."

The news only got worse and worse. If Lux was right, it was pure happenstance that she'd found her way to us.

"Well, there's only one way to know for sure. I'll come again on the next full moon," she said brightly.

"You won't come again," I said, unable to mask my despair. My voice sounded hollow.

"Of course I will."

"How old are you now?"

"Twenty-five."

"Well, if you are right about all this, then the next time you could come, you'll be nearly forty."

She looked thunderstruck. Obviously she hadn't worked it all out in her head.

"God knows where you'll be then. You could be living in Rhode Island."

I didn't say, *God knows if you'll be able to come, even if you want to.*

Years from now her life could be very different. She could be side-tracked by love. Felled by illness. Young people had no idea how quickly things could change.

"Doubtful," she said. "Stop trying to chase me off. I'm coming back, no matter where I live or how elderly I am."

"Elderly. Forty is elderly?"

"Sorry," she smirked. "Is that how old you are?"

"I am forty-two."

"Oh, just a few years younger than my mother."

Sometimes I felt elderly. Right now, sitting with this young woman, I felt like an old man.

"Aren't you going to ask me any questions, Joseph?"

"About what?"

"Life. The 1970s. What's happened in the last sixty-nine years besides two world wars and a man walking on the moon. Aren't you interested? Everybody else can't stop asking questions."

In fact, I had a million questions but I'd been holding myself back. I wasn't sure why—perhaps I didn't want to reveal my desperation to know if the progress I'd hoped to see in the world had materialized. This young woman was the personification of all my hopes for humankind, for better or for worse.

"I'm not everybody else," I said.

"Clearly," she said.


The next day Lux worked with the kitchen crew. I caught glimpses of her at each meal, behind the counter, her head in a pot, stirring jam. This time of year our food preservation efforts were prodigious. We spent a week on jams, a week on canned vegetables, and a week on drying and smoking meats. The work was relentless and somewhat boring, but every time I saw Lux she had a smile on her face.


Finally I couldn't stand it anymore. "Give me a brief summary of domestic and world events," I said that evening—our late night talks had become something of a ritual.

I saw her triumphant expression in the candlelight. Finally I'd revealed my hunger for information.

"What's your definition of brief?"

"Your highlights. You choose."

My mistake. I should have given her some parameters. She didn't stop speaking for an hour.

*The Oreo cookie invented, the* Titanic *sinks, Spanish flu, Prohibition, women granted the right to vote, Lindbergh flies solo across the Atlantic, penicillin invented, stock market crashes, the Depression, Amelia Earhart, the atom is split, Prohibition ends, Golden Gate Bridge is built, Pearl Harbor, D-Day, the Korean War, Disneyland, Rosa Parks, Laika the dog is shot into space, hula hoops, birth control pill invented, Bay of Pigs, Marilyn Monroe dies, JFK killed, MLK has a dream, Vietnam War, Star Trek, MLK killed, RFK killed, Woodstock, the Beatles (George, Ringo, John, and Paul) break up, Watergate, the Vietnam War ends, Nixon resigns, Earth Day,* Fiddler on the Roof, *Olga Korbut, Patty Hearst, Transcendental Meditation, the ERA,* The Six Million Dollar Man.

"Bloody hell," I said when she was done.

"I know. It must be a lot to take in."

"It's unfathomable. A Brit named his son Ringo Starr?"

She looked pleasantly surprised: she'd thought I had no sense of humor.

"Well, I think his real name was Richard Starkey."

Now I put my head in my hands. Countless wars. Prohibition? A bridge spanning the Golden Gate? "You can't share this information with anybody else."

"Uh—sorry. I already have."

"What have you told them?"

"I didn't volunteer any information. I just answered their questions."

"I wish you had asked my permission before you did so."

"Why? They deserve to know the truth."

"What's happening out there is nothing but a distraction. They have to focus on their lives here."

"Well, how about if I just tell them the bad stuff? About the stock market crash, the Depression, and Hitler?"

"Yes, yes, well, that would be fine. All right. You have my permission. I don't see any harm in that."

She gave me an incredulous look. "I was kidding. I'm not only going to tell them just the bad stuff. I'll tell them what they want to know, Joseph. They're not stupid. They know the world has gone on without them. Wouldn't it be worse not to know what that world was like?"

This woman was a continual surprise. I could not predict anything she would say or how she would react. When I was with her, I felt permanently off-balance.

"And for your information, 1970s San Francisco isn't so great. I thought it would be, that's why I came out west. Everything was happening here. It was the epicenter of the counterculture revolution. People were questioning the status quo; they wanted to live a different kind of life where everybody, no matter what race or class, lived happily together. It was a lovely idea, but a pipe dream. Yes, we've made some progress, but mostly things have stayed the same. I've been living in the City of Love for seven years and there seems to be less and less love. We don't care for our veterans. The Zodiac killer still hasn't been caught. The unemployment rate is something like nine percent, and in your country, it's at least double that. People are suspicious of other people. They judge. They don't give them second chances. Or any chance."

It was early in the morning now. We'd been talking for hours.

"Maybe you're the lucky ones. Did you ever think of that?" she asked.

I tried to climb into bed as quietly as I could. I didn't want to wake Martha. The floorboards creaked when I lifted my foot off the floor, and I froze in place.

"Good morning, Joseph Beauford Bell."

"You're up."

She reached out and cupped my cheek. "Of course I'm up. It's nearly dawn. Did you get your questions answered?"

"It was a Pandora's box, I'm afraid."

"You'll be sorry to see the girl go, won't you?"

"Absolutely not. It will be a relief."

"Don't lie to me. It's the most excitement you've had in—well, in sixty-nine years." She gave me a smile. "She has a certain irrepressible energy." She touched her forehead to mine. "Maybe she'll come back."

"She won't come back. She'll have the best of all intentions, but the years will pass and she'll forget all about us, I assure you."

Martha sat up in bed. "So tell me. What did we miss?"

I sighed. "What do you want to know?"

"Anything. Everything."

So I curated a list just for Martha: penicillin, Amelia Earhart, Rosa Parks, the birth control pill, man lands on the moon, the ERA and Billie Jean King.

She was silent for a good five minutes, then she said, "I always wanted to learn how to play tennis."

Two days later, Lux left.

"Goodbye, then," I said, extending my hand to shake hers. We stood at the edge of the fog.

"That's it? That's all you're going to say?"

I blinked at her.

She threw her arms around me. "Thank you for letting me stay, Joseph Bell. It's been interesting, to say the least. Magical, really. I won't ever forget you. All of you." She stepped back from me and tears streamed down her cheeks. "I'm sorry. I know you Brits don't approve of displays of emotion, but I can't help it. There's something about this place. It just burrows its way into you."

I handed her a handkerchief. "It's clean."

She wiped her eyes and tried to give it back to me.

"Keep it."

"It looks fancy. It's monogrammed."

"I have dozens more," I lied. I wanted her to take a piece of Greengage with her.

"I'll see you in a month. Well, one of your months."

"Very well." I still doubted I'd ever see her again.

"Should I bring somebody back with me?"

Over the past few days, I'd thought carefully about her offer to seek out help. Martha, myself, and the heads of all the crews had discussed it among ourselves, and had come to the conclusion that it was not a safe option for Lux. I didn't know all of Lux's history, but I knew she was a single parent and the sole provider for her son. If she returned to 1975, raving about having traveled back in time to 1906, she would at best be considered a drunk or a drug addict, and at worst, mentally unstable. I couldn't ask her to take that risk on our behalf.

"Not yet," I said.

"Can I tell anybody?"

She must have been thinking of her son. "It's not safe. For you, or for us. Keep us a secret for now."

"Okay," she agreed. "What can I bring you back? You must want something."

I mentally recited a list of everything I wanted her to bring back: electricity, ice, television, Marilyn Monroe, a yo-yo, an eight-track stereo tape player, a bottle of good scotch, coffee, a Ford Mustang—in other words, everything she'd told me about. All of it. The modern world in its entirety. Of course I would never admit that.

"As you've seen, we have everything we need right here."

"Fine. It will be a surprise, then," she said.

# LUX

✤

As I walked through the fog, back into the future, I made a list of everything I wanted to bring back with me: the heartbreaking indigo of a Greengage night sky, the sugared almonds I'd eaten in the dining hall, the hawing sound Fancy made when she laughed, the smells of freshly cut clover, sponge cake, and loam, Martha's steady gaze, the swish of my borrowed skirt.

The years streamed by; it felt like I was driving down the coast with my head stuck out the window. I was in the fog for seconds. I was in the fog for hours.

Finally I stepped into my campsite. It was morning. Everything looked exactly as I'd left it. The tank top was still draped on the bush. *The Hobbit* next to my sleeping bag along with Rose's joint.

A soft hissing sound briefly filled the clearing. The fog was gone. It had completely dissipated. I could see a thousand feet into the woods. A thousand feet of nothing but forest.

Greengage had receded into the past.

# LUX

❧

San Francisco
1975

"You're back early," said Rhonda.

She stood at the stove stirring a pot of Rice-A-Roni. I dropped my pack on the floor, ran across the kitchen, and hugged her.

"You were only gone for five days, Lux."

"It felt like years," I cried, seized with happiness at the sight of her familiar denim wrap-around skirt and knobby ankles. "How are you? Tell me everything. What's going on?"

How was I going to keep such a secret from her?

She looked at me suspiciously. "Are you high?"

"No, I'm not high. I'm just happy. Be happy for me, Rhonda." I beamed at her.

Rhonda took the pan off the stove. "Okay, Miss Happy, did you have any epiphanies out there in the wild? Benno didn't call, by the way."

Instantaneously, the pleasant, he's-in-good-hands-with-Mom feeling dispersed and was replaced by a dull, throbbing pain, the pull of the emotional umbilicus. I'd missed Benno while I was at Greengage, but I'd stopped thinking of him every other minute. I realized now what a lovely break that had been—to take care of only myself.

"Don't look so glum. That's a positive thing, Lux—it means he's not homesick. He's having a good time."

"Did you send the cards?"

"Yes. I still have one more. You can mail it yourself tomorrow."

"Maybe I should call him tonight."

Rhonda got the wine out of the fridge and poured each of us a glass. "That was a quick fall to earth."

I rummaged through my pack. I pulled out the joint and waved it at her.

"You go ahead, I have to be in early tomorrow," she said.

"How early?"

"Seven-thirty."

"What's happening at seven-thirty? You can't be seeing patients that early."

She smiled shyly. "I'm meeting somebody for breakfast."

I'd never seen that shiny look on her face before.

"Oh my God, who is it?" Rhonda was so picky about men. She had a lot of first dates, but second and third dates were rare.

"He's a doctor."

"A doctor!" That explained why it was a breakfast date, anyway.

"A pediatric orthopedic surgeon."

Somehow I knew then with utter certainty that she would fall in love with this man and she would leave me.

"My mother is going to kill me. You'll have to help me break the news."

"A surgeon? She'll be thrilled, are you kidding?"

"No, she won't. He's white, Lux. As white as they come."

Rhonda had never dated outside of her race; she was the poster girl for black pride.

"Jesus. Give me your lighter." I lit the joint, took a big puff, and handed it to her.

"Where did you get this?" Rhonda was as picky about her weed as she was about men.

"Rose and Doro."

She sighed and took a drag.

It got worse. The doctor was half Italian and half Irish. His name was Patrick Signorelli, but everybody called him Ginger because of his red hair.

"No, no, no, no, no!" I shouted, banging the table with my fist. "You are making that up. Please tell me you're making that up."

"Stop talking," Rhonda panted, clutching her stomach. "I'm going to pee my pants."

"Does he have freckles?"

"Of course he has freckles!"

We exploded with laughter again.

A pounding came from the ceiling and we heard Doro's muffled voice. "Girls, you're having entirely too much fun."

I yelled, "And it's entirely your fault! We're smoking your weed."

A second later we heard both Doro and Rose echo, "Marvelous!"

"Don't leave me, Rhonda," I said an hour later. We sat in front of the TV, stoned out of our minds, watching *Kojak*. I'd have to rethink the whole bald-men thing—Telly Savalas was pretty sexy.

"I'm not going anywhere. I'm just having breakfast with him." She tucked her feet beneath her on the couch. "Is my 'fro smushed?"

"Want me to fix it?"

She bent her head toward me. I fluffed her Afro and started to cry.

"And this is exactly why you should never smoke pot," said Rhonda.

Also, because it was like a truth serum for me. Before I could stop myself, I said, "I have to tell you something, but it's a secret—you can't tell anybody. Something happened when I went camping."

"Uh-huh." Rhonda went limp whenever somebody ran their fingers through her hair.

There were two reasons I was about to spill my secret. The obvious one: What had just happened to me was beyond belief. Who could keep quiet about something so world-changing? And the less obvious: I wanted to draw Rhonda in. She was my best friend. I couldn't bear the thought of keeping something so important from her.

"There was this weird fog . . ."

"But how did *you* find it?" asked Rhonda, twenty minutes later. "Don't you think somebody would have stumbled upon it before you? If it's been there for sixty-nine years."

Rhonda was an X-ray technician. She believed only in what the films told her. Sprained, broken, splintered, a tumor the size of an orange.

"It's been there for sixty-nine years, yes, but the only way to get there is through the fog. And the fog appears once every 13.8 years on the full moon. You'd have to find yourself exactly in that spot, in those woods at just the right time."

"Really?" she drawled. "This sounds awfully complicated."

"You don't believe me."

"Well, Lux, I'm sorry, but that is a pretty far-out story—and I'm stoned! You miss Benno. You're emotionally exhausted, I know. I sympathize."

"I don't want you to sympathize with me, I want you to believe me, and I'm not emotionally exhausted, look at me, I'm emotionally full. This is me being emotionally full!"

She pursed her lips. "Do you have any proof?"

"Wait. I did bring back something." I dug in my pocket and pulled out Joseph's handkerchief. I showed her the monogram *JBB*. "He gave it to me just before I left. Joseph something Bell."

Rhonda examined the handkerchief. "Looks old, but you could have picked it up in any thrift store."

"Christ, Rhonda! Why would I make something like this up?"

"I don't think you made it up. I don't doubt that you stumbled upon some sort of commune in the Valley of the Moon. So they wear weird clothes. They eschew the modern world. They've probably been out there for years."

"No, you're wrong. It's real. And it's not a commune. Don't say that. It's a farm."

Rhonda sighed. "Okay, go to the library and do some research on this Greengage. If the place just disappeared and hundreds of people—whoosh!—were just gone, somebody must have missed them. Is it like the lost city of Atlantis? Are people still looking for it?"

"Fine, if people are still looking for it, then will you believe me?"

Rhonda bobbled her head.

"Rhonda!"

"Yes, yes, if you find proof that Greengage existed in the early 1900s, then I'll believe."

"Spell it again for me," said the librarian.

"Greengage. Like the plum."

I'd spent the following morning at the San Francisco Public Library and had come up with nothing.

"Well, there were more than a few colonies operating in that area at the time: Icaria-Speranza—but that was in Cloverdale; Point Loma; Fountain Grove in Santa Rosa. Are you sure the location was the Valley of the Moon?"

"I'm positive. And it's not a colony. It's a farm." Every time I made that distinction, I thought of Joseph. I might be betraying him by researching Greengage, but I wouldn't betray his vision of the place.

"There's nothing here," she said, looking up from a reference book, "but that doesn't mean it didn't exist. Was it small?"

"About three hundred people?"

"Not that small, then," she said. "I'm sorry. I don't know what to tell you. It was definitely a fertile time for those kinds of communities, and it makes sense that it would be in Sonoma County. You know, sometimes folks just walked up in the hills and squatted, built their homes and lived their lives. If it was isolated enough, they probably wouldn't have bothered—"

"That's just the thing. They weren't isolated; they were well known. They sold their produce to restaurants and grocery stores in Glen Ellen and San Francisco."

"Strange. You'd think there'd be some record of them. You say your grandmother lived on the farm?"

"Um, my great-grandmother."

"Perhaps we could come at this in another way. What was her name?"

I hesitated. "Martha Bell," I said.

"Do you know her middle name? It would help to have a full name."

"No, but she was married to a British man, Joseph Bell. He had a sister named Fancy Bell. They all lived there. Does that help?"

The librarian scribbled down the names on a pad of paper. "Anybody else you can remember?"

"Lars Magnusson . . . and Elisabetta Sala. And her husband, Matteo Sala. They had a son named Nardo, too. Must have been short for something—Bernardo?"

The librarian slid a form across her desk. "Fill this out. Your name, address. We'll contact you with our results. Give it a week; it might take even longer than that. Most of the census records before 1925 aren't on microfiche."

"It's your mother!" my mother sang into the phone. "Come say hello, Benno."

I heard rustling. The sound of little feet climbing on a stool.

"Mama, I am having a great time," he said robotically. Obviously my mother had prompted him, which wasn't to say he wasn't actually having a great time.

"That's wonderful, Benno. You got my cards?"

"Yup."

"Good, good, that's good."

There was a long silence in which I could hear him chewing and swallowing something. He rarely spoke on the phone. He didn't know how to carry on a conversation.

"So what have you been doing with Grandma?"

More silence.

"Tell her what we've been doing, Benno. We went to Second Beach. We saw a play at Theater-by-the-Sea," my mother said in the background.

"The other grandma brings me jelly doughnuts in the morning," he said.

"The other grandma?"

Benno dropped the phone on the floor.

"Sorry about that," said my mother after a few seconds.

"What's he talking about—the other grandma?"

"Benno, I think *Truth or Consequences* is on. Go ahead, darling. Turn the TV on. You can watch it while I speak to your mother for a few minutes."

"You're letting him watch *Truth or Consequences?*"

"What's wrong with *Truth or Consequences?* It's really quite educational, he's learning—"

"Mom, who's the other grandma?"

My mother paused. "Your father."

"Lux, before you say anything, I have to tell you your father has simply fallen in love with Benno."

"You have got to be kidding me, Mom."

"He can't get enough of him. They spend every waking minute together. It's the cutest thing. Every afternoon they go off to—"

"You swore to me he was going to be at Lapis Lake."

"He did go to Lapis Lake."

"Well, what happened?"

"He came back," my mother said in a pitiful voice.

"Why did he come back? The weather was shitty, right?"

"The weather was glorious."

"Don't tell me that, Mom. I don't want to hear that."

"Well, it's true. He came back because he realized he was being an ass and he wanted to spend time with his grandson."

I opened the cupboard door and slammed it shut in frustration.

"Lux, your father has been nothing but admiring, attentive, and kind. He even let Benno teach him that dance. The Hustle. Imagine— your father shaking his hips. Oh my goodness, it was the funniest thing. Now, I admit, Benno is a little confused. He keeps calling us both Grandma. But I swear to you, he's fine. He's better than fine. They have a lot in common, actually. Your father is—well, I haven't seen him this happy in years." My mother's voice broke on the word *years*.

I had a vision of my father in the living room. Wearing his plaid Pendleton shirt. Standing beside the mantel, watching me walk on my hands. I was six years old.

"Monkey," he'd said, his eyes gleaming with pleasure.

I'd walked the length of the couch, my arms quivering, and finally fell in a heap on the floor. I'd wept then, from exhaustion, from an overfull heart. He'd gathered me up into his lap and held me silently. I didn't have to tell him why I was crying; he knew. He was my planet, I was his star. He orbited around me: I was safe in the knowledge I'd always be orbited. Love was so simple back then.

I put my hand over the receiver so my mother wouldn't hear me crying now.

"Lux? Lux, are you still there?"

Rhonda's prism spun in the kitchen window, splashing the wall with rainbows.

"Benno won't stop talking about you. You are his favorite topic of conversation. Mama said this. Mama said that. Mama and I did this. Mama and I did that. He sits in your father's lap and tells him stories about you. You, Lux. And your father is desperate to hear those stories. He is. He wants to know about your life."

"Right," I said.

"My God. The two of you are so alike."

"Me and Benno?"

"No, you and your father. You know, Lux, you're responsible for this, too."

"For what?"

"For this distance."

"Bullshit. Mom, it's been his choice. He's chosen to stay away. He's chosen to have little to no relationship with me or Benno. He came to San Francisco once. He met Benno once. That's it. Once."

"That's because you didn't invite him to come again."

I sucked in my breath. "He's been waiting for an invitation?"

"This is getting us nowhere," she said. "The important thing is what's happening now. Benno can be a bridge. A way back for the both of you."

I could just imagine Benno in the afternoon light, sitting on the couch, his legs swinging. His chubby hand in the bowl of butterscotch candies that was always on the side table.

"He's a little boy, not a bridge," I said.

I started a week of double shifts at Seven Hills. I needed the hours; I only had eighty-nine dollars left in my checking account. I'd splurged and bought Benno some new clothes and a suitcase for his trip to Rhode Island. I'd have to make that money up now or I wouldn't be able to buy groceries and pay bills.

On Wednesday I arrived at 10:35 and spent an hour refilling condiments and resetting the tables from the breakfast shift. At 11:30 customers started pouring in and then it was nonstop for two solid hours.

At one forty-five an elderly couple walked in the door. *Please, oh, please, oh, please don't sit in my section.* My last table had just paid up and the busboy was clearing the plates: I thought I was in the clear. There was a back-to-school meeting at Benno's school, and if I left now, I'd just make it.

They sat in my section.

Tourists. A surprised look on their faces, but that wasn't uncommon. To stumble upon Seven Hills, an Irish pub in the middle of North Beach, was like finding a four-leaf clover in Times Square. At least that's what Mike always said. Mike Mulligan, owner of Seven Hills (don't you dare mention that children's book to him, as if he hadn't been asked if he owned a steam shovel named Mary Anne a thousand times) and my boss.

"I'll take them," said Barb, my co-worker. She knew I wanted to leave.

"That's Lux's section," said Mike.

"It's fine," said Barb. "I don't mind."

"No. She was late for her shift this morning. She'll have to stay."

Mike liked to talk about me in third person, as if I weren't there. I'd been five minutes late that morning, which wouldn't have been a big deal if not for the fact that during the school year I was frequently late or calling at the last minute to beg him to find somebody to cover my shift. June had been really bad. Benno had missed an entire week of school because of a flu, which meant I missed an entire week of work. When Monday rolled around again and he still had a fever, I

was so desperate that I crumbled up two baby aspirin, sprinkled them
into his Cream of Wheat, and sent him off to school, praying by the
time he got there his fever would be gone. The school nurse, Mrs.
Lafferty, had it in for me. If she could have greeted me at the kindergarten door with a thermometer in her hand every morning, she
would have. Disapproval beaming out of her eyes. Benno's chronic
cough. His constantly runny nose. She hated us.

"Look like big tippers," Mike joked.

"Sorry," whispered Barb.

Old people frequently forgot to tip. I didn't take it personally;
watching them painstakingly count out their money was excruciating.
It was so sad it made me want to pay their bill for them. This couple
tipped me well, but it didn't make up for the fact that I was late.

I walked into the school courtyard surprised to find it still filled with
children and mothers. The picnic tables were strewn with snacks.
Bowls of potato chips. Ransacked platters of cream cheese sandwiches and peanut butter on Ritz crackers.

I missed Benno and felt vulnerable on school grounds without
him. That milky-smelling, sweaty, and, more often than not, snotty
creature whom I adored more than anything.

"Lux, we were wondering where you were," said Nancy Atkins.
She had a second grader and a fourth grader.

She smiled sympathetically at me, but it was a toxic mix of conde-
scension and schadenfreude. My tennis shoes, a splotch of ketchup
on the right toe. My cheap purse, bulging with a sweater and an unopened can of Tab.

"I'm sorry, I got a table at the last minute." I smoothed my hair
down self-consciously, knowing I smelled of french fries.

*"What's the worst thing that happened today?"* my father would ask
me when I came home from school in a bad mood. This question was
a sort of magic. A bad grade, striking out in kickball, not getting invited to a birthday party, I'd tell him. As soon as I said my reasons out
loud, my woes evaporated, exposed as the trivial things they really
were.

*Well, what's the worst thing that happened today?* I thought. Some asshole customer wouldn't deign to speak to me. Instead he communicated through snaps and pointing. Stabbed the menu with his finger. Pointed at his empty water glass. Anything to avoid treating me like a fellow human being. It was an everyday occurrence in my line of work. A man treating me like I was invisible. He left me an eleven-cent tip.

Nancy smiled. "Not to worry. You didn't miss a thing. Just the same old same old. Can the PTA afford to buy new recorders for the kids? What to do with the ripped flag—did you know there's a protocol? I mean, you can't just throw a flag away? Who knew? Anyway, we figured you had your hands full. What with . . ." She drifted off.

*Being a single mother and all. Doing it all on your own, you poor thing.* And then beneath that? The more messy truth. *Yes, we support the ERA. Yes, we fought to legalize abortion; yes, we believe you can bring home the bacon and fry it up in the pan; but really, why is your son's nose always running? Why does he wear the same pair of pants to school three days in a row? Why does he lack impulse control?*

Because he's a five-year-old boy!

In this group of mothers, all but a few were married. The few who weren't married were divorced and received alimony and child support.

"Where's Benno?" she asked.

"Covering my shift," I said.

Her eyes widened.

"I'm kidding, Nancy. He's with my mother. In Newport."

"Oh. Newport Beach?"

"Newport, Rhode Island."

"Newport!" said Nancy. "Wow, there's so much history there. Is he going to see the mansions? Surely your parents will take him to see the Breakers, Lux."

"I have no idea."

"He went alone? You didn't want to go?"

She screwed her face up into one big question mark. I screwed my face up into one big fuck-you-it's-none-of-your-business mark.

"I had to work, Nancy."

"Oh, right. Of course. I understand." She looked over my head and nodded at somebody. "I'm afraid I'm being summoned." She put her hand on my arm and squeezed. "You have a wonderful rest of the summer."

Like a school of fish, the mothers collected Nancy and swam away.

"Lux dear, it's your mother again. This is the third message I've left. I was hoping you'd call back today, but you haven't. I know you're punishing me. And I really wish we could have this conversation over the phone—I hate talking into this damned machine—but I have a feeling you don't intend to call me back at all, so here goes.

"First of all, Benno is an amazing child. He is really quite precocious for his age. Curious about everything. I can't believe he knows the name of every dinosaur in the Jurassic period. And he can already count up to a hundred. And you've done a wonderful job reading to him. Bravo! His vocabulary? Well, for a kid his age, it's astounding. Okay, so I know what I'm about to say may shock you. But I want you to take some time to think about it. George and I have hatched a plan. We've been agonizing over it, really. It's not an offer we make lightly. We may be overstepping our boundaries. You can tell us to go to hell, you may well do that, but I want to put it out there.

"What if Benno stays here with us in Newport through the fall? Your father has managed to get him a place in the first-grade class at St. Paul's. Of course you know what a coup that is. They only take the very brightest children. Your father administered some tests—Benno did very well, of course.

"He loves it here, Lux. Both of us, me and your father, have grown quite attached to him. I want you to know your father has nothing but goodwill for that boy. He wants the best for him.

"Now, I know things are tough for you out there. Money is tight. Perhaps this would be just the thing for you. To have some time and space to figure out your next move. You can't be a waitress forever—you know that, I know you do. Let us take some of the pressure off. It's just through the first term. We could send him home right after that. A little time with his grandparents. A break for you. Think about it, darling, will you?

"All right, I can't believe your tape hasn't run out. Let's try and—"


As the last four days until Benno came home slowly passed, and reality swept me under, there was a part of me that almost regretted finding Greengage. I'd never imagined a world like that existed, but now that I knew it did, it was impossible to switch off my longing for it. I'd felt so energized there, so complete. I couldn't help but contrast it with the plodding inevitability of my life here. Minute after minute, hour after hour—the days unspooling as they always did. Wake at six. Get Benno ready for school. Pack his lunch. Shower. Dress. Breakfast. Get him to school. Take the bus to work. Punch in. Punch out hours later. Pick Benno up at school. Take the bus home. Make dinner. Do laundry. Pay bills. Fall into bed. Repeat, repeat, repeat until the end of time.


It was Saturday, the night before Benno's return, and Ginger was coming for dinner. Rhonda had the entire Time-Life Foods of the World series, and had cooked her way through five of the books already. Tonight she was making jambalaya.

She glided from countertop to fridge, humming. A big pot bubbled on the stove. She'd had to make a special trip to Oakland to get the smoked sausage and another trip to Berkeley to get the proper seasonings. Apparently Ginger had been to New Orleans once when he was a kid, had tasted jambalaya, and had been dreaming about it ever since.

Rhonda was already all about fulfilling Ginger's dreams; I found it both irritating and sweet. I was happy for her, though envious.

"I don't think your mother offering to keep Benno for the fall term is such a horrible proposition," said Rhonda.

"It wouldn't be if it was just my mother. But it's my father, too."

"But isn't this what you've been waiting for? Your father to come around?"

I popped a green bean in my mouth. "Not this way."

Rhonda turned around slowly and leaned against the counter. "Lux." She was using her serious, X-ray technician voice.

"Rhon—da." I drew out the syllables of her name, hoping to pull her back from the edge of a conversation I didn't want to have.

She shook her head. "Honestly, what happened between you and your father? What did he do that was so bad? This thing started way before Benno, right?"

Yes. It started with a question.

⚜

"Does my father know you're here?" I asked.

It was the spring of 1965. I was fifteen and bursting from my girl seams; I had been ever since that last summer at Lapis Lake. I'd returned home not with a sunburn or poison ivy, but a fatal case of restlessness that now threatened to subsume me.

Dash Karras stood at the base of the ladder, a scraper in his hands.

"I sure hope so," he said.

He wore beat-up work boots, paint-splattered overalls, and a blue shirt; his hair was curly and blondish brown. He looked me up and down and it wasn't the gaze of a high school boy. This was the bold stare of a man. He'd parked his black truck in the driveway, KARRAS & SONS PAINTING in block lettering on the side.

"I'm the sons," he said.

My father hadn't mentioned anything about getting the house painted.

"George hired you?" I asked skeptically. I wanted him to think I was the kind of girl who called her father by his first name.

"Well, he hired my father, but he got me."

Dash scrambled onto the ladder. Halfway up he lost his balance and teetered on one foot. I gasped and he easily righted himself. He peered down at me. "Don't worry, I've done this once or twice before." He grinned the grin of somebody who was putting on a show.

I'd been caught. He knew I'd been staring at him. I marched into the house, my face aflame. I made cinnamon toast and spied on him through the kitchen window. Well, I spied on the ladder—that's all I could see. I turned on the radio, spinning the dial impatiently past Herman's Hermits, Bob Dylan, and Patty Duke until I found the Kinks. "All Day and All of the Night."

It was three-thirty in the afternoon and I had the place to myself. My father was holding an open house for prospective parents and wouldn't be home until after eight. My mother was working at Goodwill, likely sorting through another bin of used clothes.

I started in on my English homework and was soon lost in *The Great Gatsby*. It was my second time reading it—well, really my first: my father and I had only gotten through a few chapters at the lake. A half hour later there was a banging on the back door. Dash stood on the stoop wiping his hands on a rag.

"Yes?" I sounded just like my mother.

"Sorry to bother you, but may I use your bathroom? I won't track in dirt, don't worry." He lifted his foot and showed me the sole of his boot.

I stepped aside and let him in. "It's right there." I pointed to the bathroom door.

I didn't know what to do with myself. Should I go upstairs and give him some privacy? Or should I just sit there and be cool? Pretend it was a normal thing for me to have a man (other than my father) use the toilet a few feet away from me?

I froze when I heard the loud, ropy stream of his piss. It was so intimate. I half stood and I half sat. That's how he found me when he came out of the bathroom.

He smirked. "Please, don't make yourself uncomfortable on my behalf, George's daughter."

I sat down. "My name is Lux," I said huffily.

"Nice. Never met a girl named Lux before. The professor come up with that? You named after some literary character?"

"My father's not a professor, he's a dean."

"Professor, dean, what's the difference?" He patted his pocket and pulled out a pack of Marlboros. "Okay if I smoke?"

My parents had quit smoking. We didn't even own an ashtray anymore.

"Well, maybe—"

He opened the back door and stepped out on the stoop. "No problem."

He lit up. He was one of those serious inhalers, sucking the smoke way back into his throat, his eyes half closed with pleasure.

"How old are you?" he asked.

"Seventeen," I said without hesitation. "Almost eighteen."

He took another drag. "You look older than that. If you weren't wearing that uniform, I'd have thought twenty, twenty-one."

I pulled up my knee socks nervously. I could pass for twenty-one?

A few weeks ago I'd dreamed of Crawford Saltonstall, the captain of the St. Paul's football team. In real life he'd never given me a second look, but in my dream he sat on a blanket with me in the middle of a field. Inexplicably (we were nowhere near the water), I wore my one-piece pink bathing suit. We didn't speak. We didn't even look at each other. I may have, in fact, been looking away as he pulled the straps off my shoulders and peeled my suit down to the waist, exposing my breasts to the air.

In my dream he moaned, "God."

In my dream I moaned "God" back to him.

That was it. That was all. The bathing suit. The straps. My boobs. I was an innocent. Having a boy see my breasts was as far as my imagination would take me at that point. I'd been living off that fantasy for days now. It felt so real that when I passed Crawford Saltonstall in the hall at school, I had to look down at the ground, afraid that if he caught my eye he'd know everything.

"How old do you think I am?" asked Dash.

He was working, he had to be done with high school.

"Nineteen?" I guessed.

He nodded and took a few more drags of his cigarette. "Poor Gatsby. He never stood a chance." He stubbed his butt out on the stoop. "I better get back to it. If your father catches me talking with you—well, I'm sure he won't be too happy about it."

———

That night, long after my mother and father were in bed, I sneaked downstairs and retrieved Dash's cigarette butt from the stoop. I put it between my lips, imagining it had just come from his lips. I should have asked him for a drag—that would have been the cool thing to do.

"This is my daughter, Lux," said my father as I walked into the yard the next afternoon.

He and Dash stood at the truck. I'd heard my father laughing from a block away. He had his foot up on the bumper of the truck, like he was some handyman about to strap on his tool belt and get to work cleaning our gutters. His shiny oxford, thin black sock, and slice of hairy white leg embarrassed me.

"Nice to meet you," said Dash. He was acting as if we'd never met. As if we had something to hide.

"You as well," I said, wincing at my ridiculous formality.

Dash fought off a smile.

And so a new routine began. Every day I'd run home after school. When I was a few blocks away, I'd let my hair out of its ponytail, dab on a little lipstick, pull out *Gatsby*, and saunter slowly up the street, pretending to read.

"Afternoon," Dash would say when I walked into the yard.

I'd nod and go into the house. If my mother wasn't home, he'd come into the kitchen through the back door. He didn't knock anymore. He didn't ask permission to use the bathroom; if he needed it, he went. Most days he'd go to the cupboard, get a glass, and help himself to whatever was in the refrigerator. I'd have my books and notebooks spread out on the table, my skirt shucked high on my thighs.

"What?" I'd say.

"Shhh," he'd say.

Then he'd lean against the counter and watch me pretend-studying.

He'd stay for five, maybe ten minutes, neither of us speaking, and then he'd rinse his glass in the sink and leave. I knew this was some sort of test. Would I say anything to my father? Could I endure his stares?

One afternoon the pattern changed. He didn't come into the kitchen. Instead he called me outside into the backyard. "I need your help."

"Okay."

"Are you afraid of heights?"

"No."

"Good. Climb up on the ladder. Just a few rungs."

I hesitated.

"Don't worry, I'll hold it." He grasped the ladder and shook it. "Perfectly safe."

"I'm not scared," I said.

"I know you're not."

So, this was the moment. I'd passed the test.

It was a windy day. I held my skirt tight to my legs while I climbed the first and second rung.

"Let go of it," he said.

I looked down at him. His voice sounded different, deeper. I let go of my skirt and the wind burrowed beneath it. The pleats poofed out.

"Another rung," he said.

I climbed.

"Stop."

I stopped, staring straight ahead at the freshly painted clapboards. His gaze swam up my ankles and calves; pooled at the backs of my thighs.

"Are you all right?"

"Yes."

"Do you want to come down?"

"Do you want me to come down?"

"Not yet."

I could see the clock through the kitchen window: 4:05. My mother wouldn't be home for at least another hour.

He put his hand on my ankle. His palm was hot and dry. The breeze carried the scent of paint and bleached rags. I held my breath as he slowly slid his hand up the inside of my leg. When he reached my mid-thigh, I clamped my legs shut because I was embarrassed. I didn't know why, but my underwear was wet. It wasn't pee, but something moist seeped out of me involuntarily. I couldn't stop it. Nor could I stop his insistent fingers. They parted my legs and spidered up to my underwear. When he touched the material, he made an involuntary sound. A sound I'd never heard a man make before. I was the cause of that—I drew that sound out of him.

I'd never felt so powerful.

I don't know how long we stayed like that. His fingers lightly brushing the cotton crotch of my panties. Like a paintbrush. Back and forth. Back and forth. He kept returning to one particular spot and pressing on it. That spot was the nucleus. A wavy, thick feeling began there and radiated out.

There was this reality: his hand was up my skirt. And there was this reality: we were both pretending it wasn't.

"You'd better go," he finally said.

The next week he ignored me. He didn't greet me when I walked up the path. There was no knock on the kitchen door, no bathroom requests, nothing. He stood on his ladder and played his paint-splattered transistor radio so loudly I had to shut the kitchen window in order to concentrate on my homework. He treated me like a stranger.

I couldn't sleep. I could barely eat. What had happened? Did a neighbor see us on the ladder? Had my *down there* disgusted him?

Finally, in desperation I slipped a note under his windshield.

*Did I do something wrong?*

A schoolgirl's note. I might as well have written, *Do you like me? Circle "yes" or "no."* Then I sat in the kitchen and waited like Gatsby's beautiful little fool, stricken, unable to do anything.

He came through the front door this time. I froze as I heard his footsteps in the corridor.

"I'm sorry. I couldn't help it," I blurted out.

"Help what?"

"My panties—getting wet. I know it's gross. I think there must be something wrong with me."

He rubbed his forehead. "What? Jesus, Lux. You think that's the issue? Damn. There's nothing wrong with you."

"There isn't?"

"No. You being wet is a good thing. The fact that you don't know that is the problem."

"I don't understand!" I cried.

"That's because you're a baby. You're still in high school."

"I'm not a baby."

"Your father wouldn't agree with that."

The hair on his forearms was bleached white by the sun.

"This isn't about my father. It's about what I want. What *you* want."

"How do you know what I want?"

I remembered the sound he'd made when he touched me on the ladder. "I know what you want," I whispered.

My whole family fell in love with Dash Karras. Who wouldn't? Ridge-bellied and sun-kissed. Silver-tongued and punctual. A professional. He cleaned up after himself. When he left in the late afternoon, there'd be no sign he'd been there during the day. The ladder would be folded neatly, stored inside the woodshed. Not one drop of paint on the lawn.

He did leave things behind, however. Bruises of lust visible only to me.

"Are you feeling all right?" asked my mother.

I helped myself to another bowl of cereal. I was starving.

"Your cheeks are red. Do you have a fever?" She touched my forehead with the back of her hand.

"I'm fine, Mom."

"Sunburn? You've been at the beach?"

I picked up the bowl, draining it of milk. I was glowing because I'd been claimed. Every movement I made belonged to Dash. Tipping my head back. The sweet, cold liquid pouring down my throat. My grades were suffering. I'd quit the track team—it just seemed so silly. All I could think of was him.

"I hate it when you do that," said my mother. "Use a spoon."

My father walked into the room with the *Times*. "Ali KO'd Liston in the first round." He tried to hand the paper to my mother.

"Not at breakfast," said my mother.

I caught a glimpse of the photo, a shocking image. A snarling Muhammad Ali, arms the size of thighs, standing menacingly over a sprawled-out Sonny Liston.

"Two minutes, twelve seconds. People hadn't even found their seats and the fight was over," he said.

"We need to pay Dash. It's his last day," said my mother. "Should I write him a check or do you want me to give him cash?"

"Write him a check. I don't have time to go to the bank today."

"He did a great job," said my mother. "It was nice having him around. I'll miss our midmorning coffee breaks."

Dash had midmorning coffee breaks with my mother?

My father popped a piece of bread into the toaster. "I've recommended him to the headmaster. This fall all the buildings at St. Paul's are being repainted. I can't guarantee he'll get the job, but at least he and his father can bid on it. They should hire somebody local, a Newporter. The Karrases have been here for three generations."

"How do you know that?" asked my mother.

"I asked him."

"Dash?" I said.

"Of course, Dash. We've had quite a few conversations. He's a fine young man. I encouraged him to think about college. I'm sure he could get into URI or PC."

"What if he just wants to be a painter?" I asked.

"Nobody just wants to be a painter, Lux. He's twenty. It's time for him to get serious about his life."

I skipped school that day. I sat on a bench near Trinity Church and waited for my mother's Plymouth to drive by, then I went back home. Dash was already there, sitting on the back stoop.

I walked across the grass and sat in his lap, straddling him. "You lied to me."

"About what?"

"You're twenty."

"Who told you that?"

"My father."

"The dean. That guy asks a lot of questions."

"That's because he likes you. God, you're five years older than me!" I'd captured the attention of a man half a decade older. I was too young to realize this was a cliché.

"Two years," he said.

Time for me to confess. "Actually five. I'm fifteen."

His mouth dropped open. "You told me you were seventeen. You lied to me?"

"What's the difference? Fifteen? Seventeen?"

"I thought you were going on eighteen. There's a big difference." He pushed me off his lap. "We have to stop this. We have to stop."

"I can't believe you're saying that."

"I'm sorry, Lux, but I have a life. I have work. I can't afford . . . I mean, you're fucking fifteen!"

I stared at him, my pulse raggedy and thin. "But—I love you."

"Christ," he said.

I started crying.

"Don't do that. Don't cry. Aw, damn. Come here."

After a while I let him take me in his arms. He held me until my shuddering stopped.

"Look, this is my last day. I start a new job in Middletown on Monday. What did you think would happen? How would we see each other?"

What *did* I think would happen? I thought I'd drop out of school. I thought I'd move in with him. I thought I'd make dinner for him every night and I'd bleach his white painter pants and I'd grow dahlias in the backyard. I was fifteen. That's what I thought.

"When's your mother coming home?"

"You had coffee breaks with her every day?"

He laughed. "What was I supposed to do? She gave me Fig Newtons. She's a nice lady."

"She won't be back until supper."

"The dean?"

"Same."


And so we played house.

I made him eggs and toast. I sat at the table and watched him eat. The radio played songs it seemed were curated just for that moment. After breakfast we went to my bedroom. He undressed me. He took in each part of my body as if he'd never see it again, naming it as he touched it. Clavicle. Rib cage. Pelvis.

Sound abandoned the room.

The bedsprings groaning. Dash panting. The slap of our bodies separating and coming together. Somebody walking up the stairs. I heard none of it. I was gone.

When I opened my eyes, I saw my father framed in the doorway. His face was ashen. He stared at us, trying to make sense of what he was encountering.

"Dad!" I cried out, but it was too late.

He roared and flew at Dash, ripping him off me. Dash was no match for my father, who boxed three nights a week. In a matter of seconds, Dash's face was bloodied, an egg-size lump on his left cheekbone.

Dash scrambled around trying to find his jeans and shirt.

"Did he hurt you? Did he hurt you?" my father yelled. Before I could answer, he went at Dash again, a flurry of punches to the chest and abdomen.

I squeezed my eyes shut. "Stop, stop, stop!" I begged. When I opened my eyes, Dash was gone.


"Are you all right?" my father asked.

I drew the comforter over my head and hid. I'd swum out too far. I was caught in a rip tide. Being pulled out to sea.

"Honey. You have to talk to me." He started pacing. "Damn it. I'm phoning your mother."

His "honey" made tears come to my eyes. After last summer, we'd grown even further apart. He'd been perfectly cordial to me at school, but at home it was different. We stayed in our separate corners now. I didn't watch *Jackie Gleason* with him anymore. He didn't bring me books from the library, and on Saturday mornings he didn't invite me to walk to the doughnut store, our ritual for as long as I could remember.

Once I'd overheard my mother asking him why I wasn't going with him.

"Oh, she's not interested," he'd said.

"She told you that?" asked my mother.

"Yes."

"She said that. She didn't want to go get doughnuts with you?"

"She's got better things to do, apparently," he'd said.

"No, please don't call Mom," I said. "Please don't."

"Lux, you're going to have to talk to one of us. We need to get our facts straight before we go to the police."

"The police! Why are we going to the police?"

"Don't be scared. You've done nothing wrong. You're a victim here. It's not your fault."

And just like that he offered me a way back to my old life. To him. To the way we used to be. All I had to do was lie. I thought about it for a split second. Dash didn't love me, that was clear. Maybe he *had* used me. Maybe he *had* taken advantage of me. He'd lied about his age. But I'd lied about mine, too.

I couldn't do it. "I'm not a victim."

"What do you mean? I saw him on top of you. I *saw* him!"

I looked into my father's wild eyes, knowing I was about to break his heart. "I wanted it. I wanted him."

He backed out of the room. A minute later, I heard the sound of his car driving away.


"Does Dad have an event tonight?" I asked. It was nearly eight and my father hadn't come home yet.

My mother cut a tomato into neat slices and spread them across the plate. "He went to McGillicutty's. He should be back anytime."

I felt sick with dread. The plate I was holding slipped through my fingers and crashed to the floor.

"Don't move," my mother said.

She got on her hands and knees and started picking up pieces of the shattered plate. The sight of her hunched-over back made me want to weep. Suddenly the door opened and my father walked into the kitchen carrying his briefcase in one hand, his gym bag in the other. He was freshly showered, his hair wet. He glanced at my mother.

"What's going on here?"

"I dropped a plate," said my mother, standing. "Stupid. It just slipped right out of my fingers."

I wasn't sure why she was covering for me. Instinct, I guess.

He put his bags on the floor. His right hand was bandaged with gauze and tape.

"What happened to your hand?" asked my mother.

"Bruised it."

"How?"

"Sparring."

"You weren't wearing your gloves?"

No, he wasn't wearing his gloves when he laid into Dash, punching him over and over again.

"Of course I was wearing my gloves. Sometimes gloves aren't enough."

"Let me see it. I'll wrap it again, better. You should probably ice it, too."

"I'm fine, Miriam," he growled. He got a tumbler out of the cupboard.

"Daddy," I said, desperate. "Can I make you a drink?"

"Vodka tonic." He held out the glass like I was some waitress.

I made him the drink and my father took his vodka tonic into the living room.

Karras & Sons did not get the St. Paul's contract. In fact, I never saw Dash again.

———

For a while I tried to make my way back into my father's good graces. I joined him on the couch after dinner to watch the evening news. I asked him to help me with my trigonometry. I bought him a new pair of boxing gloves for his birthday. He acknowledged my presence, solved the equations, and thanked me for the gift, but continued to keep his distance. I felt ashamed for a long time, and then my shame slowly turned to defiance.

My last two years of high school, I lost all interest in academics. My class rank went from being in the top ten percent to somewhere around the fiftieth. I quit my clubs: French Club, Key Club, and Drama. I smoked openly in the courtyard. I flirted with any boy who would flirt back with me, and I slept with several of them. In the tennis shed. In the pool house. Once in the men's locker room. Promiscuity was an escape, a route out, a way to take my power back. I read Simone de Beauvoir, I inhaled *The Feminine Mystique*. There was something, *somebody* that lived in the country between victim and whore. I was awakening to this.

In the fall of my senior year, my father called in some favors and managed to get me into Newton College of the Sacred Heart, an all-women's school outside of Boston. I think at that point he couldn't wait to be rid of me.

My parents dropped me off at college on August 29, 1968. It was a cool, humidity-free day—fall was in the air. I could smell the Charles River as I watched the Plymouth drive away from my dorm window. When it was out of sight, I went downstairs and hailed myself a taxi.

"The Greyhound bus terminal," I said.

Three days later, I was in San Francisco.

❧

"It's a long story," I said.

"I have time. The jambalaya has to cook for another two hours," said Rhonda.

"I don't want to talk about it. It's in the past and what matters is now. What he's doing now. My father came around without me—I'm not a part of this. He's not reaching out to me."

"He's reaching out to Benno; ergo, he's reaching out to you."

"No, he's cheating. He's trying to skip the vegetable and go straight to dessert."

Rhonda ran a bunch of fresh parsley under the tap and shook it, sending droplets of water flying into the air. "You're the vegetable, I take it."

"Yes, and Benno is the dessert. Who doesn't want dessert? It's sweet and creamy and just slides down your throat. Of course my father adores Benno—he's easy to adore."

Rhonda threw the parsley on the cutting board and chopped it vigorously. "Well, at least it's something. It's a beginning. He's trying."

I sat down on a stool. "Jesus."

"Lux, he didn't go to the lake—the trip he's taken every summer for years—because he wanted to spend time with Benno. And he's offering to pay for your son to go to a fancy private school in Newport. That's amazingly generous."

"He works there; he gets a discount on tuition. And it's not that simple. There's way more to it than that—he's sending me a message. It's his way of saying I'm not taking care of my son properly. Do you want me to peel the shrimp?" I asked, hoping to change the subject.

"Sure." Rhonda handed me a bowl for the shells.

We worked in silence for a few minutes. The kitchen smelled delicious, buttery and savory.

"Benno would be better off in Newport with my parents, wouldn't he? That's what you're trying to tell me," I cried. "Admit it, that's what you think."

"No," said Rhonda carefully. "And it doesn't matter what I or your parents think. What matters is what you think. What do you think, Lux?"

"I don't know. What should I think?"

She smiled gently at me. "You're a great mother no matter what you do for a living or how much money you have in the bank. That's what you should think."

I wanted to hate Ginger Signorelli (he was stealing my best friend away), but damn, I loved him.

He was funny, guileless, and smart. He was the kind of person who made you feel endlessly interesting. The kind of person who nudged other people into the spotlight.

The first thing he said to me was, "Lux Lysander. Tell me everything about you."

By the end of the night, he was family.


Benno walked through the gate, holding tightly to the hand of his escort, the retired stewardess named Jill.

I greedily took in the sight of him in his denim overalls. He needed a haircut. Even though he'd only been gone for two weeks, he looked older. Taller. Or maybe it was just the distracted expression on his face.

"Benno, Benno!" I cried. "Over here!"

Both he and Jill swung their heads in my direction. Jill whispered something to him. Benno saw me and took a step backward, apprehension in his eyes. This was not the reunion I had planned.

I walked toward Benno, calling to him softly like you would to a feral animal. "It's me, sweetheart, it's me."

When I got to within five feet of him, he broke away from Jill and started walking in the other direction.

"Where's he going?" I asked.

"He's confused. Don't take it personally."

She went after him and he let her scoop him up into her arms while I tried not to panic. I'd known it was a mistake to send him to Newport. Had my father brainwashed him against me?

He buried his head in Jill's shoulder, exactly the way he had buried his head in my shoulder two weeks ago while we were driving to the airport. I watched as Jill comforted him, my throat swelling with guilt. After five minutes of Jill reassuring him, he finally took my hand.

We didn't speak on the walk to the car. But once we got on the road and he turned the radio to a song he liked, he relaxed. He leaned his head back against the seat and said, "Hi, Mama," in the softest of voices.

"Hi, sweetheart, hello."

"The car smells different."

"Oh? What does it smell like?"

"Popcorn."

"Really? Well, I'm not sure why. I didn't eat any popcorn in the car while you were gone."

"You didn't?"

"Of course not. I wouldn't have popcorn without you."

I got on the highway and headed into San Francisco.

"So what happened back there, Benno? Why did you run away from me?"

He shrugged. "I didn't understand."

"What didn't you understand?"

"Time got jumbled up." He knelt in his seat to see better out the window.

"It did? How did it get jumbled up?"

"It felt like I saw you yesterday. Like we were at the airport yesterday. But then at Grandma and Grandma's house, I was there for so long. And then I was back in the airport and you were there again and that was a surprise 'cause I didn't know if I'd ever see you again."

"Benno! Of course you were going to see me again. You just went on a vacation."

"The other grandma was there."

"I know, sweetheart."

"You told me he wasn't going to be there."

"I thought he wasn't. I guess he changed his mind. Was that okay? Was he nice to you?"

Benno slumped back down in the seat. "I'm tired, Mama."

"I'm sure you are. Why don't you close your eyes and I'll wake you when we get home."

Benno made a big show of closing his eyes and pretending to

sleep, his little rounded tummy rising and falling, his plump hand on the seat beside me.


Benno made me take him to the Hallmark store the next day to purchase cards to send to the two grandmas.

Snoopy for my mother and Charlie Brown for my father.

"What do you want to write to Grandma?" I asked.

"Dear Grandma," he dictated.

I wrote *Dear Grandma* in big block lettering. "You should be writing this yourself."

"You write better."

"It doesn't matter. It would mean so much more to them if it was in your handwriting."

"Grandma says my handwriting is like chickens scratching."

"Which grandma?" I didn't really have to ask—I knew.

"The other grandma."

"You mean Grandpa. *Pa* is for the man. *Ma* is for the woman."

"No, they're both grandmas," he insisted.

"Fine." In his grandparent hierarchy, grandmas were the one and only, the most important. Grandpa would just have to settle for being "other." I have to admit this made me happy.

"Dear Grandma. I miss you. I love you. Have a great day," he said.

I printed out his message and slid the card over to him. "You sign your name."

He clutched the pen laboriously and bent over the card. *B E N N.*

"You forgot the *O.*"

"I'm not done."

*E T T,* he wrote.

"*Bennett?* Really?"

"That's my name. My *real* name." He glared at me suspiciously, as if I'd withheld this information from him.

"Yes, it is. Do you want me to start to call you that? Do you want to be Bennett now?"

His eyelids fluttered, his bravado rapidly abandoning him. He wasn't ready to give up *Benno*.

"That's okay, you don't have to decide now. Do you want to do the card for the other grandma?"

"Dear Grandma," he said. He put his head down on the table and closed his eyes.

I tousled his hair. "You've got jet lag. It's five here, but eight in Newport. In Newport you'd already be in bed."

"What's eight minus five?" he asked.

"You tell me."

He stuck up eight fingers and I pushed down five of them. "Three, Benno. There's a three-hour time difference."

He looked horrified. "What happened to the hours? Where did they go?"

"They didn't go anywhere, Benno. Newport and San Francisco are in different time zones."

He shook his head. "The hours can't just go."


On Friday two letters arrived, one for Benno and one for me. He tore open his envelope. Two pieces of Juicy Fruit gum slid out and he yelped with excitement. He tried to read the card and frowned. "What kind of chicken scratch is this?"

"Let me see." It was written in my father's cursive, handwriting I hadn't seen in years.

Dear Benno,

I am already thinking ahead to your visit next summer. You will have to arrange with your mother to come in July next year, because on July 4, 1976, it will be the nation's bicentennial, and all the Tall Ships from around the world will be gathering in Newport. Eighteen ships from 14 different countries! Imagine! It will be quite a celebration. You must not miss it.

By the time you get this letter you will be back in school, I imagine. You'll be learning about the planets and the constella-

tions, mammals, farm animals and sea animals. You're a smart
boy. You already know how to count to 100 and you can read.
You will do fine in first grade. Your grandmother sends her love
and so do I. Do keep in touch.

Warmly, Grandpa

*Warmly,* Jesus. Benno unwrapped both pieces of gum and stuffed
them into his mouth. "What's a tall ship?"

"What do you think it is?"

He stuck his lower lip out. "A ship that is tall?"

"Do you want to go back next summer, Benno?"

"I must. The other grandma said so."

"Just because he said so doesn't mean you have to. It's your choice.
Think about it."

"Okay, I thought about it and I think yes."

He was so accommodating and easily swayed—how would he
ever make it in the world? I glanced at my letter. It was from the San
Francisco Public Library.

"Why don't you go down to the Patels'. Anjuli's been dying to see
you."

He raced out of the apartment.

San Francisco Public Library
200 Larkin Street
San Francisco, California 94102

Re: Census records for Martha Bell, Joseph Bell, Fancy Bell,
Lars Magnusson, Elisabetta Sala, Matteo Sala, Bernardo Sala.

August 28, 1975

Dear Ms. Lysander,

We regret to tell you there is no record of the person(s)
named above in the California census records dating from 1850

to 1910. In fact, there is no record of the person(s) named above in any of the U.S. Census records from 1850 to 1910.

If there is anything else we can help you with, please let us know.

Sincerely,

Lavinia D. Pearson
San Francisco Public Library

So there was no record of what had happened to the residents of Greengage—it was like they'd never existed. But they were a reality: people I'd sat beside, eaten with, laughed with, and learned from. They were flesh and blood, as real as Rhonda or me.

I wondered if it wasn't the absence of the fog that kept Brigette from coming back to Greengage—perhaps it was her lack of knowledge that Greengage was even there. Maybe she didn't return because she had no recollection of the place. No recollection of her daughter or mother. They'd been cast not only out of time, but out of memory.

How would I ever tell Joseph?

That night, Rhonda plunged her hands into a sink of hot soapy water and asked, "Did you hear back from the library yet?"

No, Rhonda wasn't psychic, nor had she gone snooping through my room—she was simply relentless. Until I'd given her proof that Greengage really existed, she'd keep at me. I'd have to deliver something, and soon.

"Not yet," I lied. "They said it would take weeks."

Rhonda looked out the window. "The moon's almost full."

"Tomorrow."

"You've been keeping track?"

I had, as a matter of fact. Not consciously. It wasn't like every day I got up and checked a lunar calendar. But I was aware that the moon was waxing. *Waxing*, what a lovely word.

"You seem anxious," said Rhonda.

"I'm not," I snapped.

She raised her eyebrows at me.

"Sorry, I've just got a lot on my mind. All the excitement of Benno coming home."

Joseph's formality. *Goodbye, then.* He thought he'd never see me again. The world had deserted them, but I couldn't. It was one of my own deepest fears. That I would get lost and nobody would come looking for me.

"Rhonda, what are you doing tomorrow night?"

She rinsed a plate under the tap. "Don't know. Ginger and I talked about going out for Chinese. You guys want to come?"

"Maybe you could have takeout. Maybe you could watch Benno."

Rhonda pulled the drain and the water glugged out noisily. "Let me guess. You want to go back to the Valley of the Moon?"

"I'm thinking about it," I admitted.

"What for? The fog won't be there. You said it would take years."

"I know. I just want to go. I don't know why. Just to be there. I'm the only one who knows about them."

"Except me," said Rhonda.

"Right, but you don't believe me."

Rhonda lit up a cigarette and leaned against the sink. She blew three perfect smoke rings. "Okay. Ginger and I will babysit. You'll be back on Sunday, right? In time for dinner? I'll make pork chops."

"Yes, I promise. I swear."

She picked a piece of tobacco off her lip. "All right, then. Say hello to the ghosts for me."

# JOSEPH

❧

*Valley of the Moon*
*1906*

Time is a construct, one we all inherently begin to abide by the moment we are born. Yes, we will live our days hanging from its invisible scaffolding. Morning. Noon. Night. Weeks. Months. Years. Time civilizes us. It brings order to chaos. Without it, there isn't any gravity, and no longer pinned to the world, we float away.

Lux Lysander had catapulted me out of my own time, and so, like a fool, I waited for her to return. I'd been slowly resigning myself to our fate before she'd come, but now that she'd given me a taste of the world that lay beyond the fog, I despaired.

Martha's prescription for my malaise: a change in diet. Fewer baked goods, more vegetables, fruit, and nuts. She took away my nightly glass of wine and replaced it with a tisane so foul tasting I did not dare ask its ingredients.

"Banish what she told you from your mind," she said, staring at me intently, watching me drink every last drop. As if she could hypnotize my restlessness away.

In my day I was considered a futurist. I'd had the foresight and vision to imagine a community where people of all races and classes could live together, not only peaceably but happily. I'd imagined it, planned for it, made it happen. I'd always prided myself on being a man ahead of his time.

But on the other side of that fog, I'd be a relic. From my suspenders to my bowler hat, my once progressive views on women, politics, religion, and civil rights might even be considered antiquated now. I'd be laughed out of the salons, if they even had salons anymore, and judging by what Lux had told me, salons had long gone the way of the horse and carriage. Access to what she knew was the only thing that could save me from intellectual irrelevance.

The next three weeks dragged on interminably. I threw myself into work, joining a different crew every day: fields, building, kitchen, orchard. I was the first to arrive and the last to leave. I was so exhausted I would often skip supper and go directly to bed. Sleep, that prickly bastard, played tricks on me, though: I'd fall asleep instantly and wake an hour later. I spent the early mornings on the porch, smoking the last of my cigarettes, brooding.

Finally the morning of the full moon arrived. It was impossible to believe that 13.8 years would pass in the next twenty-four hours. Approximately 3.5 days a minute. The sheer density of it was mind boggling. I had no choice but to surrender to it.


The morning after the full moon, I was spent, blurry-eyed with fatigue. We'd just finished our breakfast when Nardo yelled, "She's back!"

I watched Lux run across the meadow and my desperation finally gave way to relief. She wore a knapsack that bobbed up and down as she ran. She'd promised to bring me a surprise. I tried to wipe the anticipation from my face as she burst into the dining hall.

"Jesus, you're all here!" she shouted, searching through the crowd. Her eyes landed on me. She should be thirty-nine now, but she still looked young, preternaturally young.

"You're not going to believe it," she cried, easily reading my face. "It's only been three weeks."

"Three weeks?"

"Three weeks," she confirmed. "Well, nearly four, if you count the days I spent here."

The room filled with low but urgent whispers.

"What made you come back last night?" I asked.

"I don't know. I just had a feeling, I guess. Like something was pulling me here."

"So you're telling me we're back on the same time? One day here equals one day out there?" I said.

Had I only imagined the sensation of time speeding up yesterday? Had time begun to reset itself?

"This month, that's what happened," warned Martha. "You don't know what next month's full moon will bring."

"The fog looks different, doesn't it? Less dense," I said.

"No, Joseph," said Martha.

"What if this nightmare is over? What if we can get through?"

"Nightmare?" said Martha. "Greengage is not a nightmare. Our lives are not a nightmare."

"That's not what I meant. I meant being trapped—"

"I know what you meant."

"Then you know I have to try," I said.

"We can't afford to lose another pig," she said.

"We're not going to lose another pig." I ran out of the dining hall and across the meadow.

"Joseph!" shouted Fancy as my intentions became clear. I was going to test the fog myself.

"Stop!" screamed Martha.

"Goddamn it, Joseph!" yelled Magnusson.

The giant Swede was the only one fast enough to catch up with me. He tackled me and pinned me to the ground.

"Get a runt," Magnusson growled to Nardo.

The boy ran to the pigsty and was back in a minute. He handed the piglet to Lux.

"Again?" she said sadly.

"Again," echoed Fancy and Martha.

"How long?" she asked.

"Thirty seconds should do it," said Martha.

"Are you going to behave?" Magnusson asked me, loosening his grip.

I staggered to my feet and slapped the grass off my trousers angrily.

Lux plunged into the fog. It was over in ten seconds. She stepped back into Greengage, distraught, the dead pig in her arms.

I don't know how long I stood there, frozen to the spot. I cursed my foolishness, my embarrassing, ridiculous, and all-too-public display of emotion. The fog was no less dense. We were still trapped.

The bell rang, announcing the beginning of the workday. People drifted off to their crews. Soon Lux and I were standing alone at the edge of the meadow.

"I've caused you all such distress. I shouldn't have come back."

"Yes."

Her eyes grew wide. "Yes, I shouldn't have come back?"

"Yes, this is bloody distressing. I don't understand. It makes no sense."

She nodded. "I couldn't believe it either. When I crawled into my tent last night, the sky was clear. I could see every constellation, from the Big Dipper to Cassiopeia."

"But why were you even there? We thought the fog wouldn't appear on your side for years."

She bit her lip. "I just felt like I should come. I didn't expect to be let in."

"Did you do anything differently?"

"No. It was exactly the same. I woke up freezing and I had to pee. I stepped out of the tent and the campsite was fogged in. I watched for the light. I followed it. When I came through the fog, it was morning and I was back in Greengage."

It wasn't her fault the fog had returned, and it wasn't her fault we now knew less than we had before she first came. We'd have to wait yet another month to discover if this was a new pattern, if she even agreed to continue this little experiment. San Francisco was nearly forty miles away. She had a young son. How long could she keep coming every full moon?

"It was good of you to make the effort to get here," I said. "I'm sorry for my—"

She cut me off. "You must stop apologizing every other minute. It's a very unattractive trait in a man."

I couldn't bring myself to smile. I extended my hand. "Farewell."

She refused to shake it. "I could stay for a few hours."

"Don't you have to get back?"

"Not really. Well, not immediately. My roommate, Rhonda, is taking care of Benno. Surely you can use some help?"

Yes, we could use some help. Even though it was Sunday, ordinarily a day of leisure, most of us were working. It had been a particularly bountiful year for fruit.

"You could help in the apple orchard."

"Oh, apple picking! I'd love to."

She adjusted her knapsack and tucked a stray lock of hair behind her ears. She was dressed more conservatively than last time, in a baggy pair of white pants and a nondescript blue jumper. Her face was bare. She smelled faintly of soap—rose, not Martha's lavender.

"How was your month?" I asked, suddenly aware of our one-sided conversation.

"Not great. Same old same old."

Was she saying this to make me feel better?

"I don't need to talk about it," she said.

No, she wasn't just consoling me—I could see she'd indeed had a difficult month. I felt a strange sort of kinship with her. Both of us suffering on opposite sides of the twentieth century.

"Have you eaten?"

"Not since—"

"Last night. Let me guess. A few spoonfuls of Jif?"

She grinned. "A few shots of CC, for your information. Whiskey. I brought you a bottle. And a case of cigarettes. I thought you might be running low."

A pang of pleasure, not just because she'd replenished my supply of cigarettes but also because she'd noticed how carefully I'd parceled them out.

"The orchard crew is leaving." I could see them piling into the wagon. "If you're serious about working today."

"Of course I am," she said.

# LUX

&

Every fall, when I was a kid, my parents would take me apple picking. We'd leave Newport early on a Saturday morning. My mother
packed a picnic lunch, always the same: bologna sandwiches, short-
bread, a thermos of tea, a thermos of milk. On the drive to New
Hampshire, we'd sing songs from *Sing Along with Mitch:* "Down by
the Old Mill Stream" and "Show Me the Way to Go Home."

I'd never forget the smell of the orchard. It was imprinted on me
like the scent of my mother's Aliage perfume. Overly sweet, musty,
blossomy, leaves-turning, fruit-ripening.

The orchard in Greengage, sixty-nine years and three thousand
miles from New Hampshire, smelled exactly the same.

"Have you picked before?" asked a man, handing me a basket.

"Sure. Lots of times."

"Lower branches." He pointed to a tree. "As far up as you can
reach. Somebody will come along with a ladder and pick the top.
When your basket's full, dump it in one of the barrels. Carefully. Try
not to bruise any of the fruit." He squinted. "I'm Dr. Kilgallon. But
everybody calls me Friar."

He was a small, balding man with a horseshoe of hair. A tonsure—
he looked like a monk; now I understood the nickname. I thought of

introducing myself, but as Ilsa had said, everybody knew who I was. There was no anonymity for me here in Greengage. This was a complete contrast with my life in San Francisco, where I was one in a sea of millions. Over the years, I'd grown to appreciate the positive side of invisibility. It was liberating. I could stumble down the street dressed in pajamas or dressed like Janis Joplin—it mattered to virtually nobody, except Benno. No, the real pressure came from allowing yourself to be known. People having a set of expectations you couldn't live up to.

"You need any help, holler," Friar said. He picked up a basket and wandered off into another row.

It was a large orchard; people were scattered here and there, but it wasn't like the garden, where you worked thigh-to-thigh in the dirt. Self-conscious, I picked quickly. Was I being rude? Should I say hello to the woman at the neighboring tree? I felt like a kid in middle school looking around for a lunch table.

Soon my basket was full. I carried it to the nearest barrel and emptied the apples into it.

"It's not a race," said Friar. He was on his hands and knees, picking fallen apples off the ground. "You worked on the garden crew and in the kitchen last time?"

I nodded.

"Well, here we have an entirely different frame of mind. There's no need to rush. The apples ripen. We pick them. Or collect them, in my case." He tossed an apple into his basket. "We use fallen apples for applesauce. Don't have to worry about any bruises." He sat back on his heels. "You look anxious. Are you feeling anxious?"

"A bit," I admitted.

"Wonderful. I have just the remedy for that."

"I'm not sure I need any medication." What I needed was a shot of tequila. That would calm my nerves.

"Certainly you do. Come with me."

He picked up my empty basket and led me back to the tree.

"Pick," he instructed. "And breathe."

———

An hour later I understood why people didn't talk or hurry on the orchard crew. Picking was a meditative act. You twisted the apple off its stem. It fell into your hand. You placed it in the basket. Repeat. And repeat again. I sank into a peaceful, alert state, focused only on what I was doing.

"I thought you might be hungry," said a man's voice.

Joseph. He held a muffin in one hand, a ladder in another. I hadn't realized how hungry I was until he handed me the muffin. I finished it off in four bites.

"Thank you, I was starving," I said.

He placed the ladder against the tree and quickly climbed up the rungs. "Basket."

I handed him my basket and he balanced it on top of the ladder. He was an apple-picking pro. His hand was a blur darting in and out of the branches, expertly selecting only the ripest of the fruit.

"Fancy is having her dance tonight," he said. "She's spent the past three weeks teaching everybody to do the Scottish reel."

"You too?" I asked.

"I already know how to do the Scottish reel. A tedious dance. Unnecessarily complicated and provincial. Lots of clapping and figure eights," he scoffed.

"I think a dance is a great idea. You all work so hard. You need to have some fun."

After a long pause he said, "Right."

I'd offended him. Why had I said that? I was in no position to instruct him on what he needed.

"Listen," I said. "I wanted to tell you I thought it was brave that you were willing to test out the fog. If I was in your situation, I would have done the same thing."

He frowned at an apple just out of reach. He shook the branch, catching it before it fell to the ground. "But you are not in my situation, are you? You're free to come and go."

"To Greengage. But I'm far from free in my own life. I'm just as stuck in my own way."

I hadn't planned on being so honest; the truth just came barreling out of me. Last time I was here, I'd been so careful with what I'd revealed to him. I'd wanted to keep it simple. I was a widow with a young son and I worked as a waitress. But I hadn't told him how difficult or lonely my life really was. Suddenly, in this moment, I wanted him to know me.

"Joseph!" shouted Friar. "A little help, please!" He and another man were trying to hoist a full barrel of apples into the wagon.

Joseph climbed down off the ladder. He put his hand ever so briefly on my shoulder. Even after he left, I could still feel the heat of his palm. A calming pressure. Rooting me.

I spent the rest of the morning picking and spying on Joseph. He pitched in wherever he was needed. Doing the heavy lifting. Ferrying basket after basket to the wagon. He was clearly a leader, but one of the group as well. Everybody wanted to claim him, everybody wanted to be in his presence. They'd already forgiven him for his momentary lapse of judgment that morning. Perhaps they even liked him more for it, for proving he was as flawed and desperate as all the rest of us.

After lunch I sought out Fancy. I found her at the house, rummaging through drawers, collecting any swath of plaid fabric she could find. A tablecloth. A blanket. A scarf.

"Oh, Lux, it's tragic. I'm afraid we are quite short on kilts, and everybody knows it's not a proper Scottish reel without kilts." She sighed. "We'll have to make do with what we have."

"You're going to make the men wear tablecloths?"

"If only they would. No, these are decorations. A little Highlands flair." She eyed my knapsack. "You don't happen to have any kilts in there, do you?"

I put down my pack. "Feel free to look."

Last night I'd run around my apartment looking for things to bring to Greengage, just in case. I ended up with a time capsule of 1975: a carton of Marlboros, Canadian Club whiskey, a thumb-worn *People* magazine, and a bottle of Gee Your Hair Smells Terrific.

Fancy grabbed *People*, the August 18 edition.

"Who is this little man? And why is he wearing glasses shaped like palm trees? 'His new look: everything's slimmer but his wallet,'" she read. "Was he fat before?"

"His name is Elton John, and yes, I guess he was getting a little chunky."

"What does he do?"

"He's a musician. British, in fact." I sang a few bars of "Rocket Man."

"That is a very odd song."

"Yes, well, he's a millionaire because of it. It's one of Benno's favor-ite songs." In fact, it was the song Benno currently listened to when he wanted to induce the happy-sad feeling.

She slipped a pack of cigarettes into her pocket. Then she opened the bottle of shampoo and sniffed. "Oh my!"

"I know. Every time you move your head, you'll give off that scent."

"And if I were dancing? If I were being spun around?"

"And if you were being spun around, the entire room would smell of you."

"Oh, Lux." She threw her arms around me. "I don't care what my brother thought. I knew you'd come back. I knew you wouldn't desert us."

"He didn't think I'd come back?"

"When he wants something very badly, he won't say a word about it. He never mentioned you the entire three weeks you were gone. That's how I knew. I wanted you to come back, too. I think it's safe to say we all did. You finding us—it's made our situation tolerable. We aren't completely cut off anymore."

I worked to keep a straight face, trying not to reveal my happiness at her disclosure. They all wanted me to return. And I had no inten-tions of being a freeloader. I would pay my own way by being their conduit to the outside world.

"This dance is a very good idea. It's just what's needed. It'll perk everybody up."

Fancy's eyes sparkled. "Precisely! You just can't work, work, work all the time."

"Where's it going to be?"

"In the dining hall. After dinner we'll clear away the benches and chairs and make a proper ballroom."

"I wish I could stay."

"Can you?"

"I don't think so—it's already Sunday afternoon. My friend is watching Benno, my son, and I promised I'd be home tonight. I should be leaving right now in fact."

"But you just said Benno's safe and being looked after. Your friend will understand, and if she's a real friend she'll want you to have a little fun. Stay. Please. I desperately need your help setting things up."

I was torn. If only I could call home and ask Rhonda's permission. Speak to Benno—confirm for myself that he was fine. But of course he was fine. He was with Rhonda and Ginger. They'd have a lovely Sunday dinner, the three of them, and she'd let him watch *The Wonderful World of Disney* before bed.

"I don't know how to do the Scottish reel," I said.

Those were the magic words.

We spent the next hour in the parlor, Fancy giving me private dance lessons. She taught me the Dashing White Sergeant and the Duke of Perth. Joseph was right. There were lots of figure eights and lots of clapping. He was wrong, however, about it being tedious. Fancy and I bowed and swung and dipped around the room, laughing our heads off.

"Golly, Mummy would have loved this," said Fancy to Joseph.

The dining hall had been transformed. All the tables and chairs had been pushed back and stacked in the corners. The room was awash in candlelight. Blankets and tablecloths hung from the rafters in lieu of streamers.

"What is that smell?" asked Joseph. He leaned into Fancy and sniffed her hair. "Good God, it's you!"

"Gee, doesn't my hair smell terrific?" she said.

"It smells nice," said Martha, being diplomatic, but I could tell by the little wrinkle on her nose she thought the scent was cloying as well.

"Did your mother like to dance?" I asked Fancy.

"Oh, yes, she was a constant mover, a whirler, a swirler. Wasn't she, Joseph? She loved parties," said Fancy.

Joseph grunted.

"You think I don't remember her," said Fancy.

"You were four when she died."

Fancy's eyes flashed with anger. "I remember her."

Martha picked up Fancy's hand and squeezed it. "They're about to do the Hamilton House. Aren't you and Magnusson one of the pairs? He's waiting for you."

Magnusson was watching us intently. He'd dressed up for the occasion in a clean white shirt and a pair of pressed trousers. He'd even bathed. His face was shiny, his hair swept back. He looked quite debonair.

Fancy groaned. "Save me, Lux. He's such a bore. You dance with him."

"You didn't teach me the Hamilton House."

"Fine." She flounced off.

The fiddles started up and the center of the room filled with couples. They separated into two lines and faced each other. They advanced, *stamp, stamp, stamp,* and they retreated, *clap, clap, clap.* I watched them longingly, tapping my foot on the floor. Fancy had loaned me a green silk dress and a pair of dancing slippers; I didn't want to spend the entire night on the sidelines.

"Dance with Lux," said Martha to Joseph.

Joseph had his arms crossed in front of his chest. He did not look like he was in a dancing mood.

"That's all right. I don't know how to do this one," I said.

"Joseph does. And he's a very good dancer," said Martha.

"Why don't you dance with him?" I asked.

"Martha doesn't dance," said Joseph.

"Why not?"

A small smile crept over Joseph's face.

"Because I don't know the dance, either," said Martha.

Joseph laughed.

"All right, all right. Because I have two left feet," Martha admitted.

"Because you have no rhythm whatsoever, my dear," said Joseph.

Martha shrugged. "It's true." She gave me a little push. "Get out there. And you"—she shoved Joseph—"get out there with her."

We joined the line and Joseph faced me. I did my best to mimic the moves of everybody around me, but it was a complicated dance.

"Flirt and divert," Joseph said in a soft voice when we bowed toward each other.

"What?"

"You set to the second man in line, then turn to the third man. Then walk down the line back to me."

"I don't get it."

"It's a simple H pattern," he said. "Just keep thinking of an H."

It seemed I had two left feet as well. Joseph continued whispering me instructions until they finally clicked and finally I was part of the magic of the dance. We unfolded and folded as a group.

"I love this! This is so much fun."

He shot me a sobering look but I could tell he was enjoying himself. He was a graceful dancer, his moves practiced.

*Stamp, stamp, stamp. Clap, clap, clap.*

He went up the line without me, and Magnusson took his place. I watched the Swede's eyes continually sweep to Fancy, his original partner, who was now three people over on the other side.

When Joseph came back, I said, "Magnusson likes Fancy."

He looked startled.

"I mean he really likes her. Is attracted to her."

"You are imagining things."

"I don't think so."

"How do you know? What is your proof?"

"Look how stiffly he holds himself when he's in her presence. Look at the way he's avoiding her eye. There's your proof."

"He's avoiding meeting her eye because he doesn't like her."

"No, he's avoiding her because he likes her too much."

# JOSEPH

❦

It was well after midnight when Lux appeared on the porch; I'd begun to think she wasn't coming.

"I've got to go," she said anxiously. "I don't know what I was thinking; I shouldn't have stayed. Rhonda's going to be mad."

"If you knew your friend would be angry, then why did you stay?"

"Because I wanted to. Because I was being selfish," she admitted.

Once again I was startled by her bluntness. Her honesty landed with no warning.

She adjusted the shoulder straps of her knapsack and walked down the stairs. "I'll see you next time."

"Wait. You're leaving now? Right now?"

"I can probably get back to the city before the Monday morning rush hour. Maybe I'll even get there before breakfast."

"It's dark. I'll walk with you."

"I can find my way myself."

"I'm sure you can, but I'd rather know you got there safely."

I led her away from the house and onto the dirt path that wove between the cottages and the dorms.

"How old were you when your mother died?" she asked.

I could barely make her out. "I was nine."

"That's so young. Wow. I'm sorry."

"It was a long time ago."

"Were you close?"

I hesitated just for a moment. "She was my world."

We walked past the barn, which was stacked ceiling high with bales of hay.

"If you don't mind me asking, how did she die?"

"She took her own life."

Lux gasped.

"No. I didn't tell you so you'd feel sorry for me. I had nine years with her; Fancy only had four. If you want to feel sorry for somebody, feel sorry for my sister."

"Oh, Joseph. How terrible for you. For you both."

I could sense her staring at me. Even in the dark, her gaze was penetrating.

"She had such young children. She must have been in such pain to have to go and leave you," she said.

I was amazed to find myself near tears. Normally I was an extremely private man, but I'd never met anybody like Lux. She was open in a way women of my time were not. This morning in the orchard she'd shown me her heart. She'd told me she felt stuck just as I did. And despite that despair, she'd driven back to the Valley of the Moon. A mission of hope and faith, one that would be beyond imagining for most people in similar circumstances.

"What was her name?" she asked.

"Imogene."

"Tell me about her. What did she love? Besides the two of you?"

Nobody had ever asked me that question, not even Martha.

"She loved rhubarb pie. She loved the morning sun. She loved drying the sheets on the clothesline, even in the dead of winter. She loved a good pot of jasmine tea. She loved orange rinds and gossip and peacock feathers. She loved plums."

"Plums. Greengage plums?"

"Yes, greengage plums."

"Ah," Lux sighed as if everything had just become clear.

We'd reached the dining hall. The loaves of bread had been rising all night. In just a few hours the bakers would arrive.

"I have something to tell you," she said. "I went to the library."

I'd sworn her to secrecy; I'd made her promise not to tell anybody about us. Had she betrayed us? Had she betrayed me?

She breathed shallowly. "I got you a book. Poetry. Robert Frost. I think you'll love him, but stupid me, I left it at home. I'll bring it next time. I promise."

A few minutes later I lost her to the fog.

# LUX

❧

San Francisco
1975–76

"You should have called," said Rhonda.
        "How could I have? There are no phones there, I told you. No electricity. No radios. Nothing."

She was mad. The traffic had been terrible—there'd been an accident on 101. Despite my best intentions to make it home for breakfast, I hadn't gotten back to San Francisco until after nine. Rhonda had had to get Benno to school, which had made her late for work. Also, in order to placate him, she'd had to make up some lie about why I hadn't come home. Car trouble, she'd said. She wouldn't lie for me again.

"I'm sorry. I planned on coming home by Sunday night, really I did, but then there was this . . ." I stopped. *Dance?* I couldn't give her such a frivolous excuse.

She held up her hand. "I don't want to hear it. You have a son. You owe it to him to be responsible and come home when you say you're going to come home. He was upset, Lux. Really upset. In a rage. He picked every flower in Rose's planters. Every single one! Look, I'm not saying you don't have a right to get away. You need time off and I'll do my best to help you make that happen. But you can't just take off and not come back when you say you're going to."

———

Over the next few weeks, I tried to make it up to Rhonda. When she came home from work, I had dinner ready. I'd greet her with a can of Tab, or sometimes a glass of wine if it looked like it had been that kind of a day. My life wouldn't work without Rhonda. I couldn't afford to lose her.

I did my best to make it up to Benno, too. On Sundays I began taking him to services at Grace Cathedral, not necessarily for religious reasons, but because I wanted to give him a moral grounding, create rituals for him, things we did together that he could count on. We loved the choir, the incense, the babies crying, the smell of wood, dust, fresh coffee, and aftershave that lingered in the pews. Afterwards we'd go out to breakfast. He'd always order the same thing, corned beef hash with a side of pickles. This was good, I'd think to myself. We were creating memories. This was what real families did.

Benno knelt beside me on the porch, his hands covered in soil. We'd just finished planting geraniums in Rose's planters to replace the marigolds he'd ravaged.

"I love pink," said Benno, eyeing the flowers.

"You are not to pick."

"You told me that already."

"Yes, well, I'm telling you again. Those weren't your flowers. Rose was very upset."

"I was making you a bouquet."

Soon after Benno turned six, he'd started telling me little lies. He was trying to see what I'd let him get away with.

"Damn Henry Hobart!" he cried, clenching his fists.

"Benno!"

"I hate him!" he shouted. "He told the teacher he wouldn't share the clay with me."

I gently pried Benno's hands away from the planter and pulled him into my lap so we were facing each other. "What happened?"

"He didn't want to be my partner. He said my hands were dirty and if I touched the clay I'd make the clay dirty."

I took his dear hands, with their beautiful tea-colored skin, and cradled them in mine. "What? That's ridiculous. Henry Hobart doesn't know what he's talking about. Don't you listen to a word he says."

"He said it in front of the whole class!" he wailed.

That racist, ignorant little bastard. "Oh, Benno, I'm so sorry. That's horrible."

He nodded miserably, and kept on nodding his head like a metronome.

I cupped his ears, halting the movement. "Then what happened?"

"Nothing."

"Well, what did the teacher say?"

"She didn't say anything. Nobody said anything."

He buried his head in my chest, humiliated and heartbroken. This never would have happened in Greengage. Miss Russell, the teacher, was black, and the students were a rainbow of colors and ethnicities: white, black, Chinese, Italian, Swedish, Mexican, and Irish. Joseph had recruited as diverse a group as he could find. Benno would thrive there.

"So who did you end up partnering with?"

"I didn't have to share. I got a piece of clay all for myself."

His chin trembled. He was trying to convince himself and me that the situation had turned out in his favor.

"You're a lucky boy," I said.

We sat on the porch watching people go by. Every once in a while he'd take a huge breath, fighting down a wave of tears. Finally he was calm.

"Mama?"

"Yes, sweetheart?"

"Are you going to send me back to Newport this summer?"

"Summer's a long time away."

"Grandma wants me to come."

"Oh, she does, does she?"

"The other grandma, too."

"Really? Well, we have plenty of time to think about it. But for now let's sit here. It's a beautiful day."

He leaned against me and sighed.

———

On the next full moon, I cashed in my good-behavior chits and left for the Valley of the Moon. I was back in six hours—there had been no fog.

I suppose in the back of my mind I thought *I* might have something to do with the fog returning the previous month, despite the fact we'd theorized it wouldn't return for nearly fourteen years. I'm embarrassed to say I hoped I was the missing link. I was special. I was the reason the fog had returned so soon. But as the fogless months passed, I was forced to give up that theory and come up with a new one: there was no rhyme or reason as to how much time passed in Greengage every full moon.

Meanwhile, the fact that I'd brought up my library visit to Joseph haunted me. I'd come so close to telling him there was no record of them ever having existed, not to mention revealing that I'd broken my promise to keep their existence secret. And why had I done it? It had been a selfish impulse. I had wanted to impress him with the information I had access to, so that he'd consider me indispensable. I loved feeling needed.

To assuage my guilt, I went to the bookstore and found a used copy of Robert Frost's *New Hampshire*. I hadn't even known Frost had written a book called *New Hampshire;* it seemed a sign. I inscribed the book to Joseph. One day I'd give it to him.

Nine months went by. Nine full moons without any fog. Each full moon, I gave Benno a version of the truth—Mama was going to visit some friends up north. As long as I prepared him, he seemed to be okay.

On my tenth trip I tried to convince Rhonda to come with me. I'd arranged for Benno to spend the night at the Patels'. The only way she would believe me was for her to see Greengage for herself.

"I am not a camping sort of person," she said.

"I understand. We don't even have to spend the night. If the fog isn't there, we'll just come home."

She sighed and shook her head. "Lux, don't you get it? I don't care. I don't want to come. Look, I'm happy you found someplace that's a haven. If you like living like a colonist, that's great for you."

"It's not colonial times there, it's the turn of the century."

"Whatever."

Rhonda thought I was crazy. "Just indulge me. I have a feeling the fog will be there this time."

"Why is it so important that I believe you?"

"Because I can't stand that you think I'm lying."

"I don't think you're lying. I think you go somewhere."

Just not back to 1906.

She didn't come, and it was a good thing. No fog once again. She would have been furious with me for wasting her time.


Benno hadn't stopped talking about the tall ships since school had let out. Eighteen ships from fourteen different countries! England, Argentina. Alaska! No. Alaska wasn't a country, was it? Hundreds—no, thousands—no, millions—of people would be there. Grandma was making stuffies (baked stuffed clams). There was no better place to be than in Newport to celebrate the nation's bicentennial (my father had clearly put this into his head); San Francisco just didn't compare. Really, would they even celebrate it here? Would there even be any fireworks? What was I gonna do? Just sit around and watch *All in the Family*?

Putting him on the plane would be easier this time. I would miss him terribly, but he was looking forward to his Newport adventure with the two grandmas.

"Benno, do you want me to come with your mother to the airport to drop you off?" asked Rhonda.

Benno raced around the apartment, throwing things into his suitcase.

"I don't think you'll need a *TV Guide*, sweetheart," I said.

"How will I know what shows are on?"

"You can look at Grandma's *TV Guide*."

In went his bag of jacks. His pick-up sticks. His Go Fish deck. He climbed up on the kitchen counter, stood, and rummaged through the cabinet over the fridge. This was my private shelf. A pack of cigarettes. Three cans of Pringles, a bag of Oreos, and a jumbo pack of red licorice.

"Benno, you little monkey. That stuff is not for you."

Benno threw the bag of licorice onto the table defiantly.

"What's the big deal?" he asked, batting his eyelashes. He knew I melted when he gave me that wide-eyed look. He was such a flirt.

"Oh, okay, big boy. I'll tell you the big deal. Some things are private. That's a private cupboard, just for grown-ups. For Rhonda and me."

"I hate Fig Newtons. Why can't I have Oreos?"

Because Fig Newtons were the cookie my mother gave me. It was the only cookie I let him eat. I sighed and handed him the package.

"Benno, will you miss me?"

"No."

"What? I'll miss you. Why won't you miss me?"

"'Cause you made your choice." He held out his arms and Rhonda scooped him off the counter and deposited him on the floor.

"What do you mean I made my choice?"

This was something I said to him all the time. *You made your choice, Benno. I told you if you didn't brush your teeth you'd get a cavity. You made your choice, Benno. You chose to dawdle around this morning and now we're going to be late for school.*

"You could come. But you don't want to come 'cause you don't like Grandma. The other grandma."

In my experience six was not only the age of lying, but of brutal truth-telling. I'd spent the year being both amazed at and humiliated by the things that Benno said.

"Jesus," I muttered.

Rhonda laughed. "Ginger can come to the airport with us, too, Benno, if you want."

Ginger had really made an effort to be friends with Benno. He'd seduced him by performing little feats of magic—pulled coins from behind Benno's ear, made his thumb disappear, an ace of diamonds float. Benno adored him.

In the end we all went to the airport to see Benno off. On the way home, I shoved the eight-track of the Beatles' greatest hits into the player and cried my eyes out. Poor Eleanor Rigby. Nobody came to her funeral. And poor Father McKenzie. Darning his socks all alone in his empty, empty house. I had such a deep longing for Newport and such an ambivalence for it as well. Late June. The hydrangea would be in bloom. Those heavy purple and pink heads, drooping from the bushes in front of our house.

"Hey, at least she held it together until we got to the car," said Rhonda. "Last time she bawled at the gate."

The two of them were sitting in the backseat. I felt like a chauffeur.

"Lux, maybe you should let me drive," said Ginger.

I glanced into the rearview mirror. "You need a haircut." He had a miniature Rhonda 'fro, only his was the color of a pumpkin.

"I like it long," said Rhonda, running her hands through his hair. He leaned his head on her shoulder.

"You need to gain some weight," he said to Rhonda. "You're too skinny, babe."

"And that is exactly why I am marrying you. Because you say things like that," she said.

I gasped and Rhonda held her hand up. The diamond engagement ring glinted in the twilight. "You didn't even notice, Lux."

I started crying again. My heart was full and my heart was breaking. I'd said goodbye to Benno for two weeks, knowing he'd have a great time and knowing I'd be lost without his stabilizing presence. And now these two most unlikely of people had found each other and fallen in love. They would have gorgeous peanut-butter-colored babies with strawberry-blond hair, babies I would godmother, teach to use a spoon, and take kite-flying at the beach.

"We should have waited to tell her," whispered Ginger.

Oh, right. This meant Rhonda would be moving out of our apartment.

"No," said Rhonda. "She's good. You're good, aren't you, Lux?"

My eyes were so full of tears I could barely see. I pulled over to the side of the road. Rhonda put her hand on my shoulder.

"She gets this way sometimes," she said to Ginger. "Happy-sad. Just like Benno."

I nodded. She was right. I felt like Benno. I could feel him right behind my eyes.

# LUX

⚜

## Valley of the Moon
### 1906

I thought about Lucy Pevensie and the first time she went through the wardrobe. Rubbing her cheek against the silk of the fur coats. The musty, mothball, old wood scent. And then suddenly, a blast of crisp, cold air. Snow. She'd slipped through a crack in our world right into another, just like I was about to do.

I forced myself to walk through the fog slowly. It was difficult to do so. Once the light appeared (now I knew it wasn't a light—it was the morning sun flashing on the tin lantern that hung outside the dining hall door), everything inside of me screamed *Run, run! Don't think, don't feel, just get there!* But I wanted to gather clues. I was walking back in time. It was my duty to pay attention.

So what did my version of the wardrobe feel like? It felt like pressure. A million hands touching me at once. I pushed through time; time pushed through me.

My father and I lived in a fog like this. A deadly quiet, in-between place in which we were still stuck. I remembered a long-ago summer day he and I summited Mount Fort, the winds whipping around us at thirty miles an hour. To move forward required equal parts resistance and yielding. That's what he taught me.

Being in the fog was disorienting. I walked for hours. I walked for minutes. I counted my steps. There were thousands of them. No, only a few dozen. And then I stepped into the meadow, knowing no more about the fog than I did before, but flooded with well-being at the sight of everybody sitting at the long tables eating breakfast. The air smelling of pine resin. The grass still damp with dew.

# JOSEPH

❧

None of us acted surprised when Lux walked into the dining hall, but we were pleased. It was her third visit and we dared to hope this would be a regular occurrence. The morning after each full moon, she'd arrive. She'd be delivered to us like the newspaper, bringing news of the world, smelling of fresh ink and the outdoors.

"How long has it been?" she asked.

"It's been a month," I said.

"A month?" She looked confused.

"It's always only a month for us, remember?"

"Oh, right. God. Sorry. It's just . . ." She sighed. "It's been eleven months for me."

"Eleven months?" I asked. "Why did it take you so long to come back? Did something happen?"

She'd lost some weight. Her face was more angular; she had dark circles under her eyes. Had she been ill?

"No, no. Everything's fine. I came every full moon, but the fog didn't reappear for eleven months."

"So—every full moon we have no way of knowing how much time will pass?" Martha said slowly. She glanced at me, trying to gauge my reaction.

"Yes, I'm afraid so," said Lux.

The news was worse than before. I had begun to hope that every full moon the fog would reappear on Lux's side, which meant to me our circumstances were changing; time *was* aligning inside and outside of the fog and soon we'd be set free. Now that I knew there was no way to predict how much time would go by every full moon, I'd have to let go of that fantasy.

"I'm sorry," said Lux. "I know that's not what you wanted to hear."

The kitchen staff began talking in loud whispers.

I stood and addressed the room. "There is no need to panic. We have to be patient and collect more information. A pattern will eventually make itself clear."

I didn't dare look at Lux; she knew I was lying. I no more believed a pattern would emerge than I believed in trepanation as a cure for migraines.

"I know it's difficult not to be distracted, given Lux's arrival and this news, but we have a full day's work ahead of us. Finish your breakfast and let's gather our crews together," I said.

"Will you be staying today?" I asked Lux.

"Yes, if it's all right. It's summer back home. July. I have some time off."

July. It was October here.

"Where would you like to work?"

"Where am I needed?"

"Tubers," shouted Eleanor. She didn't like Lux, so I suspected she wanted Lux on her crew to have a little fun at her expense.

"Sweet potatoes," I clarified. "That's where I'll be working today as well."

We walked behind the wagon that ferried the crew to the fields. I felt protective: I didn't want people bombarding Lux with questions, or worse, holding her responsible for our circumstances. Eleanor watched us with a scowl, biting down hard on her pipe.

"I brought her some tobacco," said Lux. "I thought that might soften her up a bit."

"She's afraid you're going to come between her and Fancy."

"Me? What about Magnusson?"

"What about Magnusson?"

"They're a couple."

"They're a couple?"

"Why do you keep repeating everything I say? This can't be a surprise to you. I told you at the dance he liked her."

I hadn't seen them together once in the three weeks Lux had been gone.

"I knew it as soon as I saw them in the dining hall," she said.

"They were sitting on opposite sides of the room."

"Exactly. The current between them was electric. Impossible to miss." She inhaled deeply. "God, the smell of this place. There's nothing like it."

I was immune to the smell of Greengage; I'd been here too long.

"Rich, wet soil. Compost. Dead leaves. Dried hay. Indian corn. Sweet and sad," she said.

"Autumn."

"Yes—autumn."

"It rained yesterday."

"Did it?"

We'd devolved into small talk. We seemed to have only two depths of conversation. Surface, or the unlit depths of the bottom.

"So it's 1976."

"Yep," she said cautiously.

"You can tell me what's happened."

"It doesn't make you feel like you're missing out?"

I shook my head.

"Okay. Let me think. Um. Björn Borg just won Wimbledon."

"Wimbledon? The Wimbledon Championships in London?"

"I don't know, it's somewhere in England. Grass courts."

Yes, London. I'd actually attended the Wimbledon finals in 1881. It had been the beginning of William Renshaw's reign. He'd won six years in a row.

"You're smiling. That makes you happy?"

It did please me, that something remained of my old life. "The Wimbledon Championships have been going on since the nineteenth century."

"See?" she said. "Some things are exactly the same."

*Some* things. She went on to tell me that a company called Apple had manufactured the first personal computer, a two-dollar bill had been issued, and the United States had just celebrated their bicentennial on the Fourth of July—two hundred years of independence.

"Benno was in Newport for the celebration. All the tall ships came in. He was so excited to go."

"He's still there?"

"For another ten days."

"You didn't want to accompany him?"

"No," she said. "It's really more of a kid's thing." I could tell by her flushed cheeks she wasn't telling me everything. Perhaps she hadn't been invited.

"Besides, it's a good thing I didn't go—I'd have missed the fog. Who knows how long it will be before it comes back again?"

I did not want to dive down to the bottom again, where we talked plainly about unspeakable things.

"Do you have any experience picking sweet potatoes?" I asked.


I showed her how to find the crown of the vine and then, with a digging fork, carefully loosen the soil around the plant.

"Now get your fingers in there and pull," I said. "Firmly but gently."

She tugged with a soft grunt and unearthed a sweet potato. Her eyes were the exact blue-green color of the Pacific Ocean. It occurred to me I'd never see the ocean again.

She rubbed dirt off the sweet potato. "Do you wash them after you pick them?"

"They have to cure first. We'll take them to the barn this afternoon and lay them out on tarps."

She moved on to the next plant.

"Hold on. You're not done with this one. Each vine yields five or six tubers."

She thrust her fingers into the soil gleefully. "It's like searching for buried treasure."

Lux had such a captivating, childlike sense of wonder. A capacious imagination. When I was with her, everything felt a little sharper, a little brighter. She cajoled me into a better mood. No, *cajoled* was too understated a word. She whirled me into a positive emotional state—I seemed to have no choice in the matter. I was not a religious man: although I'd been raised in the Anglican Church, I didn't believe in God or angels or fate. But something about Lux being in Greengage felt divinely mandated.

"Have you given any more thought to me bringing somebody else back?" she asked, a while later. "Somebody who might be able to—figure this out?"

I'd just begun to trust her. The idea of adding another stranger into the mix was overwhelming. Never mind the risk to her safety. She seemed to barely be making it. What if she told the wrong sort of person and they reported her to the authorities or worse?

"Do you really think there's somebody out there who will be able to explain what's happened to us? Who'd be able to fix this? Alter our situation?" I asked.

She rubbed her dusty palms on her skirt and shook her head slowly. "No. No, I guess I don't."

"It's too risky for you—and for us."

As much as I sincerely doubted any scientist or other expert could help us, there was more to it than that. It was 1976 out there. If we ever found a way through the fog, how in God's name would we make our way in such a new world? And would we even want to? Perhaps we were better off staying right here.

Just before lunch she groaned with happiness. "It's just so satisfying to see the baskets filling. Abundance. There's nothing in my life like that. I feel like I'm constantly racing to catch up, and the weird thing is I have no idea what I'm racing toward. I'm beginning to doubt there's a finish line."

Eleanor approached. She'd been waiting for her opportunity. I hadn't given her one: I'd stayed by Lux's side all morning.

"Here comes Eleanor," I warned Lux.

Eleanor was a big woman, nearly six feet tall. She wore her hair in a long braid; her face was hidden under the brim of her leather hat. She strode down the rows like a cowboy, dirt spitting up from her heels.

"Break time already?" she said, her hands on her hips.

"We've been working since seven, Dear One. It's nearly noon now. Yes, I would say it's break time."

My addressing her as Dear One in public was a call to arms—only Fancy was allowed to use that nickname. I braced myself for the return of fire.

"I have something for you," said Lux.

"What could you possibly have for me?" said Eleanor.

Lux opened her pack and pulled out a pouch of tobacco. "Captain Black," she said. "Cherry."

Eleanor pulled a face but I could see how startled she was at Lux's offering. I'd known her since she was born. Beneath her brittle exterior she was desperate for connection.

"Isn't that kind of Lux?" I said. "To think of you."

Eleanor opened the package and sniffed. "It smells like a lollipop," she scoffed, but slid the tobacco grudgingly into her pocket.

"There are other flavors. If you don't like it, let me know and next time I'll bring you something else," said Lux.

I winced at her eagerness: Eleanor would devour her if she wasn't careful.

"So," said Eleanor. "Tell me, Lux, are you the kind of person who believes the future moves toward them? Or are you the kind of person who believes they move toward the future?"

Lux's brow furrowed—she had no idea how to answer that question. Eleanor sneered and turned her attention to me.

"Our Joseph was in the latter camp. He believed he was in charge. He thought he was the current; now, thanks to you, he's realized he's just a twig in the stream of time. It must come as a tremendous shock. Poor Joseph."

For once I was speechless.

"Jesus, there's no need to be so mean," said Lux. "I know your circumstances are incredibly hard. But why attack Joseph? We're all in this together."

She had a smudge of dirt on her cheek that I longed to wipe away: it undermined her authority. She was standing up for me. A useless exercise (I knew Eleanor would never back down) but endearing all the same.

"You're mistaken. We are not all in this together. You are not in this with us," spat Eleanor.

I often forgot that both Eleanor and Fancy hadn't been permanent residents of Greengage; they'd had the bad luck to be visiting when we'd been trapped by the fog. How this fact must haunt them both.

Even though I could see words of protest forming on Lux's lips, she held them back.

"I'm sorry," said Lux.

Eleanor gave her a look of disgust and stalked off.

A week after my mother died, Eleanor (who'd been Fancy's closest companion, who'd been raised as if she were one of us) was moved out of my sister's bedroom and into the maids' quarters. It took Fancy the better part of the month to stop crying herself to sleep. It took Eleanor the better part of the month to stop calling my sister Fancy and refer to her as Miss instead. They'd been making their way back to each other ever since.

"Eleanor's lonely," I said.

"That's no excuse," said Lux. "We're all lonely."

She fell to her knees and tugged on a vine.

# LUX

❦

That night, around 11:00 P.M., I went downstairs in search of Joseph. I wanted to be back in bed by midnight so I'd be in good shape for the morning. He was on the porch as usual. Perched on the railing.

"Do you want to talk about how long it took me to get back?" I asked.

He swiveled around to face me, ignoring my question. "What have you got there?"

I handed him the Robert Frost book. "The book I told you about. Poetry. I think you'll like it."

"*New Hampshire.* Your New Hampshire?"

"No, it's not my New Hampshire—it's Frost's. The title is just a coincidence. There's some good stuff in there."

"When do you have to return it to the library?"

He forgot nothing.

"I don't. It was an old copy, they were giving it away. It's yours to keep."

I was glad it was dark. He couldn't see my guilty face.

"I have a confession to make," I said. "I didn't tell you the truth about something."

"Oh?" he said carefully.

"I'm not a widow."

He didn't respond and for a split second I regretted my decision to tell him about Nelson. He was from a different era, and even though he was progressive, hearing I'd had a child out of wedlock would likely be shocking for him. It might well change his opinion of me, but I had to tell him the truth. I wanted this man to know the real me, not a prettified me.

"Benno's father was in the army. He died in the war. I didn't lie about that. It's just that I'm not technically a widow, because, well, because we weren't married. I found out I was pregnant after he shipped out. His name was Nelson King. I liked him. A lot. Maybe I would have grown to love him. Maybe we would have gotten married if he hadn't been killed. I lied to you because I was ashamed. Being an unwed, single mother in my time still carries a stigma. You'd think it would be different, but it's not."

He studied me silently.

"Say something," I pleaded, feeling utterly vulnerable.

His face was unreadable. "This widow story. Do you tell this to other people?"

"Sometimes," I said.

"And they feel sorry for you."

"I guess."

"And you like that?"

"I don't like it, but it's better than the alternative."

"Your parents? Do they know the truth?"

"Of course they do."

"How do they feel about it?"

"My mother is fine. She was fine right from the beginning."

"And your father?"

"He barely acknowledged Benno's existence," I admitted.

"But he's come around now?"

"Sort of. But it's too late, the damage is done. I don't trust him."

"Yet you sent Benno off to Newport again."

"He wanted to go," I snapped.

"But you didn't want him to go."

"I wanted him not to want to go."

"But he did."

I gave an exasperated sigh. "I'm going to bed."

"You're angry with me."

"No. Yes. Damn it, I never should have told you."

"You think I'm judging you."

"Aren't you?"

Joseph slid down off the rail. "I am in no position to judge, Lux," he said quietly.

October in Greengage. The nights were cold and the days were warm, the fields high with corn. The tomato vines had withered away, but the valley floor was a sea of fall greens: turnips, mustard, and something called bok choy. Behind the barn were acres of garlic, winter squash, and pumpkins.

I'd planned on this being a quick visit. Even though Benno was in Newport, I still felt a need to keep the home fires burning. My priority was him and our life in San Francisco. But he wasn't in San Francisco. And it was so busy in Greengage. There was no end to the work, and people were grateful to have another set of willing hands—so I stayed. Each day I joined a different crew. I wanted a chance to try everything out. How else would I know what I loved? What work I was truly meant to do. Back in San Francisco, I'd never have that luxury. Benno had Newport. Rhonda had Ginger. I had Greengage.

Everything was blissful, except for Joseph. After our conversation the first night, it seemed he was avoiding me. He was polite, but careful not to catch my eye. Every time I saw him, I was swamped with shame, transported right out of Greengage and into Safeway, my stomach a pit of anxiety, waiting for the cashier to tell me what I owed, knowing I did not have enough money in my wallet to pay the bill.

What would I put back? What could we do without?

That was the soundtrack of my life back home.

It turned out that I was right; Magnusson was courting Fancy.

"I told Dear One, but I'm afraid to tell Joseph," said Fancy.

Outside, it was drizzling. We were in the barn, braiding garlic. The pungent odor mingled with the candy smell of our lunch, sweet potatoes baking in the ashpan of the woodstove.

Fancy squirmed on a bale of hay. "Next time I'm bringing a chair."

She was dressed as usual in inappropriate work clothes. She wore a yellow silk dress and Joseph's old boots.

"Joseph already knows about you two," I said. "I told him."

"You told him? What did he say?" When Fancy got nervous, her eyelashes fluttered up and down like tiny fans.

"He didn't believe me."

"Of course he didn't." She smiled. "I'm very good with secrets."

"I don't know why it has to be a secret. I'd think people would be happy."

"You do?"

"Sure. The two of you make sense."

"Really? But we're so different."

"Well, you're not an obvious match, which makes a good match in my book."

"I suppose you're right. Yes, the difference is precisely what makes it so exciting." She squeezed the stem just above the garlic bulb, softening it so it would be more pliable. "So I have a question."

My garlic braid looked terrible. Lopsided and loose.

"Snipped or unsnipped?" asked Fancy. "I myself prefer snipped. It makes for a neat package, and oh, that lovely little mushroom cap. But I suppose there's nothing wrong with a cock in its natural state as God intended, either."

I hooted with laughter.

"Are you scandalized that I've had sexual relations before marriage?" asked Fancy.

"Of course not."

Her face fell. "Oh. Does everybody do that now? Is that the fashion?"

"Not everybody," I said. "But lots of young people experiment."

"How many men have you been with?" she asked.

"How many men have you been with?" I shot right back.

"Two," she said. "You?"

I didn't want to tell any more lies here in Greengage; either they'd accept me or they wouldn't. "Ten. No, eleven."

She smiled broadly. "One short of a dozen. Well, good for you, Luxie!"

I was stunned. I'd expected a reaction like Joseph's when I'd told him about Nelson, quietly judgmental. I did not anticipate outright enthusiasm.

Fancy leaned her head on my shoulder. "You are my role model."

"I'm nobody's role model," I said, my cheeks hot. *Role model?* Those were two words I never thought I'd hear spoken about me, especially in the context of how many sexual partners I'd had. Fancy was far more accepting than people in the supposedly open society of the 1970s were.

"Well, you're not Dear One's role model," Fancy said.

"That's obvious. Hand me that bulb."

Fancy plunked a head of garlic into my lap and I clumsily wove it into my braid.

"It's just that she's in such a sour mood all the time these days," said Fancy. "I much prefer being with you."

I sighed, feeling empathy for Dear One. "It can't be easy for her. You being with Magnusson."

Fancy huffed. "She's my best friend. She should be happy for me."

"She should be, but I'm sure it's tough feeling she's been replaced. The same thing's just happened with my roommate. She's in love." I made a face. "With a man named Ginger."

"Ginger!"

"I know, what kind of a grown man is named Ginger?"

"Ridiculous," she snorted on my behalf.

"Right, but here's the thing. He's not ridiculous. He's lovely. And he adores her. And I'm really happy for her, I am, but I also kind of hate him for taking her away from me." I laid the garlic braid on my lap. "I imagine that's a little bit of how Dear One is feeling. And there's me. I'm taking you away from her, too. It's a double whammy."

Fancy's eyes grew wide. "How can I have been so self-absorbed? I've been a terrible friend," she moaned. "Poor, poor Dear One. She's my first true love. My dearest."

"I know. Go find her," I said. "I'll finish your braid."

"I have no idea where she is."

"You know perfectly well where she is—in the sweet potato fields." Fancy grimaced.

"Yes, you'll get dirty and wet, and yes, it will be worth it. You'll make her day. Go."

Fancy handed me her braid. It was perfect, a work of art. "Don't try and pass that off as your own," she said, smiling.


After lunch Martha pulled me aside. "I need your help in the herb garden."

Nobody ever dared to ask if they could join her. Martha always worked alone.

"Are you serious?"

"Don't make me regret asking," she said.

She gave me a quick tour of the garden, pointing at plants and reciting names—bear grass, blue flax, brass buttons, cat's ear, skullcap, periwinkle, vetch, pennyroyal—then she set me to work weeding.

"You're not staying?" I asked as she walked off toward the garden gate.

"You're crushing my foxglove," she said.

She picked up a wooden carryall full of tools, tucked a spade under her arm, and walked to the middle of the lawn, where for the next hour she did nothing but stare at the grass. At least to me it looked like she was doing nothing, but clearly that wasn't the case, because suddenly she sank to her knees with a trowel and began to dig.

"Do you need any help?" I called out, curious.

She waved her hand at me, not even bothering to look up.

At first I felt insulted that she was ignoring me, but after a while I grew to appreciate the silence. With my hands in the dirt, the sun beating down on my shoulders, a now-familiar expansiveness bloomed inside of me. An internal settling. An openness through which the world poured in. I used to get that feeling at Lapis Lake. If there were a drug that made you feel this way, I'd have become an addict.

"It's called a Horologium Florae," Martha explained later that afternoon. She'd dug a large circle in the grass. The circle was sectioned off into twelve wedges.

"A flower clock. It was first hypothesized by a Swedish botanist in the 1700s. You plant a dozen flowers, each of them programmed to open and close at a specific hour. At the one o'clock section you plant a flower whose blooms open at one. At the two o'clock section you plant a flower whose blooms open at two. The blooms tell you what time it is. Like a sundial, only with flowers. Of course, I'll have to wait until summer to plant, but I wanted to mark out the space before the first frost."

She pointed at each section in turn: "Goatsbeard there, then morning glory, then hawkweed, then purple poppy mallow. Then, I'm sorry to say, I'll have to use lettuce—there's nothing else that will bloom at that hour. On to swamp rose mallow and marsh sowthistle. Then fameflower and hawkbit. I'm still working out the rest."

I was surprised to hear her talking this way. Martha wasn't the kind of gardener who forced things. She kept her herb garden neatly weeded, but she encouraged the mingling of species. She abhorred fussy plants and hothouses.

"It will really work? Each flower will open and shut precisely on the hour?"

"Yes."

"But isn't that sort of unnatural? Especially given—your situation?"

Time had turned its back on them. For better or worse, they'd been liberated of the need for clocks and watches.

"There's nothing unnatural about it!" she cried.

I'd never heard Martha raise her voice before.

"I'm sorry. I didn't mean—"

Martha took a deep breath and sighed. "No, *I'm* sorry. There's no reason for me to be shouting at you."

"It's all right."

"No, it's not. You've done nothing but try and be helpful. I just find this whole endeavor—well, quite unnerving, if I'm honest about it."

"Then don't do it," I said.

Martha tossed back her head in surprise. "When I first met you, you seemed easily categorized, Lux. Like one of my herbs. 'Nettles: a remedy for night sweats, fatigue, and releasing excess mucus.' I like things to be defined. It calms me, brings order to my life. So on your first visit, I thought, 'Lux Lysander: flighty, scared, we'll never see her again.' On your second visit, I thought, 'Sweet, a bit of a dreamer.' And now, on your third visit, it's clear I have to recalibrate once again."

She nodded briskly. "Intuitive, honest, clear-thinking, and loyal."

I looked at her openmouthed, letting the praise sink in. Each adjective was like a little firework burst, spreading its fingers of heat over the surface of my skin.

"I'm not done," she said. "Compassionate, resourceful, intelligent."

My eyes welled up.

"Worthy," she finished.

I swallowed the lump in my throat. "I thought I'd lost those parts of me."

"Nothing is ever lost," said Martha. "Only forgotten. All that's needed is one person who remembers, one person who realizes it is still there."

The door to a long-abandoned room inside me that I hadn't even known existed until this minute began to open. Sweet, fresh air poured in.

Martha knelt. "I have to make this damn flower clock. I don't know why, but I do. Will you help? Will you bring me plants?"

"I'll help however I can," I said.

# JOSEPH

✥

Late that afternoon, just before supper, I caught up with Lux. She'd barely spoken to me the entire week. I felt terrible. My response—or lack of response—to her confession was appalling. I hadn't been put off by her admission that she'd lied about being married. I was taken aback that she felt she had to tell people she was a widow in order to be accepted. And worse, that she was willing to accept the crumbs of people's pity because she felt that was the best she could get. Then there was her father, barely acknowledging her son's existence, which reminded me of my own father. It was hard to accept that the change I wanted to see in the world hadn't come even decades after my time. People still judged each other, and by all the wrong standards at that. It had put me in a pensive mood for days.

"How was your afternoon with Martha?" I asked Lux.

She sat at the kitchen table with a cup of tea. "I'm leaving tomorrow morning."

"Oh, so soon?" *Say something, you damn fool. Apologize.*

"I'll be back next month. Providing I'm welcome." She arched her left eyebrow at me.

"You're very welcome. In fact, I'd be upset if you didn't come." I joined her at the table. I swept crumbs into a little pile. "Devastated, actually."

She made a skeptical face. "Devastated?"

"Yes," I said forcefully. "I'm sorry."

She drummed her fingers on the table. "For what?"

"For being an ass."

She quickly looked to the side, trying to mask her reaction, but I could see my contrition pleased her.

"I wish things were different. I wish you lived in a world where you didn't have to tell people you were a widow."

"Yeah, so do I, but I don't."

"Well, then fuck them," I said.

Her lips slowly peeled back in a delighted smile. "My God. Look at you. Cursing like a commoner."

The kitchen was a different place with her in it. You could tell she didn't quite belong here. She pulled the light toward her.

It was my turn to confess, to reveal something to her. I wanted to even up things between us. To keep us on equal footing.

"Greengage used to be bigger," I said. "Back in 1900 there were nearly four hundred of us. We've lost more than one hundred residents in the past six years."

She brought the mug up to her lips and took a careful sip. "Why did they go?"

"Lots of reasons. Family. Money. They were bored. They wanted something different."

I looked out the window. From where I was sitting, I could see the dome of Martha's straw hat bobbing as she made her rounds in the garden.

"The day of the earthquake, it was glorious out. Temperate, sunny. That afternoon we were going to have a goodbye party for yet another family who was leaving. I was upset, but doing my best to hide it. Greengage was so perfect. I thought to myself, Who could possibly want to leave this paradise?"

She nodded. She'd asked herself the same question, too.

"'Her early leaf's a flower; but only so an hour,'" I recited.

"You read the book?" she said, looking pleased.

"From cover to cover."

"It's good, isn't it? 'Nothing Gold Can Stay.' My favorite."

It wasn't my favorite, but it was the poem that spoke to me most.

"I think I must have known that our hour was nearly up. We'd been operating for seventeen years. We'd had a good run, but I knew our numbers would continue to dwindle. People would drift away."

"Oh, Joseph. Your dream—"

"I'm not disclosing this so you'll pity me."

"I know. That's not what—"

"I have to tell you something."

"All right," she said.

I inhaled, suddenly realizing that I'd been holding my breath. "I wished, just for a moment, for time to freeze. For it to stop."

Her brow creased. "No, Joseph. You can't think that this is your fault. Everybody wants time to stop at some point in their life. Everybody."

"Yes, well, now I've been given what I wished for. We won't lose any more people, because they have no choice. They have to stay."

She didn't say anything. She took the truth of my statement in, and for that I was grateful.

# LUX

❧

*San Francisco*
*1978–79*

"Please take me to see *The Deer Hunter*," begged Benno.

Benno was obsessed with anything that had to do with war. He was eight years old now, and if he wasn't playing with his G.I. Joe, he was reading encyclopedia entries on General MacArthur. He knew everything there was to know about trench and chemical warfare. He'd read Anne Frank's diary three times. But what he was most desperate to talk about was the Vietnam War, which wasn't a popular topic. Whenever Benno and I saw vets out on the street, many in wheelchairs or on crutches, he would walk right up to them and say, "My daddy was a soldier like you. He was killed in action."

Almost all of them teared up and hugged him, and I knew exactly what Benno was thinking. *He could have been my father.* Although I did not like the idea of him going around embracing strangers, I let him. It provided him with a kind of comfort no book or movie could.

I'd seen *Deer Hunter* last week. There was no way I was going to let Benno watch Christopher Walken play Russian roulette.

"It's too adult for you," I said.

After Benno had been born, I'd hired a service to help me track down Nelson King's family. I'd had no idea where he'd grown up or if his parents were dead or alive, if he had siblings or if he was an only child. I knew what seemed like important information at the time. His favorite band was Jefferson Airplane. He loved pizza with black olives and onions. He was a rabid Doonesbury fan.

The service had found Nelson's only surviving relative, his mother, in Wisconsin. I'd written to Anna King and enclosed a photo of Benno. I also sent her copies of the letters Nelson had written to me as proof; I wasn't sure she'd believe me. There was something sort of classless about breaking the news to a stranger who'd lost her son that I'd not only had sex with him, but had a baby by him as well. A baby he'd never lived long enough to know about.

Two weeks after I'd sent the letter, it came back to me. On the envelope, scribbled in pencil, were the words *Return to Sender, Addressee Unknown*. Anna King had steamed open the letter, read it, then taped it back shut again. Whatever I'd written, whatever decisions I'd made, whatever I and her son had shared, she'd decided she wanted nothing to do with it. With us.

"I have an idea. Let's do something special tonight," I said to Benno.

"Like what?"

"Let's make lasagna. Real, authentic lasagna. We'll go to North Beach to buy the ricotta."

"Can I have Coke?"

Coke was only for special occasions in our house.

"Okay."

"Dr Pepper, too?"

I laughed. "Don't push your luck, kiddo."

I loved North Beach on a Saturday; it had a festive, celebratory air. After shopping we walked to City Lights bookstore. It was packed; a local poet was giving a reading. We stood in the corner and listened for a few minutes until the poet started reciting a poem about a blow job he'd received in the back room of a grocery store. I quickly hustled Benno out the door.

On our way home we stopped at a café to get an ice cream.

"Can we sit at the counter, Mom?" asked Benno.

"I think it's better if we get our cones to go." I'd already splurged on the ricotta for dinner. If we sat, I'd have to tip the waitress. And Benno wouldn't settle for just sprinkles. He'd want his ice cream in a dish, with crushed pineapple and whipped cream. Then suddenly it was a sundae, twice the cost of a cone.

"Please," he begged. *"Please?"*

"All right," I said, giving in. We sat down on two stools.

There were a few other customers in the café. Late afternoon—only one waitress on duty.

The manager stood at the cash register reading a paper. He stared at us. I smiled; he did not smile back. He gestured to the waitress and whispered something in her ear.

"French vanilla," Benno announced. "Can I have it in a dish?"

"Yes, you can have it in a dish." I sighed, knowing exactly what was coming next.

"Can I have pineapple and whipped cream?" He gave me such a sweet, imploring look my heart broke. How easy it was to make him happy.

"And nuts and a cherry?" I asked.

"A sundae?" His eyes opened wide in surprise. "I can have a sundae?"

"If you want."

"That's okay?"

"Yes, sweetheart."

"What are you going to have?"

"Mmm . . ." I pretended to think about it. "I think I'll have a cup of tea."

"You don't want ice cream?"

"I'm going to save my appetite for dinner."

He nodded and spun around on the stool.

The waitress came. She scribbled the order on her pad and handed me the bill.

"That's three dollars and twenty-six cents," she said.

"Okay," I said, putting the bill face-down on the counter.

She stood there waiting.

"Do you need something?" I asked.

"I'm sorry. I need you to pay the bill," she said, glancing over at the manager, who was watching us intently.

"Now? But you haven't even put in the order."

"Mom," said Benno. He reached for my hand.

"It's our policy," she said softly. "You have to pay before you get your food."

Suddenly I understood. This was their policy for people like us. Me and Benno. A white woman with a mixed-race child who looked as if they had no money, who looked as if they might run out on the bill.

"Mama," said Benno in a small voice. "It's all right. Let's go. I don't want the sundae."

I sat there, my cheeks aflame, not knowing whether to bolt out of the café or make a scene. I decided to do neither. Willing my hands not to shake, I got my wallet out of my purse and, with as much dignity as I could muster, gave her a five-dollar bill.

"I'll get your change," the waitress said.

"Keep it," I said, loud enough for the manager to hear.


Sometimes Benno and I were like an old married couple, kissing and bickering and shouting. Sometimes we were best friends, laughing and weaving into each other, slamming our cards down on the table, jamming cookies into our mouths. And sometimes, we were strangers, like that early evening when I put my key in the lock and we stepped back into the apartment. Everything felt foreign, like it didn't belong to us anymore.

"Should I get the lasagna started?"

"I'm not hungry," said Benno.

I wasn't either. "That's all right. I'll make it tomorrow night."

I drew him under my arm and gave him a hug.

"Can I watch TV?"

It was then that the longing for Greengage overtook me, so overwhelming I could only manage one word.

"Yes."

In the past two years, I'd been back only five times: the fog continued to be coy. It appeared one month, then didn't appear for another four months. Then there was a two-month stretch, then it didn't return for another year. It had been six months now and counting since I'd last seen my friends. Fancy and Magnusson had gotten married a while back. I'd given Martha seeds for her flower clock, and I continued to replenish Joseph's cigarette stores.

Knowing Greengage was there, out of my reach, beyond the fog, was unbearable.

"If you're late one more time . . . ," said Mike Mulligan.

I quickly tied my black apron. "Your watch is fast."

Benno had fallen off his Big Wheel and scraped his knee just as I was about to leave for work. He was nearly hysterical (he wasn't good with the sight of blood) and wouldn't let Mrs. Patel near him, so I had to bring him back upstairs myself, wash the wound, and convince him the Bactine wouldn't sting (that alone took an additional ten minutes).

"It's not fast."

"I'm only fifteen minutes late."

"You're twenty-five minutes late. Jimmy had to take three of your tables. Look at him. The imbecile."

Jimmy was practically running through the restaurant, a platter held high above his head, his face contorted with stress, his hair wet.

"Is that sweat or hair product?"

Mike sighed. "It better be hair product. Jesus, Lux. I can't believe we're having this conversation again. You're my best goddamned waitress and that has saved your ass until now, but I am at the end of my bloody rope."

My last week's sales had topped one thousand dollars. That was a Seven Hills record. I thought of reminding him of this fact, but he was past that point.

"I'm sorry, Mike. I'll do better, I promise."

He grunted.

"*Love Boat*'s on," Benno shouted from the living room.

Here was the wonderful thing about third-grade boys. In public they might want nothing to do with you, but in private they were snugglers. He patted the cushion of the couch.

"Oh, Julie looks good in that jumpsuit," I said, sitting beside him.

Benno had a crush on *The Love Boat*'s cruise director, Julie McCoy. Her bowl cut had been much copied, even on the streets of San Francisco.

"Want to know the title?" I asked, picking up the *TV Guide*. *The Love Boat* had two or three storylines in each episode, and I found the titles hilarious.

"'The Business of Love/Crash Diet Crisis/I'll Never Fall in Love Again'!" I recited.

Benno looked at me solemnly. He didn't like me to make fun of his favorite show. He wore his *Star Wars* pajamas and an olive green cap from the army-navy store. I fought the urge to sweep him up into my arms and cover him with kisses.

"Shush," he admonished me.

Benno was capable of doing only one thing at a time, but my God, that boy could focus. Whether he was watching TV or having a conversation, he listened with an eerie intensity. Leaning in. Never taking his eyes off yours. He dispensed his attention extravagantly and it always made me feel guilty. There was nobody I loved more than Benno, but at times there was nobody I wanted to get away from more. Not from him per se, but from the responsibility of him. I assumed it was this way for all mothers, the wild swings between claustrophobia and joy. Benno forced me to stay in the present.

Sometimes I craved this intimacy. Sometimes it made me want to run away.

The phone rang halfway through *Love Boat*. It was eight-thirty. It had to be my mother—she was the only one who called this late. I ran into the kitchen and picked up the phone.

"Can't sleep?" I asked.

She had horrible bouts of sleeplessness. I'd asked Ginger what could be causing it. Was there something to be alarmed about? Even though Ginger was a bone man, I still relied on him for all my basic medical information.

"How old is she?" he'd asked.

"Fifty-three."

"Menopause," he said. "Sleeplessness is a common symptom."

"Well, what can she do about it? She's a walking zombie."

He shrugged sympathetically. "Does your father snore?"

"Probably."

"She could sleep on the couch."

"She'd never do that."

"Tell her to get a script from her doctor for diazepam. The insomnia will pass once she's through the change."

"Did you get the pills?" I asked my mother.

"Yes."

"And—"

"And, they make me feel dead in the morning. Like I've been buried alive. I can't even open my eyelids. I'd rather not sleep."

"Oh, Mom."

She brushed my concern away. "Listen, I have to ask you something. Your father got a letter from Benno."

I no longer supervised Benno's missives to my father. I'd given him stamps, stationery, and envelopes, and he wrote to my father whenever he wanted, posted the letters in the mailbox himself. They had their own relationship outside of me.

My mother hesitated. "We're concerned. He seems a little sad. He says you have to go to work every night, almost as soon as he's home from school, that you're never home. Is that true, darling? He's exaggerating, isn't he?"

"Of course he's exaggerating," I said, but Benno wasn't exactly lying. Since Rhonda had moved out, I'd had to pick up more shifts in order to cover the full rent.

"He said he misses you."

"Mom, everything's fine. He's just going through a stage. He's a little clingy these days. I'm not sure why," I lied.

I knew why. It had been two in the morning when I got back the last time from another fogless visit to the Valley of the Moon. I crept into the house as quietly as I could. I put my key in the lock and opened the door.

"Mama?" said Benno.

Benno and Rhonda were sitting on the couch. Rhonda looked exhausted. Benno was wide awake, his face streaked with tears.

"What's going on? What's wrong?"

"Where were you?" Benno cried. He leapt up from the couch and ran to me.

"Sweetheart, sweetheart. Calm down. I'm right here."

He moaned, "You left me."

"Benno, I didn't leave you. Rhonda came to spend the night with you, like she does every month. You have a standing date every full moon. Isn't that fun?"

Rhonda and Ginger had moved to the basement apartment once they got married. She'd gotten pregnant almost immediately, but even after her daughter, Penny, was born, she still gamely came up to baby-sit on the full moons.

As for me, I had my routine down to a science. I didn't leave for the Valley of the Moon until well after Benno fell asleep, and if the fog wasn't there, I left the Valley of the Moon immediately after midnight. Most full moon nights Benno didn't even know I'd been gone.

And if the fog *was* there, Rhonda and I had worked out a deal. She agreed to cover for me, to get Benno off to school in the morning, and I agreed never to spend more than a twenty-four-hour period in Greengage. The only time I'd stayed longer was when Benno was in Newport.

Rhonda had stopped asking me about what I did there long ago, just as I'd stopped trying to convince her it was real. But Benno was no dummy. He knew my leaving on full moon nights was different from me working a late shift or going out on a date; in his heart he understood that wherever I went I was unreachable. That's what had awoken him. That was the panic.

"No, it's not fun," he wailed.

I motioned to Rhonda that she could leave. She slipped out the door.

I led Benno back to the couch and pulled him into my lap. "Benno, how old are you now?"

"Nine," he whispered. We'd just celebrated his birthday a week ago.

"Yes, nine," I said. "And you know what that means?"

He punched the cushion.

"Stop." I grabbed his hand and unfurled his fingers. "It means you're a big boy. And big boys have to—"

"Where do you go?" he shouted.

Startled by the directness of his question, I answered truthfully. "To the Valley of the Moon."

He rubbed his eyes. "What's in the Valley of the Moon?"

"Besides the moon?"

He nodded.

"Well, it's a very beautiful place. Magic, kind of, especially on full moon nights."

"Why do you have to go?"

"Because—sometimes moms forget about magic. And they need to be reminded."

He bit his lip.

"You understand that, don't you? You know about magic, too. Isn't that right?"

"Yep."

"Yep, I knew you did. You're just that kind of boy."

He threaded his fingers through the holes in the crocheted afghan. "Can you take me with you?"

"Someday. When you're in need of magic."

"When I lose mine?"

"Yes, sweetheart, when you lose yours. But let's hope that day never comes."

His face crumpled. "That doesn't help," he sobbed. "It just makes me feel worse."

"Sweetheart."

He wept harder.

"Benno. Listen to me. Okay?"

He nodded, but kept crying.

"I'll always be with you. I'll never leave you. We'll always be together."

But even as I said it, I knew I was lying. It is the pledge every mother implicitly or explicitly makes to her child, but it's the pledge no mother can ever keep.


"Well, something's going on," said my mother. "Maybe you could spend a little more time with him. I'll send you some money. Take him somewhere special. Go away for the weekend. To Stinson Beach or Petaluma."

"Mom, there's nothing in Petaluma but cows and chicken farms."

"Really? The name is so misleading. It sounds like such a pretty place."

I heard her open the fridge. Peel back plastic wrap. Leftovers.

"What are you eating?"

"A pork chop."

My mother was not a sweets person. No cookies and milk for her, even for a late night snack.

"Where's Dad?"

"Sleeping. I should warn you—he wrote you a letter."

"Dad wrote me a letter?"

I spoke to my dad through my mom. She relayed messages to me, by which I mean she said things that were out of character for her that I could only attribute to my father.

"Well, not really a letter. More of an invitation. You'll see." She tried to sound breezy.

"What do you mean, an invitation? Like to a party?"

"I can't really say."

"Oh, okay. Great, Mom. I'm going to bed now and I'm sure I'll have a very good sleep thanks to you and all this good news."

"Honey, honey, don't do that. Don't go."

I hung up the phone.

"You have to take Benno with you to Greengage," said Rhonda, when I told her about the conversation with my mother. "This isn't working anymore."

She glanced over at Penny, asleep in her playpen, her little rump sticking up in the air. Penny was nearly two now and the darling of 428 Elizabeth Street. Benno had become a big brother to her; they adored one another. Ginger had taken a job across the bay at Children's Hospital in Oakland, which meant we all saw less of him. Still, Rhonda and I made a point of getting our families together for dinner at least once a month.

"You can't be serious. He's nine. He'd never be able to keep that sort of secret."

"Then don't make him keep it a secret. Stop making it into such a big deal. Tell him the truth. It's a commune."

"It's not a commune. And what's he going to say when he sees how they dress? How old-fashioned they are? That there's no electricity?"

"Tell him they're a bunch of hippies. Or a religious sect like the Amish. He'll love it."

"And the fog? How do I explain the fog?"

"Lux, forget the goddamned fog. Just take him there."

"I can't take him. Joseph made me promise. No strangers."

Rhonda glared at me. "He is not a stranger. He is your son. Surely this Joseph would welcome him."

Would he? I wasn't sure.

"I'll think about it."

"Lux, maybe it's time for you to stop going. Maybe this place has served its purpose. Have you thought of that?"

"Mom, Mom, it's a letter from Grandpa," said Benno. He looked stunned. "It's for you, not me. Where's mine?" He started to open it. "It must be for both of us."

"Uh-uh-uh." I grabbed the envelope from him. "It's addressed to me."

Benno sat in the chair and waited. I slid the envelope into my back pocket.

"You're not going to open it now?"

"No, I'm not."

"When are you going to open it?"

"When I'm not about to leave for work."

Four hours later I locked myself in a bathroom stall at Seven Hills and tore open the envelope.

Lux,

It occurs to me Benno might be feeling unmoored because of you and me. Clearly he needs more stability in his life. I think it's time we both work on rectifying that situation. Benno is nine now and I'd like to bring him with me to Lapis Lake this summer.

I would like you to come as well. Some of my happiest memories are of the time the two of us spent together at the lake. Perhaps if we went back there, all three of us, it would start to turn things around.

Let me know,

Dad

I put the lid down and sat on the toilet. Even though he wrote that he wanted me to come and that the happiest times of his life had been with me at Lapis Lake, all I could do was read between the lines. He hadn't said it, but he might as well have. The reason Benno was unmoored was because I wasn't providing a stable enough life for him.

I hung my head between my legs, tried to catch my breath, and thought of Joseph, Martha, and Fancy. It was almost May for them. In the vineyard the buds must be breaking. The sorrel and chives would soon need to be mulched.

When I'd blown off college and run away to San Francisco, seeking freedom and adventure, I'd found just the opposite. I'd become everything my father feared I would: an uneducated, invisible, and marginalized member of society. The woman in the line in front of you, scrambling to find loose change at the bottom of her purse. The woman whose son wore the same pair of pants to school three days in a row. The woman whose hair smelled like fried fish.

I couldn't bear to see that woman reflected in my father's eyes. I felt as ashamed of her as my father did.

I crumpled up the letter and threw it away.


"We're gonna be late!" Benno cried.

"No, we're not. Your flight doesn't leave until three-fifteen. It's only two-thirty and we're nearly there."

Late July. We were only five miles away from SFO, but we were stuck in wall-to-wall traffic on 101. Everybody was trying to get to the airport. I'd known I'd need to leave plenty of time, but not this much.

"I'm supposed to be there an hour before my flight."

"Stop worrying. I'll get you there."


He'd been angry the moment he woke up that morning. I heard him slamming things around in his room. He poured himself a bowl of Froot Loops (he was a creature of habit—he ate the same thing for breakfast every day), plopped on the couch, and turned on the stereo.

I pretended to read the paper and he raised the volume, wanting to get a rise out of me. I wasn't about to give him one. I wanted us to part on a positive note. I needed that desperately.

"Are you looking forward to going to Lapis Lake?"

He shoveled a spoonful of cereal into his mouth.

"It's really amazing, you're going to love it. It smells incredible there, pine needles and campfires and leaves."

"If it's so incredible, why don't you come?"

I'd never told him about my father's letter. I'd meant to respond with a card politely declining, but I'd never gotten around to it. Then another month had gone by and the window had passed. When I'd spoken to my mother about Benno's flights, neither of us had brought it up.

"What are you gonna do for a month while I'm gone?" Benno asked suspiciously.

I'd agreed to let Benno stay an extra two weeks this year. If Benno and my dad were going to the lake, my mother had to have her time with him as well.

"Oh, Benno. I'm going to work. What do you think I'm going to do?"


I got him to the gate just as it was closing. He no longer needed an escort. He'd been making this trip for four years.

Benno darted past me and into the Jetway.

"Wait, give me a hug!"

The stewardess tapped her foot impatiently, giving me a dirty look. It was too late for hugs.

I watched Benno until he turned the corner and was gone.


The traffic back into the city was even worse. I showed up for my 4:00 P.M. shift at 5:28.

Mike met me at the entrance of Seven Hills. "No," he said, blocking the door. "You're done here. Go home."

"I'm sorry, I had to drive Benno to the airport and we got stuck—"

He gave me a grim look.

"For tonight, right, Mike? Go home just for tonight?"

But it wasn't just for tonight. It was for all the future nights.

I was out of a job.

# JOSEPH

❧

*Valley of the Moon*
*1907*

L ux walked across the meadow instead of running.

"Something's happened," said Martha.

*Something.* A personal setback, or an event of a more global nature? Had war broken out? Had there been another earthquake? Was Benno sick?

"Does she look older to you?" I asked.

"She looks worn out," said Martha. "And a little older. I'd guess maybe a year has passed."

Nine months, she told us. She emptied her pack right there in the dining hall: toothpaste for Fancy, seeds for Martha. The Betty Crocker cookbook for the kitchen crew.

"Are you feeling well?" asked Martha.

"I'm tired. I've been working too hard. Double shifts."

"Benno?" I asked.

"It's August. He's in Newport. Well, actually he went to Lapis Lake with my father."

I'd known Lux for nearly a year now. If Newport was a blow, Lapis Lake was a shot to the heart. I could see it on her face.

"Any news we should know about?" asked Martha.

She pursed her lips. "There was a blizzard in New England in February. They caught this serial killer, Ted Bundy. Scientists discovered a moon orbiting Pluto."

"Anything else?" asked Martha gently, hoping she'd reveal something of a more personal nature.

Emotions flitted across Lux's face. Fear. Worry. Despair.

"No. Nothing that matters, anyway."

Thirty minutes later we were mucking out stalls.

"You don't have to do this. You've just arrived. Why not take on an easier job today? The domestic crew is making rag rugs," I said.

She raked the horse dung into a pile. "I don't want to make rugs. I want to do something that requires muscle. Something that tires me out."

I was in the stall next to hers but could hear how aggressively she was raking.

"You think I don't know how to roll up my sleeves and dig in!" she shouted.

I propped my rake up against the wall and walked into her stall. "What in God's name is going on?"

"Nothing."

"I find that hard to believe."

She dumped a load of dung into the wheelbarrow. "I don't care if you don't believe me."

"Something's happened."

She wore a pair of loose brown trousers, a vest, and a blouse.

"And why are you dressed like a man?" I asked.

"I am dressed like Annie Hall, for your information. One of Woody Allen's most brilliant feminist creations. *This* is a style." She practically stamped her foot at me.

"You're sad," I said.

"Fuck you," she said.

"You're angry."

"Fuck you," she repeated, her face crumpling.

I grabbed both her hands. Startled, she pulled back, but I kept a firm grip on her. "What's happened? You must tell me."

"Why *must* I tell you?"

"Because I want to know." Because—I was surprised to realize—I cared deeply about her well-being.

She huffed. "There's a new video game called Space Invaders; Benno is addicted to it. Kentucky beat Duke in the Final Four. Bianca and Mick Jagger are getting divorced."

"That's not what I want to know."

"What do you want? A confession? Fine. Here you go. I'm a terrible person."

"No," I said steadily. "You are a fine person. A good person. Who thinks about others. Who means well."

"No. I'm irresponsible and I can't be counted upon and my boss just fired my ass." Her face reddened and she held up a finger. "Don't. Don't say a word. I don't want your pity."

This was one of the qualities I'd grown to admire most in Lux. She truly did not want my pity. She could stomach anger, criticism, neglect, even abuse, but she couldn't abide having somebody feel sorry for her. She had so much pride.

"Well, it's about bloody time," I said. "You're far too intelligent for that job."


"Are you crazy?" she asked. "A doctor? A lawyer? A banker?"

It was 1979. Women were barkeeps. Surely they were doctors and lawyers and bankers, too. Why shouldn't she aim high?

"Do you know how many years of school I'd need for any one of those jobs?"

"Then go back to school."

"And just who will pay for this school? And what will Benno and I live on while I go back to school?"

I sighed. "All right, then we'll set our sights a bit lower, but not much."

"Humph," she said, her arms crossed.

"Lux, this won't work unless you remain open to new possibilities."

"I'm open, Joseph; I'm just not unrealistic."

"All right. How about a store?"

"What kind of a store?"

"Whatever you're interested in. What are you interested in? What sort of products?"

She smirked. "I like candy."

"That's it—you can open a sweets shop!"

She glowered. "You can't be serious. They sell sweets, as you put it, in every bodega on the corner of every block. Besides, I'm sure that the profit margin on candy is quite slim, not to mention my lack of money for start-up costs."

She rolled her eyes at me.

"I can see now is not a good time to discuss your future. Perhaps when you're in a better mood." I walked out of the stall.

"No, no. I'm sorry. Don't go." She groaned. "I just feel so hopeless. I appreciate you trying to help. I really do. Keep asking me questions, please. There's nobody else who talks to me like this. Who would ever think I had it in me to be a doctor." She smiled softly. "Or a banker. Imagine that."

"You *should* imagine that," I said to her.

My mother had imagined that. And she'd fought for that. And ultimately she'd died for that: that one day women would have the same opportunities as men.

"You should set high expectations for yourself," I said. "Nobody else will if you don't."

"You really believe I can pull something like that off? With *my* life the way it is? With Benno? At my age?"

For God's sake, the woman was only twenty-nine. She was acting as if her life was over. She was so beaten down. If I could, I'd have paid for her education, for her start-up costs, for whatever she needed to begin again.

"I believe you can do anything if you work hard and put in the time," I said.


I watched Martha performing her nightly ablutions. Washing her face vigorously with soap. Patting it dry gently with a flannel. A dab of lavender oil applied to her cheeks in feathery, upward strokes.

"She's staying a full month?" asked Martha.

"That's what she says. What else does she have to do? Her son is in Newport. She lost her job."

"Shouldn't she be looking for a new job?"

"She needs a rest."

"Greengage is a rest?"

"For her it is."

Martha pulled back the covers and climbed into bed. "She brought me sundrop seeds. I can't plant them now, it's too early."

"Then we have something to look forward to," I said.

"That is the plan."

That was always the plan with Martha. That's why she loved gardening so much. It was an act of hope. Of promises yet to be fulfilled. Of future joys. It was a simple calculus. You planted and waited.

# LUX

❧

Perhaps my father had done me a favor. Now that Benno was going to the lake, I could let go of it. I could pass that baton on to my son, along with all the regrets and nostalgia that went with it. I'd lost my place at the lake and I'd lost my place out in the world. But in Greengage, I was found.

I belonged here. Everything felt familiar now. I'd worked on practically every crew and was capable at all of them, although I most loved the kitchen, winery, education, and the herbal apothecary. Martha had taught me how to make a simple tincture. She'd even let me peek at her family's herbarium.

Today I was working with Friar in the infirmary, not that he needed much help: he hadn't had any patients in days. I dropped the metal implements into the soapy water.

"Let's launder the bandages, too," he said.

"Are they soiled?" The bandages appeared freshly washed.

He scratched behind his ear. "I guess not." He was searching for things to keep me occupied.

"Throw them in," I said.

I'd been here a week and was starting to feel hopeful. Maybe I did have a future. I'd told Joseph the only legal, non-restaurant jobs available for a woman with a high school diploma were menial: receptionist, secretary, salesclerk. Any of those would be better than waitressing, he'd said: more stable hours, potential for advancement, less physically taxing.

That was the first phase of the plan. The second was that I get myself back in school. I could attend City College at night and in two years' time have an associate's degree.

The front door of the infirmary swung open. Ilsa shuffled in. She looked pale. Her eyes were glazed. Two bright splotches of red shone on her cheeks.

Friar helped her into the examination room. "My God, you're burning up," I heard him say.

A few minutes later he told me, "Find Martha."

In the next hour three more people came into the infirmary with the same symptoms. I wanted to stay and help but they kicked me out.

"Go tend the lavender," commanded Martha.

She had a separate lavender garden. Ten long rows of it. I'd spent hours tending that garden. I knew its pests, its contours, its dry soil, like I knew the N-Judah bus schedule. She didn't have to tell me what had to be done.

Late that afternoon, Joseph came back to the house. He'd spent the day on the building crew, installing new shelves in the root cellar.

"What's happening in the infirmary?" I asked.

"Six people are ill now."

"Oh God."

He gave me a perplexed look. "There's no need for alarm. It's a simple flu. Martha and Friar have it well in hand."

"Are they taking precautions so they don't get sick?"

"Martha has a hearty constitution; however, she's not taking any chances. She's been exposed and doesn't want to get anybody sick. She'll sleep at the infirmary tonight," he said.

Joseph was right: Martha and Friar had it well in hand. It was a quick-passing influenza. It began with a sore throat. Next the fever spiked and then came the nausea. A couple of uncomfortable days in bed, but by the third day, up and walking around again.

Even though I assured Martha I had been vaccinated against and exposed to every kind of disease known to twentieth-century man, she advised me to go home. I gently refused. Instead I tended her plants and cut back the grass around the flower clock. She still hadn't completed it. She'd managed to get ten sections of it working, the blooms opening and shutting on the hour, but the section between eleven and twelve still eluded her. In the apothecary I turned the jars of tincture every morning so that each blossom and root and stem had its daily light.

In short, I tried to make myself indispensable.

"Are those diaries?" I asked.

Joseph sat at his desk in the parlor, a pile of unopened notebooks in front of him.

His eyes narrowed. "No."

"Don't worry, I'm not going to read your personal journals."

"There's nothing personal in there. They're market notebooks. It's how I keep—how I *kept*—track of the fields. Evaluate the crops. Calculate yields and productivity. Money in, money out. Distribute profit checks. Obviously, there's no need to do that anymore."

"Well, maybe that's a relief not to have to worry? Only having to provide for yourselves?"

"I'm not sure what it is."

When I'd first met Joseph, he seemed so much older than me in every way. I was twenty-nine now and I'd known him for four years. Even though he'd aged only nine months in that time, I felt like I was rapidly approaching his age. It helped that he treated me as an equal.

"I think this flu has run its course," he said.

About a quarter of the people in Greengage had cycled through it. We hadn't seen much of Martha for the past two weeks, but only a few people remained in the infirmary now.

"Martha will be home tomorrow for good."

"You must be happy about that."

"She's exhausted. She needs to sleep in her own bed."

"It's strange," I said. "How slowly things change. I mean, you know things will change, of course they're going to change, they always do, but when you're in the moment sometimes it feels like that moment will never be over."

"Time elongates."

"Exactly, it stretches. And sometimes that's a good thing, if it's a good moment and you don't ever want to leave it. And sometimes it's a bad thing."

He finished my thought. "And you find yourself trapped in a terrible moment forever."

"Yes," I said. "This is not a terrible moment, you know that, right?"

# JOSEPH

❦

Martha grimaced as she worked the bar of soap between her palms. Her hands were raw from washing them so much.

"Why don't you let me heat the water?" I asked.

"There's no need, Joseph."

I made her some toast and a soft-boiled egg. Even though she'd barely slept in days, Martha was full of energy. Her leg jittered up and down under the table and her eyes were bright. She thrived in a crisis.

"We're down to John," she said. "His temperature was normal today but we kept him one last night just to be sure."

She sopped the rest of her egg yolk up with her toast.

"Shall I make you another egg?"

She pushed her plate away. "No, thank you."

"Some tea."

"No."

"A biscuit."

She gave me the faintest glimmer of a smile. "I'm tired. Let's go to bed."

"It's only seven and you said you're not tired."

"Bed," she whispered, taking me by the hand.

Oh. *Bed.* I followed her up the stairs.

———

The next morning Martha slept in. I went back to the house at lunchtime to check on her, and she'd just risen. She bustled around the kitchen, wiping down counters, tossing a rotten apple into the compost bucket.

"When is Lux going? The moon will be full in two days."

"Today or tomorrow," I said, guessing. I hadn't spoken to her about it. She'd stay as long as she could, I suspected. She might never have an opportunity to put her life on hold for a month again.

I spent the afternoon mulching garlic, Fancy by my side.

"I'm famished, Joseph. Did you bring any sweets?" she asked.

"Why, yes, right here in my pocket."

"Really?"

I raised my eyebrows at her.

"I should know better than to count on you," she said. "You only think of yourself."

She was teasing me; still, there was something about the comment that stung.

"I'm going to get some water. Would you like some?"

"No, thank you."

She stood and squinted. "Who's that?"

A man on horseback galloped toward us, clearly in a hurry. As he got closer we could see it was Magnusson, a grave look on his face.

"Dear God, what's wrong?" said Fancy as he approached.

Magnusson slid out of the saddle and handed the reins to me.

"Martha," he said.

"I'm fine," said Martha.

"You passed out," said Friar, taking her pulse.

"It's because I haven't been sleeping," she muttered.

John had been deemed well enough to go home and Martha had been cleaning up in the infirmary, stripping sheets, wiping down counters, when she'd collapsed.

Martha tried to sit up and Friar gently pushed her back down.

"You're not going anywhere," he said.

She shook her head angrily.

"She does look fine," I said to Friar.

"How's your appetite?" Friar asked.

"She's been eating like a horse," I answered for her. "Finished everything on her plate last night."

"Why are you people so concerned with my appetite?" snapped Martha.

Friar stood. "Just do me a favor. Stay here for the rest of the afternoon. Let me keep an eye on you. You don't have a fever but you feel a little warm."

"That's not how the other cases presented. The fever was immediate and high. A sore throat for two or three days prior. My throat feels fine. You are being ridiculous, Friar."

"I am being careful, Martha."

A few hours later Martha had a temperature of 102.


"What's wrong, darling?" she asked.

We'd agreed it was best for her to stay at the clinic overnight.

"What's wrong is that you just called me darling."

"Why shouldn't I call you darling?"

"You should call me darling, you just never do."

"I don't?"

I kissed her on the forehead. "Go to sleep."

I was at the door when she called out to me. "Don't forget to buy sugar at Poppe's. And tea. Jake set some Twining's aside for me."

Poppe's was the general store in Glen Ellen, and Jake Poppe had likely been dead for some fifty years.

"Of course. And how about some grape taffy?" I teased her.

"Oh, yes."

"And some butterscotch drops?"

"Lovely."

Martha had such a gallows sense of humor. It was one of the things I loved most about her.

The next morning Lux came downstairs dressed in her modern clothes.

"You're going home?" I asked.

"The full moon is tonight. I don't have a choice." She looked at me sadly. "Thank you for being so good to me. I don't know what I'd do without Greengage."

"You have a plan. All you have to do is execute it now."

"Right." She slung her backpack over her shoulders. "Walk with me to breakfast?"

"I have to stop by the infirmary first," I said.

"I'll go with you. I want to say goodbye to Martha."


"I was just going to send somebody to get you!" cried Friar when we walked in the door. "Her fever is 104. I don't understand. I checked on her just an hour ago and the fever had gone down. I thought she was out of the woods."

Martha lay on the bed with the sheets pulled back, her nightgown nearly transparent with sweat, her hair wet, like she'd just come out of the bath. She moaned; the cords in her neck tightened.

"Ice," she whispered.

"She's been asking for ice all morning," said Friar.

"Ice," she moaned again, delirious.

"It's coming, darling. I can hear the ice wagon now," I said.

"We have to cool her off somehow," said Friar.

"The creek." It was 55, maybe 60 degrees this time of year.

"What can I do?" asked Lux, frantic.

"Just stay out of the way," said Friar.

I wrapped Martha in the sheet and carried her out to Friar's buckboard.

"I can get you close," Friar said, "but I won't be able to get down the bank with the rig."

"I can manage."

Martha clung to me as we drove.

"If we get the fever down?" I asked.

Friar frowned.

"Will that be enough? Will she be all right?" I demanded an answer.

"Nobody has had this high of a fever. I'm inclined to believe this is a different virus. Or maybe it's the same and it's just hit Martha harder."

"Why would it hit her harder?"

"I don't know. I'm sorry, Joseph."


I waded into the water with Martha.

"No," she whispered. "It's too cold."

"Yes, my darling. We have to cool you off."

"But what about the summer solstice party? Have the tables been moved from the dining hall? I have to get dressed. People are arriving at five."

"We've got plenty of time," I said.

I held Martha out in front of me and slowly lowered her into the water until only her face was above the surface. She sighed. Her blond hair fanned out from her head. I rocked her back and forth.

Friar called down from the top of the bank. "Is she all right?"

"She seems to be."

"Good. Keep her in there as long as she can bear it."

Martha bore it for about five minutes, then her lips turned purple and she started to shiver. I staggered up the bank with her. Friar met me with a woolen blanket.

Martha's color slowly returned to normal.

"I'm fine, Joseph. Why are you all making such a fuss?" she asked.

Friar felt her forehead with the back of his hand. "The fever has gone down. Let's get her back to the infirmary and into some warm, dry clothes."

# LUX

❧

Before Friar shut the door behind him, I caught a glimpse of Joseph sitting by Martha's bedside. They were talking softly. This was a good sign.

"She's doing much better," Friar said to me.

"Can I see her?"

"Maybe later. Why don't you go get some lunch and come back."

Lunch? What happened to breakfast? "What time is it?"

"Nearly three."

I'd been in the waiting room for six hours? It felt like only twenty minutes had passed.

"No, thank you." I wasn't moving until I knew Martha was all right.


Martha's fever didn't rise. By the evening she was sitting up and drinking broth. Finally I was allowed into the examination room.

"Tell me again what I said?" Martha was asking Joseph.

"You asked me to get Twining's from Poppe's. You said Jake had set it aside for you."

Roses bloomed on her cheeks. She looked like a flaxen-haired Snow White.

"Goodness. You must have thought me a lunatic."

"I thought you were joking," he said.

I stood there quietly by the door, suffused with happiness at the sight of the two of them conversing like normal.

Martha noticed me. "Lux," she said. She motioned me to the bed. She reached out her hand. Her palm was dry, but her skin felt warm. The last little bit of fever. "You're still here."

"I had to make sure—" My throat throbbed.

I wanted to tell her how much she meant to me. That knowing she loved me and believed in me gave me courage back out in the world. But all I managed to squeak out was, "I'm so glad I'm here."

"You love Greengage?" she asked.

"I do."

"More than home?"

I didn't answer, but I didn't have to. We all knew the truth.

"You can live the same sort of life in San Francisco, you know that, don't you?" she said.

I shook my head. "I don't think so. It's not possible, it's—"

"Tell me. Why are you so happy in Greengage?"

I shrugged. "Because I feel like I have a place here. I'm part of a community."

"And because you're in service to something larger than yourself," said Martha.

"I guess so. Yes."

"So what are you going to do about that?" asked Martha.

"Keep coming to Greengage?" I said slowly.

"No, that is not the answer," said Martha. She yawned and turned to Joseph. "I'm so tired." She looked at him bewilderingly, and then suddenly her back arched.

"Friar!" shouted Joseph.

Her fingers and toes curled up. Her limbs grew rigid. She bucked on the bed.

Friar ran into the room. "She's seizing."

Joseph cupped Martha's face in his hand, murmuring, "It's all right, my love. It's all right."

"Hold her arms, Joseph, and you hold her legs, Lux," said Friar.

I threw my upper body across her calves. It took all my weight to keep her still on the mattress. Friar placed a cotton cloth in her mouth so she wouldn't bite her tongue.

The one terrible moment Joseph and I had spoken about? We were in it. Pinned fast. Unable to escape.

Finally Martha stopped writhing. The room was filled with an overly sweet smell, like pears. Friar took her temperature: 105.4.

Joseph cradled an unconscious Martha in his arms. I don't know how long we sat there before she came to. It was like watching somebody rise from the bottom of a lake.

Her flesh was searing hot. The whites of her eyes yellow.

"Tell Fancy to shut the window. A storm's coming," she said.

A few seconds later, she was gone.

It was stunning how fast life could change. How the solid ground that was your long-held, never-questioned beliefs could reveal itself to be nothing but shale and crumble into dust.

Joseph pressed Martha's small body to his chest and began to keen. It was an involuntary sound, ripped from him. A wail of disbelief and grief, so private and piercing I had to look away.

Through the open window, I saw the full moon hanging high in the sky.

Friar tracked my gaze, glanced at his pocket watch, and his face grew pale.

"What time is it?" I whispered.

He shook his head sadly and I had my answer. It was well after midnight; I'd stayed through the Greengage full moon. The roulette wheel was spinning. The tiny ball of my fate was skittering around, and I had no idea where it would land.

Time had already begun to speed up on the other side of the fog.

# LUX

❧

*San Francisco*

My car wasn't in the parking lot. Filled with dread, I dug some change out of my wallet and called Rhonda on the payphone. No answer. I called Doro and the Patels. They weren't home either. Then I saw an eight-by-ten piece of paper taped up on the side of the phone booth.

*Have You Seen This Woman?* It was a photo of me at Stinson Beach. On that day Rhonda and I had taken Benno to the beach, but it had been too windy to fly our dime-store kite. Minutes after Rhonda snapped the photo, we'd packed our things and gone back to the city.

The notice had my height, weight, age, and hair color.

*Last seen August 2nd. If you have information please call 415-289-3434.* Rhonda's number.

Desperate, I called Seven Hills. Mike answered in his familiar South Boston accent.

"Mike?"

"Speakin'." He didn't recognize my voice.

"Mike, it's Lux."

"*Lux.* For fuck's sake. Lux. Everybody's been looking for you. We thought—we thought. Goddamn it."

I started crying.

"Okay, okay. Calm down. Take a deep breath. Are you all right? Are you hurt?"

He paused, waiting for my answer. I couldn't get any words out.

"Jesus. Are you in a safe place? Lux, tell me you're in a safe place. Say yes or no."

"Yes," I managed to squeak.

"Okay, good. Where are you?"

"In a parking lot."

"Where?"

"Valley of the Moon. Jack London State Park."

"Okay, sit tight. I'm coming to get you."

"Wait, wait, Mike?"

"What, darlin'?" He'd never called me darlin' before. I'd heard him call other waitresses darlin', but never me.

"What's the date?"

"August thirty-first—"

I started weeping again with relief. Benno had probably just come back from Newport. He hadn't even started school yet.

"Nineteen eighty."

It took a few seconds for it to sink in. I'd been gone a year.

Mike dropped me off at 428 Elizabeth Street. We'd barely spoken on the ride home and I was grateful he hadn't interrogated me. I stared out the window trying to think of what I was going to say. How I was going to explain where I'd been.

"Someone's in there?" Mike asked. "You're not gonna be alone, right?"

"Rhonda." I could see the lights on in her apartment.

He reached over me and opened the car door. "You be good, Lux." He gave me a sad smile.

I knocked on Rhonda's door. I could hear the TV and Penny singing to herself.

"It's open, Sunite," Rhonda shouted. She thought I was Mrs. Patel.

*The Jetsons* were on. Penny waved as if she'd just seen me yesterday: she was three now, her baby fat nearly gone. Rhonda was folding laundry in the kitchen.

"It's me," I said in a wobbly voice.

Rhonda took a step backward in shock. "There you are," she said calmly. She didn't want Penny to see her reaction.

I walked into the kitchen and closed the door behind me. Rhonda, a pillowcase in her hand, stared at me.

"What the fuck, Lux."

"I'm sorry," I said. "I'm so sorry."

"Where the hell have you been?"

"I got—stuck. In Greengage. It was an accident. I didn't mean to stay through the full moon. I didn't, I swear."

"Oh my God. Are you fucking serious? You can't imagine. Oh my fucking God."

She came around the table and hugged me. The familiar scent of her perfume, Charlie, incited a fresh round of tears.

"Christ, Lux," she murmured, but it wasn't an admonishment, it was more of a *Thank God you're safe.* Finally I pulled away from her and sat down. I could see she was crying now, too. It was hard for me to meet her eyes and even harder to ask the question.

"Where's Benno?"

She looked down at the table guiltily.

"Jesus, Rhonda, tell me. Is he all right?" I cried.

"I tried to keep him here with me, I swear to you, I did. Ginger was okay with it. He could have shared a room with Penny, she has bunk beds." She chewed the inside of her lip. "He's not here. Your father insisted Benno stay in Newport. He never came home. After you didn't." She couldn't bring herself to say it.

*After I didn't come back.*

Rhonda explained what had happened. When I hadn't returned, they'd gotten the police involved and a formal search had ensued. My car had been in the Jack London State Park lot, and all Rhonda knew was that Greengage was in the Valley of the Moon. They'd scoured the valley and all of Sonoma County, but there was no sign of the farm anywhere.

"That's when I started to believe you about Greengage," she said. "I kept your secret, but it was damn hard, Lux." She shook her head, tears welling. "I mean, why didn't you tell me?"

"I did tell you," I said. "Over and over again."

"You're right. You did. I didn't listen. It was just so crazy."

I reached across the table and squeezed her hand. "I don't blame you. Nobody would believe in Greengage unless they saw it."

She nodded. "I'm your best friend. I should have come with you. I should have at least tried."

"You didn't tell anybody?" I asked.

"No. I stuck to my story. I may have played up the commune bit. Don't be mad at me. I had to. Nothing else would have made sense. Your father flew out when the formal search ended, and he hired a private detective, but that went nowhere."

I couldn't think about my father. Not now.

"What did they tell Benno? What does he think? Does he think I'm—*dead*?"

Rhonda gave me the most miserable look, and I had the answer to my question. Of course. It was even worse than him thinking I was dead; he thought I'd abandoned him.

I put my head in my arms, convulsing in sobs.

Alarmed, Penny pushed open the kitchen door with her chubby hand and waddled over to me. She stuck her face into mine.

"Lux sad? Lux cryin'?"

Her face scrunched up with empathy. She deliberated for a moment and then smoothed my hair. "Don't worry, noodle," she crooned.

That was what Rhonda said to her when she got a splinter or fell off the swings at the park. I pulled her toward me. She smelled of my past, of powder and Johnson's baby shampoo.

Benno was ten now.

———

"I've got to go to Newport. Tonight," I said to Rhonda.

"Uh-huh. So what's your plan? You're just going to waltz in like Rip Van Winkle and say, 'Hello, I'm back from the dead'?" she asked.

"Oh God. What am I going to do? Should I call?"

"No, you should think about what you're going to say first. How you're going to explain where you've been for a year."

I gulped painfully. My throat was raw from crying. "I didn't just stay for no reason."

Rhonda waited for an explanation.

"Martha, Joseph's wife, died the night I was supposed to come home. It was sudden. One minute she was fine, the next she was having a seizure. I couldn't just leave. I mean, we were trying to save her—"

"You knew Martha well? You were close?"

"She was like a sister to me."

"Oh, Lux. I'm so sorry," Rhonda said.

Penny had gone back to the living room. She knocked over a tower of blocks—they clattered to the floor and she clapped her hands joyously and whispered to herself, "Again." That had been Benno's favorite word when he was Penny's age. *Again, again, again.*

"How am I going to explain where I've been? They looked for Greengage, they know it's not there."

"Maybe you could tell them the community moves around. Say you got swept up. It's like a cult. You went on the road with them. They brainwashed you but finally you came to your senses and got out."

"But they're not a cult. And it's my fault I stayed, not theirs."

"Look, if you want to get Benno back, then I think that's your only choice."

My apartment was exactly as I'd left it, only cleaner. Rhonda told me my father had hired a maid to come once a month and he'd continued paying the rent. He'd also stocked the cupboards with canned and dry goods.

This made me feel even guiltier. How would I ever face him? It would have been better if he'd just let my apartment go to shit. I didn't deserve to have people keeping my home fires lit. And the fact that it was my father who'd kept vigil, the most unlikely person to be looking out for me, was stupefying.

I showered and then crawled into bed. My flight left at six in the morning. I hadn't called home; I couldn't bring myself to do it. Rhonda was going to phone once I was in the air and let my parents know I was on my way.

The next day my taxi barreled down I-95. I sat in the backseat with the windows open. The closer I got to Newport, the more panicked I became. Labor Day weekend. The traffic was backed up half a mile to the tolls on the bridge. We inched alongside cars filled with teenagers and families. On weekends Newport's population doubled. They came for the beaches, to tour the mansions, and to party. The restaurants and bars on Thames Street and Bowen's Wharf would already be packed, the line for Dairy Queen dozens of people long.

My parents lived in a middle-class neighborhood. Not glamorous by any means, no historical society placards on the clapboards, but well-maintained houses, the gutters clean, the driveways re-tarred like clockwork every ten years. Houses on my street rarely changed hands, and when the taxi pulled up and I saw the blue light of the TV in the house next door to ours (that TV had been on twenty-four hours a day since I was a girl), I was bowled over with nostalgia. Nothing, nothing had changed.

"You're late," said my father when I walked in the door.

That was an understatement.

He and my mother were sitting side by side on the sofa.

"Benno?" I gasped.

My mother got up and embraced me. I held myself stiffly against her, not deserving of her affection.

"Benno's not here," she said. "He went to see *The Empire Strikes Back* with his friend Billy. He'll be back in a while. We thought it was best if he was out of the house when you arrived. Give us time to catch up." She stepped back and gave me the once-over. "You look starved. Did they have you on some sort of a special diet? Were you even allowed to eat?"

How could she be talking about diets? I was so desperate to see Benno—I couldn't think of anything else.

My father looked at me like a stranger, dry-eyed and emotionless. "Did you contact the police?"

"I haven't had time yet. I came straight here."

"You'll have to tell them everything about this Greengage. Where they are. How they operate. Were there others trapped there like you? Other outsiders?"

"No, it was just me," I said, cringing at the word *trapped*.

"Just you? Really? You're the only one they recruited?"

I thought of Joseph, cradling Martha in his arms. The animal sound he'd made as he wept.

"I wasn't recruited. I—joined. Voluntarily."

My father gave me a stony look. "I suggest you leave out the 'voluntarily' part when you speak to the police."

"But then they made you stay, right?" asked my mother. "You wanted to come back, but they wouldn't let you."

"It's not that simple, Mom. They didn't force me to stay, I could have gone, but I didn't want to." I was trying to have it both ways. A little lie and a little truth.

My mother whispered, "You could have come back?"

"No, no, no, that's not what I meant. Let me try and explain. Being with them, being there—"

"Where?" interrupted my father. "Exactly where were you? We searched the Valley of the Moon, every square inch of it. There were no encampments, no buildings, nothing. Those woods were empty."

"Where doesn't matter," I said. "Let me finish. Being with them—it was like I was under a spell. Like I fell through time."

My father snorted. "Are you hearing this, Miriam?"

My mother waved her hand at my father, shushing him. "Are you under this *spell* now?" she asked.

Did she think I was high?

"Of course not. Look at me. I'm perfectly lucid."

My father got up from the couch. "I can't listen to this anymore. She went somewhere, God knows where or with whom, some drugged-out hippies, a bunch of losers, it doesn't matter. She left her job, her friends, her family, *her son* behind. She's an unfit mother, she's—"

"Mom?"

Benno stood in the doorway, his face drained of color.


"You didn't tell him I was coming?"

"Look who's here, Benno. Look who's come back. It's your mom. We're so happy she's home," said my mother.

"Benno," I murmured. "Sweetheart."

He shook his head, almost like he couldn't believe what he was seeing.

"It's me. It's really me."

He ran across the room straight into my father's arms. This was a punch to my gut, but I held in my emotions and took inventory of him.

He'd gotten taller and he'd lost weight. He had biceps. Had my father been teaching him to box? I wondered how I looked to him, if I appeared one year older as well. I felt ten years older, watching my father hold my son as if I were somebody Benno needed to be protected from.

"How was the movie?" my mother said.

Benno grabbed onto her query like a life raft, hauling himself back into my childhood home, back into his new life with his grandparents, where it was safe, where there was supper at the same time every night, where the three of them sat in the living room and watched *Truth or Consequences* together.

"When they were filming, they made a full-size model of the *Millennium Falcon*," he said.

"Really?" said my father. "How do you know that?"

"Billy's mother read it in *People*."

Forty-eight issues of *People* had been published since I was gone. They were acting like I wasn't even in the room.

"Did you eat?" asked my mother.

"We went to the mall afterwards. I had a burger and an Orange Julius."

Benno kept his gaze focused on my parents.

"Well, there's some leftover American chop suey, if you want it. I made it for your mother. It's her favorite food." My mother was trying to find a way to bring me into the conversation.

"That's right. Grandma made it once a week when I was a kid," I said.

"I'm tired. Can I go to bed?" asked Benno.

"Of course," said my mother. "Why doesn't your mother bring you up? I'm sure you'd like some time alone with her."

Benno finally looked me in the eyes. "Where the fuck have you been?"

My mother shouted, "Benno!" My father crossed his arms over his chest; he wanted the same answer.

Despite the time difference I was up at five the next morning, as was my father. He sat in the dark with a cup of coffee.

"You can put on the light," he said.

I flicked the switch. His hair was combed, the creases in his pajama bottoms crisp, his feet shod in his leather slippers with the custom lifts.

I poured myself a cup of coffee.

"There's no cream. Your mother and I have given it up. Actually, she gave it up for me. Everything we eat is fat-free."

"That's all right. I don't use cream."

"Since when?"

In high school I couldn't stomach coffee unless half the mug was cream.

"Since—I don't know, Dad. What does it matter?"

I sat down at the table with him and took a few sips. My mother bought real coffee beans; she didn't use Sanka. Every month she made a special trip to the Italian grocery store in Cranston to stock up.

My father's hands were splayed out on the table. His nails short and groomed. Little tufts of hair on each knuckle. "So just what is your plan?"

"My plan?"

"Yes, why are you here?"

"I'm here to see Benno. My son."

"Right," he snapped.

"Look, Dad. You have every right to be angry. I know I fucked up. I know I—"

"That's what you call this? Fucking up? You left. You just got up and left and didn't come back for a year."

I clasped my hands together. A conciliatory gesture. "I'm sorry."

"I'm not the one you should be saying you're sorry to." He shook his head in disgust. "I don't believe your story, Lux. I don't believe one damn word of it."

"Well, that's your prerogative, Dad. You can believe what you want. But it's the truth."

He glared at me, and then he slammed his palm down on the table. "This is the life you chose. You chose it, Lux, nobody forced it on you." He got up from the table and walked over to the sink. He leaned against the counter, breathing heavily. "How the hell did you get so lost?"

As I sat in that kitchen—having driven my father into such a state that he was unable to bring himself to even look at me, his only daughter—a headline ran through my mind. *Everybody Who Loved You Is Gone.* They were done with me, they'd given up on me. And I deserved it. My precious Benno—bar nothing, the best thing I'd ever done in my life—I'd left him with no word, no explanation. My disappearance had ripped him out of his old life and hurled him into a new one, and he would probably never fully recover from it. And my father? He'd extended many olive branches over the years, and to him it must have looked as if I'd rejected all of them. I hadn't so much rejected them as felt unworthy of them. And now, I truly *was* unworthy.

Once, I'd worked with a waitress who'd lost her dad in a car accident when she was in her teens. She'd never gotten over it. Even though her mother had eventually remarried, there was always a hole in her heart that no amount of new paternal love could fill. The world had shown her its cracks. Her protector was gone.

Well, my father wasn't dead, he was standing in the kitchen not a few feet away from me, but I was dead to him. This was far worse.

I crept silently from the kitchen and walked up the stairs to my old room.

Benno was still sleeping, an arm flung over his eyes. His face was soft and relaxed. As he slept I could imagine he still loved me. I sat on the edge of the bed, fighting the urge to lie down beside him. I'd lost that right, hadn't I?

A while later he began to stir. He opened his eyes. For a second he forgot what had happened.

"Mama," he whispered, a look of pure happiness breaking over his face.

"Sweetheart," I cried softly, inhaling his familiar smell, freshly washed cotton pajamas, the sweet hay scent of his hair.

His face shuttered closed.

"Please," I pleaded. "Let me explain."

I'd tell him about Greengage. About Joseph. About Martha dying so suddenly and me doing everything I could to try to help and accidentally staying through the full moon. He was a compassionate boy. He'd understand. He'd forgive me. I just had to give him the truth. He was ten now, old enough to be trusted.

"I have something to tell you," I said. "A secret. I think when I'm done you'll understand everything. Why I was gone. Where I was."

"No," he said, shaking his head.

"Benno?" I said. "Come on, now. Be fair. Give me a chance to explain."

He turned his face into the pillow.

"Please," I begged.

Was he going to pretend I didn't exist anymore, like my father?

His small shoulders began to shake. I immediately began crying. There was nothing that could make me cry more instantly than the sight of my son weeping. It was unbearable. I had to do something, anything, to make it stop, to comfort him, to make him feel better. If he was in pain, I was in pain. Would it always be this way? Would he call me as a fifty-year-old man, weeping about a lost job or a failed marriage, and would a seventy-year-old me begin crying, too?

I took a chance and put my hand lightly on his back. He let it stay there for a minute, and just as my chest began to flood with hope, he said, "Get off me."

A week later my mother drove me to the airport. I was all cried out. I'd accepted the current reality; Benno had refused to come home with me. Our emotional umbilicus had been severed. He treated me like an acquaintance, cordial but distant, clearly counting the days until I left. What else could I do but return to San Francisco and start working on a plan to win him back?

"Will you go back to waitressing at Seven Hills?" asked my mother when she pulled up to the curb.

"I have to figure something else out. Something better. Being a waitress isn't enough. For me or for Benno."

She smoothed the pleats on her skirt. "When you were young, Lux, your father and you were so close. Sometimes I used to be jealous of you two. Especially in the summer when you went off to the lake."

I was shocked to hear this. She'd put on such a good front. Reveling in her solitude. Going off on jaunts with her friends.

"You could have come with us, Mom."

"No. I wanted you to have that time together. You had such a special relationship—you and him."

I picked at a cuticle, not trusting myself to speak.

"There are things you haven't told us," she said. "Things you're holding back, right?"

I nodded.

"I don't understand. We're your family. Why can't you tell us?"

"It's just—I made a promise."

"I see," she said coolly.

"Mom, please don't be mad at me. Everybody's so mad at me. I couldn't bear it if you were, too."

"I'm not mad, Lux, I'm just confused."

I had to tell her something. "I was gone so long because somebody very close to me died."

"Somebody in San Francisco?"

"No, somebody at the farm. The place where I was. At Greengage. I'm not making excuses. There's no excuse I could possibly give you or Dad or Benno for being gone so long, but—"

Her face crumpled up at the sight of my crumpled-up face. She picked up my hand and held it.

"I didn't tell you to get your sympathy," I croaked.

"Well, why not? You deserve sympathy, Lux, just like anybody else."

"Okay," I said. "Okay." I brushed the tears from my eyes. "I've gotta go. The plane leaves in an hour."

"Don't give up on your father," she said. "He just needs some time."

I opened the car door. "Please don't let Dad say horrible things about me. Don't let him turn Benno against me."

"He would never do that." She grabbed hold of my arm. "It's a balancing act now, you understand? It's the hardest thing about being a parent. Holding on and letting go simultaneously. Don't worry. We'll take good care of him until he's ready to come home."

Twelve hours later I put the key in the lock and opened my apartment door. It smelled of Lemon Pledge and Fantastik. The maid had come while I'd been gone. My father had paid one last time for my place to be cleaned.

The next morning Rhonda knocked on the door. I'd been up for hours already and was wired from three cups of coffee and adrenaline. I didn't know where to start. How to begin to put my life back together again.

Rhonda looked around the apartment. "Benno didn't come back

with you." She poured herself a cup of coffee and sat down at the table.

"You're not surprised," I said.

"No."

"Right. Why would you be? Why would he come back with me? How could he possibly trust me? I just disappeared with no word, for a year."

"Did you tell him it wasn't your fault? That it was a cult? You were brainwashed?"

"No. I can't lie to him anymore."

"So he thinks you just checked out of your life for a year?"

"Pretty much."

"Christ. So what is your plan?"

"To try and win him back."

"How?"

"I'm going to start by getting a job."

Rhonda went with me to the police station. I told the truth; that I'd chosen to stay with the Greengage community voluntarily, there'd been no brainwashing, and they were not a cult. The last thing I wanted to do was give anybody reason to try to hunt them down.

I was remorseful. I told the policeman my son was now living with my parents in Newport and I was going to do everything I could to get my life back on track and then bring him back to San Francisco. He took my statement with both disinterest and contempt.

"Well," said Rhonda, putting her arm around me as we left the station. "The good news is you've hit rock bottom. It can't possibly get any worse."

I called Newport that night. The answering machine picked up and my mother's voice said, "Hello, you've reached the Lysander residence. I'm afraid we're not here to answer the phone. Please leave a message after the beep."

"It's me. Lux. I was just calling to say hello." I did my best to inject a breeziness into my voice. "I made it home okay. I just wanted—"

"Lux," my mother panted, out of breath.

"You're there? Why didn't you pick up?"

"I was in the basement doing laundry."

I could hear the TV. "Can I speak to him?"

"Hold on a sec." She covered the mouthpiece with her hand. A few seconds later she said, "He's not here, darling. I guess he and your father went out. They were talking about going to Bowen's Wharf for ice cream."

She was lying, I could tell because the TV abruptly shut off. I felt like a robber; like I had no right to have entered their house, even with a phone call.

"I'm sorry," said my mother.

"How is he?"

"He's well. He's great!" I heard a door squeak open and shut and I knew she'd walked into the pantry with the phone. "Honestly, it's been very difficult since you left," she whispered. "He doesn't want to talk about what happened."

"He's furious with me, isn't he?"

"I think it's more like shock. You have to give him some space."

"Should I not call?"

"No, you should call. He may not want to talk to you for a while, but believe me, it will mean a lot to him that you make the effort. He's got big ears. I'm sure he's out there in the living room listening right now."

The pantry door squeaked open again. "Okay, I'll be sure to tell him. I'm so glad you got home okay. Yes, yes. You take care, too. Bye now."

She hung up the phone.

"How fast can you type?" asked the recruiter.

"Seventy words per minute."

"How far did you get in math?"

"Straight A's in almost every math class from elementary through high school. St. Paul's in Newport, Rhode Island—I can get the transcripts if you want."

"And where did you attend college?"

I clutched the handles of my patent leather bag nervously. I'd borrowed a suit from Rhonda and it was too snug across the chest. The heels were from my mother, a birthday gift. "Every woman should own a pair of black pumps," she'd said.

"I didn't go to college."

"Junior college?"

"No."

She scribbled on the pad. "With your background and education, you're well suited for secretarial work. Or perhaps sales. Have you ever worked retail? I have something in the lingerie department at Macy's. All employees get a twenty percent discount, not just in their department but store-wide."

She eyed my ill-fitting suit compassionately, and that's when I knew I had a chance. She'd probably risen up the ladder herself over the years, sat in plenty of interviews like the one I was currently in and been told the same thing: you're only good enough to be a secretary or salesgirl. The placard on her desk read MS. HENNESSEY. Either she wasn't married or she was a feminist, both of which would work in my favor.

I sat forward in my chair. "Look, Ms. Hennessey, I don't have a college education, that's right. But I'm really smart, and I'm a fast learner, and I don't give up. I promise you that. All I need is a chance, please. I can't afford to be in a dead-end job. I need a job with a future. I have a son. His name is Benno. He's ten. I'm a single mother."

Ms. Hennessey took off her glasses and looked at me with kind eyes. "I understand. Things happen sometimes that are out of your control and you find yourself—well, you find yourself in the last place you ever expected you'd be." She smiled. "Let me see what I can do."

When I got home, the red light on the answering machine was blinking. I had an interview for a teller position at Baytelco Credit Union on Wednesday.

A credit union! Practically a bank! Wait until I told Joseph! Without his and Martha's support, I never would have dared to ask Ms. Hennessey if there was something better out there for me.

Oh God, Joseph. What had the last week been like for him? Had there been a funeral? Had he given a eulogy? Did he go straight back to work, in need of the distraction of physical labor? Or had he locked himself away in the parlor, the shades drawn, smoking the last of his cigarettes? It killed me that I wasn't there. That I couldn't speak with him, sit with him, help him feel his way into this new life.

I said a silent prayer.

*Joseph. I'm here. I'm here.*

I called Newport in the late morning, knowing the house would be empty. I was desperate. I'd called home every night for the past three nights, and every night Benno was mysteriously "out." I wanted to leave a message that required nothing out of him. He could choose to listen to it or, with one punch of a button, erase it. Erase *me*. It was up to him.

The answering machine beeped.

"Benno." I bit back "sweetheart." I tried to remember what it was like to be ten. Double digits. Standing in front of the mirror staring at myself. It was a limbo age. I'd stepped off the shores of girl, yet the rocky coast of teenager was still a thousand miles away. It was easy to feel lost at ten, even in the best of circumstances.

"I'm calling to see how you are. I hope things are going well in school. Grandma tells me you're getting invited to all sorts of parties and the kids have nicknamed you California. That's a hoot! Do you like that? Well, things are boring here without you. Practically every day Anjuli asks me when you're coming back. She's gotten really tall and she babysits for Rhonda after school most days. And Penny, you wouldn't believe how big she is. So I have some good news. I have an interview tomorrow that I'm really excited about. It's at a credit union called Baytelco and it's for a teller position. Can you imagine? Me, a teller? I think I have a good chance. I'm a fast typist, which probably means I'll be fast on an adding machine. Wish me luck, I'll need it!

Okay, well, I guess that's it. I'll call again tomorrow. I'm thinking of you."

I didn't say "I love you": I knew I had to earn back that right. I'd been so cavalier in my *love yous*. Tossing them to him like fastballs, never thinking for a minute he wouldn't be there to catch them.

In the end I realized I'd invested twenty-five dollars in a new suit for nothing—I may have looked the part but I didn't sound it: I'd blown the interview.

1. *Why do you want to become a teller?* Because I've always loved money.
2. *Why did you choose our credit union?* It was chosen for me. You're looking for a teller?
3. *What are your strengths?* I don't give up.
4. *What are your weaknesses?* I don't give up.
5. *What would you do if you saw an employee take fifty dollars out of the register?* It would depend on the circumstances.
6. *Under what circumstances would that be okay?* Um, if he really, really needed the money. Like if he couldn't afford food for his family.
7. *Do you mind repetitious jobs?* Is that a trick question?
8. *No.* So you want me to answer honestly?
9. *Yes.* Yes.
10. *Have you ever been fired?* Um—maybe.
11. *What would your last boss say about you?* Is there a bathroom I could use?

Once I got home, I called Ms. Hennessey at the employment agency. She'd asked me to check in after the interview.

"How'd it go?" she asked in an upbeat voice.

"I'm not sure," I hedged.

"Well, how did you leave things? What did Mr. Ludwig say?"

The branch manager, Mr. Ludwig, was in his mid-thirties. A pleasant guy, but I'd found his crew cut a bit distracting. Whoever cut it hadn't done a great job; they'd left a quarter-inch ridge of hair running down the middle of his scalp. I couldn't stop looking at it and I couldn't stop wondering why a bank manager who obviously made a good income had such an incompetent barber.

"You mean his exact words?"

"Yes."

"He said it had been interesting to meet me."

"Oh," said Ms. Hennessey. "Oh dear."

That afternoon I put in applications at five bars and three restaurants for waitressing positions. Then I called Mike at Seven Hills.

"I'm desperate. Will you give me a reference?"

"That depends. Are ya going to be able to make it in on time for your shifts? 'Cause this is a small town and I have a reputation and I love ya, Lux, and I feel sorry for ya, but there's no way I'm giving you a reference unless you swear to Our Father that you will be on fucking time from this day forward. Do ya swear?"

"I've changed, Mike. I really have. I swear."

"Okay, darlin'." He hung up before I could say thank you.

"Hi, Benno. It's me. I thought you might want an update. I had the interview today and I think it went pretty well. But nothing's set in stone. So I'll just say I'm cautiously optimistic. I hope you had a great day at school. I put a care package in the mail today. Some of your favorite treats and a drawing from Penny. So, listen, I also wanted to tell you I'm sorry. I know you've heard it before, but I'm going to tell you again. I didn't take care of you the way I should have. I'll never forgive myself for that. I don't blame you if you never forgive me either, but I'm sorry. I'm sorry. I'm sorry. Okay. It's Wednesday. *Diff'rent Strokes* is on tonight. I wonder if you'll be watching. I think of you every minute of the day."

I only allowed myself to fall apart at night when I was in bed with the lights off. It was then that despair pinned me to the mattress.

Benno was gone. Martha was dead. Greengage was seventy-three years away.

I was living in a world that didn't approve of me. My father was right: this was the life I had chosen and this was the life I had to inhabit. The problem was that I knew there was another life out there that suited me so much better. A world where I was known, accepted, and loved.

I hadn't wanted to admit this to myself because of the futility of the situation. What good would it do? I had a son who belonged in this world. A *Star Wars*–watching, Burger King–eating, Levi's-wearing, 1980s kid.

I had to find a way to belong here, too.

The next morning the phone rang.

"Hello, is this Ms. Lysander?"

"Speaking." I didn't recognize the voice. Maybe it was one of the restaurant managers.

"This is Mr. Ludwig, from the Baytelco Credit Union."

Mr. Ludwig? Why was he calling me at home? To tell me personally I hadn't gotten the job?

"I have a question for you," he said. "If you wouldn't mind."

"Okay. Sure."

"In the interview. You kept staring at my head. May I ask why?"

Oh God.

"Are you going to ask me if I'd like you to tell me the truth?" he asked.

"Uh—yes."

"Then, yes, I'd like you to tell me the truth."

I tried to think of a lie, but I was too anxious to come up with a good one.

"Okay. Your barber did a shitty job on your hair. There's a ridge, maybe a quarter inch long, running down the middle of your head. It makes you look sort of like a Charonosaurus. From the Late Cretaceous period. It's one of the lesser dinosaurs. You probably haven't heard of it."

He made a strange sound. Something between a bark and a cough. "Are you a paleontologist in your spare time, Ms. Lysander?"

"No, my son is."

I heard the sound of his pen scribbling on paper. "All right then, thank you very much."

"That's it?" I asked.

"That's it. Goodbye, Ms. Lysander."


"So what happened with Baytelco?" asked Rhonda.

"I screwed up the interview."

She made a sad face.

"I should have taken the job selling underwear at Macy's. What was I thinking?" I was too embarrassed to tell Rhonda I'd applied for waitressing jobs all over town.

"You were thinking you wanted to be more than a salesgirl. You wanted a real career. A career with a future. There's nothing wrong with that."

"What's wrong with that is that I'm not qualified. I never went to college, Rhonda. The only thing I'm qualified to do is type, sell bras, or waitress. That's it."

Rhonda gave me a stern look. "Stop feeling sorry for yourself. Call the employment agency back and get them to send you on another interview. There are other credit unions. Other banks. Get on it."


My father answered on the second ring. "Lysander residence."

Since when had he become so formal? He wasn't expecting it to be me. I'd called at 8:00 A.M. his time, 5:00 mine. I wasn't sleeping well these days.

"This is Lux," I said.

"Oh. Your mother is out jogging."

My mother had taken up jogging? "I wasn't calling to talk to Mom."

He paused. "Benno's here but he doesn't want to talk to you."

"How do you know? You didn't ask him."

"Benno, your mother is on the phone!" A few seconds later he said, "No go."

"Okay," I said, trying to keep my voice from wobbling.

Just as I was about to hang up the phone, he said, "He listens, you know. To your messages. He plays them over and over again. Keep calling."


The next morning I got up early, went for a jog myself, stopped at the Golden Gate Bakery, and even though it wasn't Saturday, delivered mooncakes to Doro and Rose, all before ten. When I got home, Ms. Hennessey from the employment agency called to tell me Mr. Ludwig had offered me the job. Apparently two things had impressed Mr. Ludwig quite a bit. My honesty. And my attention to detail.

Well, that was one way to spin my shortcomings.

I started a week from Monday and the salary was $195 a week. "Would that be acceptable?" asked Ms. Hennessey.

I spent the rest of that day in a sort of delirium. I had a job, a good, stable job. One that required me to dress like a grown-up and wear L'eggs pantyhose. Benno wasn't speaking to me, but he was listening to my messages. The world had been closed to me. Now it had opened the door, just an inch.

# LUX

✤

*San Francisco*
*1981*

At precisely 5:45 P.M., Mr. Ludwig asked, "Is anybody short?" He made a concerted effort not to look at me.

I raised my hand. "Sorry."

He sighed; I was the only teller whose drawer was ever short. Mr. Ludwig had been patient with me at first, but I was months into the job now.

"How much?"

"Twenty dollars," I confessed. This was not an inconsequential amount. Tellers kept only five hundred dollars cash in their drawer.

"Can you stay late?" he asked.

Reconciling my drawer would require me to call every member who had made a withdrawal that day and ask them politely if they wouldn't mind checking their wallets to see if I'd accidentally given them too much money. Some people didn't have answering machines and I'd have to wait until they got home from work to reach them.

That was the bad part. The good part was that I knew nearly every member and some of them were like family to me. They'd come in every week and they'd tell me about their kids, their vacations, and their holiday plans. If my drawer was short, inevitably it was right before payday, when people were stressed out and trying to stretch their paychecks. Their roof was leaking and needed to be repaired. Their child had gotten sick and they had an unexpected doctor's bill.

I'd see their tense faces and some unconscious part of me would slip them extra cash, a ten-dollar bill mixed up in the ones, a twenty in the tens.

"Absolutely," I said.

He walked back into his office and I could tell by the way he pulled his shoulders erect that he was annoyed.

My fellow tellers were packing up, putting on their lipstick, and flashing me sympathetic looks. We'd become close. All of us young women, and all, except for me, college graduates. But not for long. This winter I'd start attending night school at City College.

I'd called five members (reached three, left a message at one, no answering machine at the other) when Mr. Ludwig stopped by my desk.

"Any luck?"

"Not yet."

He held his briefcase stiffly by his side. "May I ask you something?"

"Sure."

"Do you enjoy being a teller?"

I enjoyed talking to people and hearing their stories. But the math? The counting? The endless filling out of forms? The constant *tap, tap, tap* of the adding machine? No.

"Of course, why do you ask?"

He cleared his throat. "It's been four months since you started. Is something distracting you?"

Oh God, was he going to fire me? "No, I promise you, nothing. When I come here, I'm fully focused. There's no place I'd rather be."

I'd worked so hard at being a model employee. I was the first to show up in the morning and usually the last to leave. I took on extra work. Covered people's shifts when they were sick. I couldn't lose this job.

"Look, you have to stop being so sloppy. This isn't Monopoly money you're handing out. We're a team here. Your drawer constantly being short affects all of us."

I picked up the phone. "I swear it won't happen again."

At 8:05 P.M. I found the missing money. I'd given it to Mrs. Ortiz, a telephone operator. Her landlord had just raised her rent and she couldn't afford to stay in her apartment; she'd confided to me that afternoon that she didn't know what she was going to do. Mrs. Ortiz promised to return the money tomorrow. I told her it was the bank's mistake, not hers, therefore she was entitled to keep it.

The next day I withdrew twenty dollars out of my own account and gave it to Mr. Ludwig.

I hadn't made the drive out to the Valley of the Moon for six months now. Instead, on the night of the full moon I called Benno. He was the elusive fog, he was the other world I was trying to get back to. Our primary method of communication was my parents' answering machine. It had become a confessional, a place where I poured out my heart. Where I apologized, begged for forgiveness, recited poetry, and told stupid jokes. I played songs I thought he'd like. Blondie's "The Tide Is High." Bruce Springsteen's "Hungry Heart." I talked about San Francisco: the Niners' slump, the Giants' winning streak. Once I called and just said grace. *For what we are about to receive, may the Lord make us truly thankful.* I hoped my mother would play it before dinner and it would seem like I was there in some way.

I spoke to my mother regularly. She filled me in on all the details of Benno's life. He had a friend named Sal who was somewhat of a tomboy. He'd tried out for the basketball team but didn't make it, so my father installed a hoop over the garage so he could practice. It had snowed ten inches, school was canceled, and my mother took Benno and Billy sledding at Fort Adams State Park and afterwards out for hot chocolate and glazed doughnuts. I was happy to hear he was thriving, but heartbroken he was thriving without me.

In February, instead of a valentine, I sent him a copy of *The Lion, the Witch and the Wardrobe*. A week later he called.

"I got the book."

I'd spoken to him only a few times since last summer. He was eleven now and his voice was deeper.

"Oh, good," I said, acting as if we'd just talked yesterday.

"Why did you send it?"

"Because it's one of my favorite books." I was going to tell Benno about Greengage, but I had to do it in precisely the right way. Ease him in gently. Otherwise he'd freak out.

"So what did you think?"

"I liked it okay, but Edmund was totally annoying. And who would want to eat Turkish Delight? I mean, it sounds delicious but it's actually disgusting. Squares of pink jelly."

"Tell me some of your favorite parts," I prompted him.

He paused, thinking. "When it was snowing in the wardrobe. And Lucy saw the light in the middle of the forest and she followed it."

If he gave me the chance, I would show him the light that pierced through the fog and we would follow it together.

"I thought it was cool how they spent years in Narnia, but when they went home only minutes had passed."

"That would be nice, wouldn't it, if it worked that way?" In my case it had been just the opposite. I took a deep breath. "It's good to hear your voice. I'm happy you called and I'm happy you liked the book. Will you call again?" I asked.

"Maybe," he said.


I missed Greengage so much. I thought of it every day, just as I thought of Benno every day, thus I tried to keep both my lives alive. Every night before I went to bed, I recited a litany of their names. *Joseph, Fancy, Magnusson, Friar, Elisabetta,* and on and on. I begged for their forgiveness, too. Nine full moons now that I hadn't shown up. The fog could have been there every month, or for two of those months, or three. Or perhaps it hadn't even been there at all. That was the best-case scenario. I couldn't bear them thinking I'd abandoned them, too.


"They can't just do that. They can't just take the money out of my paycheck without my permission!"

Mr. Templeton stood in front of me, struggling to remain composed. A lineman at Bay Tel, he'd been working for the company for nearly twenty years. He'd taken out a loan to pay for his eldest son's college tuition, and he'd been late on his last two loan payments.

"I'm sorry, Mr. Templeton," I whispered, "but they can."

Mr. Pease, the collector, had begun garnishing his wages. I'd known this was coming. I'd gone to Mr. Pease and begged him to give Mr. Templeton another few months, but Mr. Pease refused. He was a smarmy man who delighted in others' misfortune. Sometimes I thought he approved loans for sport, when he knew the applicant would default.

"Perhaps if you went and spoke to Mr. Pease," I said. "He might be willing to work out a new payment plan."

Mr. Pease would likely do nothing of the sort, but I couldn't bear to leave Mr. Templeton with no hope. I slipped him an extra ten when I counted out his cash. I wouldn't tell Ludwig I was short—I'd simply add a ten of my own to the drawer at lunch.

The time I'd been at Baytelco had done me a lot of good. On Friday nights my colleagues and I had a standing date at Dino's for fried cod and half-price beers. Despite the limitations of my job, and my obsession to get Benno home, I got up in the mornings feeling like I had a purpose. I was part of the working world.

A week later Ludwig called me into his office.

"Shut the door, please."

Oh shit.

"Sit down."

I remained standing. "Please—"

"Sit down, Lux. I have something to discuss with you."

I sat and bowed my head, waiting for the blow.

"Clearly you're not all that happy in your current job."

I'd gotten a Meets Expectations on my six-month performance review along with a list of things to improve.

"That's not true, Mr. Ludwig. There are things I love about it."

"Like what?"

"The people."

"I'm sorry but that's not going to cut it. We have to face facts. You're not a good teller. It just doesn't come naturally to you."

"But I'll make it a good fit. I'll do anything. I'll try harder, I swear."

"There's no need to try harder." His mouth was set in a hard line.

He'd already made up his mind and there was nothing I could do to change it.

I nodded. "How long do I have? Can I stay until the end of the week?"

Would he give me a reference? How would I explain another gap on my résumé to a future employer?

He gave me a confused look. "I'm not letting you go, Lux. You're one of the most hardworking employees I have. I'm promoting you to loan officer. Your customer service numbers are through the roof: members love you. There's a fifty-dollar-per-week salary hike, and the downside, obviously, is that you'll have to work with Pease—"

"Tell me you're not fucking with me, Ludwig." I couldn't believe he'd just put me through this.

His cheeks turned red. "I am not fucking with you."

"Oh my God!" I leapt up from the desk and threw my arms around him.


Being a loan officer was a natural fit for me. I loved hearing people's stories. When applying for a loan, they were always vulnerable, so I made sure to put them at ease. I had a photo of Benno on my desk, a great conversation starter. *Oh, you have children, too! Tell me about them. How old? What are their names? Where do they go to school? Yes, the cost of clothes has skyrocketed. Forget Macy's, Penney's has the best sales.*

Once we'd made a connection, then they'd tell me why they needed the loan. College tuition. A new car. A vacation. To pay for their kid's braces. Their mother's nursing home. A leaky roof. I easily spent an hour with each potential customer, something Mr. Pease was constantly giving me crap about. "Half an hour tops is all it should take," he said. Sometimes I'd see him timing me with a stopwatch. He could tell whether an applicant was a good risk as soon as they approached his desk.

"Just look at their shoes," he told me. "Are they scuffed? Do they need a shine? Do they need resoling? Are they out of fashion? Have they been purchased at Goodwill? The shoes will tell you everything you need to know."

I'd looked at plenty of shoes in my lifetime, and I agreed with Mr. Pease: they revealed quite a bit. *What* they revealed was highly subjective, however. Scuffed to him meant *desperate*. Scuffed to me meant *hard worker*. Out of fashion to him meant *given up, doesn't care about how they look*. Out of fashion to me meant *frugal, knows where they spend every cent*.

When I had to reject somebody for a loan, I made sure I did it in a way that preserved their dignity. I never sent them away without hope. I gave them a list of things they'd have to do in order to get that loan, and many of them reapplied successfully in the future.

Even though we butted heads quite a bit and I'm sure Mr. Pease would have liked to fire me, he couldn't. My customers adored me and made sure to trumpet their satisfaction to the credit union staff. Aluminum-foil-wrapped paper plates covered my desk. Homemade baklava, cookies, biscotti. Frequently I received flowers—not from the florist, but hand-picked bouquets from backyard gardens, the stems wrapped in damp paper towels. I secured my customers' loans. Their kids graduated high school, and gave their valedictorian speeches while flashing perfectly straight teeth.

I was the patron saint of the out-of-date, the invisible, and the left behind.

Benno began calling every Sunday at four. All week long I looked forward to our phone date. I kept a notebook of things I wanted to share with him. Penny's latest escapades. The new bodega that had opened on Divisadero. The plate of empanadas a grateful member had given me.

He in turn played me his favorite songs. Confessed how much he hated his Latin teacher. And asked me about his father. Did he have any extended family on Nelson's side?

I told him that when he was very young I'd hired a private detective and found Nelson's mother in Wisconsin. A little town called Folsom Lake.

"Just his mother? No father? No brothers or sisters?" he asked. Obviously, he'd been fantasizing about having a big family. Aunts and uncles. Cousins.

"That's it, as far as I know."

"Did you call her? Did you tell her about me?"

"Benno, are you sure you want to hear this?"

"Why? Is it bad?"

"I don't think it's what you want to hear, which is why I haven't told you before."

"Well, now you *have* to tell me."

"All right. I wrote to her. I told her about meeting Nelson in San Francisco before he shipped out. I told her what a lovely man he was, how much I enjoyed our time together. I even made copies of the letters he'd sent the first couple of months he was in Vietnam. I wanted to make sure she believed me."

"You have *letters*?"

"Yes, and I'd be happy to let you read them if you'd like. You'll get a real sense of him. He was funny and honest and full of heart, just like you."

Benno went silent.

"I also told Anna King about you. That was the real point of the letter. I enclosed your picture and offered to come to Wisconsin to visit."

"Did we go?"

"No, sweetheart."

"Why?"

"Because she opened the letter, read it, and then taped it back up. Then she wrote *Return to Sender* on the envelope and mailed it back to me."

It took a moment for Benno to take that in. "She didn't want us. She didn't want me!" he cried.

I heard my mother in the background and Benno telling her to go away. He covered the mouthpiece with his hand. A minute later he came back on.

"She didn't know you, Benno. If she'd gotten to know you, she'd have wanted you. Who knows why she wasn't capable of responding? Maybe she was scared. Maybe she thought I was lying. Maybe she was in so much pain from Nelson's death that she couldn't bear the thought of dredging it all back up. I don't know."

He hung up soon after that. What more was there to say? I anguished. Had I done the right thing? Should I have given him a less painful version of the truth? Should I have lied and told him Nelson had no family? But Benno called me the following night, and the night after that, and soon we were speaking daily. Making our way back to one another.

On June 28, 1981, Benno came home. I met him at the airport gate, nervously holding a box of See's chocolate creams. When I saw him coming up the ramp with his shaggy hair and ripped jeans, I threw the box in the trash. This was not a visiting dignitary, this was my son.

"Hey," he said.

"Hey," I said back.

He made no move to hug me and I kept my distance; I'd take my cues from him. We walked through the airport, at least a foot between us.

"The car smells funny," he said when I opened the trunk.

"Like what?"

"I don't know. Rotten apples. Or bananas."

"Oh—sorry."

"No prob." He shook his hair out of his eyes. "Can we stop somewhere and get a milkshake?"

He sucked down his black and tan frappe.

"Good?" I asked.

"You don't know how much I've been craving one of those."

"Awful Awful's didn't cut it?"

"I got sick of them after a while. Too thick. You had to eat them with a spoon."

The adolescent cool dribbled down his face, exposing the boy. "What now?" he asked nervously.

"Home?"

"I guess. Will Anjuli be there?"

"She should be. She's got a regular babysitting gig with Penny."

"Rose and Doro?"

"Of course. Everybody is so excited to see you. To welcome you back."

"You didn't plan some kind of a surprise party, did you?"

I tried to read his face. Should I have? Did he want one? "I thought you'd want to settle in first. But we could have a party this weekend. That's a great idea."

He signaled to the waitress for the check. He looked exactly like my father in that moment; clearly he'd copied the gesture from him.

The waitress put the check face-down on the table, and I went to pick it up. Benno grabbed it first.

"I've got it." He slid his wallet out of his back pocket and extracted a ten-dollar bill.

"Did Grandma give you money?"

"It's my money. I earned it at McGillicutty's. I worked there on weekends. Sweeping up. Doing laundry."

My father made him get a job?

"It was fun. And it was my idea, not Grandpa's."


When we got back in the car, Benno fiddled with the radio dial. He spun past "While You See a Chance" and "Jessie's Girl." He stopped on Elton John's "Tiny Dancer."

"I love this song." He turned his face away from me so I couldn't see him crying.


On the next full moon, I took him with me to the Valley of the Moon. We tramped through the forest. Every ten steps or so, he'd stop and look up at the sky. I hadn't told him anything about Greengage. The only way to explain it was for him to see it. My plan was to bring him here every full moon until we were let in.

We walked up the creek bank. He carried the knapsack and our gear, loping along easily. All I'd told him was that we were going camping overnight. If the fog appeared—well, then I'd tell him everything.

The last couple of weeks had been awkward and sweet as we tried to figure out how to live with each other again. In a way we were strangers. Instead of calling me every night, he called Newport. My parents were a safety net now.

He liked that I had a proper job. Liked that I left the house at eight wearing a dress and heels. He'd become quite independent. In the mornings he'd take off soon after me and make his rounds: to the dog pound to visit the strays, over to Tower Records, skateboarding in Golden Gate Park. In the afternoons he kept Anjuli company while she babysat Penny for Rhonda.

"This way," I said, directing him to the clearing of redwoods.

He put the knapsack down by the fire pit. "You've been here before?"

"A few times."

We hadn't talked yet about where I'd gone. He knew what he'd been told by my parents: I'd joined some commune called Greengage, but he hadn't wanted to know more and so I hadn't offered. What kind of a place could have exerted such a pull that it kept me away from him for a year? It was clearly easier for him not to ask.

"It's like Lapis Lake," he said.

He didn't have to tell me what he meant. The Valley of the Moon had a timeless feel, just like the lake.

"You came here alone?" he asked.

"Yep."

"You were never scared?"

"I was scared, sometimes."

"But you came anyway?"

"Uh-huh."

"Why?"

I shrugged. "Because sometimes fear is the thing that makes you feel most alive."

It had taken Benno a long time to learn to hold his breath underwater. He was five, nearly six, when he finally did it.

"Keep your eyes open," I'd told him, that long-ago day at the Y.

"Don't let go of me," he said.

"I won't. I promise."

We slipped under the surface of the pool together, holding hands. His cheeks bulged. His little legs kicked wildly. He gazed at me with a death stare, and I remember I just kept nodding, silently transmitting *You're okay, you're okay* to him.

Now he said softly, "I want to feel alive."

Five hours later, Benno yelled, "Mom, Mom, wake up!"

The tent was unzipped; Benno was outside. I stepped into the fog. It swirled around me.

"I've never seen fog like this. It's so thick, like a blizzard. You could get totally lost," he said, a look of wonder on his face.

Or found. I took his hand.

# JOSEPH

❧

*Valley of the Moon*
*1907–8*

It is naïve, I know, but you never think the unspeakable thing will happen to you. That is something that happens to other people. That is the accident you watch from the side of the road, unable to tear your eyes away from the mangled body in the street, a stranger, somebody's mother, somebody's daughter, somebody's sister, somebody's wife. *Somebody's* beloved, but not yours. Never yours. That experience has always resided outside of you. You are the observer. That is your birthright. You will go home, whole and intact, having come face-to-face with your mortality from a safe distance, and everything will be heightened for a time. You will be grateful. For the full coal bin in the basement. For the sound of your loved ones in the kitchen at dusk, laughing quietly as you sit in the parlor, an unread book on your lap, feeling vibrantly, exquisitely alive, because you were not the one, you are never the one.

Today, I was the one. And for all the rest of my days, I'd be the one, too. The man who'd lost his wife so brutally and so suddenly there was no time to say goodbye. I recognized the stunned look in my friends' eyes. Astonishment and relief. I didn't blame them. I'd been standing erect on the side of the road all my life, and now it was my turn to kneel in the street. The question wasn't why this had happened. The question was why I ever thought I'd be spared.

Decisions had to be made. Where would Martha be buried? We were only in our forties, we'd never discussed the particulars of our deaths. I knew Martha would not want a religious service and she'd want to be buried somewhere beautiful. I chose the meadow that abutted our backyard. In the spring it would be full of poppies.

At first I was remarkably clear-headed. Driven by tasks. Fancy and Eleanor washed and dressed her body. Magnusson made a beautiful coffin out of walnut.

There was a service. People wept. People paid tribute. I did not. My sorrow was a private thing. Each night I grieved behind the closed bedroom door. I allowed myself one week of this emotional indulgence, then I packed Martha's things away: her clothes, her lotions, her knickknacks. I left virtually nothing in the bedroom but the bed, a side table, and the washstand.

The weeks crept by. The moon waned and waxed. Lux did not come. I was disappointed, but not surprised. She'd accidentally stayed through the Greengage full moon, and while she'd done so, time had most likely accelerated on the other side of the fog. She would have had no idea what she was walking into, how much time would have passed. Even if it was only a month she'd been gone, she'd have to account for where she'd been. Had she told her family about us? Had she given away our secret? I found myself not caring either way.

A second month went by; it passed even more slowly than the first. I'd thought I'd have acclimated to Martha's death by now, but grief was a tapeworm, relentlessly burrowing its way inside me. Every night, when I finally drifted off to sleep, I'd forget she'd died. In my dreams we'd meet and have ordinary conversations that felt utterly real. The calendula was late to flower. What a lovely, surprising August rain. Would I like a biscuit, some jam for my toast, some peppermint tea? And when I woke in the morning, I would have to remember that she was gone.

Greengage had slipped out of time; now I slipped out of time, too, incapable of anchoring myself to anything.

Nine months. Nine full moons. No sign of Lux. I was desperate to see her now, convinced she was the only one who might be able to bring me back, to fasten me again to the hours. The night Martha died was a bullet, lodged in my chest. I hadn't spoken of it to anybody, not to Friar, who'd been there, not to Magnusson, my closest friend, not even to Fancy, who was now eight months pregnant. I knew the bullet needed to be excised, but the only person I felt safe excising it with was Lux. I had to go back to that night, relive it in order to put distance between myself and the experience. Until I did, I'd be stuck in that moment, watching her die over and over again.

*A storm's coming.*

I was haunted by Martha's last words.

On the morning after the tenth full moon, Lux walked into the dining hall with a boy. His skin was a few shades darker than hers, his hair a mass of black curls. He wore a puzzled look on his face. I knew immediately it was Benno.

I felt both happiness and fury at the sight of her. I'd thought I might never see her again. I thought she might have abandoned us, abandoned *me*. I would not have been able to withstand that. Where had she been? Why had she taken so long to come back?

"How long has it been?" asked Lux.

Our positions had been reversed. Normally I was the one asking her how much time had gone by in the outside world.

"Ten months," I said.

Lux winced. "Jesus. Joseph, I'm sorry." She gave me a beseeching look, letting me know there was much to be said but our conversation would have to wait. First things first. This startled young man.

She put her hand on the child's back. "This is Benno. Benno, this is my good friend Joseph."

"Why are you dressed like that?" asked the boy. He looked around the dining hall. "Why are you all dressed like that? What is this place?"

Lux smiled at him. "Welcome to Greengage, sweetheart."

His mouth fell open.

"You didn't tell him where you were bringing him?" I asked.

"Not exactly."

"*This* is where you were, Mom? This place? For a year?"

So a year had passed when she'd stayed through the full moon. Her life must have been in complete and utter disarray when she got home. Now I understood why this boy was standing in front of me. There would have been no way to explain where she'd been other than bringing him here.

"What do you know about us?" I asked him.

"That you're a commune."

"We are not a commune. We're a working farm—"

Lux sighed. "Okay, Benno. I know you're going to find this hard to believe, but you know how in *The Lion, the Witch and the Wardrobe*, Lucy goes through the wardrobe and it's not an ordinary wardrobe, it leads to Narnia? To another world? Well, this is the same. Only the fog is like the wardrobe and Greengage is what's on the other side. Only Greengage isn't really another world. It's our world, just—"

Brevity had never been Lux's strong suit. "Young man, it's 1908 here. Nineteen seventy-nine—"

"It's 1981 back home, Joseph," Lux said, shrugging, as if to soften the blow.

Nineteen eighty-one? Another two years had passed? Was there anything that I could count on?

Benno looked from me to his mother and back to me again. "Why is it only 1908?"

"Because we got stuck here," I said.

"Why?"

"I have no idea."

"Well, do you like being stuck?"

"No, we don't like being stuck."

"Then why don't you leave?" he asked.

My head pulsed, the beginning of a migraine. The sun was far too bright.

"You'll have to pardon me. I'm not feeling well at the moment." I could barely converse about normal things like crops and weather, never mind be expected to indoctrinate another stranger into our situation in Greengage.

"Ask Fancy. She'll explain everything," I said.

I caught my sister's eye; she nodded, got up from the table, and approached us.

"She's pregnant!" gasped Lux. "Fancy's pregnant?"

I left the dining hall. A few minutes later Lux came running after me.

"I had no choice. I knew he wouldn't believe it until he saw it," she said.

All I wanted was to retreat back to the house. I'd been waiting for months. I needed her to attend to me. I'd forgotten she'd have needs as well.

"Joseph, please. I never stopped thinking about you, about Greengage, but I couldn't return. Benno was living with my parents in Newport. It was so terrible. It took me a year to get him back. He's just come home and we came straight here. You can trust him. He won't tell anybody about you, I swear."

"This is not some sideshow. We are not animals in a zoo."

Her face collapsed, and even though I felt guilty—Lux was the last person in the world who would exploit us—I couldn't control my emotions.

"I would never—you've never . . . ," she stammered.

"Go back to your son," I said harshly.

But she didn't have to go back. Fancy brought him to us. So I was forced to listen as Lux told Benno our story.

She began on April 18, 1906, the morning of the earthquake. She told him how the wall of fog had encircled us. She explained in detail about the full moon nights. How time sped up. And she ended with her fatal mistake, accidentally staying through the full moon.

"I was on my way back to you. I was leaving the night before the full moon. I thought I had plenty of time," she said to Benno. "But I didn't."

I registered Lux's omission. She hadn't used Martha's death as an excuse. Once again, I was overcome with guilt. I wasn't fit to be in public.

"I'm very glad you're finally here," said Fancy, holding out a hand to Benno. "We've been waiting for you a long time."

"You have?" The boy's cheeks grew pink with pleasure.

Thank God for my sister, doing my job, taking over for me, making the boy feel welcome.

"Certainly. We knew your mother was bringing you, we just didn't know when. We've got your bedroom all set up," she said.

Lux flashed Fancy a grateful smile.

"I have a bedroom?" Benno asked.

"Of course. But I imagine you're hungry. Shall we get a bite at the dining hall before I take you to the house?"

"What kind of food do you have at the dining hall?"

"Pancakes. Bacon. Cornbread. If you're lucky, some of yesterday's leftover rhubarb pie."

Fancy led Benno back across the meadow.

# LUX

❦

I was torn. Should I go with Joseph or should I stay with Benno? Benno was putting on a good face as Fancy brought him from table to table, introducing him, but I knew he must be stunned. I'd just told him he'd traveled back to 1908. What must he be thinking?

"Go," said Joseph, making the decision for me.

"Are you sure? You're okay?"

"It didn't happen yesterday. It's been ten months, Lux," he snapped. "How long are you here for?"

Oh God, he was furious. In the years that I'd known him, I'd seen him worried, anxious, despairing, but never enraged. Was I responsible for this? Had I failed him?

"How long?" he repeated.

"Just the afternoon."

Should I have tried to make it back to Greengage? For a brief check-in, just to let him know I was there, I was thinking about him, I hadn't forgotten about him?

He gave me a clipped nod.

"Can we talk later?" I asked. "After Benno's settled?"

He shrugged. And that shrug—his attempt to look as if he couldn't care less—told me everything. How bottomless his grief. How broken he still was.

"I stayed away too long," I said.

He looked at me, his eyes pooling. "I am—" He couldn't finish the sentence.

"I know," I whispered. "I know. Me too."

I trailed Fancy as she showed Benno around the kitchen and got him a plate piled high with his favorite breakfast foods. The dining hall quickly emptied out.

"Where are they all going?" asked Benno.

"To work," said Fancy.

"What kind of work?"

"They have all sorts of different crews, Benno," I explained. "Kitchen, garden, animals, building, fields. That's just some of them. You can choose wherever you want to work."

"Come be on my crew," said Fancy. "Entertainment." She winked at him. "It's the best crew. You don't have to get all mucky. I'm thinking about mounting a play. *Much Ado About Nothing*. Yes, I know Shakespeare is ambitious, but I'm certain we will rise to the occasion. You would make a lovely Don Pedro, Benno, by the way. You're a little young, but I think you could pull it off. With the proper costume you'd be rather dashing."

"How far along are you?" I asked Fancy.

"Eight months."

"And how are you feeling?"

She beamed. "Good. Better than good, actually." Her hands drifted down to her belly.

"I'm so happy for you!" I cried.

Fancy nodded at me and swayed back and forth, as if listening to some internal music.

She smiled at Benno. "My, you are a handsome young man. Look at that face. So expressive. Tailor made for the stage. So. Will you join my crew?"

"I don't think we'll be here that long," I said.

Fancy pouted.

"Please, Mom. Can we stay? Just for a while," Benno pleaded.

If I had any misgivings about him being able to handle the reality of Greengage, they were rapidly diminishing. He looked positively gleeful as he shoveled a big piece of pancake into his mouth. I remembered what it was like to be his age. How I courted impossibility, as if it were only a matter of seducing it, convincing it to come out of hiding and reveal itself to me. It was the same for Benno. He had a satisfied, almost smug look on his face, as if something had been resolved.

"Benno, do you have any questions?" I asked.

Déjà vu. That long-ago day at the airport. *Mama, I'm busy. Doing what? Leaving.*

He shook his head.

"Let the poor boy eat," said Fancy.

After breakfast, Fancy and I brought Benno back to the house and gave him a quick tour. Then Fancy passed him off to Magnusson, who immediately put him on a horse. We sat on the porch while they trotted by, Benno's expression shifting between terror and joy as he struggled to keep his seat.

"Isn't that horse too big for him?"

"A baby could ride Apollo," said Fancy.

"Where are they going?"

"Who knows? Up to the springhouse? Lars has been doing maintenance up there all week."

"Should I go with them?"

"Whatever for?"

"I'm just—shouldn't I be there when Benno experiences all this for the first time? See what he sees? See how he reacts?"

"How do you think he'll react?"

"I don't know. I hope it's a positive experience for him."

"What was it like for you?"

"Good. Centering."

"Do you feel that way at home?"

"Sometimes."

I gazed out at the lawn. Martha's flower clock was completed— every section planted.

"You finished. You found the flower for the eleventh section," I said.

"Joseph found it. It's sweet alyssum," she said.

I could smell it even from the porch. Its scent was like newly mown hay mixed with honey.

"And it works? Each flower opens on the hour?"

"I guess. To be honest, I don't spend a lot of time watching it. It reminds me too much of Martha."

"So how have these months been for you?" I asked gently.

"Oh, Lux. It's still impossible to believe that Martha's not coming back. I keep expecting to come round a corner and hear her voice." Fancy flinched and grabbed my hand. "Golly, she just kicked. Feel." She pressed my palm to her belly, which rippled beneath my fingers.

She groaned. "I'm scared to death of giving birth. I told Friar he should knock me out. I just want to wake up when it's over. Is that terrible? Does that make me a terrible mother?"

"No. I had anesthesia when Benno was born."

"You did?"

"Yep. And he turned out just fine."

Fancy turned to me. "I don't know if Joseph's going to get past this, Lux. He won't speak about it. About Martha. I can barely get him out of the house. It's like he's just given up. And we need him. I need him. I need my brother."

"I think you just have to give him some time," I said.

"I know. I know I do."

"But you're afraid."

"Yes."

"What are you afraid of?"

"That I've lost him—that we've lost him for good. Maybe you being here will help," she said.


Everything about Greengage fascinated Benno: the lanterns, the outhouses, Magnusson's workshop, the one-room schoolhouse with the Walt Whitman quote painted on the wall. I was shocked at how nonchalantly he took it all in.

"Benno, isn't this weird for you?"

"Nah."

"You just believe all this? The fog? That it's 1908 here? Just like that?"

I expected him to test things. Demand proof, as I had when I first came.

"I thought you'd be happy," he said to me. "Isn't this what you wanted? For me to see where you'd disappeared to for a year?"

That stung. "A night, Benno. I stayed one extra night here in Greengage."

His eyes narrowed. "But that one night was a year in San Francisco."

"I know. I'm sorry, Benno. It was so hideous, not being able to explain. Having you think I'd just abandoned you."

"So why didn't you tell me?"

I sighed. "I wanted to. I tried, sort of. When I came to Newport."

He shook his head. "You didn't try very hard."

"You're right," I said. "I guess—I was afraid."

"To share this with me?" He looked wounded.

"No, sweetheart. I was afraid of what this place would ask of you."

"What will it ask of me?"

"It will ask you to split yourself in two. Because now that you know about Greengage, you'll always live a sort of double life. And there's no way to unknow it, no way to take it back. You'll reside in two worlds now. Half past. Half future. That's your new life. *Our* new life."

"And that's a bad thing?"

"I won't lie. Often, it's a difficult thing," I said. "But incredible."

"Benno!" a girl's voice cried out.

Benno looked impatiently over my shoulder.

Miss Russell had introduced Benno to a group of kids his age, and now they were all going swimming. It was barely spring. The creek must be freezing, but they were children, they didn't care.

"Mom, can we spend the night? Please? I have a bedroom and everything."

It was Saturday and I had the weekend off—potentially we could.
"I'll think about it."

He sprinted off.


I finally caught up with Joseph in the parlor just before dinner. He
stared at me vacantly.

"I brought you something," I said. "It's called a Walkman."

Joseph examined the black and silver square, turned it over in his
hands.

"The batteries will last for a while. At least through the month.
Provided you don't listen to it nonstop."

I popped it open and slid in a cassette of the Beatles' greatest hits
from 1967 to 1970. I handed him the headphones and showed him
how to put them on.

"Ready?" I asked.

He nodded and I pressed Play. I'd cued the tape up to "Let It Be."
The music leaked out of the headphones—I listened alongside him.

When the song ended and he slid off the headphones, tears were
streaming down both our faces.

"I can't—" he said to me, "get out of that goddamned room."

I knew exactly the room he was talking about.

"I can help you," I said.

He cried out and bent over, hiding his face from me, a hank of his
thick, black hair falling over his forehead, like an unruly schoolboy.
My heart swelled with tenderness for him, for the motherless child he
once was.

"Let me help you," I whispered, sitting beside him.

He didn't push me away, so I put an arm around his heaving shoulders as the sounds of his agonized sobs filled the parlor. We time-
traveled back to that night. Back to the room in which Martha had
died, was still dying for him.

He knelt on the floor of that room, riding waves of shock. Unable
to absorb what was happening. Martha's body, lying still and rigid on
the bed.

"She's gone?" he croaked.

"Yes."

"It happened? The worst has happened?"

"The worst has happened," I confirmed.

Saying the unsayable was a sort of magic. An incantation. It lifted the binding spell and released him. He got himself up from the floor of that room. He walked backward until he was standing in the doorway next to me.

I stood there with him for a long time, until he was able to look upon the scene not without emotion, but without being undone by it.

Time spun forward again. We floated out of that room and into this one.

He looked up at me, his eyes red and swollen. "The worst has happened to you, too."

It had. I'd lost Benno.

"Let me help you," he said.

I hadn't admitted even to myself how truly horrendous this past year had been for me. I'd screwed up so royally that I didn't deserve to think about my own feelings. I'd left them in that examination room, too, the moment Friar told me it was past midnight and the reality of what I'd done began to sink in. I'd been stuck in that room as well. I needed Joseph to rescue me as much as he needed me to rescue him. Each of us held the power to release the other. To shove the other back into the present. Back to life.

"Tell me everything," he said.

# JOSEPH

❦

The boy clattered down the stairs early in the morning. I'd been up for an hour already and was on my second cup of mint tea. He ran into the kitchen, banging into a chair with his hip.

"Oh Jesus, I'm sorry. I didn't think anybody else would be up."

He sounded exactly like his mother. Jesus this. Jesus that.

"Do you want a cup of tea?"

"Do you have any hot chocolate?"

"This is not a restaurant."

"Tea would be great," he amended.

"Teacups are in the cupboard, kettle on the stove." I wasn't about to wait on an eleven-year-old.

"That's all right. I don't really like tea." He sat across from me at the table, his hands tucked under his thighs. "So, you're the leader?"

"Everybody here has a job. Everybody is the leader of something."

"But you're the leader of everything."

"Why do you think that?"

"Because everybody looks to you."

I took a sip of my tea.

"How long has my mother been coming here?"

"That depends. If you're talking our time, she's been coming here for a year and a half. If you're talking your time, she's been coming since 1975."

"I was only five in 1975," he gasped.

"Yes, and as I remember it, the first time she came you'd just gone to Newport to spend some time with your grandparents. So it wasn't as if she up and left you." I felt the need to defend Lux.

He chewed on his lip. The wounds of his abandonment were fresh, right below the surface.

"What did you think when she didn't come back?" I asked.

His face clouded over. "Sometimes I thought she was dead. Sometimes I thought she'd just moved somewhere else. Got bored with life, with me. Most of the time I just tried not to think about it."

I could see the boy was fighting back tears.

"Your mother has been coming to Greengage for six years now. Every time I've seen her, all she talks about is you. What you're doing. What things you're interested in. She never would have intentionally left you."

"But how could she have missed the full moon?" he cried. "How could she have let that happen?"

He was a handsome boy. He and Lux had the same full mouth; it was quite disconcerting.

"She hasn't told you everything about that night."

He visibly startled. He was not expecting me to be so candid.

"I knew it!" he cried.

"What do you know?"

"That she lied to me."

"She didn't lie. She just didn't tell you the whole story."

"Why not?"

"Because she probably felt it wasn't her story to tell."

Benno pressed his lips together in frustration.

"And she didn't want to use what happened as an excuse."

"Jesus. What happened? Tell me already."

I took a breath. "My wife, Martha, died."

Talking with Benno, I was crossing some border, making good on a promise I'd made to Lux last night to rejoin the world.

"If you want to blame anybody, you should blame me. I should have ensured she left. But she couldn't bear to leave, not until she knew Martha was all right."

"But she wasn't all right."

"No. She died just after midnight."

"I'm really sorry," he said.

"Thank you."

He gulped. "That's terrible."

"Yes, it is. It was."

A not uncomfortable silence ensued between us.

"Do you have kids?" he asked.

"No."

"I figured."

"Why?"

"Because you treat me like an adult."

"You are almost an adult."

"Not where I live."

"From what your mother has told me, it seems children are trapped in childhood long past the time they should be in 1981."

Benno exhaled shakily. "My father was a soldier. He was killed in the Vietnam War."

"Yes. Your mother said."

"I have a grandmother I've never met. She doesn't want anything to do with us. With me."

"Then she's a damnable idiot."

He smiled shyly. The hours drew me back into their arms.

# LUX

❦

*San Francisco*
*1981*

I interrogated Benno on the way home.

"So what do you think?"

"About what?"

"Greengage!"

"I think it's cool."

"You think it's cool."

"Yeah."

"That's it—cool?"

"What do you want me to say?"

I wanted him to tell me he forgave me. Tell me he understood now why I'd been gone for a year. And to share in my love of the place.

"Can you please stop staring at me and look at the road while you're driving?"

"You seem different."

He sighed.

"I'm not kidding. Going through the fog changed you. It does that." I took a quick glance at him. "You look older."

"Stop it, Mom," he said, but I could tell he was pleased at the "older" part of my comment.

He was silent until we went over the Golden Gate Bridge. Then he hugged his knees to his chest and said, "I feel bigger. Like there's more room inside me."

"Really? That's an interesting way to put it. What else?"

"I don't know. Peaceful, I guess."

I felt peaceful, too, although I knew the high wouldn't last. I'd crash tonight and tomorrow morning I'd have to drag myself to work. I paid for my visits. Every time I went, it was a little harder to return to the modern world.

That weekend, all the occupants of 428 Elizabeth Street caravanned to Stinson Beach. It turned into an impromptu welcome-back party for Benno. He played host, setting up the volleyball net. He distributed ham sandwiches and made sure everybody got an even share of strawberries, the last good ones of the summer.

The peacefulness he'd described to me in the car *had* lasted. He was still riding a long, slow wave of contentment.

"Throw the Frisbee to me, Penny!" he yelled.

Penny ran to him with the Frisbee and slammed it into his stomach, then grabbed him around the thighs, toppling him into the sand. He took her down with him and she shrieked with delight.

"I said throw it to me, not bash it into me!"

She clung to him even tighter.

"That's it. He's officially ruined her. She's never going to get over him," said Rhonda.

"Rhonda, Penny is four."

"So? She's in love with him."

"She's a baby. She's too young to be in love."

"You have no idea what it's like with girls. She may as well be fifteen."

Benno jumped up, grabbed Penny by the hands, and swung her in a circle.

"I should have listened to you and brought him to Greengage years ago. He wants to go back on the next full moon," I said.

"What day is it on?"

"A Tuesday."

"How are you going to manage that with his school?"

"I have no idea. How many days a month can you miss before you become truant?"

"I can't believe you're asking me that question."

"Well, he's not going to let me go alone."

And honestly, I didn't want to go alone anymore. Going without him was out of the question.

"Goddamn, what I wouldn't do for a beer." Rhonda was pregnant with her second child.

I handed her my can of PBR. "A sip won't kill you."

She took a furtive sip and sighed. "Even warm, it's the nectar of the gods."

"I saw that!" yelled Ginger. He ran across the sand to our blanket. "How dare you ply my pregnant wife with alcohol?"

"She begged me."

"It's true, I begged her," said Rhonda.

"You are a very bad influence," said Ginger. "Give me that beer."

I handed it to him and he drained it. "Benno, my boy!" he shouted, his other hand raised. Benno leapt into the air and the yellow Frisbee arced across the sky.

School started and we fell back into our regular routines. I never realized this was a privilege, to know what the day would bring. To wake every morning, sit up in bed, look through my open door across the living room and see Benno, bleary-eyed and pajama-bottomed, searching for a clean shirt in his dresser drawer.

Before, this might have made me feel trapped. The tedium. The same thing every day. Now that I'd introduced Benno to Greengage, my life expanded. Here on the other side of the fog, time was pliable and elastic. It bulged and kicked, like Fancy's unborn child. Possibility and hope bled into my world, *our* worlds. Benno and I were in on it together. This changed everything.

On the full moon we'd leave right after I finished work. We'd stop at McDonald's before getting on the highway, and Benno would do his homework in the car. After that I'd usually lose him to the Walkman. Van Halen or the Stones. He'd stare out the window, his fingers tapping the beat out on his thighs, and I'd listen to public radio, collecting the news of the day for Joseph. Finally we'd pull into the lot of Jack London State Park, get our backpacks out of the car, and make the trek to our campsite. I'd set up the tent. He'd start the fire. At five in the morning we'd wake, pack everything up in the car, and drive back to San Francisco, just in time to get him to school.

We performed this ritual for four months before the fog returned.

# JOSEPH

❦

*Valley of the Moon*
*1908*

I didn't realize how I'd been waiting for their arrival and how slowly the weeks had passed, until I saw them standing in the meadow.

"How long has it been?" I called out to Lux when they drew near.

"Four months."

Benno lifted his chin at me and held up a red package. "Brought you some Skittles."

"Candy," translated Lux.

Benno tore open the package, poured a few into his palm, and offered them to me. I chose the least offensively colored piece and popped it into my mouth. I spat it out immediately.

"What's wrong?" he asked.

"It's appallingly sour."

"They're supposed to be sour. That's the point," he said.

He bobbed up and down, twitchy. He seemed pent up, as if he'd been counting the days until he and his mother would be let back into Greengage. This pleased me, to know they'd been waiting anxiously on the other side of the fog as well.

"What should we do now?" he asked me.

"Are you hungry?"

"Not really."

"Thirsty?"

"No."

"Well, then, would you like to go on a ramble?"

"What's a ramble?"

"It's a stroll. A walk."

"Where?"

"Wherever our feet take us. That's the point of a ramble. You don't have a destination."

"All right. Yeah. Cool, man."

"Fancy?" Lux inquired.

I nodded. "A girl. Gennie. She arrived last week."

Lux clapped her hands and squealed. "Everybody healthy? How's Fancy holding up?"

"Both mother and child are fine."

"Magnusson?"

"He's fine, too."

She smiled proudly. "My God. You're an uncle! How does it feel?"

It felt unnatural, to be honest. I had virtually no experience with infants. Benno, impatient, shook his bag of Skittles in an effort to regain my attention.

"I assume you won't be joining us? You'll want to go straight to Fancy?" I said to Lux.

"Yes! I'm dying to get my hands on that baby!"

Lux ran toward the house, her full pack bouncing on her back. She never came empty-handed.

"She loves babies," said Benno. "She can't get enough of Penny."

Penny was Rhonda's daughter: Lux had told me all about her. Lux was a surrogate aunt to Penny just as Rhonda was a surrogate aunt to Benno, part of the makeshift family she'd built for herself over the years.

"Let's go," I said to Benno.

His head swiveled from left to right as we walked. The boy took in everything with a starved expression on his face.

"Was it strange when you went back home last month?" I asked.

"What do you mean—strange?"

"Was it difficult to comprehend what had happened? Where you'd been?"

He stuffed his hands in his pockets. "Sort of. But not really. I didn't think about it. I mean, I didn't question it too much. You're here. You're a reality. I didn't dream you all up."

We walked past the vegetable garden. The gardeners were on their knees, jabbing tiny onion bulbs deep into the ground.

"They have hundreds to plant," I said. "They'll need to last us for an entire year."

"What's the date here?" he asked.

"April 19th."

"The day after the earthquake."

Yes, yesterday had been the two-year anniversary. I'd thought of that briefly at breakfast. Should I stand up and say something? Acknowledge it? In the end I'd decided against it. The dining room had been filled with happy chatter. People didn't need to be reminded.

I led Benno past the garden toward the chicken coop. I thought we might gather some eggs.

"My mom worries about you," said Benno.

"Does she?"

"Yeah. You're always on her mind. She gets this faraway look in her eyes and when that happens I know she's thinking about you."

"About Greengage."

"No, you. Jesus, that chicken house stinks. You're not going to make me go in there, are you?"

I steered him in the opposite direction. "Is your mother doing well?"

"She got a really good job. She's a loan officer at a credit union."

Lux had shared this news with me last time she was here. "Is she enjoying it?"

"I think so." He looked at me, then looked away. "I don't understand. Why don't you want anybody to know about Greengage? There could be people who could help you get through the fog, help you get back."

"There's nobody that can help us, and besides, it's too late for that. We've been gone for seventy-three years. There's no *back* to get back to."

A wagon rumbled past. The field crew. They held up their hands in greeting.

"So you've just given up," he said.

"No, we've accepted our fate."

He gave me a perplexed look. "I know that sounds good and all, like what you should say as a grown-up, but I think it's bullshit. You could come back. You could adapt. You just don't want to."

"That's ridiculous. Why wouldn't we want to?"

"Because you're scared."

Was I? Thanks to Lux, I'd grown lazy, used to having the future spoon-fed to me. Delivered verbally, or through a magazine or newspaper, or the Walkman. Safe in my parlor, I sat and slowly absorbed the news. But actually being there, on the frontlines of the modern world—that was something I felt quite ambivalent about. Perhaps the boy was right.

"This way," I said.

"Where are you taking me?"

"Back to the house."

"Back to the house. Why, did I do something wrong?"

"No. I just have the sudden urge to see my niece."

That was not a lie. But mostly I realized I wanted to see Lux's reaction to my niece. How she looked when she met Gennie—the proper way one should look when meeting the baby of somebody you loved for the first time.

Benno made a face. "Does the baby do anything besides sleep and drool and spit up?"

"Not that I've seen."

He groaned.

"I'll drop you off at the schoolhouse."

He brightened.

"But you must promise to sit in the back quietly. You mustn't disturb the lesson."

He nodded, though we both knew his arrival would indeed disturb the lesson. His role was to deliver the future to the younger generation, via his clothing (a black and pink harlequin print shirt), his expressions (*Cool, man*) and sweets (Skittles). They'd enjoy the candy, of that I was certain.

---

Lux had brought Gennie a stuffed elephant and something called a lightsaber.

"The Force is strong with this one," she said. She gazed down at Gennie in her crib. "God, she's so long."

"Twenty-three inches," said Magnusson.

The day after she'd been born, he'd taken his daughter to the woodshop and measured her himself. Of course Gennie would be tall; Magnusson was a giant.

"And you're all living here in the house?" Lux asked. "That's so cozy."

Yes, Magnusson and Fancy had temporarily moved into the wing after Martha had died. I'd tried to convince Magnusson they should live in one of the cottages (surely they wanted more privacy), but Fancy wouldn't hear of it.

"She wants her uncle," said Fancy, handing a bundled-up Gennie to me.

I held her for a moment, an awkward smile on my face. The thumbprint of her fontanel, her green eyes, her snow-blond hair, made me distinctly uncomfortable. She was as alien to me as one of Nardo's piglets.

"Here." I slid the baby into Lux's arms.

Lux was a complete natural. She expertly held Gennie in the crook of her arm, shifted her hip to the side, and began swaying back and forth. I unwittingly began moving in time to her rhythm.

"I'd forgotten about their little starfish hands," Lux said.

"Joseph—are you *dancing*?" asked Fancy, smirking.

For God's sakes. Could I get away with nothing? "I'm going to the dining hall."

"Bring me back something sweet, I'm starving," said Fancy. "This little one is eating me out of house and home."

This was entirely too much information. The other day I'd stumbled upon Fancy breastfeeding in the kitchen. Yes, she was covered, a blanket shielding her, but I could still hear what was going on. And then my sister tried to carry on a normal conversation with me. But the suckling! The gurgling! She'd seen my stricken look and admonished me.

"This is not Victorian England. Nor do I have the luxury of a wet nurse, Joseph."

"But—"

"But what?"

"You look like you're enjoying it."

She'd laughed then. "Why shouldn't I enjoy it? I'm feeding my daughter, Joseph."

"Hold on, I'll go with you," said Lux. She carefully handed the baby back to Fancy.

Lux shivered. It was a cool day. I took off my jumper and handed it to her and she pressed it to her nose.

"It smells like you." She put it on; it came nearly to her knees. We walked across the yard and I watched as she took stock of Martha's gardens.

"The flower clock—I can't believe you made it work. It's beautiful."

"I'm not sure it's really working," I said. The clock required constant attention. Some plant was always on the verge of dying. And whether the blooms opened or closed exactly on the hour was anybody's guess. I couldn't bring myself to watch it, or time it. I'd only finished it as a tribute to Martha.

"I brought you a greengage seedling," Lux said nervously. "Please don't be mad at me. Now, I know you said they're notoriously hard to grow and there's probably a perfectly good reason why you named this place Greengage Farm and there are no greengage trees on the property, but I just thought maybe—"

I held up my hand, stopping her. "You brought me a greengage plum seedling."

Two pink spots appeared on her cheeks. "Yes. Yes, I did."

"Really?"

She bit her lip.

"That does me no good."

"Fine, I'll take it back with me. I knew I shouldn't have—"

"Because greengages can't pollinate themselves. In order for the tree to bear fruit, I'll need at least two other seedlings, different varieties, maybe the Monsieur, and the Royale de Montauban."

"You want to keep it?"

She looked flustered and happy and I felt a piercing stab of gratitude for her. For knowing what I needed well before I knew and just getting it for me.

"It's time we grew into our name," I said.

We walked past the schoolhouse. I heard the children singing "Meet Me in St. Louis." We caught a glimpse of Benno sitting in the back of the classroom, leaning forward, trying to learn the words to the song.

"Do they ever sing anything else?" asked Lux.

She was right. Miss Russell had a tiny repertoire of songs: "Meet Me in St. Louis," "By the Old Oak Tree," and "Tippecanoe and Tyler Too."

"Benno should teach them some modern stuff." She popped up on her toes and then did a little spin. "Michael Jackson. Probably not your style."

We made our way across the meadow toward the dining hall.

"So what's it like for you, having a new baby in the house?" she asked.

"She wakes every morning at two and at five."

Lux laughed. "God, I don't miss that, I have to say. Infant time. The hours warp when there's a baby around."

"How are you doing?" she asked a moment later, meaning *How are you doing about Martha?*

I'd gotten to the point where Martha was dead in my dreams. I didn't have to wake up anymore and remember she was gone. I knew this was a good thing, a sign of my moving on, but I missed the dark hours of the night when my unconscious gave me a brief holiday, when all was as it had been before.

"It's a little easier every day."

"I miss her so much," she said. "I've tried to live the way she encouraged me to. Fully inhabiting my life. Both lives. Here and at home."

Something was changing between us. Now we could conduct our nighttime talks in the bright light of day. There was no clearing of throats. No small talk. Was it because of her son? *Here,* she said. *This is my life. Take him. Take us.*

"Is it working?"

She nodded. "Bringing Benno here makes that possible. I don't know why I didn't figure that out sooner. Thank you for making him feel so welcome."

We approached the dining hall. The smell of baked potatoes. Roasted chicken. Rosemary and thyme. My stomach growled. My appetite had returned.

"I'm only sorry Martha didn't get to meet him," I said.

"You are? *Really?*" said Lux.

"She would have loved him," I said.

# LUX

❖

That night, just before midnight, Joseph and I met on the porch. He needed a haircut. His chin was stubbled, he hadn't shaved in days. He had a sort of rakish look about him. Not unkempt, but loosened up.

"I did not come from money," he said.

Recently he'd started launching into conversations in the middle of them, acting as if we'd been talking for hours. I guess it was the nature of our friendship, with month-long interruptions on his end and even longer ones on mine. We couldn't afford to ease into it every time we picked back up.

"My mother was a scullery maid and my father was the gardener's son. He was desperate to make something of himself, to leave his past behind."

He lit a cigarette. Pulled on it, his eyes drawn nearly shut, then wordlessly handed it to me.

"He did what he had to do. He weaseled, he finagled, he hustled. He worked from dawn until midnight. He failed and he failed and he failed again, but he never stopped demanding he be let in to the hallowed halls of the moneyed class. Finally a door opened. He made a fortune in textiles."

"Good for him," I said.

"No, it wasn't. He was a royal son of a bitch, to his colleagues, his employees, and to us. After my mother died, he sent me to boarding school. He wanted nothing to do with me."

He wagged his fingers impatiently. I took a quick drag and gave the cigarette back to him.

"He never met Martha, did not attend my wedding. Never visited Greengage. He spent his whole damn life trying to buy his way into a higher class. And for what? He probably died alone in that enormous goddamned mansion."

"What was his name?"

He took another drag. "Edward." He flicked the ashes over the railing into the dirt. "I've been thinking a lot about him lately. I've spent years resenting him."

So, we were alike in this way.

My father came from nothing, too; he'd worked his way up and out of his circumstances. But unlike Joseph's father, he'd never left his past behind. Every summer at Lapis Lake he embraced it; it was the foundation upon which he built his life.

"And now I'm done," said Joseph.

"You're done?"

"Hating him. It's what Martha would have wanted. Maybe we would have eventually reconciled. Maybe when his children vanished off the face of the earth, he changed. Maybe he spent the rest of his years looking for us. I'd like to think that he did."

My heart hammered with guilt at the knowledge that nobody had looked for him or for Fancy. There was no record they'd ever existed.

"I'm nearly the same age he was when I last saw him. How can that be? Christ." He handed me back the cigarette. "I feel sorry for him. He must have been such a lonely bastard."

I knew that kind of loneliness. I'd lived it until I found Greengage.

"We have to leave the day after tomorrow," I said.

"Oh?"

He was so hard to read. Was he just being polite? Or was he masking his disappointment?

"It's a long weekend. Benno doesn't have school tomorrow, but he does on Tuesday. I can't have him missing school. People will get suspicious."

"And there's your job," he said.

"Yes, my job." There was no way to call in sick from Greengage.

"A loan officer," he chuckled.

"What's so funny about that?"

"Do you remember the look on your face when I suggested you become a banker?"

"I am not a banker," I huffed.

"You're a banker."

"I'm the complete opposite of a banker. I work at a credit union. I work for the people, not Wall Street."

He grinned.

"I don't know why you think this is funny."

"It's just—you remind me of somebody," he said.

"Martha?"

"No, not Martha."

"Fancy?"

He sighed. "You remind me of my mother, Lux. And trust me, that is a compliment. Before my father had her committed, she was just like you. Full of ideas, enthusiasm, gumption, pluck."

His mother was committed? By his father? To an institution? Why hadn't he told me this before?

"Was your mother emotionally unstable?"

"No. At least she wasn't before she was institutionalized."

"You told me your mother killed herself."

"That's right."

"She killed herself after your father had her committed? At the institution?"

"No, *after* she came home from the institution."

"She came home. So she got better?"

"No," he said impatiently, probably regretting now that he'd told me. "After she came home, she changed. It was like watching somebody slowly drowning. And I—I couldn't do anything to pull her back up to the surface. None of us could. My father arranged to have her committed once again. And on the night before she was due to go back, she killed herself."

"Oh, Joseph," I gasped.

He waved his hand at me. "Sending your wife away wasn't such an uncommon thing back then. Women—lively, outspoken women whose husbands couldn't control them, or just didn't like them, or wanted to shut them up—were institutionalized. An easy, sterile solution. Just put them away for a while."

"My God. That's unspeakably horrible."

"That's the world I grew up in. You can see why I was so anxious to leave it."

This new information required me to recalibrate. Here was the last big puzzle piece sliding into place. Now Greengage made total sense. Joseph's utter devotion to it. To the memory of his mother.

"She would have liked you," he said. "She would have tried to recruit you for one of her causes."

"What were her causes?"

"Women's rights. Workers' rights. Land preservation. The list is endless. Anything that needed fighting for."

"Did that include you? And Fancy?"

"Yes, me and Fancy, until she wasn't able to. Gennie is named after her."

"Really? I didn't know that. That's such a lovely tribute."

"Gennie looks like her, too. They have the same eyes."

"Is that difficult for you?" I asked. "Their similarities? Being reminded of her?"

He smiled. "On the contrary. It makes me very happy. It's as if she's finally made it here. After all this time, she's come home."

# JOSEPH

❦

"Here. This is for you," I said to Benno the next morning, handing him a box.

Benno was a big talker. Over the last few days, I'd learned a great deal about him and his mother, more than I'd ever learned from Lux. I barely asked any questions and he expounded. He told me all about Newport, his grandmother Miriam and his grandfather George. His year at St. Paul's, and Lapis Lake, where he and George went every summer.

He examined my gift. "Eastman Kodak Brownie Camera. Is that supposed to be a brownie?" He pointed to the illustration of a little man with a huge stomach and froglike face. "Creepy. Are you sure you want to give this to me? It looks brand-new."

The camera was basically brand-new. I'd bought it in January of 1906.

"Have you ever used a camera?" I asked.

"Once or twice. I haven't done much photography."

"I can see you taking photographs all the time in your mind. You look, you focus, and you snap. You take a mental image. I think it's the way you make sense of things."

"It is?"

"Yes."

"You saw that in me?"

"You're an observer, Benno."

Much like his mother, he was forthright, which I appreciated. There was no need for small talk—we just forged right into things. I liked to think I was a good role model, that I was giving him something that would help him make his way back in his own life. But the truth was I was getting something from him, too. He was a stitch to my shredded heart. Although our circumstances were entirely different, we were both of us fatherless, paternally unmoored.

"I'll take good care of it, I promise."

"It's not a loan, it's a gift. It's yours to keep."

"You're sure?"

"I am quite sure, young man. Go, now. Capture the world."

# LUX

❦

*San Francisco*
*1982–83*

And so the next two years flew, a blur of work, school, and visits to the Valley of the Moon. Sunday night arrived and I blinked and it was Sunday night again. The old cliché seemed to be true. The older you got, the faster the days passed. I raced through time. I was acutely aware of it, but helpless to slow it down. I was not the driver. All I could do was sit in the passenger seat and gaze out the window as life streamed by.

Rhonda had another girl; they named her Sophie. Overcome with jealousy, Penny pinched Sophie and bit her tiny finger. When questioned, she burst into self-righteous tears and blamed it on the cat.

I took Penny for the weekend and smothered her with attention. I made her breakfast-for-supper (pancakes and bacon) and brought her to see *The Great Muppet Caper*. She spent the entire movie in my lap. I breathed in the sweet apricot smell of her shampoo. Afterwards we went home and I painted her fingernails magenta. She did my hair up into two lopsided pigtails. She stared at me moon-eyed, asking me, when would she be old enough to wear a bra? When would she be old enough to wear rouge? I soaked up every minute.

———

Benno turned thirteen. No longer did he come home from school and tell me everything about his day. I barely knew the names of his friends.

The sounds of *Thriller* seeped through his closed bedroom door. I wanted to run in there and hurl myself on the bed next to him. Tuck him under my arm and read him all of his old favorites. *Goodnight Moon. Petunia.* Instead I alphabetized my cookbooks, threw out old spices, and scrubbed the sink with Comet. Finally I heard his door open. He padded into the kitchen.

"I'm hungry."

"There's leftover mac and cheese. I can heat it up for you."

He got the milk out of the fridge. "Cookies?"

"There's some Fudge Stripes left."

"No, there's not. I ate them."

My eyes flitted to the fine black hair above his upper lip. I could see the beginnings of a mustache.

"Do you think I should shave?" he asked, following my gaze.

"What do you think?"

He stroked his chin. More and more I'd seen him trying out these manly gestures.

"I'll buy you some razors. You should have some anyway. If you don't shave now, you'll be shaving soon enough. So how was the movie?"

He and Anjuli had gone to see *Fast Times at Ridgemont High*. It was rated R, but I'd told them if they could figure out how to sneak in they could see it.

"Fine."

*Fine?* That was all I was going to get? How had his first boob sighting affected him? Did they look like he thought they would look? I wanted to tell him so many things, but, most important, I wanted him to know that most girls' breasts didn't look like Phoebe Cates's breasts.

He opened the cupboard and plucked a few sticks of uncooked spaghetti from the box. He chewed on a strand. "Do you have plans with Steve tonight?"

I'd been casually dating an accountant. In fact, he'd asked me to attend the symphony with him tonight, but I'd declined. He was nice enough, but a little boring.

"No."

"You canceled on him."

"Yep."

"Why? He was nice."

Benno had taken a sudden interest in my love life. I dated occasionally, but never seriously. Men weren't a priority. Benno, work, and Greengage were.

"Why are you so concerned?" I asked.

"I just don't want you to be alone."

"I'm not alone, I'm with you."

"What happens when I leave?"

"You're in seventh grade. You're not leaving for a long time."

"Time is nothing but a construct."

"You sound just like Joseph."

He smiled. "I'll take that as a compliment."

# JOSEPH

❧

*Valley of the Moon*
*1909*

The heat was unbearable. Two weeks of unrelenting high temperatures.

"We are living in hell. Go home," I told Lux when she arrived after breakfast.

I didn't mean it. I could tell by her face she was relieved to be here, which meant it had been more than a few months since the fog had come, but I wanted to appear cavalier, as if I could do without her monthly visit.

"Jesus, it's hot." She batted the air, trying to swat the heat away.

"Benno?"

"Newport."

It was the only time of the year he didn't come with her to Greengage, his annual visit to his grandparents.

"How can you be wearing a long-sleeved shirt and pants?" she asked. "Aren't you dying?"

What did she expect me to wear?

"You're not serious?" she asked. "About me going home?"

I said nothing and she scowled.

"I'm from New England. The summers are incredibly humid. This is nothing for me." A bead of sweat appeared in the indentation above her upper lip, and she wiped it away with her finger. "I'm staying."

"Then may I suggest you join the building crew with me today? We're digging out a new root cellar."

It was a dirty job, but at least you weren't working under the blazing sun.


She dug frantically, chipping out large blocks of dirt. The rest of us went about our work in a measured way. We knew from experience that was the only way to survive the heat.

"Slow down. You're no good to us if you faint."

She dug even faster.

"Are you staying for a few days?"

"Yes, of course."

"There's no reason to work so hard."

"What other way is there to work?"

"I'm only looking out for you."

"I don't need anybody looking out for me."

"Yes, you do." I grabbed a shovel and started digging beside her.


That night it was too hot in the upstairs bedroom, so I grabbed a blanket and my pillow and went outside on the porch. I lay on the wooden floor praying desperately for a small breeze. I must have drifted off, because when I awoke, Lux was standing in front of me.

"I can't sleep," she said.

Her nightgown was white, sheer, without sleeves.

I sat up. "Come with me."


"I'm hungry," she said when we went past the vegetable garden.

She had tucked her nightgown into the legs of her drawers. I would have been shocked, but it was dark, I could barely make out her thighs. Besides, I felt the urge to strip myself, the air was so stifling.

"Carrot? Radish? Onion?" she asked.

"Carrot."

She stooped, plucked two carrots out of the ground.

"They're a little dirty," she said, wiping one carefully on her night-gown before handing it to me.

I heard her teeth bite into the crisp orange flesh. "Where to now?" she asked.

I brought her down to the creek.

"God, yes," she breathed as we stood on the bank. The carrot fell out of her hand. I dropped mine beside hers, then I led her into the water.

The water bound our clothes to our bodies. It was like being swaddled in a cool bandage. She moaned softly with pleasure.

"Now under," I said.

We dove down to the bottom and stayed there until we could hold our breath no longer. Then we swam up to the surface, gasping.

"This is just what I needed," she said.

I'd never seen her with a head of wet hair. Rivulets of water streamed down her cheekbones and shoulders. Her nightgown pooled around her.

"Good?"

"So good." She floated on her back.

We didn't speak after that. What was there to say?

When finally we climbed back up the bank, our wet clothes plastered to our skin, we both politely averted our eyes, but I was incapable of diverting myself from the fact that Lux was standing beside me in a transparent nightgown, giving off a golden light like a firefly.

# LUX

❧

*San Francisco*
*1984*

My mother melon-balled in my kitchen. My father sat on the couch watching the news. In a few hours a mob of people would descend upon the apartment for my graduation party. I hadn't wanted one, but my mother and Rhonda had insisted. I'd finally gotten my associate's degree in business at City College, and according to them, this was something that had to be celebrated.

My mom looked up, her fingers covered in watermelon smush. "Your father's sitting in front of the boob tube again?"

"It's fine, Mom."

I didn't mind that my father spent so much time watching TV; it gave us both a break. We were deeply uncomfortable around each other. Even though I'd gotten my life back on track, he'd never forgiven me for abandoning Benno. There was a part of him that would always distrust me.

After Joseph told me about his father, the dull ache of our estrangement receded somewhat: I wasn't the only child who'd been such a disappointment. But every once in a while, triggered by some sense memory of Lapis Lake—the smell of a charcoal grill or suntan lotion—a tidal wave of regret plowed me under.

"Where's Benno?" asked my mother.

"I sent him to the store for ice."

"That's an errand your father could have done."

"Are we finished in here?" I asked.

"Pretty much." She flicked her fingers at me. "Take a shower, get dressed. Have a little rest before the guests arrive."

"You're sure?"

"Yes, this'll take me five more minutes and then your father and I are going back to the hotel to clean up. We'll be back at . . ." She looked at the clock. "Four-thirty. Half past. Okay?"

I did exactly as she said. I took a shower, got dressed, did my makeup, and stretched out on my bed. Who was I kidding? There was no way I could nap. I opened my bedroom door. My father was already back, sitting on the couch. He'd changed into a pair of khakis and a blue sports jacket with gold buttons. He'd had that jacket for years.

"Where's Mom?"

"She's still at the hotel."

"You came back early?"

"I wanted to give you this." He held out a white envelope.

"Mom already gave me a card."

"This is from me."

I took the envelope and put it on the mantel.

"You're not going to open it now?"

I opened the envelope. *Congratulations, Graduate* the card said in sparkly letters. Inside was a check for one hundred dollars.

"Thanks, Dad. That's really nice." I slid the card and check back into the envelope. "Do you want something to drink? A beer? Scotch?"

"I'll take a beer."

I walked into the kitchen.

"City College," he called out. "That's a good school."

I got a glass. He hated to drink out of the bottle.

"Do you have a coaster?" he asked when I handed him the beer.

"No."

"You don't use coasters?"

"No, Dad, we don't."

He blinked at me. "It's good you have your degree. Without a degree you can only go so far."

"So I've heard."

"You hit the ceiling and then they won't let you go any further."

"Right."

"I didn't want that for you. I didn't want that to happen to you," he said in a shaky voice.

I heard the sound of footsteps on the stairs, and my mother and Benno burst through the door.

"George! You just left without telling me you were going!" said my mother.

"Here's the ice," said Benno, stuffing the bag into my arms.

My father gazed down into his lap. He looked so small sitting there. Had he lost weight?

"Is everything all right? Did we interrupt something?" asked my mother.

"Everything's fine," said my father quietly.

"Dad got me a card."

"Did he?" said my mother. "You got her a card, George?"

Oh, the pleasure that radiated across my mother's face. She wanted nothing more than to see us reconciled.

"Some money, too," I added.

"You should do something special with it," my father said. "Go out to dinner. Give yourself a break."

"Well," said my mother, smiling. "Well."


Everybody came. Rose and Doro; the Patels; Rhonda, Ginger, and the girls, and Rhonda's mother, Betty.

Betty had slowed down quite a bit: she had angina. She greeted me, then retired to the living room, sinking into the recliner with a groan.

"Is she okay?" I asked Rhonda.

"It's the beta blockers," said Rhonda. "They do a great job of slowing her heart down, but they wipe her out."

Penny was seven now, Sophie, two. They were the most adorable children. Light auburn hair, freckles, caramel skin. They wore party dresses and patent leather shoes. They smiled at me shyly.

"Hugs, right this very instant." I held out my arms. "My goodness, don't you look beautiful! Like princesses."

The doorbell rang. Into the apartment poured friends from school and colleagues from work. Even Mike turned up, carrying a pony keg of beer on his shoulder.

"I fuckin' knew you had it in you," he said, hugging me. "All the way, baby, you're going all the way."

Who wasn't there? Whose absence could I not speak of? Fancy and Magnusson. Eleanor and Friar.

*Joseph.* A little shiver ran through me. What was he doing this very moment? Mucking out the stalls? Working in the vineyard? Did he think of me as often as I thought of him? The time that separated us had been pulled taut. I could feel his presence from seventy-five years away. The charge between us was so strong, sometimes it felt like he was in my apartment with me. His parlor superimposed on my living room. I frequently envisioned him sitting in his leather chair, staring into the fire, waiting. Waiting. For what?

I filled a glass with ginger ale and brought it to Betty.

"I'm so proud of you," she said weakly.

I put the glass on the side table and sat down next to her. "Are you feeling all right?"

"I'm fine, Lux."

"Rhonda said you're on medication?"

"Beta blockers."

"Do they help?"

"They're very effective—it's just that I'm so tired all the time."

Back when I first started going to Greengage, I'd interrogated Friar about what happened when somebody walked into the fog. Joseph was the only one who'd made it back alive. What had he reported? His heart rate had sped up to four hundred beats a minute, Friar told me. Another few seconds in the fog and he would have died, too.

"They lower the amount of oxygen my heart needs," said Betty.

"By slowing your heart down."

"Yes, I believe that's how it works. Why are you so interested? Is there somebody in your family who has heart issues?" she asked.

I kissed Betty on the cheek. "Yes."

# JOSEPH

❧

*Valley of the Moon*
*1909*

The small blue tablet looked unremarkable. I held it in the palm of my hand. Could this really be the fix?

Lux's eyes bored into mine. She'd just handed me a medication that could potentially end our captivity. I should feel just one overriding emotion. *Joy*. Instead, fear and longing dueled it out inside me, making it quite difficult to summon up the appropriate response.

"Thank you, I'll think about it." I handed the pill back to her.

"You'll think about it? What is there to think about, Joseph?"

"I have responsibilities here. I can't just leave."

"There are plenty of responsible people here. Everybody, in fact." She crossed her arms. "I understand. You're worried about how long it will take for the fog to return. Not knowing when you'll be back. That's the big question. But I've given that a lot of thought and I think this is a good time to risk it. The fog's been coming more regularly now. In the past four years, it's never stayed away longer than four months. There were even a few times it came every month. If you average it all out, the fog has been coming roughly every two months."

When I'd first met Lux, she was twenty-five. Now she was thirty-four. She had a single crease on her forehead. Faint lines around her mouth. She'd learned to inhabit her beauty; she lived now in all its rooms.

"Two months! I can't be gone for that long," I protested.

"Why not? Eight weeks is nothing. It will take that long to get acclimated, anyway, assuming you do make it through. We're probably getting way ahead of ourselves."

I could tell by the high color in her cheeks how much she hoped the pill would work.

"What am I going to do in San Francisco for two months?"

How would I pass—a man of 1909 in 1984? And did I even want to pass? What if I hated the late twentieth century? What if the fog never returned? What if I got stuck there forever?

"You'll be with me. I'll walk you through everything. Yes, it will be shocking, you'll be disoriented just like I was disoriented when I first came to Greengage. But you were a patient guide. I'll be the same for you."

"I don't know."

She frowned. "Yes. That's right. You don't know. None of us knows anything. There are no guarantees, ever. Are you going to let that stop you?"

"What if 1984 isn't right for me?"

"Then you'll come back."

"What if others want to leave?"

"Then they'll go. Jesus, Joseph, it's time. If you don't try the beta blockers, somebody else will. And I don't want it to be somebody else. I want it to be you. You're the one who needs to do this."

She walked up and stood beside me, so close our arms touched. I knew etiquette required that I take a step to the left, reestablishing a proper distance between us; instead I increased the pressure the slightest little bit and waited for her to move her arm. She did not. We both stared straight ahead and pretended our limbs weren't touching. I thought of that hot summer night down by the creek, Lux in her transparent nightgown, water streaming down her body. How difficult it was to look away from her. The jolt of that realization.

She was the main reason, perhaps the only reason, I would consider this madness. I was haunted by her. She was the first thing I thought of when I woke in the mornings, and the last before I closed my eyes at night.

What would it be like to live with her? To wake and see her pad across the room in her pajamas. To wait for her to come home from work every evening. To see her gloriously alive and competent in her own time.

"I know it's scary," she said. "But aren't you also curious to see everything I've been telling you about all these years?"

I'd given up the idea that we'd ever get out of Greengage long ago. Hope was a torn sail lying on the deck. Lux was the breeze that poked at it.

"What if it doesn't work?"

"Then you go back to this lovely, lovely life. Don't you see, Joseph? There's no way to lose."

Oh, but she was wrong—there was everything to lose. Once you let yourself want something, you could never take back the wanting.

I swallowed the blue tablet anyway.

# JOSEPH

❦

*San Francisco*
*1984*

" You took off," panted Lux.

She was bent over, hands on her knees.

Once I realized it wasn't going to kill me, I'd ridden the fog like a wave right out of 1909, seventy-five years into the future. I'd run as fast as I could away from Greengage.

"The trees. The vegetation. It looks exactly the same," I gasped.

"How do you feel? Is your heart racing?"

I took a few deep breaths. The medication was holding my heart rate back. A slightly uncomfortable pressure, but other than that, I felt normal. "I'm fine."

Lux looked over my shoulder. "The fog's still here. Usually as soon as I come through, it vaporizes. It makes this funny sound, a kind of backward whooshing."

The fog was far less menacing on this side. It was a puffy, lacy sort of mist.

"Let's wait a few minutes, see if it goes," she said.

We stood in the clearing for five minutes. When five minutes was up, she checked her watch and mumbled, "Ten minutes more."

When those ten minutes had passed, she shook her head bewilderedly. "It's like it's watching. It knows one of you is out here. I don't think it's going to evaporate, Joseph. Maybe it won't—not while you're on this side. It's keeping the door open for you, so to speak."

She turned to me, her eyes bright. "You know what this means? You don't have to wait—you can go back anytime."

I felt strangely cheated hearing this news. Once I'd finally decided to go and had committed myself, I wanted the door to be completely shut behind me. I wanted to be forced to stay in 1984 for a few months so I could experience the heightened reality of being exiled with her.

"I guess I should go back," I said. I had a responsibility to tell everybody that it had worked, that they could take a beta blocker and leave Greengage, too.

"Do you want to go back?" asked Lux.

Her braid had loosened. Two long tendrils crept down her neck.

"No."

"Then don't. You're not expected for at least a month. After everything you've been through, nobody would begrudge you that."

She nodded at me, seeking my approval. We were making some private decision that could only be made because we were standing together on the other side of the fog.

I heard a rushing sound far in the distance. And closer by, music. A radio?

"The highway," she said. "And—" She listened for a moment. "Steely Dan. An oldie." She laughed. "Perfect! 'Reeling in the Years.' It's a sign."

# LUX

❦

I hadn't realized how much I wanted him to stay until he was con-
fronted with the opportunity to go straight back to Greengage.
These past weeks I'd lived in a sort of in-between place. The bottle of
pills ever present in my purse, a reminder of my longing and intention
to set him free.

I opened the trunk of my car and pulled out a canvas bag.

"You can get dressed in there," I said, pointing to the bathroom.

He peered in the bag and frowned.

"You can't go around looking like that," I said.

Joseph wore his typical daily uniform—wool trousers, suspenders,
boots. And today, it being a special occasion and all, a bowler hat.

I'd bought clothes for him: a pair of Levi's, a white T-shirt, and a
blue cotton sweater. When he emerged from the bathroom, the
change was stunning; he'd been transformed into a modern man. My
stomach fluttered. I tried not to stare as he sat down in the passenger
seat of my Camry.

I pulled out slowly and he gaped at the dashboard. I'd seen the
Model T Ford rusting away in Greengage. All it had was a gearshift
and odometer.

I wanted to impress him. "Hot?" I asked, and turned on the air
conditioning.

A minute later he put on his hat. Something from home to ground him.

I'd been new to his world once. I remembered well how this went. The disorientation. The embarrassment that you didn't know what something was or how it was used. I could easily put myself in his place, imagine all his questions. So I just started talking.

"That's a Pontiac Grand Am. That's a Chevrolet Caprice. This is Highway 101. The price of gas is one dollar and thirty-two cents a gallon. The speed limit is fifty-five, but you can safely go sixty-five without getting stopped by a cop. This is the Golden Gate Bridge. Don't ask me why it's painted red and not gold—I have no idea. That pointy skyscraper? The Transamerica Building. Those skates are called Rollerblades. That woman is wearing a cowl-necked sweater. That's what's called a yuppie. Macy's. Amazing windows at Christmas. McDonald's—Benno practically lives there."

Finally we pulled up to 428 Elizabeth Street. My apartment would be empty; Benno was sleeping over at a friend's house this weekend.

Joseph hadn't said a word since we left the Valley of the Moon. We climbed up the stairs and I blabbered on.

"Rhonda and Ginger used to live in the basement apartment, but they moved because it was too small once they had Sophie. The Patels live there." I pointed down at the first floor. "Top floor is Doro and Rose, and this is me."

I unlocked the door and we walked through the living room into the kitchen. He stared at me as if to say *What now?*

"Let's take that off," I said, putting his bowler hat on top of the fridge. "How about some tea?"

I put the kettle on. Then, because I couldn't think of what else to do, I went around naming and explaining more things.

"Microwave, garbage disposal, VCR, answering machine. Häagen-Dazs, Hamburger Helper, eggs—about ninety cents a dozen. Nylons—I have to wear them for work; a Rubik's Cube—try it, Benno can do it in six moves. FM radio—KFOG is the best station; phone; Lip Smacker; junk drawer—if you need anything, just take it (*what's a tampon doing in there, Jesus!*); futon couch—folds out into a bed; afghan my mother made me. Benno's room. Let's just leave the door open and air it out a bit, shall we? My room. Guest room—you'll be sleeping in there. Albums. Cassettes. Stereo. Tape player. Help yourself to anything. I want you to feel at home."

The teakettle whistled. I sounded like I was on speed. Maybe *I* should take a beta blocker.

Joseph sat down and rubbed his temples.

"What's wrong?"

"I have a headache."

I gave him two Tylenol and tried not to panic. *It's just a headache. He's fine. Don't make a big deal of this.* I plunked teabags into mugs and poured boiling water over them. I brought the mugs to the table. Having him here, sitting in my kitchen, felt unreal. I had to fight to stay in my body, to not reject this reality. I could see he was doing the same.

He took a small sip of the tea.

"This is not a mistake," I said. "You being here."

He rubbed the back of his neck.

"Are you sorry you came?"

His eyes drifted to the window as an ambulance went by, filling the room with the wailing of its alarm.

"An ambulance. You want me to shut the window?"

He closed his eyes.

"It's overwhelming, isn't it? All that you saw on the ride?"

"Yes."

"Was it terrible? Was it ugly?"

"It was just—different."

Joseph was usually so precise in his language. That he defaulted to an adjective like *different* told me how overstimulated he was.

"Look. We can take it slow. We can stay right here until you feel safe. We don't even have to leave the apartment for the rest of the day. Benno won't be home until Sunday. We can order in Chinese."

He nodded wearily. "Does Benno know about the beta blockers?"

"I didn't tell him. I didn't want to get his hopes up. But he'll be happy. My God, the kid will be beside himself."

This man adored my son. He knew him intimately. His weaknesses, his foibles, his quirks, and he loved him anyway.

"I'm so happy you're here," I said to him. "I'm beside myself, too, in case you were wondering."

Something happened to Joseph's face then. The worry slid away and was replaced with something involuntary and true.

*Hope.*

"The clothes suit you. You look good," I added with a grin.

He glanced down at his sweater, his jeans.

"Handsome," I said.

He blushed. I blushed.

I looked at the clock. It was 3:00 P.M. What the hell. Screw the tea—I grabbed two beers out of the fridge.

# JOSEPH

❧

We got a little drunk. And why not? How else to blunt the shock? Fog lag, she called it.

I drifted and she continually pulled me back with her words. She talked endlessly and I was grateful to her for filling the space, for naming things and telling me their proper uses. She anticipated every question I had. She didn't require me to ask anything.

Seeing her in her proper time was edifying. In Greengage it had taken her many visits to find her footing and her voice. Here, in San Francisco in 1984, she was firmly stitched in.

But as bedtime approached, we became more formal with each other. We retreated to opposite sides of the couch.

"Well, it's been a long day," she said.

"It's late," I agreed, suddenly perfectly sober.

"The sheets are clean in the guest room. There's a towel and facecloth on the dresser. An extra blanket in the closet."

I stood. "What time do you wake in the morning?"

She'd asked me the same question on the first night she'd stayed in Greengage.

"It's Saturday, we can sleep in. Nine or ten. Or however late you want to sleep is fine."

She looked up at me, her feet tucked beneath her, her face unguarded.

The moment billowed, as if caught by a sudden wind. I found myself bending toward her. What was my intention? Touch her lightly on the shoulder? Kiss her cheek?

I gave a little bow. "Sleep well."

A tide of color rose from her chest to her neck to her cheeks.

"You too," she said.

# LUX

❦

The next morning I handed him a beta blocker and poured him a cup of coffee. "How did you sleep?"

"Fine, thank you."

He'd showered; he smelled of my Pantene shampoo.

"Are you hungry?"

"Not yet."

He stared at the coffee like he didn't know what to do with it.

"Cream? Milk?" How many times had I uttered those words when I was a waitress?

"Neither."

"I can put the kettle on for tea."

"No, coffee is fine." He took a sip of the coffee and gave a small groan of pleasure.

"How long has it been since you've had coffee?"

"I can't remember," he said, taking another sip.

I wiped down surfaces, emptied the dish rack. I felt his eyes on me. Every gesture I made felt exaggerated.

"What should we do today?" he finally asked.

"What are you up for? Do you want to take it easy? Have a lazy morning? I can get the newspaper."

He considered my suggestion for a moment. "Let's go out."

"You're sure? We've got plenty of time. We can take it slowly."

"I'm sure. Do I pass muster?"

He was wearing the jeans and blue sweater again.

"Yes, but we're going to have to get you some more clothes."

"I can make do with what I have."

"You can't wear the same thing every day. We'll go to Macy's and get you a few things."


As we walked down the street he kept accidentally bumping into me and apologizing.

"I don't know what's wrong with me," he said. "My balance feels off."

"It's going to be fine. You just have to get used to being here."

I knew what he was wondering: Was he experiencing this disequilibrium because he didn't belong here? Had he broken some law of physics by leaving Greengage?

I reached for his hand. His palm was cool and dry, callused from hard work.

"Just until you get your balance back," I said.

Liar. I saw an opportunity to get physically close to him and I took advantage of it. I felt ashamed.

"Lux," he said.

I dropped his hand. "Sorry."

He gave me a sad look.

"I'm fine. It's nothing," I said, embarrassed.

"Lux," he whispered urgently.

I'd never heard anybody say my name like that. In that *Lux* was everything. An entire vocabulary of longing. Of things desired. Things unspoken. Things about to happen.

"It's not nothing. We are not nothing, damn it," he said.

He entwined my fingers in his.


The world contracted. We waded through a sea of people on Market Street, but it felt like we were the only ones there. My hand brushed the side of his thigh. He walked a pace in front of me, protectively.

A group of giggling Filipino schoolgirls in plaid skirts surged around us.

"Are we really doing this?" I asked.

"Doing what?"

"Going—to Macy's," I stammered. *"Now."*

"Are we almost there?"

"Yes."

"Then yes, we are going to Macy's."

"Then what?"

Abruptly he turned right and led us out of the flow of pedestrian traffic. The air smelled of sandalwood incense and popcorn. He backed me up against the concrete wall.

"Then this," he said, staring intently at me. He ran his thumb over my lower lip.

"Joseph."

Then he kissed me.


I, of all people, knew that life could change in a split second. You could walk through a fogbank and find yourself in the past. Or you could be strolling down the street with a man you'd considered nothing more than a friend until that man kissed you. And then you could find yourself on a cable car, him standing behind you. A Macy's bag filled with his new clothes pinned between your knees.

It felt impossible. It felt—inevitable.

"Stop thinking," he said.

I leaned back into him as the cable car jostled from side to side. I let myself be supported. I let myself feel what it was like to not be alone.

# JOSEPH

❦

There was before. There was after. And there was the seam separating before and after. She sat on her bed. I knelt in front of her. The sky just before it begins to rain. The smell of condensation, grass, and lightning in the air. The parlor just before dusk, before the lamps are lit. The kitchen, clean and quiet, just before dawn.

Her breath, ragged.

"Are you sure?" she whispered.

I unbuttoned her shirt.

# LUX

❦

It was fast. Urgent. We couldn't get to each other's bodies quickly enough. A button flew off my blouse. We wriggled out of our pants.

This was metamorphosis. In a matter of minutes, we went from being friends to being strangers.

We were gentle. We were rough. We said dirty things to each other. We whispered tender words of love. And when he finally slid inside me, there was only this. The swelling and need. Building and thrusting. Hip bones rising up to meet hip bones. Backs arching. Fists clenched and unclenched.

Afterwards, like astronauts, we floated back down through the atmosphere to earth. Our beacons? The faint sound of traffic through the open window. A garlic-scented breeze from the pizzeria on Douglass.

"Did you expect this?" I asked.

He drew me under his arm. "Expected, no. Hoped, yes."

"You hoped?"

My heart, saturated with joy, fastened me to this moment forever.

He nodded. "I did, but it was still a surprise. You were the surprise, I suppose. That you wanted this, too." He frowned. "But why do you look so forlorn?"

"I'm afraid that I've taken something that I shouldn't have," I whispered.

What would Martha have thought of Joseph and me? Had we betrayed her in some way? I couldn't bear to ask the question. Surely Joseph must be thinking of that, too?

"You've taken nothing that wasn't freely offered," he said carefully.

"You don't feel guilty?"

"I feel—possibility. You, Lux, are possibility."

"I am?"

"You are. How can you not know that?"

He tipped my chin up, forcing me to look at him.

"You are all the doors opening at once," he said.

My insides felt liquefied, spreading, like warm yellow yolk, like sun.

I put my finger on his lips, silencing him. "Stop talking. It's too much. I can't take it in."

"You're going to have to."

"I can't."

His face blurred. I couldn't hold his gaze.

"How long has it been?" he asked.

"Since when?"

"Since somebody has cherished you the way I do."

*Never.*

Time slipped through my fingers. A common expression, so often and casually said it was almost trite. The truth—it was an incomprehensible sentiment that was so profound all we could do was let it wash over us. Watching our child play in the sandbox at the park. Lighting the candles on the birthday cake. The smell of waffles. The first day of school. Pumpkins on stoops. *Oh my God, it's snowing.* The unexpected gift of a warm March afternoon.

In the most literal sense, this was what I'd been experiencing with Joseph since the day I met him. Every time I left Greengage, the moment I stepped back into my present, the hands began flying around the clock. This wasn't an ephemeral, fleeting feeling, it was reality—my life moved quicker than his; I aged faster than he did. We never knew how long it would be, or how old I'd be when we'd see each other again.

And it made what was happening between us now almost impossible to bear.

"Joseph's here," I told Rhonda late the next morning, on the phone. "He made it through."

"What?" she said. "Where here?"

"Here, standing-right-in-front-of-me here. In the kitchen. Currently eating a bologna sandwich and making a face. There's no such thing as bologna in 1909. I don't think he's a fan."

"Don't fool around with me, Lux."

"I'm not. Joseph, say something." I held the phone out to him.

"Um—hallo."

I put the phone back to my ear and heard the sound of something slamming. Rhonda's fist on the table. "For fuck's sake!" she cried.

"Yes, exactly," I said.

"How is he?"

"I don't know. Let me ask him. How are you, Joseph?"

He gave me a lazy, post-sex look. Heavy lidded, content. Again I was struck by the foreignness of him.

"I'm very well, thank you," he said.

"Are you giving him the beta blockers? Have you taken his pulse? Forget it, I'm coming over right now."

"There's no need—"

"There is a need and I am coming. I love you. I am coming and you can't stop me."

With that, Rhonda hung up.

"Your pulse is a little high. I think you should bump the dose up. Take one in the morning, one in the evening, okay? As long as you do that, you should be okay. Don't do anything that would overexert you. No running, no exercise. Don't let Lux drag you to aerobics class," said Rhonda.

I could just imagine the look on Joseph's face seeing all those women in striped leotards doing the grapevine. If anything would send him straight back to Greengage, that would. But what about sex? Did that count as exercise? Is that why his pulse was raised? I studied Joseph's face. There was no sign of any stress; in fact it was the opposite. He looked stoned. I probably looked stoned, too. Our eyes kept meeting and then quickly we'd look away. We were too new.

Rhonda unpacked a bag of McDonald's. French fries. Big Macs and apple pies. She slid a plate over to Joseph. "Dig in."

The two of us watched Joseph take his first bite of a Big Mac. In Greengage he ate nothing but the freshest produce and meat. Would the burger taste like cardboard to him?

"Mmm," he said.

"You like it?" I asked.

He nodded and took another big bite.

"It's the secret sauce," said Rhonda, biting into her Big Mac.

"Well, now that you've eaten McDonald's, you are truly one of us," I said, stuffing a handful of fries into my mouth.


Later I walked Rhonda down the stairs.

"You realize that man is in love with you," she said.

I played dumb. "What?"

I wanted to keep us a secret for a while. Just until I knew for sure that it was real.

"Are you crazy?" I said.

She stopped. "Look at me."

"No." I pushed ahead of her on the staircase.

"Lux, what the fuck. Look at me."

I spun around and faced her, my hands on my hips. She broke into a broad smile.

"My God, you're in love with him, too."

I groaned.

"What's wrong? That's not a bad thing. That's a really good thing."

"Don't tell anybody."

"Who am I going to tell?"

"Ginger. *Benno*."

"Where is Benno?"

"He's staying at a friend's house. He'll be back tonight."

"But why don't you want to tell him? He adores Joseph. He'll be thrilled."

I hung my head. "I don't want to get his hopes up. What if it's a fling?"

"A fling? You've been traveling back in time for almost ten years now in order to see this man, and he risked life and limb to get to San Francisco. He put all thought of his own safety aside—that's how much he wanted to be with you here."

She grabbed me by the upper arms and shook me a little. "You have loved each other through time. A fling. Please, Lux. Don't insult what the two of you have."

"I'm an idiot!" I cried.

She hugged me. "No, honey. You're just scared. You have something to lose now."

After Rhonda left, Joseph carried me to bed again, like a child or a bride; I felt like both.

He carefully undressed me. After he slid off my underwear, he climbed into bed next to me, shirtless, but still in his jeans. I could feel his erection through the material, stiffening against my leg.

I got a condom out of my bedside table. We hadn't used one before, but I'd just finished my period, so I was safe.

"Here." I pressed the condom into his hand.

He looked confused, then embarrassed. "I don't need this. We don't need this."

I sat up. "Look, last night was an anomaly. What happened between us—it was so unexpected I didn't think. But I'm thinking now and you have to wear a condom. The chances are slim I'd get pregnant, given where I am in my cycle, but I can't risk it."

"I wouldn't have done that to you. I wouldn't have put you at risk." He grimaced. "I'm sterile. I'm unable to have children. We don't have to use any kind of contraception." He rolled over onto his back and stared dejectedly up at the ceiling. "The reason Martha and I never had children was because I wasn't able to."

I'd just assumed they hadn't had children because they were so devoted to the farm; Greengage was their child.

"I had no idea. You and Martha seemed so content."

"Nobody knew, except Fancy."

"Did you want children?"

"God, *yes*."

He was so amazing with Benno. Such a natural. "I'm so sorry, Joseph." He laid his head on my chest and wept.

# JOSEPH

❦

I found myself counting to eight over and over. It took me a few hours to realize this was happening. At first it was the quietest of background noises, virtually impossible to detect unless you brought all your focus to bear on the sound. One. Two. Three. Four. Five. Six. Seven. Eight. Like a ringing in the ear that drifts in and out. But soon, just in.

I took a shower to try to rid myself of it. I let the water pound on my head. It worked. The numbers receded, but once I was dressed they returned.

"I keep counting to eight," I told Lux.

"What do you mean?"

"Counting off."

"Numbers?"

"Yes. One, two, three, four—all the way to eight."

"And then what?"

"Then I start all over again."

"Really? Are you doing it now?"

"No, Lux, I can't count and talk."

"So keep talking."

"That's not a solution. I can't talk all day long."

She frowned. "An inner-ear thing? You still feeling off-balance?"

"A little."

"Maybe you're just anxious. When I get anxious, I repeat a phrase over and over again in my mind. A silly thing, like 'Green, yellow, green, yellow.' It gives me distance. Allows me to step outside the anxiety. Maybe that's what you're doing. Mentally trying to keep calm."

Fine. Anxiety it was. I grabbed onto that explanation and for the rest of the day forced myself to believe it. Until Benno burst through the door that evening, dropped his bag on the floor, and looked at me with disbelief and delight.

One, two, three, four—the numbers unspooled, faster and faster.

"What the hell," said Benno. "How are you here?"

"Beta blockers," said Lux. "They slow down your heart. I got them from Rhonda. I don't know why I never thought of it before."

His eyes shifted back and forth between the two of us.

"Well, Jesus." He leapt forward and hugged me.

I stood stiffly, my arms down by my sides; we'd never embraced before.

"Welcome to San Francisco, man. Welcome to the modern world. How long are you staying?" he asked.

"I'm not sure," I said.

"Does this mean you'll be coming back and forth like we do? Does this mean everybody in Greengage can come?"

"Whoa, you're getting ahead of yourself, Benno. He's only been here since Friday night," said Lux.

"This is awesome." Then Benno's face clouded over. "What are we going to tell people? How are we gonna explain him?"

"He's an old family friend, that's all you have to say."

Benno grinned. "I can't believe it. You're standing right in front of me. In our living room," he caroled.

He threw his arms around me again and this time I embraced him back.

Lux and I didn't have a minute alone for the rest of the night, but I really didn't mind. Benno wanted to show me everything: his Nintendo, his Rubik's Cube. His photographs.

The Brownie camera I'd given Benno had been the beginning of an obsession for him. He'd taken a photography course. He'd spent hours at the library poring over books of photos. His tastes were eclectic. On his last visit to Greengage, he had rattled off names of famous photographers that he loved—none of which were familiar to me: Henri Cartier-Bresson, Diane Arbus, and Walker Evans. Man Ray, Ansel Adams, and Mary Ellen Mark.

Now I had the opportunity to examine Benno's photos. The subject matter was varied, some portraits and landscapes. Buildings. Crowds. In some instances he'd shot so close up I couldn't tell what the image was. His photos had a grit and beauty that belied his fourteen years.

"Do you like them?" he asked. "I know some of them aren't so great. This one's sort of overexposed and . . ."

I glanced at Lux. Here was all her hard work. Here was her undying love.

"Tell me more," I said.


Lux announced she was going to bed.

"I'm not going to bed yet. It's too early," said Benno. "I want Joseph to see MTV."

"Does Joseph want to see MTV?" she asked.

"It's fine," I said. In truth, I was exhausted, but I didn't want to let Benno down.

"Okay. Don't stay up too late. It's a school night," she said to Benno.

Benno jumped up from the couch to change the channel. Lux went to the bathroom and closed the door.

I stared at the bathroom door, willing her to emerge. Finally she came out, dressed in her nightgown, her hair loose. She looked down at the floor, then boldly swept her gaze up to me.

I hadn't told Lux, but today I'd had to take three beta blockers.

One, two, three, four. Five. Six. Seven. Eight.

I knew what the counting was now. My heartbeat—speeding up. Meting out the days.

# LUX

❦

On Monday I called Mr. Pease and told him that I had an urgent family matter I had to attend to, and therefore he would need to find somebody to fill my shifts all week. I didn't give him a chance to say no.

Joseph looked pale.

"I'm worried," I said. "I should take you to my doctor."

"And say what?"

"Say you have a heart problem."

He shook his head. "I'm fine."

He didn't look fine.

"Please don't worry," he said.

"I should just give you some time?"

"Yes."

"Okay. Fine. I'll give you some time."

He nodded tiredly.

"But why do you look that way?"

"Good God. What way?" He pulled himself erect. Widened his eyes.

"Have you changed your mind?" I asked. "About me? About us?"

"No," he practically shouted.

"It's not a stupid question. You might feel over your head. You might feel like you made a mistake. I would understand if that's the case."

I was losing him. I could sense him pulling away from me.

Joseph scraped his chair back and walked around the table. He yanked me out of my chair and into his arms.

"Listen to me. There is nothing I wouldn't do to stay with you and Benno. Nothing. No matter what happens, you have to know that."

"Then stay," I begged him. "Don't leave before you have to go. I know you're scared; I know this is a lot to adjust to. You're not going to be able to absorb everything in a week. We have all the time in the world for you to adjust to life here. Weeks. Months, if you want it."

He hesitated and murmured, "All right. Yes."

# JOSEPH

❧

That afternoon we picked Benno up from school and the three of us took a stroll down Market Street. I caught a glimpse of our reflection in a store window. We looked—like a family. *Remember this,* I told myself.

I'd taken three beta blockers already today. Soon I'd be in need of a fourth.

"Oh, look, Benno. Lotta's Fountain," said Lux. "Let's show Joseph."

"Who's Lotta?" I asked as we approached the cast-iron fountain.

"I think she was a singer or a showgirl," said Lux.

"She was a vaudeville performer," said Benno.

"How do you know that?" asked Lux.

"We came here on a field trip in sixth grade. Her big claim to fame was that she had the most beautiful ankles in the world."

"People gathered here after the 1906 earthquake," explained Lux. "This was the meeting place. Where people came looking for their loved ones."

The fountain was in utter disrepair. The lion heads defaced with red paint, all the panes of glass on the lantern either missing or cracked.

A sudden rage washed over me. Why had no one come looking for us?

"They should clean it up. Paint it or something," said Benno. He glanced at me. "They should take care of it better."

"Oh God, Joseph. I didn't think. I shouldn't have brought you here," said Lux.

"I have something to tell you," Lux said, just before dinner. "Something I feel terrible about."

A chicken was roasting in the oven. A loaf of bread sat on the table, slathered with butter and garlic. Benno was in the living room watching TV.

"I've kept something from you. The first time I came back from Greengage? I went to the library." She shook her head. "Stupid. I was so stupid. I was trying to prove to Rhonda you existed. I knew you existed. That should have been all I needed."

"But it wasn't."

"No, it wasn't."

I sighed. "What did you find?"

"Nothing," she said sadly. "There was no record of Greengage and no record of any of you. I had the census reports checked back to the 1850s. It was like you never existed. I should have told you right away. But I just thought, what's the point? Why hurt you unnecessarily? Wasn't it better to just let you go on thinking your families had looked for you? That you'd always be remembered?"

My vision blurred. The room spun.

When I came to, I was on the floor. Benno and Lux hovered over me.

"Did you forget to take your meds this morning?" asked Lux.

"No." It was the only word I could manage, my heart was beating so quickly. I pressed my hand on my chest in vain, as if I could slow it down.

"Can you swallow?" asked Lux.

Benno gently propped me up. Lux gave me two pills.

"I want you to rest now. Stay in one position. Don't even move your head," she instructed me.

I stared at the ceiling obediently.

"Close your eyes," she said.

I closed them. A racehorse in my chest. Galloping, galloping. I blacked out again.


When I woke, I was in the car. Lux was driving. Benno sat with me in the backseat.

"He's awake," Benno said.

"Hold on. We're almost there," she said.

I felt dizzy and nauseous.

"I gave you a Valium along with the beta blocker," said Lux. "To keep you calm."

"Where are we going?"

"Home."


I don't remember walking through the woods. Lux told me they half carried, half dragged me. I have a faint recollection of somebody crying, then the scent of bacon and freshly baked bread. When we stepped into Greengage, my heart rate went back to normal and I knew I would never see 1984 again.

# LUX

❧

For four short days I thought I could have it all. With the help of the beta blockers, Joseph could pass freely between my world and his. Now we knew that was a fantasy.

"You could stay," he said. "Both you and Benno. You could stay."

He looked so miserable. It was midmorning; everybody was off working. Nobody except the kitchen crew even knew we were back.

Elisabetta and Benno sat about twenty-five feet away from us at a table. Benno shoveled food into his mouth—bacon and a roll smeared with butter. That boy could eat three breakfasts every morning if I let him. Elisabetta kept glancing at us nervously.

"We can't stay, Joseph. Benno has school. He's already been absent five days this semester. He can't miss any more."

"He can go to school in Greengage."

"His life is back home."

"He has a life here, too."

"Yes, he does. But it's not the same for him as it is for me. I'm thirty-four. I've had plenty of time in my world. I could stay, I could make that choice, God knows I've thought about it. But Benno's only fourteen, not old enough to make a mature decision, and he isn't ready to commit to Greengage. Maybe someday. But not yet."

Aware of the kitchen crew's eyes on me, I did not reach out and touch him, although it took everything I had not to throw myself into his arms.

"I'll be back before you know it," I said.

He looked down at the floor despondently and I knew what he was thinking. Who knew how long it would be for me?

"A month. Maybe two. The fog is coming more regularly. The stretches have been shorter and shorter," I reminded him.

"How can you be so hopeful?"

"Because I understand now," I said. "The hours, the days, the months are irrelevant. Joseph, don't you see that?"

The fog had brought us together; it would not keep us apart.

# LUX

❧

San Francisco
1984–86

B ut the fog did not materialize the next month or the month after that. I was distraught—it physically hurt to be away from Joseph; my body ached for him. The only thing that kept me sane was knowing he had no idea. Time was passing normally for him. He could look on his calendar and mark the days until he saw me again. I, however, avoided the calendar; it was too painful of a reminder.

So it wasn't until the second fogless month that I realized I'd missed my period.

I'd believed Joseph when he said he was sterile. Apparently he'd had sex without contraception with Martha for twenty years and never impregnated her. How did they test men for sterility back then? Clearly it wasn't foolproof, because it must have been Martha who'd been barren.

There should be a word to describe the particular combination of shock and fate one feels when faced with unimaginable news. I didn't tell anybody for a while. Instead I stood on the shore of this new reality, testing the temperature. Despite my panic and burgeoning list of questions (How would Joseph feel about this? When would the fog return? What about my job? How would my parents react?), the most delicious anticipation began to flutter through me. The utter rightness of this conception.

Joseph would be elated. We would figure it out.

I wanted to do this for him—for *us*. A child. Our child. I had the sense she or he had been there all along, waiting, as I'd been waiting, as Joseph had been waiting all these years.

As soon as we'd returned from Greengage, I'd told Benno about me and Joseph.

"Great," he'd said.

"That's not a big deal? That's not weird for you?"

"It would be weird if you weren't together. I mean, anybody could have seen that coming."

Okay, fine, being a couple was one thing, but being pregnant with Joseph's child was another. What would Benno think? Here I was, in the same position I'd been in with him. A single mother, pregnant again.

I tried to soften the blow with waffles at Mel's.

"You're not hungry?" Benno asked after I'd broken the news.

"I don't have much of an appetite these days." Actually, I was trying to keep from gagging at the smell of the fake maple syrup.

He chewed thoughtfully. "I think you should keep it. Him. Or her," he added. "But I think it's a her."

"You do? You—?"

He reached across the table and put his hand over mine. "This is a good thing, Mom."

"Even if I have no idea when we'll be able to get back to Greengage? Even if I'm all alone?"

"You're not alone. You have me. Besides, I was sick of being an only child: all that attention, all that pressure to succeed. I'm sick of getting straight A's. Let somebody else get straight A's!" He grinned.

Benno did not get straight A's. He did okay in his classes, but what he really excelled in was the arts. Drawing and painting, and of course photography. He was never without his camera. It hung from his neck now.

"Smile," he said. He snapped my photo. "For Joseph."

How I loved his optimism.

By the fifth month I couldn't hide my pregnancy any longer, and Rhonda brought me over a box of her old maternity clothes. They were dated, smocks and tent dresses in cheerful madras.

I tried one on.

"Looks great!" Rhonda said.

"Liar. Why can't I be like you? You couldn't even tell you were pregnant from the back. Why can't I have a perfect little basketball of a stomach?"

I studied my reflection in the bathroom mirror. The smock made me look even more pregnant. I was better off sticking to my oversize shirts.

"Because you're thirty-five," said Rhonda.

We'd spent many long nights discussing my situation. I'd been back to the Valley of the Moon every full moon for the past five months, but there'd been no fog.

"How are you feeling?" Rhonda asked.

"Okay."

"Morning sickness?"

"Nope."

"Ankles swollen?"

"Not yet."

She folded a shirt. "Lonely?"

I sat down on the bed. "God, I miss him, Rhonda. I don't know what to do. Where to put this ache. It hurts so much. It's like a contraction that never stops."

"I can't even imagine what you're going through. It's so crazy that he doesn't know, that you don't have any way to get word to him."

I'd never been more acutely aware of the inequity of the difference in the way time unfurled in each of our worlds. In three of his weeks, I could not only find myself pregnant but quite possibly have his baby.

She sat down next to me and put her hand on the swell of my belly. "But that doesn't mean it's not right. This baby is your fate, Joseph's fate. She's going to be the bridge that links the two of you together."

I looked down at her familiar hand. The shell-pink nails. The slightly crooked middle finger. Her unadorned gold wedding band.

"You really think so? Really?"

"Really," she said.


I named her Vivien, Vivi for short.

"Where's the proud father?" asked the maternity nurse.

I'd listed Joseph Bell as the father on the birth certificate.

"He's on his way," I said.

Vivi! Twenty-two inches; seven pounds, six ounces; from the breaking of my water to the final push—three hours and twenty-two minutes. A full head of black hair, eyes blue. She was perfect in every way except one. Her heart beat a little too fast.

The doctor listened intently with his stethoscope, then abruptly pulled the instrument out of his ears and smiled.

"I'm sure it's nothing to be worried about, but just in case, let's get an EKG and a chest X-ray, and set Mommy's mind at ease."

Mommy's mind would not be at ease. Mommy suspected why her daughter's heart beat a little too fast, and if she was right, there was no medicine in this world that could fix it.

They wheeled her away. Benno, Rhonda, and I sat in my room in silence. An hour later the doctor brought Vivi back himself.

"There's nothing to be worried about. She's got something called supraventricular tachycardia, a fancy name for arrhythmia. Nine times out of ten they outgrow it." He handed a swaddled Vivi to me. "This gal is just in a hurry. She'll be an active one."

"Can I bring her home?" I asked.

"Of course. But let's keep an eye on her." He scribbled a name on a prescription pad and gave it to me. "Tim Walker—an excellent pediatric cardiologist. Set up an appointment with him in a month's time."

Another prickle of worry ran down my spine, but I quickly banished it.

"Can I hold her?" asked Benno.

He took her in his arms. I'd never seen such an unguarded look on his face. A fierce, protective tenderness. Joy.

_____

I'd finagled three months of maternity leave. Pease had not been happy when I'd told him I was pregnant; I'd never forget the look of contempt on his face.

"Who's the father?" he asked.

"That's none of your business," I said.

I knew what he assumed—that I'd stupidly and carelessly got knocked up again—but I didn't care. I owed him nothing.

I didn't want Joseph to miss out on anything, so I began keeping a journal, a record of Vivi's daily activities.

> She woke at 5. Nibbling toes. Laughing. One curl plastered to her cheek. Cranky morning. Gas? A trip to Dolores Park. Put her on a blanket under the trees. She stared up at the leaves and cooed for nearly twenty minutes. Suspect she's thinking deep thoughts. Suspect she's highly intelligent. Fell asleep on the breast. Stayed asleep through the evening news. Woke at 9— gave her a taste of smushed-up banana. Surprise, disgust, and yum flickered across her face.

The days were a year long. The days passed in a second. I'd forgotten how time slid when you had an infant. I caved to its rhythms. The only thing fastening us to reality was breakfast with Benno and his return after school.

Vivi was a movie that was always running; a life preserver, bonding Benno and me together in a profound way. She was a fragile thing to be protected at all costs. And she was, of course, a source of great delight. An actress, a natural comedian. She had us in constant fits of laughter. Gurgling and burbling. Inviting us to poke a finger into her Pillsbury Doughboy belly. She'd do anything for attention.

She had a Mohawk of ebony hair. Her eyes hadn't yet settled on a shade. At breakfast they were light blue like Joseph's. At lunch, a green-blue, similar to mine, and at dinner, navy. Her resting face was a half smile, as if she were about to be tickled. She was merriment incarnate.

She wasn't an observer like Benno. She was a doer. An investigator. The first day she learned to crawl, she got her hand stuck under the fridge. She had to be watched constantly, and watch her we did. She was a one-baby show.

Every day after school Benno would run home and sweep her up in his arms. She called him Ba. She had a special laugh just for him. A high-pitched *hee-haw-hee* that brought tears to his eyes.

Only two things disrupted the routine every month. A fruitless trip to the Valley of the Moon and a visit to Tim Walker, the pediatric cardiologist. I dreaded both.

"Is she sleeping more?" asked Dr. Walker.

"No," said Benno. Benno accompanied me to every appointment.

Dr. Walker smiled at me. At times Benno acted more like Vivi's father than her brother. He'd taken his role as man of the house seriously.

"How long does it take her to fall asleep?"

"Depends," I said. "If she's tired, boom, she's out. But if she's awake, which is most of the time, you can't keep up with her."

"She has fifty words already," said Benno.

"Well, there's no doubt she's a smart girl," said Dr. Walker. "But tell me what you mean by 'boom, she's out.'"

Benno and I exchanged glances.

"I'm exaggerating," I said. "She's like any kid. If she's tired, within five minutes her eyes are blinking shut."

"No, Mom," said Benno. "It is *boom*. One second she's awake, the next second she's asleep."

My stomach roiled; I had been intentionally understating things. "Is that a bad thing?" I asked.

"It is if she's fainting," said Dr. Walker.

"But she's not fainting, she's sleeping."

"It might look like sleeping. But it could be that her heart has sped up so much she just sort of passes out. A baby can't tell us what's happening. When she's older, she'll be able to report to you and let you know if she feels dizzy or light-headed."

When Vivi had an episode, her heart rate could elevate to a staggering 250 to 300 beats a minute.

Dr. Walker looked at the chart. "Let's see, she's eleven months and two days. Her resting heart rate when she was born was 160 beats a minute. Each month, it's gone up a beat or two, and today we're at . . . 180." He looked at me over his glasses. "Normal for a child her age, almost a year old, is 80 to 130. The number should not be increasing, Lux. It should be decreasing as the heart muscles get stronger, as she gets older and stronger."

He squatted down next to Vivi, who was buckled in the stroller, chewing on her stuffed monkey's tail.

"Hey, cutie pie," he said. "How about you cut down on your coffee intake and give up smoking? Can you do that for me?"

She promptly yanked his glasses off his face and flung them across the room. We all heard the plastic frames crack.

"Vivi!" I yelped.

Dr. Walker laughed, walked to his desk, and pulled out another pair of identical glasses. "And that's why I buy them in bulk."

"I'm so sorry," I said.

He nodded, looked at Benno and me. "Frankly, I'm concerned."


Vivi wailed all the way home, batting her chest, trying to pull off the event monitor.

"How the hell are we supposed to keep that on?" I cried.

Dr. Walker had given us two choices. Have her wear a monitor or start her on beta blockers. I didn't want to medicate her, and I doubted the beta blockers would be a long-term solution if Vivi's heart issues were a result of her being Joseph's child (which I firmly suspected they were). I had begun to believe the only real solution was to bring her back to Greengage.

"We have to dress her in layers so it's impossible for her to get to it. Poor baby, she doesn't know what it is. But you'll get used to it, won't you, Viv?" Benno crooned, reaching into the backseat and holding her hand.

I looked into the rearview mirror and watched as she calmed, her eyes blinking shut.

"Did she just pass out?"

Benno shook her gently.

"Isn't that thing supposed to give off some sort of an alarm?"

"I don't think so; it just records. Vivi, Vivi." He squeezed her hand. Her eyes opened. "Ba," she said.

"Oh Jesus. Jesus, thank God!"

"Mom, calm the hell down. It doesn't do any of us any good if you freak out, does it, Vivi? We don't like it when Mom freaks out, do we?"

"Nil," said Vivi, her word for vanilla ice cream.

"She wants Nil," said Benno.

I put on my blinker and turned right, trying not to cry. A few minutes later I pulled into a Denny's parking lot. Just an ordinary family out for an ordinary meal, I told myself. I'd put her in a high chair. Benno would turn his paper napkin into an origami swan, and we'd order a plate of fries and bowls of ice cream. Salty and sweet. Happy and sad. That's the way we all liked it.


"I can't believe Benno's a sophomore," said my mother. "It seems like almost yesterday that I was at the airport waiting for a five-year-old to arrive."

She'd come bearing suitcases of presents. For Benno, clothes. For Vivi, she'd just about emptied the shelves at the Toy Soldier in Newport. I told her it was far too much, but she told me it was far too little. She was trying to make up for my father's absence. He'd flown out with my mother for a visit just after Vivi was born, but we hadn't seen him since.

Vivi squealed in her high chair and waved her arms. "Gamma!"

I handed my mother a banana. "She's hungry, you better hurry up."

What had I told my mother about Joseph? There was a father. He lived abroad. It was complicated. We were in love. What else was there to tell her? Until something changed and Greengage opened its door to us, there was nothing left to say. She'd accepted it just as gracefully as she'd accepted my story of Benno's origins. She'd asked only one question: was she expected?

"She wasn't an accident," I'd told her. I'd grown into that truth—both Benno and I had. All you had to do was take one look at Vivi and you knew that this baby belonged in the world. She had enough life force for two worlds.

"Your father wanted to come, but he was feeling under the weather," my mother said. She gave Vivi a piece of the banana and took a deep breath. "I have something to tell you. *We* have something to tell you, me and Dad. Your father has prostate cancer, Lux. We've known for a few months."

My mouth fell open in shock.

"Oh, no, please don't look at me like that," she pleaded. "I've been under orders not to tell."

"He's got prostate cancer? Are you kidding me? Mom, why didn't you let me know?"

"It was his idea. He didn't want to burden you. Besides, you have your own medical crisis here."

"God, you've known for two months?"

"Well, actually a little more than a year," she confessed.

I gasped.

"Gamma," said Vivi, aware her grandmother's attention had wandered. "*Harry Dirty Dog?*"

My mother leaned over and kissed Vivi on the cheek. "I'll read to you in a little while. After you finish your snack. Has she had her medicine this morning?"

Last month, when it became clear Vivi had been fainting—not often, but often enough to scare the hell out of us—we'd given in and put her on beta blockers. They were helping and I was hopeful.

"I can't believe this," I said. "I'm coming back with you. I'll book the flight right now. Sunite Patel can take care of Vivi, and Benno's very independent."

"No. There is no need for you to come back to Newport. I'm telling you now because he's doing okay. He's much better. He's been through two cycles of chemo. He's weak, but officially in remission. That's the good news. That's what I wanted to share with you."

"How long will he be in remission?"

She gave me a weak smile. "Could be a long while, the doctors say."

"That's good, Mom. That's really good."

A month later she called to say he was dying.

# LUX

❧

*Newport, Rhode Island*
*1986*

"Mom." I opened the screen door and stepped into the living room. "Mama, I'm here."

No answer. I heard the water running; she must be upstairs. I put my suitcase on the floor and tried to slow down my jackrabbity heart.

They'd gotten a new Sony TV and there were stacks of VHS tapes piled on top of it: Jane Fonda's *Low Impact Aerobic Workout*, *Out of Africa*, and *Tootsie*. The radio still sat on the windowsill above the kitchen sink. Memories came flooding back. The Kinks. My plaid skirt. My fifteen-year-old tanned and muscular legs.

On the fireplace mantel were three photographs, one of my father and a gap-toothed Benno sitting at the counter at Newport Creamery. The second was a photograph my mother had taken of Benno and Vivi in my kitchen. The third was of me on my first day of kindergarten, Dad holding my hand. My braids so tight my eyes were almond shaped.

"You're here," said my father from the top of the stairs.

Once he'd had a full head of thick brown hair. Now he was bald, his scalp covered with age spots. His eyebrows were sparse and wiry, his lips thinned to two lines. He looked like an ancient toddler.

My breath caught in my throat—his appearance was so shocking. Had the decline happened slowly or had it suddenly ramped up in the last month? I hadn't been here to witness it, to be with him and my mother.

He clutched the banister.

"Do you need help?" I asked.

He shook his head.

I thought of Benno and Vivi and my heart clenched. I could just picture Vivi in bed, clutching her stuffed monkey to her chest. She'd be sleeping in her Winnie-the-Pooh onesie. Sunite was staying with them, but Benno would be the one to retrieve her in the morning. The lucky one to have his cheek patted with her tiny hand. "Ba, Ba," she would say, a dazed look in her eye, the same look she had on her face every morning. *I'm still here?* She was so new.

My father walked carefully down the stairs and sat on the couch.

"Can I get you some water?"

"I have a favor to ask," he said.

"Where's Mom?"

"Your mother has gone to the store."

"At nine o'clock at night?"

"We've run out of whiskey. It's my last vice."

He sounded so grave. Was he going to ask me to give his eulogy? Help him pick out a plot?

"What is it, Dad? What do you need?"

He looked down at his lap. "Would you come with me to Lapis Lake one last time?"


The next morning, my mother raced around the kitchen. She packed a cooler full of sandwiches, some cut-up celery, and grapes. She poured whiskey into a flask and filled two thermoses, one with tea, one with orange juice.

"Is the whiskey for him or me?"

"It's for whoever needs it. If his blood sugar plummets, we'll give him the juice."

"*We'll* give him the juice? You're coming with us to Lapis Lake?"

"Well, I suppose that depends."

"On what?"

"Am I invited?"

"Jesus, Mom, of course you are. You don't need an invitation."

"Then I'm coming."

She was coming. My mother was coming to Lapis Lake. I tried to imagine her using the outhouse. Knowing her, she'd hold it all day and make us stop at a gas station on the way back. Well, we'd have a picnic and be back on the road within a few hours. That's all the excitement my father could tolerate anyway.

My father slept all the way to the New Hampshire toll booths, then he woke with a start.

"We've crossed the state line?"

"A few miles back," I told him.

He shifted around, trying to find a comfortable position.

"Do you need another pill, George?" asked my mother. The two of them were sitting in the backseat. He'd stopped chemo a month ago. The only thing he took now was pain medication.

"Not yet. Damn."

"What's wrong?" I asked.

"We missed the state liquor store."

When I was a kid, we always stopped at the liquor store and loaded up, because the booze was tax-free. He got beer. I got red licorice whips.

"I packed you a flask," said my mother.

"She likes it when I drink now. She pushes it on me."

"Yes, George, I want you drunk."

"She wants you to be happy," I said.

"She wants me unconscious."

"Dad!"

"You think I don't know I'm a pain in her ass?"

He rolled down the window and tipped his nose up like a dog, sniffing the wind.

"Humph, not so rural anymore," he said, when I turned onto Rural Road 125. I had the same butterflies in my stomach I'd had when I was a child.

"When did they pave it?"

"A while ago."

"It's nice. Easier on the suspension."

"It's not nice. The dirt road was fine. Now that it's paved, leaf peepers come down here. I had to put up a No Trespassing sign."

"George, you only come up a few times a year. You can afford to be generous. Let other people enjoy it, too," said my mother.

I drove slowly down the maple-lined road. The leaves were brilliant shades of orange, red, and yellow. It was peak foliage season. Woodsmoke hung in the air.

"I don't think I've ever been here in the fall," I said. My father had always come alone on Columbus Day weekend to close down the cabin for the winter.

I pulled into our driveway and parked.

"My God," my mother said. "It looks exactly the same. Like no time has passed at all."

"I can smell the lake," said my father.

He excitedly swung his legs out the car door, but even that tiny effort cost him. He closed his eyes and breathed heavily for a minute or two. When he opened them, he looked defeated.

"Give him a minute," said my mother.

"Where's the key, Dad?"

"In the usual place," he said. "Go with her, Miriam."

"I'm staying with you. I want to make sure you're okay."

"Go with her, I'm fine," said my father.

"You might want to wait, Mom, let me air things out a bit."

"Go ahead, Miriam," said my father.


I ducked under the porch and retrieved the key, which hung from a rusty nail. My father hadn't visited at all this summer, which meant the place had sat unused for over a year.

"Brace yourself," I said to my mother.

I slid the key into the lock and opened the door hesitantly, anticipating the stale cardboard scent of decaying mice. Instead the cabin smelled pleasantly of cedar and lemon cleanser.

We stepped into the cabin and gasped. Every surface had been scoured clean. The curtains were pulled and fresh air streamed through the open windows. A pot of mums sat on the counter.

I opened the fridge and was hit by a blast of cool air. Not only was it running, but it was fully stocked: strawberries, a quart of milk, a pint of cream. A roasted chicken. A container of potato salad. A jar of pickles. A six-pack of Coors Light. A wedge of cheddar and sliced salami. A package of Oreos and a bottle of Boone's Farm apple wine, my mother's favorite.

We peeked in the bedroom. The bed was neatly made up with fresh sheets. There was a stack of clean towels on the dresser and a candle on the bedside table.

"I feel like Sara Crewe in *A Little Princess,*" I said.

My mother had her hand cupped over her mouth, her eyes wet. "He did this for us."

"He did it for you," I said.

She nodded. "I suppose this means we're spending the night."

"I think that's the idea."

"Lux!" my father shouted.

"I'll get him," I said. "You stay."

I took my father's arm and helped him out of the car. "It's like Christmas in there."

"Did she like it?"

"Yes, she liked it."

"Was she surprised?"

"She certainly was. How did you do it?"

"I hired a caretaker. She looks after the place. After I got sick, it was too hard to open and close up the cabin by myself."

Slowly we walked around to the front of the cabin and climbed the porch stairs. He nodded in satisfaction at the two rocking chairs, each of which had received a new coat of glossy green paint. When we stepped into the cabin, he grinned.

"George," said my mother.

"Miriam," said my father.

"You little sneak. This isn't a day trip. We're not going home this afternoon, are we?"

He sat down in a kitchen chair. "One night. All right? That's all I want. One last night here with my family."


I was the only one awake. My mother had fallen asleep on the pullout couch. My father snored raspily in the bedroom. The loons were calling, that distinctive, forlorn cry. *Hoo-hoo-hoo*. My thoughts were forlorn, too: *Vivi is so sick. I may never see Joseph again. My father is riddled with cancer.*

I put on my bathing suit and walked down to the lake. I dipped a toe into the water. Not too bad. I dove in before I could change my mind.

The water was glorious. I'd always loved night swimming the best. I stayed in as long as I could bear it, but when I started to shiver uncontrollably I went back to the cabin. My mother was still conked out on the sofa; she'd had three glasses of wine, two glasses past her limit. I thought about making coffee but I didn't want to wake my parents. Instead I lit a candle and perused the bookshelf. There were lots of paperbacks, mostly thrillers, John le Carré and James Patterson, along with the classics my father had read to me when I was a girl. On the topmost shelf I found the copy of *The Lion, the Witch and the Wardrobe* I'd sent Benno the year we'd been apart. On the inside cover in pencil he'd written, *Property of Bennett Lysander.*

Had my father read it to him?

I didn't hear him snoring anymore. I opened the door and his bed was empty. He must have gone to the outhouse. But his slippers were neatly lined up beneath the dresser. He'd left the cabin without shoes?

I checked the outhouse. He wasn't there.

"Dad?" I called. "Dad?"

I checked the car. Empty. I started to panic.

It was four in the morning. I got a flashlight and began making my way through the woods. I walked through our neighbors' yards, then back along the waterfront. I kept calling his name. I'd alternate between "Dad" and "George." Finally, on my fourth round, I heard his tremulous voice: "Lux."

Three cabins down from ours, I found him. He was on the ground in front of the Harrises' outhouse. He was barefoot, in his pajamas. I could just make out his face.

"I had to go to the bathroom. I didn't want to bother your mother." He'd fallen.

"Why aren't you wearing shoes?" Of course he'd fallen. Not only was it dark, but one of his legs was two inches shorter than the other. "Let me look at your knee."

"No, goddamn it. I only skinned it."

"Okay. Can you stand if I help you?"

He grunted and I stooped beside him. He put his arm around me and I gently hauled him up. We hobbled back toward our cabin.

"Why did you go to the Harrises'? Why didn't you go to our outhouse?"

He gave me a confused look. He thought it *was* our outhouse.

"I woke and you were gone."

"I went for a swim. I couldn't sleep. Look. Here we are now."

We stood at the bottom of the stairs.

"Come on, let's get you back into bed," I said.

We climbed the stairs, but when I opened the front door he said, "I don't want to go to bed. Not yet."

We settled into the chairs that still smelled of fresh paint.

He was disheveled. His hair mussed, his bloody shin exposed. I felt light-headed with guilt. Finally, here we sat, all these years later, on the porch of our beloved cabin. No real rapprochement in sight and my father was dying. He was *dying*. How could I have let so much time pass?

He coughed. "That summer. Nineteen sixty-four. The last summer you were at Lapis Lake? I knew you didn't want to be here. What was I thinking? That we'd have this, the two of us, forever?" His voice cracked on *forever*.

"Dad, stop. You have to conserve your energy. You can't afford—"

He looked at me with an anguished face. "Just listen. Please."

I sat back in my chair, my heart racing.

"You were a teenager. You were bored. You wanted a bigger life. Of course you did—that was only natural. But I couldn't bear to see it end. Only a damned fool thinks paradise will last." He ran his hand over his scalp. "It can't last; it's not meant to. Look at this place. Run-down, falling apart, mice in the rafters. Why the hell would you have wanted to stay here?"

Was he seriously asking me that question? "Because it *was* paradise, Dad."

"It was?"

"Yes," I said softly, letting the truth of that sink in.

"But you—"

I interrupted him. If I didn't say this now, I never would.

"I feel like I've spent all my life trying to find my way back to Lapis Lake, not literally the lake, but, you know, you. Us. The way we were. The way things were here."

He blinked hard.

"I should have come when you asked me to. When you first brought Benno. It was such a nice gesture for you to invite me along. To give us a fresh start."

"I didn't hear back from you. I thought maybe you didn't get my letter."

"I got it. I was just—ashamed. My life was such a mess. If I'd have come back, the person I was then, I would have ruined this place for you. I didn't want to do that. My memories of us at the lake are sacrosanct. What you taught me here. How you believed in me here. The way you loved me here—that's what I built my life on. That's how I got to this. To who I am now. To Benno. To Vivi."

*To Joseph.*

He hung his head in despair. "It was my fault. I was such a stubborn, narrow-minded ass. I just couldn't get over my disappointment that you hadn't made the same choices I had, that you didn't value the same things. I'm not talking about wanting to be at the lake—well, maybe that was the beginning of it—but I'm talking about school. Your education. The ways you got distracted."

*Distracted.* That was a civilized way of putting it. Dash. Dropping out of college and moving to San Francisco. Getting pregnant at nineteen.

"Well, Dad, I certainly gave you every reason to be disappointed. I was young and stupid. I lost myself for a while. For longer than a while, actually."

"You didn't lose yourself, Lux. I left you and I'll never forgive myself for that. I made some attempts over the years to make amends, to reach out to you, but it hasn't been enough." He steepled his fingers in order to stop his hands from shaking. "Benno. Vivi being so sick. How do you manage?" he rasped.

I went inside and got a box of tissues and a glass of water. I placed them on the table next to him. He took a sip of the water and stared out at the lake, trying to compose himself.

"I manage, Dad, because I am loved. Because I found my own Lapis Lake. My own little paradise."

"Noe Valley?"

"No, no." I took a deep breath. "Greengage, Dad."

"Greengage?" he echoed.

I hadn't spoken the name to him since that terrible visit to Newport in 1980.

"Benno and I go there pretty regularly now. It's where Vivi's father, Joseph, is from."

His eyes narrowed. "Your mother told me about this Joseph. Where is he?"

"He's in Greengage."

"Well, why isn't he with you now? He's got a daughter—a deathly ill daughter!"

"He would be with us if he could. I promise you."

He squinted in disbelief.

"Dad, you're just going to have to take my word for it. We're doing everything we can to be with each other. It's just complicated. Getting to Greengage isn't easy."

I grabbed a tissue and pressed it to my eyes, willing myself not to cry.

"I don't understand, Lux," he finally said.

"That's because it's impossible to understand."

He took my hand. It had been years, perhaps going back to childhood, since my father had held my hand.

"Tell me. You love this Joseph? You love this place, Greengage?"

"More than anything!" I cried. "And Benno loves it, too. And Vivi will, I know it, if I can just get her there. All this time, I've been living two lives. My heart in two different worlds. It's just been so hard."

I began to sob. I had my eyes shut but I could feel his body shaking—he was crying, too. I breathed raggedly, trying to catch my breath. After a few minutes, I looked at him and he nodded.

"Lux?"

"Yeah" was all I could manage to say.

He gave me a heartbreaking smile. "Darling girl."

Would anybody ever call me *darling girl* again?

"You deserve a world that wants you," he said.


A month later I got the call that he'd died in his sleep. Benno, Vivi, and I flew back to Newport for the funeral, then the following day we drove north to Lapis Lake to scatter his ashes.

Vivi dropped a handful of ashes on the ground by the car. "Bye-bye," she said, clutching my pant leg. She was too young to understand what was going on, how final death was. That she'd never see her grandfather again.

I picked her up. She burrowed her face into the crook of my neck. She spent a lot of time there. If a neck could have had a head-shaped indentation worn in it, mine would.

Benno was somber, placing handfuls of ashes in carefully chosen spots that my father had loved. At the base of Mount Fort. At the foot of the dining hall stairs.

I rubbed my father's ashes into the porch railing. How many times had he sat there, a book cracked open, reading to me? The smell of Coppertone drifting through the air.


"I'm going to walk out on the branch one last time," I said, just before we were about to go.

"Careful," said my mother. "Don't fall into the water."

I took a mental snapshot of her sitting on the steps, a steaming mug of tea in her hand. A sight I'd never seen and would likely never see again.

"Don't worry. I've done this hundreds of times," I said, traversing the maple bough, arms outstretched for balance.

I saw my name from three feet away. Etched into the wood with the dull blade of a Swiss Army knife.

*LUX WAS HERE.*

Years ago, my father had made me sand it out of the bough.
Years ago, he'd carved it back in.

# LUX

❦

Finally we were allowed to take Vivi home from the hospital. She'd had a procedure called a radiofrequency ablation. It was a last-ditch effort to stop her ever more frequent episodes. Dr. Walker told us that in most cases the procedure was ninety-five percent effective, but Vivi had been in the hospital for nearly three weeks, and when she got out, she was weaker than ever. It hadn't made a damn difference.

Only six months had passed, but she was a shadow of the little girl she'd been on her first birthday. She spent most of her days under a blanket watching reruns of *Leave It to Beaver*. "Hello, Mr. and Mrs. Cleaver," she'd say to us when we walked into the room. She had an uncanny talent for mimicry. She belonged on the stage, not on the couch.

She learned how to live with the constant light-headedness. She walked in a wide stance, making sure one foot was firmly planted before shuffling the other foot forward. She'd throw up in the morning upon waking, and once more in the late afternoon. She was thirsty all the time: always sucking on ice chips. But when she saw me or her precious Ba, she'd shriek with glee, hold out her arms, and wave like a concertgoer, and for a second the old Vivi would bust through.

Benno had captured this moment perfectly with his camera, and I'd had the photo framed. In fact, Benno had documented just about every minute of Vivi's life. He couldn't stop taking pictures of her; it was a compulsion. I'd tucked every photo carefully away. A visual record for Joseph, to supplement my journal. Vivi loved being photographed, of course. She had a particular face she'd put on when she knew her brother had trained his lens on her. She'd dip her head and bat her eyelashes. "Act natural, Viv!" he'd cry. "Pretend I'm not taking a picture."

She wasn't capable of it.

In January, my mother had sold the house in Newport, donated her old Lilly Pulitzer shifts to Goodwill, and moved into the basement apartment at 428 Elizabeth Street. We told her about Greengage then. Whether she believed us or not, I didn't know, but she believed we believed, and that was enough for now.

She'd taken over Vivi's care during the days while I was at work. All in all, we had a fine support system set up, and Vivi couldn't have been more loved. Still, we all knew the truth. These days were numbered. If I didn't get Vivi back to Greengage soon—I couldn't bear to think of what would happen.

"I don't know if we should bring her," said Benno. "The party did her in."

It was 11:00 A.M., usually Vivi's most wide-awake time, but she was asleep on the couch. Yesterday we'd celebrated her half birthday with great fanfare. We'd taken her down to the Embarcadero to see the circus and then afterwards out to her favorite restaurant. She'd had one spoonful of ice cream and promptly thrown up. It was too much.

I understood Benno's reticence. This would be my twenty-seventh useless trip in a row to the Valley of the Moon, and I was despairing as well. In my darker moments I wondered if I was being punished for having Joseph's child. In my darkest moments I wondered if Vivi was being punished for being born. Did her existence break some fundamental law of time? Could a creature who was half of the future and half of the past live? Would we be banished from Greengage forever?

"Why don't I have Grandma take me?" said Benno. "If the fog is there, I'll call you from the parking lot. There won't be any traffic. You can borrow the Patels' car and be there in an hour and a half, tops."

No, I couldn't take the chance. What if the fog was there? Sick or not, Vivi would have to go, as would I.

# JOSEPH

❧

*Valley of the Moon*
*1909*

Two figures emerged from the fogbank. Lux looked exhausted and Benno was two, maybe three inches taller. How long had it been for them? Not for the first time, I was struck by how much easier I had it. I knew I'd see her every month the morning after the full moon, but when she said goodbye to me she never knew when she'd see me again.

She clutched something to her chest. A doll for Gennie? The doll slid out of her arms. The doll walked toward us. Then the doll began to trot.

"Vivi, wait!" Lux shouted.

The doll was a little girl with a head of black curls. She did a strange sort of stagger-run at first, ungainly, like a colt taking its first steps, but she gained strength as she went and soon she was cantering across the field. I heard my father's voice in my head. *"Faster, boy, faster."*

"Well, hello," said Fancy as the girl stopped short in front of us.

Lux and Benno were halfway across the meadow, and Lux had a stricken look on her face. Had this girl sneaked through the fog with them somehow? Become separated from her family?

"Hello, Mr. and Mrs. Cleaver," the girl said.

"For God's sake," said Fancy. "Would you look at her eyes?"

Lux and Benno ran up. Benno nodded solemnly at me and Lux

squatted and grabbed the little girl by her chubby arms. "Don't you ever, ever do that again, Vivi." Then she burst into tears. "Did you see, Benno? Did you see? She ran. She ran!" She pressed the girl to her chest. "Look at you. Look at you. Oh, you big, strong, beautiful girl."

"Her eyes, Joseph. Her eyes," said Fancy.

They were the exact same glacier blue as my own.

"Stop it," said the little girl, trying to wriggle out from Lux's arms. "Mama, let me go."

# LUX

&#10070;

The change had been immediate. Like Sleeping Beauty, as soon as we stepped through the fog, Vivi awoke and her body flooded with life. Within a minute she went from slack in my arms, barely having the energy to raise her head from my shoulder, to galloping across the meadow.

I hadn't planned what to say to Joseph. Honestly, I'd almost given up on the fog ever appearing again.

He stared at Vivi and then at me. "Is it true? Is she mine?"

I nodded; I could barely see through my tears.

# JOSEPH

❦

How can I describe the next few days? They passed at a feverish pitch. That this creature existed, that she had been alive for a year and a half without my knowledge—it was impossible to digest. I'd long ago given up on my dream of being a father, long ago reconciled myself to a life without children, yet here she was in front of me; Vivi was no dream. She was decidedly of the flesh. Dipping and swaying. Flipping her hair. Talking without taking a breath. Darting between my knees. Exploring. Investigating. Touching. Sighing. Singing. Crying. Laughing. Tragedy—a dead spider! Triumph—an iridescent green beetle skittering across the floor! Sitting on my lap, her sweet-smelling head nestled into my chest, her eyelids fluttering, on the verge of sleep.

This late in life, to have a second chance at love and a first chance at being a father—it was exquisite. Once cursed, now doubly blessed.

After I'd returned from San Francisco, I had broken the news about Lux and me to Fancy, knowing it was the quickest way to ensure the information would spread throughout the community; I had no intention of sneaking around or hiding our relationship when Lux came back. I was prepared for people to be stunned. Instead they'd acted like it was inevitable. They'd seen what we hadn't long before we had.

So in this sense, at least, Vivi's arrival was less shocking than it might have otherwise been.

Vivi ran amok in the dining hall. She ran amok in the vineyard. She ran amok everywhere and we let her. She rapidly became everybody's darling. She was a miracle, you see. A child of two times. She gave us roots. She gave us a future.

And Lux? My darling Lux. Even though only a month had passed for me since I'd seen her last, I felt the two-plus years as if I'd gone through them as well. It was heart-wrenching to think of how she'd suffered, not knowing if she'd ever make it back and if Vivi would live. I didn't let her out of my sight. We went everywhere together, some part of our bodies always touching. Again and again I thanked her.

"When you found out you were pregnant, you must have considered—"

"Never. Not for a moment."

She hadn't given up on me, on Greengage, or on our daughter. I owed her everything.

# LUX

❧

After four glorious days together as a family, I finally spoke the words I'd been dreading to Benno.

"We've got to get back. You've already missed two days of school."

"And two days at Morty's," he said.

Benno had an after-school job working at Morty's Camera. He loved showing customers the cameras. Helping Morty run the photo lab he loved a little less: any monkey could do it, he said. He was old school. He liked to develop his own film in the darkroom. He'd become a master of light, of stop baths and wetting agents. He was trenchantly against special effects, but I suspected that would change as he got older. He would be seduced. He would dabble and find a way to mix the old with the new. That was his fate.

He put the camera up to his eye, sighted Vivi and Joseph in the lens, and frowned. "Hey!" he shouted. "Turn the other way. Face the sun."

Vivi and Joseph ignored him. He photographed them obsessively; even Vivi had grown tired of posing.

"Wait until Grandma sees her," I said. "And Rhonda. And Dr. Walker."

"What are you talking about?" asked Benno.

"How are we going to explain her sudden recovery? 'Well, Doc, the ablation finally took. Better late than never.'"

"Mom, Jesus. Vivi isn't coming back with us."

"Of course she is. Why wouldn't she? She's better. She's great."

"She's great because she's here in Greengage, Mom. She won't be great in San Francisco."

"She'll be fine at home. All she needed was this little visit back in time," I said defensively.

Benno let the camera fall heavily against his chest. "You think she's healed now? Permanently?"

"Yes, I do. I think so."

"You can't just think. You have to know. It took us over two years to get here. What if as soon as we get home she goes back to being sick? If that happens, she won't last another month, Mom. God. I thought you and Joseph had talked about Vivi. I thought you had it all worked out."

Joseph and I *had* talked about Vivi. Every night. Her personality traits. Whose genes she'd inherited. The constant devilish look in her eyes. What we hadn't talked about was what happened next.

"I thought he knew that Vivi would be coming home with us. I thought that was obvious."

"And he thought you knew Vivi would be staying. He—*we*—" he amended, "all thought that was obvious."

"You did?"

"Yeah, Mom."

"Well, why didn't you tell me?" I cried.

"'Cause we didn't think we needed to."

Joseph heard us arguing and swung Vivi up in his arms. They headed away from us, toward the herb garden.

"Stop!" I yelled. "Bring her back."

Joseph immediately put Vivi down on the ground.

"Vivi!"

She ran across the grass and hurled herself at me, screaming, "Tickle me!" I obliged and she writhed in paroxysms of joy. I lifted up her shirt and gave her a loud raspberry on her stomach.

"Do you know how much your mama loves you?"

"How much?" She threw her arms up into the air and preempted my answer. "To the moon and back."

"Yes," I said. "That goddamned moon. That much."

"You could stay here with her," said Benno as we watched Joseph and Vivi walk off to the dining hall. "I was going to tell you that. It would be okay with me. I'd be fine."

"You're only seventeen. I'm not leaving you alone."

"I wouldn't be alone. I'd have Grandma."

"No, Benno, forget it. I left you once before. I'm not doing it again."

"But now you're leaving Vivi."

"It's different. I'm leaving her with her father. If I stayed in Greengage, you'd have no parents. At least this way each of you gets one of us."

"She's a baby. She needs you more."

"It will be easier for her. It will. She'll be able to count the days. She'll know exactly when she'll see us next."

Neither of us said what we were thinking: that it would not be the same for us.

# LUX

❧

*San Francisco*
*1987–88*

B ut it was. Every month after, the fog appeared and Benno and I went back to Greengage. I got to see my daughter grow.

I concocted a story to explain Vivi's disappearance to everyone but Rhonda and my mother, both of whom knew the truth. People were aware Vivi had been sick, and I'd told a few people her father lived abroad. Abroad—a vague definition that suited my purposes perfectly. Vivi was temporarily living abroad with her father, getting treatment at a children's heart clinic.

I put on a good show, but the loss of Vivi in my daily life was crushing. I carried her photo with me. Dozens of times a day, I'd take the picture out of my wallet and look at her. I'd carry on a conversation as if she were there in the room with me. I'd wonder what she'd had for breakfast. If she'd napped that afternoon. What adventure Joseph had taken her on. How many stories she'd begged for before bed.

My mother missed Vivi terribly, too. I pleaded with her to come with us to Greengage, but she wasn't able to make that leap yet. Instead she wrote letters to Vivi and I carried Vivi's letters back to her. In this way they stayed in touch.

Back in Greengage, Vivi acclimated to her new life quickly. Even though Fancy and her family had eventually moved to a cottage of their own, Gennie frequently spent the night at the house. The wing was filled with the sounds of shrieking and laughter. Little feet pounding down the hall. The quiet hour. Dusk. Two girls freshly bathed, swatting away sleep, awaiting their bedtime lullabyes. They were more than cousins, they were super cousins. Bound together through time.

It was stunning to see Joseph with Vivi and Benno. I'd never experienced parenthood with a partner, let alone one who was as invested in my children as I was. It felt like a sort of miracle. The way he gently instructed them, nudged them. And the way he listened to them. The look of continual wonder on his face, that these two young humans belonged to him, to us.

I wondered if there would come a day when I wouldn't have to travel back and forth every month. I didn't imagine Benno would be ready for that anytime soon; he was only seventeen and as firmly embedded in 1987 as he was in Greengage. After high school he wanted to go to art school. And after that he dreamed about moving to New York City. Or to Barcelona. Or Paris. He was young—he wanted everything. I wanted everything for him, too. But whenever he told me of his plans, my heart stopped. How could he do all that and regularly come to Greengage, the only place we could all be together? He couldn't.

He'd eventually leave San Francisco. We wouldn't see him every month. Maybe we'd see him once or twice a year. The idea of this separation panicked me, but wasn't this what most children did? Sought out their fortunes? Left home? Moved to a different city? Only saw their parents a few times a year? Yes, it was—but there was one big difference. The fog. Although it was coming regularly now, I still didn't completely trust it. I found myself praying all the time. *Please, God, please. Let this continue. Just let me have this. Let us have this.*

But for now, I tried to live in the present.

In April, Doro and Rose were in a car accident. They swerved to avoid a bicyclist and were broadsided by a truck. Rose died instantly; Doro passed a few days later. Neither of them had children: they were the last of their lines. I was stunned to find out that they'd left 428 Elizabeth Street to me.

The lawyer delivered a card along with the paperwork. Snoopy in a red plane, sailing off into the sunset. Written in Doro's spidery scribble . . .

*Take care of our grand old lady!*

They donated the rest of their fortune (and it was quite sizable) to the Lesbian and Gay Alliance in San Francisco.

How I would miss them.



Benno and Joseph had their own relationship outside of me. They took frequent long walks—rambles, they called them. I was never invited.

"What did you talk about?" I'd ask Joseph when they'd come back.

"Oh, this and that," was always his answer.

"Do you give him advice?"

"Only if he asks for it."

I'd continue to push him for details, but Joseph remained mum, so I had to imagine their conversations. What does a father figure teach a son? How to hold your liquor. Always carry a handkerchief (a bandanna in Benno's case), never make excuses, tell the truth except when it will hurt someone's feelings. And women. They must have talked about women. Did Benno have a girlfriend? I had no idea until the day Benno asked if he could skip going to Greengage that month.

"Your sister will be devastated," I said.

"No, she won't."

"She will! She lives for your visits."

"She'll be fine. I'll write, and I've been making a cassette for her."

"A cassette of what?"

"Music. Thoughts. Conversations. Silly things. Jokes I know she'd like."

"Well, what am I going to tell her?"

"Tell her I had to see my girlfriend."

"You have a girlfriend?"

"Don't act so surprised."

"You can't see her on another night?"

"I want to take her to see the Smiths at the Fillmore. A bunch of our friends are going."

"Who's this girl?"

"A girl. You don't know her. One month, Mom. Come on. Please."

"I'm sorry—no. We need you in Greengage," I said.

Benno stomped off to his room. He wouldn't speak to me for two days.

"He's eighteen now," said Joseph. "He's been so devoted. You can't expect him to come back to Greengage every month."

He was *only* eighteen. Yes, I could.

Eleven full moons had passed since we'd left Vivi in Greengage, and eleven times the fog had appeared. Joseph and I had a hypothesis. The fog was coming every month and would continue to come every month because of Vivi. She was a bridge, just as Rhonda said she would be. She was holding open the door between the past and the future. The wall of fog still encircled all of Greengage, but time no longer sped up during the twenty-four-hour period of the full moon. Greengage was back on the regular calendar.

"Let's surprise Vivi and Joseph. Let's stay through a full moon this summer," I said to Benno.

Benno held up a threadbare sweater. "Toss or keep?"

We were going through his drawers. He'd grown two inches—he needed new clothes.

He would be attending the San Francisco Art Institute in September. He'd applied to Pratt and RISD as well, and had been rejected by both. Secretly I was thrilled he'd be living at home for another few years.

"Toss," I said.

He pressed the blue wool sweater to his nose. "But I love this sweater."

"Then by all means keep it." I sat down on his bed. "Did you hear what I said?"

"I heard you."

"Well—what do you think? Time isn't speeding up anymore. The fog has been coming every month for nearly a year."

"That would mean we'd get there the morning after the full moon and stay through the next full moon? That would be almost two whole months. That's a long time, Mom."

I still felt bad about not letting him go to that concert. But I was also scared I was losing him. Every day he became more independent, more insistent on making his own choices.

"It's a big deal, I know, but it means a lot to me. I won't ask you to do this again, I promise. If you want to skip a visit now and then this year, it's okay with me. But let's have this one long visit, the four of us. Please."

"What about work?"

"I have a month's vacation time saved up and I think they'd let me take a month more as unpaid leave." Pease had retired. I ran the loan department now.

"What about my job?"

"Tell Morty it's a family trip. He'll understand. You've been with him for so long."

"Would you stay through the full moon if I didn't go?"

"No, of course not. The only way I'd stay is if you agreed to come."

"Can I think about it?"

I wasn't going to force him. "Sure. But imagine what it would be like for all four of us to be together for an extended period of time."

He raised his eyebrows at me. "Let's be honest. Imagine what it would mean to you. You don't want to stay without me, and you still feel guilty for staying through the full moon when I was nine, right?"

I nodded, my throat swelling. As long as I lived, I would never forgive myself.

"Well, don't. You had a good reason. Martha had just died."

"That's not a good enough excuse. I wasn't thinking about you."

"Yep, you weren't thinking about me. That's true. I wasn't the first thing on your mind. But how long are you going to beat yourself up over it? One day I'll be a parent and I'll fuck up, too; I'll stop looking for just a second. I'll make the wrong call, I'll forget to do what I said I'd do, and it will be inexcusable and there will probably be consequences. I know that will happen. And I also know I'll probably carry that guilt with me, because isn't that part of what being a parent is all about? But maybe that guilt isn't a bad thing? Maybe you felt that guilty because you loved me so much. Isn't that good?"

Suddenly he teared up. I hadn't seen him cry in years. I started crying, too.

"You don't have to prove anything to me. You don't have to rewrite the past. It's okay, Mom," he whispered.

A week later he told me he was in.

We decided we'd leave the day of the July full moon and return the day before he had to start his classes. I couldn't believe we were really doing it.

When I told my mother, she basically moved in for the weeks remaining until we left.

"Mom, you see me every day, you live right downstairs."

"That's not enough."

The days passed in a flurry of activity. I put in long hours at work to prepare for my absence; I didn't want to let anyone down. My mother made dinner for us every night—my old favorites, American chop suey, corned beef and potatoes. I let myself be mothered.

I also did some mothering of my own. I took Benno shopping and bought him some new clothes. We browsed Tower Records and hiked from Muir Beach to Tennessee Valley.

And my excitement grew ... we were about to have the longest time together as a family that we'd ever had by far.

# LUX

❧

*Valley of the Moon*
*1910*

Benno and I were completely absorbed into the community. July in Greengage was my favorite time of year. I worked in the garden, harvesting sugar snap peas and melons; Benno spent most of his time helping Matteo in the vineyard. We rose before first light and fell into bed the moment it got dark.

Oh, the incredible luxury of not having to leave a few days after we arrived. We began to talk about the future as if we had one. The following Wednesday. Next Saturday. A week from Sunday. I couldn't stop staring at the three of them. There, in front of me, my family. Eating, walking, laughing, playing cards. I hadn't realized how starved I'd been for this. Forget jewelry, or vacations, or a new car.

The most precious gift you could give somebody—time.

# JOSEPH

❦

"The flower clock," said Lux. "What happened to it?"

She sat between my legs on the porch step. Tomorrow was the full moon. She and Benno had been here a month and we still had a month to go.

When Lux and I first became a couple, I agonized over what Martha would have thought about us. Would she have felt betrayed? Once a week I went to her gravesite with a pair of clippers. I kept the grass neatly cut and the stone free of moss, but really I was searching for a sign. I looked for her approval in birdsong, in a squirrel scampering up a tree, in a particularly beautiful spider web. Eventually I realized I was making this far more difficult than it needed to be. Martha loved me. She loved Lux. She would have been happy for us.

"It never really worked, no matter how much attention I gave it. So finally—I just decided to let it go," I said. I still felt guilty when I looked at it. The weeds had taken over. The plants, so carefully chosen, had dried up and browned.

"It never made sense to me," said Lux. "The whole idea of it was the antithesis of Martha. Forcing flowers to open and shut at a certain hour. Trying to control time. To control nature."

"Martha didn't show it, but sometimes she felt desperate, just like all of us, trapped by our circumstances," I said. "The flower clock was her way of fighting back."

"Do you think she knew it wouldn't work?"

I nodded. "Yes, but working on the clock kept hope alive in her. That was reason enough for the undertaking."

Lux tipped her head back and smiled. "Aren't you going to ask me?"

"Ask you what?"

"If I'm staying. Tomorrow."

"Why would I ask you if I know the answer?"

"To make sure I hadn't changed my mind."

I gave her braid a gentle yank. "Have you changed your mind?"

She smiled. "I'm staying. We're staying through the full moon. Can you believe it?"

No, I couldn't believe it. I was so used to getting her in bits and pieces. A day here. An overnight there. A week, if we were lucky. This month had felt like a dream. Similar, in a strange way, to how I felt that first month after the earthquake, when we realized we'd been trapped by the fog. A drifting, but a drifting toward something. A shared future.

"You're sure?" I asked.

She gave me a long, sweet look. There were no words.

# LUX

❦

"So how are you feeling?" I asked Benno after dinner that same night.

We were sitting on a boulder down by the creek.

"About what?"

After spending a month in Greengage, Benno was the color of teak and had muscles in places he hadn't before. My beautiful boy. Dressed as usual in Levi's and a flannel shirt. Scuffed Timberlands. A leather cuff around his wrist.

"Tonight. Staying through the full moon. Having you around full-time, I've never seen Vivi so happy."

"I've never seen you so happy," he said.

"Yes, well." Somehow my happiness felt disloyal to Benno.

He grinned at me and jumped off the rock. "Gotta go."

"Wait. Where are you off to? Do you have plans for tonight?"

He shrugged noncommittally; he always wanted to keep his options open. He was quite popular in Greengage, just as he was back in his own life: I'm sure he had lots of invitations.

For a split second the boy surfaced in his manly face. His dark eyes glittered. A vulnerable softness around his mouth.

I slipped off the rock, hoping to get a hug, but he was eighteen, I couldn't just thrust myself upon him anymore.

He made no move toward me.

"Okay, I'll see you tomorrow."

"Yeah. See ya, Mom."

He loped off.

I woke after midnight. The room was spinning.

"Joseph!" I cried out.

He bolted up, immediately awake.

"Is it an earthquake?"

"No, it's not an earthquake." He drew me under his arm. "Stay still."

"I feel dizzy. It feels like I'm falling."

"Just close your eyes."

Panicked, I cupped my ears with my hands, trying to slow the whirling.

"You're safe here. We're safe together," he murmured.

In the morning we walked to the dining hall and Joseph seemed distracted. I held Vivi's hand and she toddled along slowly, stopping every five minutes to examine something. A ladybug on a blade of grass. A rock flecked with mica.

"God, I must have eaten something bad last night," I said. "I still feel like my equilibrium is off."

"Hurry," Joseph said.

"Why?"

He didn't answer.

"Why?" I pressed him, picking Vivi up.

She made a cry of protest.

"Give her to me," said Joseph. He carried her piggyback, her fat little hands clasped tightly around his neck.

"Do you feel dizzy?" he asked me.

I stopped. "Yeah. Sort of. It's the weirdest sensation. It's like I'm standing still but everything is flying by me."

He pressed his lips together grimly. "Time is speeding up."

"What?" I gasped.

"I'm sorry, Lux. I'm guessing more than a day passed outside the fog last night."

It took me a moment to process this information.

"But you said on full moon days time had been passing regularly. It's been that way for months," I protested.

"It was—until last night, I think."

We walked into the dining hall. He deposited Vivi on the floor and she ran off to join Gennie and Fancy. He scanned the room.

"Where's Benno?"

"I don't know."

"Who was he with last night?"

"Joseph, you're scaring me."

"I don't see him. He's not here."

"I assumed he was sleeping in. His door was shut and I didn't want to wake him."

"He's not in his bedroom—I checked. And all his friends are here. There, at that table."

All his friends *were* there, laughing, spearing sausage links with their forks.

"What did he say to you yesterday? What did you two talk about?" he asked.

"I don't know. It was just chitchat."

"Come on, Lux. Think. There had to be more."

I got a mental image of Benno's profile. Once, he'd let Penny put mascara on him, and his lashes were so thick and long they'd nearly touched his brow bone.

*He said he'd never seen me so happy.*

We went back to the house. It was Joseph who finally spied the note on the mantel in the parlor.

*Mom, went to meet a friend. Don't worry, I won't leave you stranded. I'll be waiting for you in the parking lot on August 30th.*

He hadn't stayed through the full moon. He'd gone through the fog.

———

"You have to go," said Joseph.

"What about Vivi?"

"I'll take care of her."

"What if—"

He put a finger to my lips, silencing me. "Go find him."

# LUX

❧

*San Francisco*

**B**enno wasn't in the parking lot. Neither was my car. Déjà vu. Only this time there was no payphone, no piece of paper taped up on the side of the phone booth saying *Have You Seen This Woman?* The only thing there was a bus stop.

I ran out to the road. What was my plan? To flag down a car? To hitchhike? Everything was eerily quiet. Judging by the deep blue shade of the sky, I surmised it must be early in the morning. Just after dawn.

I went back to the bus stop and sat on the bench. Okay, how bad could it be? How much time could have passed? Three, four months? Longer than that? I let myself imagine a year. Jesus, what if it was a year? What if I'd missed another year of his life! But it would be different this time. First of all, Benno was eighteen, not nine. Second of all, he wouldn't have felt abandoned, because he'd have known exactly where I was, in Greengage—exactly where he was supposed to be. I took a deep breath. A year, okay, a year, his first year of college. My mother would have kept an eye on him; she would have moved into our apartment. Made sure he ate well. She would have taken him to the cathedral on Christmas Eve. To Stinson Beach on Labor Day. She would have made a cake for his birthday.

*His birthday!*

*Oh, Benno—what were you thinking? How could you have done this? I never would have stayed through the full moon if you hadn't agreed to stay, too.*

A bus pulled into the parking lot, a San Francisco express. I hadn't even heard it approach. No squeal of brakes. No roar of a diesel engine. It was silent. The door opened, beckoning me in. I hesitated. Just as the door began to close, I ran up the stairs, reaching for my wallet.

"How much?" I said, but there was no driver, only a panel of electronics. I clutched the handrail. "Oh God," I whimpered.

"Please take a seat," said a disembodied voice as the bus pulled onto an empty road.

I made my way down the aisle, my anxiety skyrocketing. There were three people on the bus, all sitting in the back: a sleeping man buttressed by two suitcases, and a young couple who were making out.

The bus was driving itself? I'd have to readjust my estimate: three years? Five? I started to hyperventilate, then I remembered my father's advice. *If you ever get lost in the woods, the worst thing you can do is panic. Act like a scientist. Observe. Take note of your surroundings. Be patient. You'll find the way back.*

The sky slowly brightened. The highway was a vibrant green, made up of hexagons. We were joined by other early morning commuters. Mostly buses and some cars, all of them driverless as well, their passengers in the backseats, reading or sipping cups of coffee. Driving had apparently been outsourced.

*Five years, five years.* If I said it loud enough, maybe the fates would hear me and feel sorry for me and I would lock in the five years and be done with it. Five years was not so bad. Benno would be twenty-three.

There was a small screen embedded in the seat in front of me, and advertisements scrolled across it. The weather. A sale at Macy's. An entreaty to ration water.

The screen spoke. "Your destination?"

I was so surprised I answered immediately, like a schoolgirl being addressed by the principal.

"Noe Valley."

"Address?"

"Four twenty-eight Elizabeth Street."

"Adding your destination to route. Will arrive at the corner of Douglass and Elizabeth Street in approximately thirty-one minutes," the voice informed me.

I glanced behind me. Was everybody else getting the same sort of special treatment? Would they be driven directly to their destinations as well? But the man slept. The teenagers sucked face. Maybe the screen had already asked them.

I gripped the armrests. My fingernails dug into the leather. *Ten years. Ten years. Do you hear me? Not a week more than that.* Breathless with dread, I stared out the window, searching for some sign that it was going to be okay.

We stopped just before going over the Golden Gate Bridge to let the teenagers out. They scrambled down the steps, still clinging to each other, and on we went to San Francisco. Downtown looked jarringly different. Gleaming glass skyscrapers thousands of feet tall. Rooftop parks. A building that looked like saucers stacked one on top of another.

The man with the suitcases awoke and got off in Union Square, and then it was just me on the bus. When we got to Douglass Street, I asked the screen, "How much?"

"All public transportation in the city of San Francisco and its environs is free. If you wish to make a donation to the San Francisco Transportation Department, you may do so now."

I was directed to press my thumbprint onto the screen. Blindly I did so.

"You are not in the system." A list of countries appeared. "Please input your country of origin."

Not knowing what to do, I jumped off the bus. Panting, I stood on the street corner for a good fifteen minutes, trying to calm myself. *Please, please, please.* Please what? *Please don't let this be as bad as it looks. Please let this still be the twentieth century.*

*Please, oh, Benno, please.*

———

My neighborhood appeared much the same. The same Victorians, the same tiny driveways. In the early morning light, the houses looked like they were breathing.

I stopped in front of 428 Elizabeth Street. I'd stood here just four weeks ago and the trim was peeling. Now the house was painted a glossy dark gray. I couldn't shake the sense that it was staring at me. I half expected it to speak as the bus had.

I walked up the stairs to the front door. Was it too early to ring the buzzer?

I needn't have worried. Before I'd done anything, the door swung open and the smell of freshly brewed coffee drifted out. "Just a sec," said a man's voice. A little scratchier, a little throatier. Unmistakably older. Benno.

I prepared myself for what I might find. My son in his late twenties. I wouldn't be angry at him. There must have been a good reason he left.

It wasn't Benno. A man in his sixties, with rumpled silver hair, came down the stairs to greet me.

"Good morning," he said, after a pause.

"Um—hi. Is Benno Lysander here?"

He furrowed his brow. It *was* too early; I had probably woken him. "He's not, but please come in." He held the door open for me.

"How did you know I was here?" I asked.

"I didn't know, the house knew."

"And it just opened the door? What if I were a burglar?"

He laughed. "Then it wouldn't have opened the door. Would you like some coffee?"

I must have had a suspicious look on my face, because he gave a small bow. "I promise *I* am not a burglar."

I was unsure of what to make of him, but I had nowhere else to go, no other way of obtaining information about my son, so I followed him up the stairs.

"Thank you. I'd love some coffee," I said as we walked into the apartment.

"How do you take it?"

"Cream. Teaspoon of sugar."

"Cream. Teaspoon of sugar," he said under his breath, and I heard the beans being ground in the kitchen. "This way."

I bristled. I knew the way to the kitchen. *My* kitchen.

"I'm sorry if this sounds rude, but what are you doing here?" I asked.

"I live here."

"In this apartment?"

"Yes, in this apartment."

"With Benno?"

"No, with my partner, Alejandro. I'm Lucien."

He reached into a cabinet and pulled out a box of cereal. Froot Loops. The coffeemaker churned, gurgled, and spat a thick black liquid into a waiting mug.

We stared at each other awkwardly. He broke the silence.

"My name means light, just like yours, Lux."

A ghastly coldness settled inside my breast.

He lowered the boom as gently as he could. "It's 2064. I'm your grandson."


It was 2064? Seventy-six years had gone by?

I braced myself against the wall, pressing my legs together, trying to keep them from shaking, unable to bring myself to ask the obvious question. Where was Benno?

A figure seemed to appear on the surface of Lucien's left eye. He was wearing some sort of contact lens. I saw a tiny woman sitting at a desk.

"No. Something has come up," he said, apparently speaking to the woman. "A family emergency. Reschedule the meeting to seven A.M. PST tomorrow."

The woman disappeared. "Everybody wears lenses," he explained. "We conduct business with them, shop with them—they do just about everything for you."

My eyes darted around the room, frantically looking for something safe, something familiar. The cereal box. Toucan Sam. *Follow your nose. It always knows. The flavor of fruit. Wherever it grows.* Froot Loops was Benno's favorite breakfast.

"Is—" I sputtered.

He sighed. "I'm so sorry to have to tell you this. My father is gone. He passed away in 2060. My mother, Karen, died a year later."

I gaped at him, trying to make sense of what he was saying. I was confused, my mind grasping. His father?

"Your father?"

He gave me the gentlest of looks.

"Benno," he said.

"My son? You're talking about my son?"

"I'm afraid so."

I wobbled and took an involuntary step to the right. He reached out to steady me and I flinched. The last thing I wanted was for him to touch me. This man who was delivering to me the worst news of my life.

My son, Benno, who I just saw yesterday? Who needed to shave his sideburns? Who'd taught his little sister all the words to the Stones' "You Can't Always Get What You Want"? Whose dirty laundry sat in a pile back in Greengage, waiting for me to wash it on Sunday?

"I don't believe it," I whispered.

"I'm so sorry," said Lucien.

I shook my head vigorously, as if I could shake out what he was saying. The gesture was all Vivi's—she did this whenever I said no to her.

"But he was only eighteen!" I cried.

"Actually, he was ninety, Lux. And he lived a good, long life."

"Don't tell me that," I choked out, as I realized the disassociation I was feeling was because we were talking about two different people.

We weren't mourning the same Benno, because we didn't know the same Benno. I could only speculate about the man Benno would become, as I'd done so often while he sat at the kitchen table doing his homework. Would he marry? What would his spouse be like?

Where would he work? What would he name his children? What kind of a grandmother would I be? What city would he finally settle in? Would his favorite meal always be pot roast and mashed potatoes?

That this stranger standing in front of me held all the answers was unthinkable.

No, we weren't mourning the same Benno, because my Benno was not even out of his teenage years. To my knowledge he'd never been in love, never had sex, never eaten Peking duck—never even been out of the country. My son and Lucien's father were as unrelated as they could be. Neither one of us knew the one the other mourned.

I slumped to the floor. Benno was gone? Oh God, that meant my mother was gone, too! I wheezed, my breath shallow.

Lucien crouched down and put an arm around me.

"Breathe," he said.

Breathing was an impossibility.

"Look at me," he commanded. "Just look at me."

I focused on his face.

I thought of that night when Benno was nine, when I'd come home in the wee hours of the morning from the Valley of the Moon. The way he'd clung to me on the couch. I'd promised him I'd always be with him. That we'd always be together.

And Rhonda and Ginger? The Patels? Mike Mulligan? My colleagues at Baytelco? All of them? Dead?

"It wasn't your fault. You have to know that. It was nobody's fault," said Lucien.

"Why did he leave that night?" I cried. "We were supposed to stay through the full moon. I didn't force him. He agreed. He'd wanted to."

Lucien nodded. "He came back to go to a party. It was my mother's birthday. She was turning seventeen."

I looked at him dumbly. A party? I'd lost him to a party?

I thought back to the summer of '64. How I'd sneaked out after my father had gone to sleep. How I'd flirted with the bartender who'd poured me drink after drink. I was bored. I wanted action. I couldn't wait for my life to begin.

"They were kids," said Lucien. "And he was cocky; he thought he could have it both ways. You had it both ways for a while, didn't you? The fog came every month? He assumed that would continue. He went back the following full moon, but there was no fog. He went back every month after that. Nine hundred and forty times. He never missed a full moon; he never stopped trying to get back to you. I wasn't surprised when I saw you on the doorstep, because he'd prepared me. He knew you'd come back someday. I'm only sorry it wasn't sooner."

When Lucien's father died, he must have been sad, but it probably wasn't unexpected. As he'd said, Benno had lived a good, long life. As pleasant as Lucien seemed, I couldn't help but resent him. He'd had a lifetime with Benno. His grief was the clearest of lakes—you could see right down to the bottom of it. Mine was a waterfall with a hundred-foot drop that I'd just been shoved off involuntarily.

I searched for Benno in Lucien's face, but I could find no trace of him. My grandson was a stranger.

I have no idea how long we sat there on the floor or how long I wept. Occasionally Lucien would pass me a tissue, urge me to drink some water. Finally the tears subsided. A younger man entered the kitchen. Alejandro. Lucien handed him a cup of coffee. "Come back in a little while, honey," he said.

I thought, *Okay, Lux. Sit up. Try to speak. Be kind.* My mouth was so dry.

"You have some toothpaste here," I said, touching my chin to show him.

Lucien dabbed at his chin with a napkin. I kept being bowled over by swells of disbelief: this man was old enough to be my father. I felt numb, my blood frozen in my veins.

"Karen? Your mother? Tell me about her."

"They met in high school. She was an artist. A painter. They were in the same calculus class."

Was this the girlfriend he'd wanted to take to the Smiths' concert?

"Do you have siblings?"

"Two sisters. Iris, she lives on the top floor with her husband, and

Mary, who lives in Walnut Creek. Iris's son, Thomas, his wife, and their two kids, your great-grandkids, have the flat below ours. Mary's daughter lives in the basement flat. Alejandro and I moved in when Mom passed. They're going to be so thrilled to meet you."

"They all know about me?"

"The adults do, not the kids. As soon as we were old enough to be trusted to keep the secret, Dad told us. I went with him to the Valley of the Moon hundreds of times over the years."

I started to notice what my brain had refused to take in when I'd first walked in. The apartment was unrecognizable, furnished with a mix of mid-century and modern furniture.

"I had a futon couch there. You don't know what a futon is, I'm sure," I said.

"I know what a futon is. I slept on one all through college."

"Where did you go to college?"

"Cal."

"What did you study?"

"International relations. Minor in economics."

"What do you do now?"

"I'm a lawyer. Immigration issues. Civil rights. I handle mostly pro bono cases for the firm now."

I drank a glass of water and asked for another.

"Tell me the truth. Was he happy?"

He gave me a deeply empathetic look. "Come. You can see for yourself."


"Sit here," he instructed me.

I sat in a recliner in the middle of the room.

"Are you comfortable? I can adjust it. You're much smaller than I am."

"I'm fine."

The recliner was no La-Z-Boy. It was made of the finest leather, and sitting in it felt like a warm embrace.

"Lights," he said.

The lights in the living room went off.

"Activate walls."

How can I describe what happened next? The walls seemed to burrow around me.

"It's called a Timestream. My father—Benno—invented it. Sold hundreds of millions of them. They're as common as TVs; everybody has them now."

I felt uncomfortably weightless. I clutched the arms of the chair.

Lucien made a small adjustment, tipping me forward a degree. "Better?"

"Yes."

"He made this stream just for you," said Lucien.

An image slowly moved toward me. As it came closer the colors brightened and it sharpened into a photograph of an elderly man dozing in a chair, a book open in his lap. When it had enlarged to life size, it stopped and bobbed, like a seal poking its head out of the sea.

"This was him two days before he died," said Lucien. "I took that photo."

An ancient Benno. His face creased and weathered, jowled, age-spotted, wearing Joseph's bowler hat and a Grateful Dead shirt. Seeing him as an old man felt unspeakably unnatural. He'd died and I wasn't there. But of course I wouldn't have been there; even if I had been back in San Francisco, I'd have been long gone. How many mothers outlived their ninety-year-old sons?

The image passed through me, or I passed through it, I couldn't tell—it felt so real. Another photograph floated toward me.

"That's my mother," said Lucien.

Karen and Benno standing on the front porch, their children and grandchildren sitting on the steps in front of them. Their hands were clasped. Their faces full of pride.

"Thanksgiving, 2052. We all had the flu and didn't know it yet," said Lucien.

I sat spellbound as Benno and Karen slowly went from elderly to late middle age to middle-aged. Their hair from white to salt-and-pepper to blond and black. Their bodies from stooped and fragile to muscled and upright. I saw my mother's eyes in Mary. My father's chin in Iris. My grandchildren became young men and women, then they metamorphosed into children. Then my mother suddenly appeared, sitting in front of a computer in the basement apartment.

I cried when I saw her. The technology was so good, so crisp, I could almost smell her Aliage perfume. She'd been my ballast. She'd never, not once, given up on me. But at least she and Benno had had each other; at least they weren't alone all those years. That gave me some comfort.

Now here was Sunite Patel in the kitchen chopping peppers. Iris and Mary playing on the floor. Ginger and the girls (the girls no longer girls, but women, with families of their own), and Rhonda, that old hippie, flashing the peace sign at the camera.

Photo after photo flew by. Here were the people I loved drinking cold Coronas, listening to bluegrass, swimming at Lake Tahoe. And here were the people I loved getting younger and younger. Shrugging off the years.

Then Vivi and I appeared. Standing in front of a circus tent. Eating cotton candy. She and I napping on my bed. All photos Benno had taken before our last trip to Greengage. Then abruptly Vivi was gone.

Then it was just me, sitting in a booth at Mel's. The day I'd told Benno I was pregnant and he'd snapped my picture.

Still the years unwound. Benno at the seventh-grade science fair. The first day of middle school, Benno in the throes of a punk phase. Benno with my mother on Bowen's Wharf, posing in front of a tall ship, Miriam in her Lilly Pulitzer shift. My father in his office at St. Paul's, chatting with a student, leaning back in his chair. Benno standing in line for Del's lemonade. My precious, dearest, sweetest Benno with the happy-sad feeling beaming out of his eyes.

"Shut it off, please," I said. "I can't take any more."

"It's almost over," said Lucien.

Benno in Rhonda's arms, eating a lime Popsicle. Benno snuggled into the couch, the afghan covering him, mesmerized, watching *Love Boat*.

Benno hadn't been able to find his way back to me through my portal, the fog, so he'd used his portal, his camera lens. He'd done it so that I could go back into the past and find him, so that I wouldn't miss his life.

I knew what the last photo was before it came into focus. The Polaroid Rhonda had taken of a five-year-old Benno at the airport, his mouth ringed Hi-C orange on his way to Newport. The first time I'd had to let him go.

I pressed my fingers to my lips, kissed them, and held them up as the image passed.

The next few weeks, Lucien kept me busy. Everybody wanted to meet me. My grandchildren, my great-grandchildren. Their wives and husbands and partners. Their dogs, their cats, and their hamsters.

If I could have, I'd have stayed in bed, where a continual Timestream of my own making ferried me into the past. I inhabited my memories like a house. Each day I visited a different room. Here was four-year-old Benno at the zoo, shrieking along with the monkeys. Here were Rhonda and I driving down 101, singing along to the radio. Here was my mother mixing up a glass pitcher of Kool-Aid on a hot summer day. Here was the sound of my father's key in the lock.

I didn't want to leave the apartment, but Lucien insisted I get up, and dress, and eat a proper breakfast. He was a firm believer in distraction. Each day he had some family event planned. He shuttled me from apartment to apartment. From house to house. Dinner with Iris. Lunch with Mary. Little Gary's violin recital. Dolly's gymnastic tournament. We traveled from San Francisco to Bodega Bay. From Orinda to Danville. It seemed we missed no corner of the Bay Area.

The truth? This was my family, but they were strangers. Kind, interesting strangers, but strangers nonetheless. I counted down the days to the full moon. All I wanted to do was get back to Greengage to be with Joseph and Vivi. There was no other place for me now.

When the moon was full, Lucien drove me to the Valley of the Moon, but there was no fog.

"I'll bring you again next month, I promise," Lucien said.

I wept my way back to the city.

"There's something I want to show you," said Lucien a week later. "Have you ever been to Lotta's Fountain?"

"Yes, but it's been a while."

"How long?"

"Sometime in the eighties."

"Ah, yes. Well, I think you'll find it much changed."

We walked down Market Street. I saw the golden glow of the lantern from fifty feet away. The lamppost in the snowy forest. The light flashing off a tin lamp.

"The entire fountain was completely refurbished," said Lucien. "That's an eternal light. It will never go out. No matter how big the earthquake, that light will shine."

Water spouted out of the lion's mouth. The copper-hued iron gleamed.

Lucien read the plaque out loud. "'The fountain survived the 1906 earthquake, at which time it became a meeting place for people in search of their families.'"

He led me around the other side of the fountain to another plaque, which read GONE BUT NEVER FORGOTTEN.

What followed was a list of thousands of names.

"Look under the *B*'s," he said.

Babineau, Baggett, Batteulo, Baumann, Bayliss, Bayne. *Bell.* Joseph Bell, Martha Bell, Fancy Bell, Vivien Bell.

"Benno did this?"

"He was on the board of the restoration committee. Keep looking."

I found Dear One and Magnusson, Elisabetta and Matteo. Miss Russell, Friar and his wife, Sarah. I found all 278 of the original Greengage residents; my name was there, too.

Benno had remembered us all.

When three fogless months had gone by, it became clear I needed a more permanent living situation. Against my protests, my granddaughter Iris and her husband vacated the top-floor apartment and gave it to me.

Rose and Doro's old flat was a gorgeous space, flooded with sunlight, the kitchen outfitted with all the latest appliances. Unfortunately, the only way to operate them was through the lenses, which I refused to wear. I did not want to be plugged into a feed like some robot. What I would have given for a simple coffee percolator, the kind my parents had in Newport.

Without a current social security number, I was unable to work. Anticipating this possibility, Benno had set aside money for me in a trust fund. This was good and bad. Good because I didn't have to worry about how to support myself. Bad because I had nothing to do. If you tell a person they're useless, they become useless: one of the first things Joseph ever said to me.

I forced myself to leave the house every morning with my family. They went to work and school; I spent my days at the San Francisco Public Library. The library had evolved, just like everything else. Instead of being issued a library card, I was given a digital reader. If I wanted to read a book, within seconds all I had to do was download it to my device.

The library was furnished with long couches and comfortable chairs. There was a coffee shop and a bar. Floors filled with row after row of computers, but not a book to be seen anywhere, except in one room on the top floor. I spent almost all my time up there, inhaling the familiar smell of leather, paper, and dust while working my way through the library's archive of magazines and newspapers. I didn't belong here anymore, that was clear, but that didn't mean I shouldn't make an effort to understand what had happened in the years I'd been gone. Soon I'd be back in Greengage and Joseph would expect a full report.

*Soon* started to feel like a pipe dream. Every month I went to the Valley of the Moon and every month I returned, heartbroken. Was I doing something wrong? Perhaps if I tried to re-create the exact same conditions from before, I could somehow conjure up the fog again.

With Lucien's help, I went online and found the exact same North Face tent I'd had back in the seventies. I purchased a Marmot sleeping bag and an L.L. Bean camp chair, also exact replicas of our old gear. Everything smelled pleasantly musty. The sleeping bag held the faint odor of weed. These items, touchstones from my past, felt imbued with magic, and they made me ache for Joseph and Vivi. That I had no idea how long it would be before I could be with them again was devastating. The only thing that comforted me was knowing it would be just a month for them. They wouldn't suffer like I was suffering.

I couldn't have borne that.


The gear was not magic, of course it wasn't. It did nothing to change my fate. The fog did not return.

Despair was the most insidious of killers. A vampire, it drained me of energy and will. I stopped leaving the house. Stopped reading books or listening to music. Even Benno's Timestream, which I'd watched constantly over the first few months I'd been in San Francisco, ceased being of interest to me.

A year passed. Two years. I became more and more reclusive. In the months leading up to my fortieth birthday, I started to drink. At first it was a nightly glass of wine, but soon I was polishing off an entire bottle by myself. I'd pass out and wake a few hours later, unbridled fury coursing through me.

I'd stopped caring what happened to me. I'd walk in the most dangerous places in the middle of the night: Golden Gate Park, the Tenderloin. I courted violence, but it did not court me back. I was invisible. An exiled creature. I had the stink of alien on me. People kept their distance.

In the mornings, after my bender, I'd drag myself to Grace Cathedral up on Nob Hill. It was there, with the light streaming through the stained glass windows, the smell of wood and aftershave and incense, that I felt the presence of Benno, Joseph, and Vivi most strongly. There it was safe to cry.

---

"I see you," said the man from the end of the pew.

He was a regular. He arrived at the cathedral promptly at seven every morning and left fifteen minutes later. He was younger than me, maybe early thirties. Always dressed impeccably in a suit.

I shook my head at him. I was so used to being ignored that the sound of his voice felt like an assault.

"I see you," he repeated.

"Please don't talk to me," I said.

The next morning I came at 7:45. The man sat in the fourth pew from the front. His head bowed. His neck exposed.

What was he doing here? He should have been long gone by now.

I sat in a folding chair to the left of the sacristy, deep in the shadows. A minute later he got up and surveyed the cathedral. I sank low in my seat, but there was no use trying to hide, he was on a mission, hunting me down. He approached, walking quickly, his heels tapping on the floor. He stopped at the top of the row and I held up my hand to ward him off.

"You've lost somebody," he said.

"Shut the hell up." I was furious he'd invaded my privacy.

He flinched but didn't move.

"Jesus. Why are you looking at me that way? Do I know you?"

He made a strange sort of croaking noise. "I lost somebody, too," he said.

By then it had been four years. Lucien and the rest of my extended family were well intentioned and kind, but I knew they thought I should have moved on by now. They wanted me to put down roots in the present, move past Benno's death, past the Valley of the Moon, past my desperation to get back to Joseph and Vivi.

But this man's simple act of confession? The communal recognition of our loss? It made me feel like my grief was okay, maybe even appropriate.

"I can't shut it off," I said. "They want me to, but I can't."

"Some things can't be shut off," he said, absolving me. "They can only be borne."

My pain was bottomless. Benno was gone. My baby. My first. There would be no fighting it. No forgetting about it. No putting it behind me. I would carry it with me forever. This shattering truth. I walked this earth and my son did not.

The ride to the Valley of the Moon was the only time I felt free. It was time out of time. Past and present collided. I was twenty-five, having just sent Benno off to Newport, my backpack in the trunk, stuffed with Slim Jims, a copy of *The Hobbit*, and Rhonda's stolen peanut butter. I was forty-three, grooves around my eyes, my hair graying at the temples, and thin, so thin, whittled by loss.

I drove down the highway as I had every month for five years, spring, summer, winter, and fall. Nothing had ever stopped me. I'd come when Napa was burning. When the drought was at its worst and the price of water was as high as the price of oil.

*Joseph, Joseph, Joseph. Vivi, Vivi, Vivi. Benno, Benno, Benno.*

Their names were my open sesame. My prayer.

Lucien's car parked itself in the lot. The trunk popped open and I grabbed my pack and set out. A cool October day. The temperature would plummet at dusk. I'd need to gather firewood.

I'd learned not to have any expectations. So when I awoke in the middle of the night, freezing cold, needing to pee, and I unzipped my tent and the fog swirled around my head enthusiastically, like it had never abandoned me, never betrayed me, never exiled me from those I loved—I simply said, "Hello."

I surrendered to it, relief flooding through me. It would bring me home.

And when I stepped into the sunlight moments later, hours later, 1,792 days later, there they were. Joseph and Vivi. In the meadow, waiting for me.

"Is that Mama?" I heard Vivi ask.

"That's your mama," said Joseph.

I immediately began sobbing. I had years' worth of tears stored up.

The wetness on my cheeks felt primal and life-sustaining, like milk letting down.

Vivi squinted. "Where's Ba?"

Joseph came striding toward me—the expression on his face a mixture of alarm, concern, protectiveness.

I fell into his arms.

# JOSEPH

❧

*Valley of the Moon*
*1910–11*

L ux started from the very beginning; she didn't leave one thing
out. The bus that drove itself. Her escalating panic. The way the
door to 428 Elizabeth Street had opened without her even knocking.
The sound of her grandson's voice. The way Lucien's face had looked
when he gently broke the news to her that it was 2064.

Her horror at hearing Benno was gone. The Timestream he'd left
for her. The futility of trying to understand what had happened and
what it meant. The duality of it all. The timely and untimely, the natural and unnatural loss of her son. Her desperation to get back to us.
Her drinking. Her wanting to die. The man in the cathedral. The
desperate measures she'd taken. The North Face tent, the Marmot
sleeping bag.

The five long years she'd had to wait for the fog to return.

That I was not with her when she learned of Benno's death was
devastating. I would carry that guilt forever.

Vivi was so young—she struggled to understand that her brother
was really dead. For her, only a month had passed since she'd last seen
Benno. It was virtually impossible to explain to her that in those four
short weeks, on the other side of the fog, eighty-one years had gone
by. Benno had married, had children and grandchildren. The last time
she saw him, he still had baby fat. He'd barely had to shave.

———

"Ba's never coming back?" she asked as we were putting her to bed. She'd asked that question every night for the past three weeks.

"No," I said.

"But Mama came back!" she cried. "Why can't Ba come?"

"Because he's not there anymore," said Lux.

"Where is he?"

Lux and I exchanged glances.

"He's here," she said, reaching under Vivi's pillow for the photo.

In the photo Benno was five. It had been taken at the airport, just before he boarded a plane for Newport. The look of anticipation on Benno's face must have hurt Lux deeply. She'd had no idea what was ahead of her, that later that night she would stumble into Greengage.

*Um, hello.* The first thing I'd ever heard her say.

Vivi traced the outline of Benno's face with her finger.

"He looks like me," Vivi said, her eyes filling.

"Yep, he does," said Lux. "You guys have the same nose. And the same eyebrows."

Vivi's face crumpled. "Ba," she sobbed.

I remembered standing in my father's drawing room in London, telling him of my plans for Greengage. The last thing I could remember him saying to me was "Well, you've made your choice." Meaning I'd chosen my dreams over him.

If only our heart's desires could be reduced so simply. My father had traveled so far from the life he'd been born into, but in the end he couldn't escape the binary mindset of a gardener's son. Water the plants and they would grow. Forget to water and they would die. If his son wanted to throw away his life, well, that son was not a son of his any longer.

We made a choice at that moment, Lux and I, and even Vivi. Benno was gone, but he would never be lost to us. He was an autumn wind that bent the trees. He was the soft polished wood of the kitchen table, the leafy smell of the creek on a warm October night.

We live because we are remembered.

———

Lux was forty-three, I was forty-six. I woke up stunned to find her there next to me in bed day after day. That we would be together now permanently was the bright spot amidst our sadness.

Slowly the months passed and slowly my family emerged from the cave of our loss. Benno's death had irrevocably changed us. We were rooted to the earth in a way we hadn't been before. This wasn't a bad thing. It was a reminder of our mortality. From this ground we'd come, to this ground we would return.

The nights grew cold. We picked the last of the corn, canned pumpkin and squash. Thanksgiving came and went. And two days before Christmas—snow. Five inches! In all my years at Greengage, we'd never even received a dusting.

We put on our coats and boots and stood in the yard, the three of us. Vivi's face was pink with wonder, her cheeks tipped up to the sky, her mittened hands outstretched as if in supplication.

"It's the first time she's seen snow," Lux whispered to me. "She has no idea what to do."

Lux grabbed Vivi by the waist and pulled her down to the ground with her. "Lie next to me, here," she instructed.

I watched them, my daughter and my beloved, their sweet heads turned toward one another.

"Now do like this," said Lux, waving her arms up and down.

Vivi imitated her.

"Do you get it? Do you understand what we're doing?" asked Lux.

Vivi shook her head.

A beatific smile spread across Lux's face. "We're making wings," she said.

Four months later, just before dawn, Lux awoke me with a scream. "Joseph! Earthquake!"

She tore the covers off and sprinted down the corridor to Vivi's room. I followed her, the floors buckling beneath me. I heard a deafening crash from downstairs. The granite slab of the fireplace mantel cracking in two. Chunks of plaster falling from the ceiling. Crockery shattering.

Lux transferred a trembling Vivi into my arms. She'd already outfitted Vivi with the Walkman; music was the best way to calm her down. Vivi had spent much of the last months with those headphones clamped over her ears. She paid homage to her brother by listening to all his favorite bands: the Rolling Stones, the Grateful Dead. Queen and Prince.

"Daddy," she whimpered.

"Everything's going to be fine," I said. "Close your eyes and press Play."

I held her close to my chest, shielding her head with the palm of my hand.

We made it down the stairs just before the staircase separated from the landing; it dangled from the second story like a loose tooth. We ran out of the house and stood in the yard, unsure of what to do. Other families stood in front of their cottages just as we did, similar stricken looks on their faces.

The earth groaned and creaked. Chimneys collapsed. Porches sagged. The full moon was a bone-white orb in the sky.


People staggered around us, making their way toward the meadow. We all knew the protocol. Earthquake, fire, flood—congregate at the dining hall.

The schoolhouse, the cottages, the dormitories, the winery, the barn, the cooper's shed, the workshop, every structure had incurred heavy damage. The grain silo had tipped over, crushing the chicken house. My mind immediately conjured up the earlier earthquake that had brought no damage. This quake was its polar opposite.

"Joseph!" shouted Fancy, catching up with us.

Vivi slid out of my arms and ran to her cousin. I embraced my sister. I hadn't realized until that moment that I'd been holding my breath. "Magnusson?"

"He's all right. He went to check on the horses. Dear God," she said.

The earth rumbled again, an aftershock. Vivi threw herself back into my arms.

By the time we got to the dining hall, sidestepping debris, climbing over fallen branches, the sun had risen.

It took another hour or so for everyone to gather. We were lucky— other than a few minor injuries, everybody was fine.

Greengage, however, was in ruins.

# LUX

❧

Despite all the mess—broken china, cutlery scattered all over the floor—the dining hall was structurally sound. The kitchen crew brought out a meal of bread, butter, and fruit. Those who had an appetite ate in stunned silence. Vivi sat on my lap wearing her headphones.

Suddenly Joseph stood. "Did you hear that?" he said.

People looked up from their food.

"Hear what?" I asked.

He bent forward, listening intently. "*That*. That rumbling."

"Another aftershock?" I clutched Vivi.

"No, it's not an aftershock. It sounds—like a wagon," he said.

Joseph ran out into the meadow, the rest of us trailing behind him. He stopped fifty feet or so from the fog. A moment later we heard the unmistakable sound of an axe slicing through the air and a dull thunk as it hit wood. Then a man's voice.

"This way!"

The fog swirled and then a patch cleared. For the first time in years, the mist dissipated enough to allow a glimpse into the forest. A wagon was revealed. And then another. And, oh my God, there was a group of men clearing a path.

One of them saw us and lifted his hand in greeting. "There are so many trees downed! We got here as soon as we could."

The fog gathered, swirled, and thickened again, and the man disappeared.

Joseph turned to me, his eyes wide. "That's Jake Poppe. He owns the general store in Glen Ellen."

"The fog!" shouted Fancy. "It's lifting."

And it was. The wall of fog that had briefly reasserted itself began to lift again—for good. Great chunks of it floated off. It thinned to a mist, and in a matter of minutes was gone.

Jake Poppe walked toward us, axe slung over his shoulder.

"Joseph," he said. "Goddamn. Looks like you were hit pretty bad, too. I'd hoped you'd fared better. I'm sorry."

Joseph pulled Vivi behind him, shielding her from Jake's view. With one quick movement he palmed Vivi's headphones off and passed the Walkman to me.

"Do you smell that?" asked Jake.

I dropped the Walkman into the tall grass, then focused on trying to make sense of what had happened. Time had reset itself. It was 1906, the morning of the first earthquake.

And that smell?

That was San Francisco burning to the ground.


This was how great change happened. Suddenly and all at once—fate jumped the tracks. An airplane flew into a building. A cough was diagnosed as stage four cancer. A fertilized egg embedded itself in a womb.

All of us lived on fault lines. We just pretended we didn't.

"Don't worry," said Jake, clapping Joseph on the back. "I know it looks bad now. But we'll clean this up. We'll rebuild. Who knows what the future holds?"

We, in fact, knew exactly what the future would hold. In eight years the world would be at war. In twelve years 50 million people would die of the Spanish flu, and on October 29, 1929, the stock market would crash. Ethnic cleansings were coming. Genocides. The clearing of the rain forest. Cultures would be lost. Animals would go extinct. A man would walk on the moon and a woman would walk on

Mars. There'd be droughts, floods, and blizzards. There'd be a third world war. There'd be another flu—this one so virulent, 100 million would perish.

I looked at my family, at their dear, familiar faces. I thought of the face that was missing. *All* the faces that were missing. I gathered them in my heart.

We would do this together. We would begin again.

Time no longer tethered us. Love did.

# ACKNOWLEDGMENTS

I'm very thankful to the following people who read early drafts of this novel and offered their expertise, editing, and encouragement: Joanne Hartman, Robin Heller, and Anika Streitfeld. To those who gave their support in myriad different ways: Kerri Arsenault, Brigeda Bank, Laura Barnard, Elizabeth Bernstein, Deni Chambers, Rodes Fishburne, Katie Fox, Sara Gideon, Kaarlo Heiskanen, Roberto Horowitz, Pat Jimenez, Jacob Marx Rice, Lisa Ruben, and Mary Ann Walsh.

I'm extremely grateful to my editor, Jennifer Hershey, for her tireless efforts, as well as the rest of the wonderful crew at Ballantine: Gina Centrello, Susan Corcoran, Caroline Cunningham, Sanyu Dillon, Deborah Dwyer, Kristin Fassler, Kim Hovey, Steve Messina, Paolo Pepe, Sharon Propson, Allison Schuster, Matt Schwartz, Scott Shannon, Anne Speyer, Kara Welsh, and Theresa Zoro.

Thanks to Lynne Drew at HarperCollins.

Abiding thanks to my agent, Elizabeth Sheinkman, as well as Tracy Fisher, Amy Fitzgerald, and Alicia Gordon.

And finally I couldn't have written this book without the support and love of Ben Gideon Rewis and Ben Hunter Rewis.

# A Q&A with Melanie Gideon

**What was your inspiration for writing *Valley of the Moon*?**

The main inspiration was the musical *Brigadoon*, which is about a village in the Scottish highlands that is stuck in time (none of its inhabitants can ever leave). Every evening when the villagers go to bed, a hundred years pass in the outside world but only one night passes for them. Gene Kelly stumbles upon Brigadoon. He falls in love with Cyd Charisse and has an impossible decision to make – either leave Brigadoon by nightfall, never to see his beloved again, or stay with her and be trapped for a century at which point everybody in his life will be long gone.

**Did you always have ambitions of becoming a writer?**

I knew I wanted to be a writer when I was eight years old. But the desire to write sprung from the books I was reading at the time. Is there any more immersive experience than reading? It seemed like magic to me when I was a girl, and it still does. Where else but between the pages of a book can you find yourself skipping pebbles on a lake with a girl named Caddie. Stepping into a musty old wardrobe, pushing your way past fur coats, the smell of mothballs in the air, and then—suddenly—it's snowing. Enchantment! Bewitchment! Real life paled in comparison. One week I lived in an attic in Brooklyn. I was an assistant pig keeper the next week. A piano-playing child prodigy the next. Reading showed me that anything was possible. I time travelled. I sharpshooted. I gathered and I received. In essence, books taught me what it meant to be human.

## What is your writing process like and how has it changed from book to book?

My writing process is the same for all my books. I'm a serious plotter.

I never start a book until I have a comprehensive outline. After I've outlined I just dive in and I don't stop writing until I have a first draft.

## What has been the most challenging part of the writing process?

*Valley of the Moon* was the most challenging book I've ever written. In fact, I wrote the book once and then realized it was stillborn, so to speak, so I wrote a second completely different book. Same conceit, different approach. It was quite difficult to pull the time travel piece off, to organically integrate the supernatural element. Ultimately, the solution was to ground the book in character development. That's usually the solution by the way.

**Your characters, and especially Lux, face almost impossible choices – was it a challenge to get into their mindset and explore their choices?**

I think the first step is knowing your characters really well. Who they are. Where they came from. Why they might do the things that they do. Their strengths. Their flaws. Their deepest wounds and their biggest secrets. Once you know those things the story flows.

**Would you say that you identify with any of the characters in the book? Which ones and why?**

This was the first book I've written where the characters were completely unknown to me and not autobiographical in the least bit. That said I do identify quite strongly with the mother/son relationship between Lux and Benno. I have a son and I drew heavily on my own feelings for him. Imagining what it would be like if we were separated—if I held back such a secret from him for so many years.

**Did you always know how the novel would end?**

I thought I did, but when I was working on the third draft a sort of coda came to me that felt like the last puzzle piece falling into place. I pitched the new ending to my editor and she wrote back one word – Yes!—and I knew I had it.

**What would you ideally like your readers to take away from the novel?**

I hope first and foremost that they are entertained and that they're transported and moved. *Valley of the Moon* is about loss and redemption. About families, about the unbreakable bonds between parents and children, and the bittersweet nature of the passage of time. I also hope that the book would hold up a mirror to their own lives.

**Each of your previous books have a very distinct tone and subject matter.**
  **How do you see *Valley of the Moon* as similar to or different from those previous books?**

Although *Valley of the Moon* might seem like a departure from my last two books, both *The Slippery Year* and *Wife 22* had the theme of time set squarely in their sights. *Valley of the Moon* is for me, the ultimate meditation on time: how it constricts us, traps us, and also frees us.

**Greengage is such a special place – was it inspired by a real community in your life?**

Greengage is an amalgamation of the farm in South County, Rhode Island where my family lived when I was a child, and the camp I attended from the ages of 12–18. The farm was a magical place where I developed a profound connection to the natural world. Camp was a yearly plunge into communal living, a way of life I still long for today.

**Time travel is clearly a subject that has fascinated the popular imagination for a long time. Why do you think the fantasy of travelling through time is so appealing?**

Because who wouldn't want to step through a portal into another time, if only for a few hours? To sneak in and experience the middle ages, ancient Greece or the Gilded Age and then pop right back out into your own time. Of course in all the best time travel books there's always a caveat, a price to be paid for that experience. You can't time travel without being fundamentally changed or fundamentally changing your environment. That's part of the thrill and the heartbreak of the fantasy.

**What are some of your favourite books or movies that deal with the theme of time?**

*The Lion, the Witch and the Wardrobe*, by C.S. Lewis. Not a true time travel book, but a book that plays with time. *Time and Again*, by Jack Finney in which the protagonist lives for months in a perfect replica of a 19th century apartment in New York City, convincing himself through self-hypnosis that it's 1882. *Kindred*, by Octavia E. Butler, where a woman in 1976 finds herself hurled back through time to a pre-civil war plantation. And finally *The Time Traveler's Wife*, by Audrey Niffennegger, unique in that it's told from the point-of-view of both the time traveller and the wife he leaves behind.

**Lux finds a place that seems to feel like home in a time very distinct from her own. Do you personally ever wish you could have lived in another time? When would it be?**

The late 1800s, just like Lux, and the place would be a community similar to Greengage. I suppose I created the world for Lux that I wanted most to time travel to.

**Was there any special research you had to do to bring the 1900s and 1970s to life so vividly?**

For the early 1900s one of my best and inspirational sources was Jack London's novel *Valley of the Moon* which was published in 1913. I also read books on farming methods from that time period, as well as guides to Victorian life. One indispensable treasure trove was the *American Decades* series, comprehensive tomes addressing everything from world events, to the arts, to fashion, to medicine and health. For the 1970s, I looked partly to my own memories and sense of that time, and for a more cultural perspective of 1960–1980s San Francisco, David Talbot's *Season of the Witch*.

# Book Club Questions

What are the key themes of the novel?

The villagers of Greengage are surprised when Lux returns – if you were Lux would you have ventured back through the fog?

Lux attempts to return to Greengage every full moon for 11 months. What do you think drove her back every month? Was she right to keep returning to Greengage?

Who do you think was responsible for the deterioration of their relationship, Lux or her father? From this, who do you think should have been the one to bridge the gap?

Though at first she doesn't appear to like her, Martha is the first person to vocalise that Lux is more than a mother calling her 'compassionate, resourceful, intelligent.' What words would you use to describe Lux? How would you describe Joseph?

Would you have believed Lux about Greengage after she'd disappeared for a year?

The novel deals with the concept of ageing and death several times. Was there any moment surrounding these events that you empathised with?

How did you feel about the ending? Is it what you were expecting?